BREACH OF TRUST

VICKI THARP

BREACH OF TRUST

1

There's a reason why the calm before the storm is so ominous.

Saxon Gray's seventeen-year-old self would have laughed his ass off if Saxon had returned from the future and told him that he'd be a father of five humans by the time he was thirty-two. Yet here Saxon was… living the dream.

That was sarcasm.

But only a little.

Because ever since Saxon had aged out of foster care without a security net, he'd wanted to be that safety net for other LGBTQ kids who aged out of the system and had nowhere to turn.

If he got technical, these humans he was responsible for were adults and not biologically his. And maybe he was more of the big brother they all needed kind of thing than him being a father figure, but you get the idea.

And with the new grant from the beautiful state of California, Saxon had secured the money to build out the third floor and add five more beds to the group home if he budgeted carefully and did most of the work himself.

If that meant one more Friday night alone, hanging out on the third floor hanging drywall by himself instead of, you know, having any kind of a love life or even a social life, then so be it.

From his small office off the kitchen, which might have been a butler's pantry at some point in the old house's history, Saxon heard the peal of laughter from upstairs, the clump of feet, and the *tic-tac, tic-tac* of high heels on the ceiling above him.

He shut down his computer for the night as Oliver ran down the stairs with the biggest cheek-to-cheek grin on his face, lighting the house's entire first floor.

"Ohmygod,ohmygod,ohmygod, wait until you see Phoenix," Oliver said. His body practically vibrated. He wore skinny jeans, an orange crop top with his hair slicked back, and a fresh coat of matching nail polish on his fingernails.

Sophia came down next, just as dressed up and just as excited.

"Tell him to close his eyes," came Phoenix's voice from somewhere up above.

Saxon rolled his eyes but closed them when Sophia said, "You heard her, old man."

"Old man," Saxon grumbled. "Thirty-two is *not* old."

"Yeah," Oliver said. "Keep telling yourself that."

Saxon heard the teasing in his voice. One of the things he loved about his kids was that they felt comfortable enough around him now to give him a hard time. It hadn't always been that way with them, and he loved how the group had bonded around giving him a hard time.

"Are his eyes closed?" Phoenix called down.

"Yes," Oliver said. Saxon heard Oliver go up a couple of the steps. "You can come down now."

The tell-tale tapping of Phoenix's high heels trailed down the treads. The kids had pooled what spare money they had and bought Phoenix's shoes for her nineteenth birthday the week before.

Step by step, she came down. "Don't peek."

Oliver moved behind Saxon and covered his eyes, even though Saxon wasn't trying to spoil the surprise.

As Phoenix's heel hit the ground floor, he heard the more solid clack. "Okay. You can look." The excitement in her voice sent goosebumps over his arms.

If Saxon could bottle up her glee, he'd be rich a million times over. This is what Phoenix's parents were missing. They'd missed this when they'd kicked her out of their home for being transgender. They'd never hear the sheer delight in her voice at something so simple.

And that was their loss.

Saxon swallowed down the sudden thickness in his throat as Oliver dropped his hands and gripped Saxon's shoulders.

Saxon opened his eyes, and he immediately had to blink back tears. "Holy cow. I mean that—" Saxon tried again. "You—you look—"

Sophia laughed. "You rendered him speechless, Phoenix."

Phoenix giggled and turned in a slow circle. The dress had a form-fitting bodice and a skirt that flared out at the waist and hit her just above the knees.

The hem of the skirt flew in the air as she twirled. "Well? What do you think?"

Saxon took in the sight of her. From the jewel-toned thrifted dress that complemented her dark skin to the gifted high heels to the smile on her face that went on forever.

"You look gorgeous," Saxon said.

This would be the first time that Phoenix went out in public in a dress and makeup in one hundred percent complete girl mode.

Saxon was so fucking proud of her. "You're gonna knock them dead tonight."

The tears welled in Phoenix's eyes, but with that radiant smile, Saxon knew they were tears of joy.

"Where are you three headed tonight?" He had to ask. It was the protective father in him.

"Under 21," Phoenix said.

The new under-twenty-one club had opened a month or two before. Although with the way the three of them were dressed, any of the bouncers at the regular nightclubs would've let them in.

"Addi and James not going with you?"

"Addi is working a late shift tonight," Sophia said, clearly bummed.

"And James is at his boyfriend's place." Oliver made lovey-dovey eyes, but Saxon saw the flash of… jealousy? No, that wasn't jealousy. More longing, perhaps.

Oliver was a sweet, handsome kid, but his shyness around people he didn't know well fed into his social awkwardness. It made dating for him harder than it did for James, who had never met a stranger, and flirted easier than Saxon's lying, cheating ex.

Sophia got a mischievous glint in her eye. "*Ooooh*, look who's going to be home alone tonight."

Oliver's eyes brightened. "Got a hot date, old man?"

The heat ran up Saxon's cheeks even though he had no plans. "The only hot date I have is with 4 x 8 sheets of drywall and an extra-large box of screws."

"You're not going out with your boyfriend?" Phoenix asked.

Oliver cut his eyes toward Phoenix, and with a loud stage whisper out of the side of his mouth, he said, "ixnay on the oyfriendbay."

"Ix, what?"

Exasperated, Sophia said, "He's trying to say that Saxon doesn't have a boyfriend anymore. They broke up. Remember?"

"Yeah, the asshole cheated—"

"Okay, okay," Saxon said, "Enough about my private life."

"Who would cheat on Saxon?" Phoenix said. "He's, like, the nicest person ever."

Oliver reached out and poked Saxon in the abdomen. "And it feels like he has some abs under there. He hasn't completely gone to pot in his advanced years."

Saxon laughed. God, he loved these kids. "Don't you three have a club to go to?"

Saxon's phone pinged with a HotDix notification. Within six seconds, it pinged again."

All three sets of eyes dropped to his front pocket where he had his phone, then back up at him. They all knew the sound of the dating app.

"Are you going to check that?" Oliver asked, ever hopeful. "We'll wait."

"No," Saxon said. "I'm done with dating for now. I've got my hands full with you guys and the renovations."

"You could give that one guy a call," Oliver suggested.

If Saxon ever needed a wingman, he knew who to call.

Before Saxon could answer and act like he didn't know who the hell Oliver was talking about—even though when Oliver said *that one guy*, Saxon's thoughts went immediately to Cesar Morales, Sophia chimed in. "What guy?"

"Oh my God," Oliver said. "Don't you two ever pay attention? That guy… you know, the one he had coffee with a few weeks ago and came home smiling like a hyena."

"I wasn't smiling like a hyena," Saxon grumbled, even though he remembered his cheeks tiring from all the smiling. That kiss he and Cesar had shared might have had something to do with it.

Something must've clicked because Phoenix snapped her fingers, and she grinned. "Oh yeah, I remember now. He was all smiles and in an extra good mood the next day. He let us order takeout instead of having to cook."

At this rate, he'd never get them out of his personal life, get any of the drywall hung, and the kids would never have their night out.

Saxon stepped over to the front door and held it open for them, gesturing with his hand. "Out. Everyone out."

"All I'm saying," Oliver said as he followed Sophia and Phoenix out the door, "is he should give that guy a call. No one wants to die alone and horny."

CESAR MORALES TOOK A SIP OF HIS COFFEE AND SETTLED IN HIS seat in the stake-out car, prepared for a long, boring night.

His partner, Derek Watts, sat in the passenger seat beside him, his seat pushed back to stretch out his legs.

"You know," Derek said, "You don't have to be here. We're not staking out some fugitive's hideout. This is a simple divorce case. I can sit on this guy's house myself. It's not a two-man job."

"This is my job." Cesar took his eyes off the house, not too concerned he'd miss anything since their target had already come home for the night. If this night were like the other nights that they'd staked the house out, they'd do nothing but watch a dark house until morning. "And this is my car."

Derek's beater of a surveillance car was so dilapidated that in an affluent neighborhood like this one, someone would've called the cops on them in the first five minutes after they'd pulled up. And if they'd been in Derek's daily driver, a Mercedes Roadster, they would have caught everyone's attention.

They'd tried to use the Roadster on a stake-out before, and people kept coming up to the car and taking selfies in front of it.

At least Cesar's late-model sedan was non-decrepit enough that no one looked at it twice.

"I've borrowed your car before."

Derek dug his keys out of his pocket and held them out for Cesar. "It's Friday night. You've done nothing but work these past few months. Now that things have slowed down, you should take time for yourself. Maybe go see what Saxon Gray is up to."

Cesar just looked at him, and Derek laid his keys on the console between them. "I'm sure Saxon has other plans on a Friday night. Besides, it's not like we're a thing or anything. We had coffee twice."

And the man had been on Cesar's mind every day since.

The first time they'd met, he'd accepted the invitation for coffee more out of curiosity as to why Cesar's ex's ex-boyfriend wanted to talk to him.

Did they really have anything in common besides being dumped by the same manipulative asshole?

"Besides, Saxon has a house full of kids and a complicated life. I don't think he needs me to muddy it more."

"Those *kids* are adults. He doesn't have to babysit them twenty-four seven. Besides, did Saxon *say* he wasn't interested in seeing you again? You know," Derek said, with the most annoying sly grin, "that time you two locked lips."

"You're an asshole." Even as Cesar said it, he couldn't keep the smile off his face. Derek smiled as well. "No. He didn't say that. But I'm a good PI. I can read between the lines. And if he were interested, he could have contacted me. He's the one who asked me out for coffee. He's got my number."

"If I'm not mistaken, you have his number, too. Communication goes both ways, right?"

Fuck. "What are you saying?"

"I'm saying, get your ass out of the car and go see that man."

"Look at you, Mr. Matchmaker," Cesar said as he palmed Derek's keys. "Just because you and Max are sickeningly happy doesn't mean the rest of us can't be happy single."

"I didn't say that. But it's nice to have someone to come home to. Someone who loves me as much as I love them. You should give it a shot."

In answer, Cesar squeezed the door latch and popped it open. "Are you going to be in the office tomorrow so I can get my car back?"

Derek popped his door as well to switch into the driver seat. "I'll stop by your place tomorrow, and we can exchange cars. Unless you want to do the exchange at Saxons place?"

"Ha ha, asshole."

Derek laughed and got out of the car, careful not to slam the door when he closed it. Cesar dropped Derek's keys into his pocket and waved at him over the roof of the car.

He walked down the dark street for a few blocks and called a ride-share to take him to the office to pick up Derek's car.

By the time Cesar climbed into the Roadster, he considered heading straight home and calling it a night. After all, was sharing the same ex something you could build a relationship on? The only thing it said about them was that they both had the same bad taste in men.

Though, to be fair, Aiden had been a commonality they could bond and bitch over.

And Cesar's inability to get Saxon out of his head said something. When was the last time he couldn't dislodge a man from his brain?

His ex notwithstanding.

It wasn't just the prospect of a hookup with Saxon that interested Cesar. He genuinely liked the guy as a person. Saxon had given up his career as a high school counselor to sink his savings into Stonewall House and do whatever he could to support LGBTQ kids aging out of foster care.

That said a lot about Saxon.

Cesar used to think big, buff men were sexy. As it turns out, finding a guy with more heart and more compassion in his little finger than Aiden possessed in his whole body was enormously attractive.

Well, hell.

Cesar pulled out his phone to call Saxon. After all, what did he have to lose?

His heart added an extra beat as he waited for Saxon to

answer. Right before the call went to voicemail, a breathless Saxon answered. "Hello?"

At least Cesar thought it was Saxon. With all the grunting and heavy breathing, it was hard to be certain.

Oh shit. Did Saxon have somebody over? And if he did, why the hell would he answer the phone?

Only one way to find out.

"Hey. It's Cesar. Did I catch you at a bad time?"

"Hang on. One sec." Saxon sounded like he stood at the bottom of a deep hole. Or maybe he had Cesar on speaker phone. Cesar heard the *zip zip* of a drill driver and a heavy clunk in the background.

Saxon came on the line again. "Sorry about that. I'm hanging drywall on the third floor."

"You got the state grant?"

"Yeah, I got it."

Cesar heard the grin in Saxon's voice… and the pride. He deserved to be proud of himself. What he was doing for those kids was life-changing.

"Is there something I can do for you?" Saxon asked.

"I was calling to see if you wanted to go out for a drink… Or something. But you're busy."

"You could always come here." The hope in Saxon's voice made Cesar sit up and take notice. "I could always use another set of strong hands. I mean, you know, for construction."

Cesar considered whether he should go home and change first, but he wasn't wearing such nice clothes that he had to worry they'd get ruined. "Have you eaten?"

"Yes."

"Oh, okay." Cesar didn't know what to say to that.

After the mildly awkward silence, Saxon said, "But Cesar?"

"Yeah?"

"A little dessert sounds good."

The way Saxon lowered his voice to say *dessert…*

Had Saxon been flirting with him?

Or was Cesar reading more into it?

Either way, Cesar took the open invitation. "Dessert. Right. I'll see you in a little bit."

Cesar knew the perfect place. He checked his phone. If he made good time, he could make it to Biscuits and Beans before closing for the evening.

Biscuits and Beans was a coffee shop and bakery combo best known for its lattes and cherry pies.

Thirty minutes later, Cesar stood at the door of Stonewall House with a bag of pies in one hand and a tray with two lattes in the other.

He put the bag down to knock. One of the third-floor windows stood open, and Saxon turned down the classic rock radio station before calling down. "Is that you, Cesar?"

Cesar stepped back from the door to see Saxon leaning out the window, his brown hair tousled and sweaty. Cesar had to tamp down on his wild imagination when he thought about a different situation where Saxon would be shirtless and sweaty with a satisfied smile.

Down boy.

Cesar smiled up at him. "It's me."

"I'll buzz you in." Saxon pulled his phone out of his pocket. A few seconds later, the lock on the front door disengaged. "Come on up."

Cesar entered and locked the door behind him. Stonewall House wasn't in a particularly bad neighborhood, but it wasn't in a particularly good one either. It sat in one of those areas where if you were looking for trouble, you could probably find it very quickly.

But no way could Cesar have been able to afford a house the size of Stonewall House in a nicer part of town. The San Fernando Valley priced you out of the market pretty quickly.

Immediately upon entry, he was met by the older house's

wooden stairs. Cesar smelled the fresh paint. Saxon had told him how he'd painted the entire first two floors after he bought the place six months before.

As he climbed from the second story to the third, the fresh paint gave way to tattered floral wallpaper peeling off the wall. It was all Cesar could do not to put the drinks down so he could rip off one of the layers.

"Hello, hello," Cesar called out as he made it to the third floor landing a little out of breath. Saxon had left the door cracked, and Cesar used his foot to push it open.

Saxon stood on the far side of the room, a 4 x 8 sheet of plywood in his hands over his head. He braced it against the wall and held it in place.

Cesar watched the play of muscles in Saxon's back for a second as he wrestled the large sheet of gypsum.

"Can you give me a hand?"

Cesar shook his head, trying to dislodge the image. Good thing. It wouldn't be easy hanging drywall with a hard-on. Besides, this wasn't a booty call. He needed to remember that.

He set the pies and the lattes at his feet and hurried over to help. Saxon bumped a hip out toward Cesar. "I ran out of drywall screws, but I think I still have a few in my front pocket. Can you get them out for me?"

That close, Cesar saw the drywall dust in Saxon's hair and mixing with the sweat on his shoulders, back, and chest. Saxon's jeans sat low on his hips with the leather tool belt slung around him.

Cesar reached into Saxon's front pocket and wrapped his hand around the screws. With his hand full of screws, he struggled to get it out of Saxon's pocket. He wiggled his hand around until he inadvertently brushed against Saxon's semi-hard cock

Cesar stilled.

Saxon flushed.

Dropping the screws, Cesar slipped his hand out of Saxon's

pocket and pressed his hands to the drywall. "I'll hold the drywall. You screw it in."

Saxon cleared his throat, and his smile went straight to Cesar's dick. "Great idea."

Saxon used the remaining screws to secure the wallboard.

"You can let go now." Saxon dropped his drill driver into the holster on his tool belt. "Whatever you brought smells delicious."

"Are you ready for your break?"

Saxon unhooked the belt and laid it on the nearby stack of drywall. "Definitely."

They walked over to where Cesar had left the lattes and pies.

"Damn, that smells good." Saxon stuck his nose in the air like a dog sniffing for bones.

Cesar pulled one of the cups out of the carrier and handed it to Saxon. "Soy, caramel latte with extra whip."

With a grin, Saxon said. "You remembered."

Was it creepy that Cesar remembered Saxon's coffee order from several weeks ago?

Cesar dug the pies out of the bag and distributed the forks and knives. He opened each box. "I didn't know what you liked. I got a cherry, an apple, and a blackberry pie."

"Blackberry," Saxon said without hesitation.

"I like a decisive man." Cesar handed Saxon the pie. He took the cherry pie for himself, and they both sat with their backs against a section of drywall Saxon had already hung.

Cesar avoided the line of carpet tack strips on the floor near the wall left over from where Saxon must have ripped up the old carpet to reveal the hardwood floors beneath.

With his pie on the floor, Cesar started cutting a piece with his knife. He glanced at Saxon, who had removed the blackberry pie from the box. He held the pie in one hand and the fork in the other.

Like someone who'd been raised by wolves, Saxon dug straight into the center of the pie and shoved a forkful into his mouth. Saxon's eyes rolled, and the most delicious-sounding *Mmmmm* rolled out of the back of his throat.

That sound did little to help the semi Cesar tried to hide behind the fly of his jeans. Saxon's eyes popped open. Cesar must've had a funny look because Saxon cocked his head. "What?"

"Did you wake up this morning and choose chaos?"

2

———

Saxon swallowed a delicious bite of pie. The crust was the buttery-est, flaky-est crust he'd ever eaten, and the blackberry center struck the perfect balance between tart and sweet.

He forked another bite but didn't bring it to his mouth. "Eating pie from the center out is not chaos. It's what works for me. The middle is my favorite, and I like the outside edges the least. I'm eating it in a spiral from the center outward. It's not like I'm a complete monster and am taking bites from random locations all around the pie."

Saxon could have gone downstairs and gotten them both plates, but where was the fun in that?

"What if one of the kids wants some of that blackberry pie? Or are you not going to share?"

"No. No no no. This pie is mine. If those fuckers want pie, they can have the apple one."

Of course, when Saxon called them fuckers, he meant it as a term of endearment.

Saxon glanced down at Cesar's pie. He'd cut a healthy-sized wedge, taking careful, nibbling bites to ensure he only ate from the wedge he'd cut and didn't mess up the rest of the pie.

Saxon pointed at Cesar's pie with his fork. "Tell me, Mr. PI, have you always lived your life inside the lines?"

Cesar glanced at his pie. A blush rose to his cheeks—completely, simply, kissably adorable. Saxon wanted to lean in and kiss that embarrassed smile off Cesar's face, but even though they'd kissed before, he held back.

And he'd thought about that kiss every night—and most days —since. They had chemistry. No denying that.

Then again, Saxon and his ex, Aiden, had had chemistry, and look at how that turned out. No, this time, Saxon wasn't leaping in dick first. He liked Cesar. And thought he'd like him even more once he got to know him. There was no rush.

Saxon playfully nudged Cesar with his shoulder. "Go on. I dare you. Eat from the middle and work your way out. It's liberating."

Cesar leaned away, switching hands to get his pie farther away from Saxon. "You eat your chaos pie over there and leave me to my nice, orderly, perfect little slice over here."

No. That wasn't going to work at all.

Saxon lunged, stabbed the middle of Cesar's pie, and scooped out a big bite, the cherries falling off.

Cesar barked out a laugh. "Dios mio. What the hell are you doing?"

"Open wide." Saxon moved the fork toward Cesar's mouth. Cesar shrieked like a little kid who'd had enough of his blended peas.

"No." Cesar laughed.

"Oh, yes." Saxon pushed Cesar's pie away and set it down beside their lattes.

Cesar tried to get away, laughing the entire time. Somehow, Saxon ended up on top, straddling Cesar's hips. Cesar outweighed Saxon, and at any moment, Cesar could have tossed him aside, but Cesar didn't even try.

Not really.

Saxon trapped one of Cesar's hands, the red cherry filling dripping onto Cesar's chin. "Open up."

Cesar pressed his lips together and shook his head, but he still had a smile and didn't push the fork away with his free hand.

Instead, that free hand landed on Saxon's hip, just above the waistband of his jeans.

"Eat it or wear it. Your choice."

Cesar opened wide, but at that point, only a single cherry and a bit of crust remained on the fork. Cesar caught Saxon's fork between his lips, and Saxon yanked to get it free. Cesar glared up at him, a drop of filling on his chin and another near his cheek.

Saxon sucked the drop from Cesar's chin. The smile fell from Cesar's lips, his eyes dilating and his nostrils flaring. His heated gaze shifted from Saxon's mouth to his eyes and back again.

With a finger, Saxon swiped away the spot of filling near Cesar's cheek and sucked his finger clean to tease him.

Cesar's other hand landed on Saxon's other hip, his thumbs tracing small circles on Saxon's lower abdomen, which did nothing to help the semi he had growing in his jeans.

Saxon pointed to his own upper lip. "You've got a little right here."

"You get it for me."

Saxon reached out, but Cesar clasped his wrist and shook his head. "Not with your finger."

He spoke barely above a whisper, but there was very little noise on the third floor in an empty house. The mild breeze blowing through the open windows wasn't strong enough to rattle the raised blinds. Saxon swallowed hard and braced his hands on either side of Cesar's head.

Saxon nibbled the spec of pie filling off Cesar's upper lip with his lips and tongue. Cesar's hands slid to Saxon's sides and skimmed up his bare back. The sweat had mostly dried, but he felt the scratchiness of the drywall dust beneath Cesar's fingers and the stickiness from the dried salt on his skin.

That didn't stop Cesar from pulling him in tighter and deepening the kiss.

All Saxon wanted to do was stretch out between Cesar's thighs and grind against him.

But that wasn't taking things slow.

He didn't think he could take another heartbreak like Aiden.

Saxon broke the kiss and sat back on Cesar's thighs. Cesar raised, bracing his weight on his elbows behind him. "What's wrong?"

"Nothing."

Cesar smiled, but it was only a half-smile and kind of sad. "Want to try that again?"

"It's about Aiden."

"Aiden?" Cesar scooted back until he was no longer beneath Saxon and crisscrossed his legs. "Don't tell me you're still hung up on him. He cheated on me with you and then cheated on you with who knows who else. He's a player unworthy of your time, let alone your heart."

Saxon crossed his legs, mirroring Cesar, and bowed his head, unable to meet his steady gaze. "I know it's foolish to allow him space in my head, but I don't know if I could handle being cheated on again. To have invested myself so fully and then have Aiden do what he did…"

Saxon shook his head. "I don't need that kind of complication in my life. These kids already take a lot out of me. And I'm happy to do it. I signed up for that. But I don't need that added instability."

"Look. Saxon. I don't know where this is going. Or even if it's going anywhere. I know I like you and want to see more of you. But no matter where that takes us, I won't cheat on you."

Saxon had to laugh and glanced up at Cesar. "Now that I think about it, I know you won't."

"How? We barely even know each other."

"You can't even eat a pie outside of the lines. I think it would be even harder for you to live your relationship outside the lines. The galling thing about Aiden was that he didn't have to cheat. I was amenable to a little openness in our relationship. With rules, of course. But he couldn't even manage that."

"You want an open relationship?"

Saxon couldn't tell if that idea intrigued or horrified Cesar. "I'm not opposed to a degree of openness within a set of mutually agreed-upon boundaries."

Cesar nodded. His non-committal, "Good to know," made Saxon's heart thud a hollow note in his chest. Had he killed the prospect of a new relationship with a hot, kind, thoughtful man before he'd even had a chance to see where it might go?

Then again, if they weren't close to being on the same page from the start, they might be better off as friends.

"Want to chill? Maybe watch a movie?" Saxon offered, hoping he hadn't scared Cesar off.

Cesar pushed off the floor, his jeans filthy with construction dirt and dust, and wiped his hands on his pants before offering Saxon a hand. "I'd like that."

Saxon allowed Cesar to pull him to his feet, a tingle of anticipation making him lighter on his feet, banishing some of the construction exhaustion from his body.

About the time Saxon expected Cesar to drop his hand, he did the unexpected and pulled Saxon closer, his voice low in Saxon's ear when he said, "Just so we're clear and there are no misunderstandings, you didn't scare me away with the consensual non-monogamy stuff."

Cesar let go of Saxon's hand, his fingertips skipping across Saxon's palm as he did.

"No?" Saxon asked when he met Cesar's gaze.

Even in the harsh light of the third floor's bare bulbs, Cesar had the most beautiful, deep brown eyes. Saxon had seen eyes that brown before, but they'd never drawn him in the way Cesar's did. Cesar had a way of looking at Saxon as if he could visualize his essence. His being. That unique substance that made Saxon, Saxon.

"No," Cesar confirmed. "And I agree, clear boundaries are needed, and most importantly, open, *honest* communication is needed."

"Agreed." Saxon took a step back. All he wanted to do was curl up on the couch in a dark room and maybe share a few more of those kisses that made his heart beat faster and his mind forget about a certain asshole who wouldn't know an honest thought if it came up and bit him on his dirty, cheating ass. "Let's close up here and head downstairs. You can pick out something to watch while I take a quick shower."

"Sounds great."

Saxon closed the windows. The third floor was unairconditioned and would probably remain so for the next few weeks. He'd managed to get an amazing deal on a new air conditioning unit plus installation with the caveat that he had to wait until the installer could do the work between other jobs. For the price differential, the deal was worth the extra days he'd have to spend sweating.

Cesar stacked their pies in the boxes and balanced the now cold lattes on top. "I've got it," he said when Saxon tried to help him carry things downstairs.

Cesar led the way, and Saxon pulled up the rear, closing the door to the third floor to keep from losing too much of their precious cool air to the empty space.

Cesar slotted the pies into the fridge and pitched the half-drunk lattes into the trash.

"Um... the TV remote is on the coffee table," Saxon said, starting to feel inexplicably exposed without his shirt.

Maybe it was the way those dark eyes drifted up and down his body as if cataloging all the amazingly naughty things they could do together if they both got naked.

Saxon swallowed audibly, and Cesar tore his gaze away from Saxon's bare chest. Saxon wasn't built like a guy who spent several hours a day in a gym for the past five years, but more like a man who did what he had to do to improve people's lives.

Something that Cesar found damn sexy.

"It'll only be a minute." Saxon reluctantly took a step back and headed for his shower.

Cesar figured that with all the people living under the same roof and using the same common space, function over feng shui prevailed.

Perpendicular to the couch, a love seat sat pressed against one wall, and on the wall directly opposite were two recliners that looked like they'd been thrifted.

Cesar found his way into the den and sat on the three-seater sofa that faced the TV in the over-furnished den at the front of the house.

He picked up the remote, thumbed over to one of the streaming services, and scrolled through the movies until he found a comedy he hadn't seen yet. He queued the movie up and paused it until Saxon returned.

He looked fresh and clean, dressed in athletic shorts and a comfy tank, his hair still damp and mussed as if he'd ruffled his towel over his head and not taking the time to run his fingers through his hair in his hurry to rejoin Cesar.

"Find something?" Saxon asked. He plopped down on the sofa and stretched his legs to the coffee table.

Cesar spun the remote in his hand, but he had more interest in Saxon than the movie. He angled toward Saxon, and his knee pressed into the side of Saxon's thigh.

How long did he have Saxon to himself? He reached over and played with a couple of the wet strands of hair at the back of Saxon's neck. "So, what time do the kids have to be back?"

Saxon grinned, his hand moving to rest on Cesar's knee. "They're adults. They don't have a curfew. Stonewall House isn't supervised like a halfway house for people coming out of prison. Our goal is to help LGBTQ kids who've aged out of the system or have previously been unhoused and have no support."

Saxon patted his chest, his pride mesmerizing. "We are their support. We give them an affordable place to live, help teach them how to manage their bank account, get a job, and learn to be responsible for themselves. All the things a parent should teach their kid. That's something a lot of these kids lack.

"Wow," Cesar said. He felt the grin spread across his face, loving how Saxon got so animated and passionate about his work.

"Why are you looking at me like that?"

"You're amazing. I don't know much of what you do here, but I can tell just by your compassion and passion and how your eyes light up when you talk about this place that those kids are so lucky to have you in their lives."

The red immediately came to Saxon's eyes. They got glassy, and Cesar worried he'd said something wrong. "I'm sorry. I didn't mean—"

Saxon waved him off. "No, no. It's okay. I just… I'm—It's just been a long road getting here. I don't have much support navigating this myself, and that was probably the nicest thing anybody has ever said to me."

"I take it Aiden wasn't supportive."

Saxon rolled his eyes, and a half-laugh escaped him. "Oh my fucking god, that prick…" Saxon got thoughtful before he said anything else. Then, as if deciding Cesar was trustworthy, he added, "He'd get real pissy if I had things going on with the kids and had to break a date or reschedule or be late. It wasn't like it happened all that often, but when you have this many people to deal with, it can happen more often than not. He'd call me selfish and say I wasn't a good boyfriend or that I must not love him if I had to take time away from him to help the kids."

Cesar scrubbed a hand through his hair. Even though he had nothing to do with how Aiden had acted, he still said, "I'm sorry."

Saxon shrugged the apology off. "Not your fault. I'm glad I found out he was a lying, cheating, manipulative asshole before I'd gotten any deeper than I already was."

Desperate to change the subject and see the light return to Saxon's eyes, Cesar asked, "Tell me, how does Stonewall House work?"

Saxon tilted his head. "What do you want to know?"

"Anything? Everything?"

"That could take all night."

Cesar slouched farther down on the couch, resting his sock heels on the coffee table. He tugged on Saxon's hand until Saxon laid on his back, his head in Cesar's lap. He ran his fingers through Saxon's still damp hair and massaged his scalp. Saxon groaned. "That feels fucking amazing. Don't stop."

"Now, tell me about Stonewall House."

The corners of Saxon's mouth dropped, and Cesar couldn't quite read him. "Is something wrong?"

"No. Nothing's wrong. It's that… It's that every time I've tried to talk to Aiden about anything to do with Stonewall House, he would immediately change the subject. I mean, I get that not everyone is interested or cares about it, but—"

"I'm not Aiden, Saxon."

Saxon blew out a heated breath and relaxed more deeply into Cesar's lap. "Yeah, I'm beginning to see that."

"Can we make a promise?"

Saxon rolled more toward his side so he could see Cesar's face. "What's that?"

Cesar leaned down and pressed a kiss to Saxon's forehead. "Can we make a pact not to mention Aiden's name again? At least for today?"

"Yeah. Sorry," Saxon said. "I'd love that." After a few moments, he continued. "You want to know how things work here?"

"I do." That simple response brought a smile to the sweetest face and the most kissable lips Cesar had seen in a long time. It took everything he had not to bend down and kiss those lips and have this precious time devolve into something that Saxon clearly wasn't ready for yet. If Saxon wanted to go slow, Cesar could do slow.

"We were lucky enough to get state funding to run the home," Saxon said. "The kids are encouraged to pursue an education of some kind that'll help them support themselves. It could be college or community college or trade school or apprenticeship, anything like that. Those kids qualify for a stipend that helps pay for their room and board at Stonewall House.

"If the kids prefer to work, there's no state subsidy, but they're only charged a small fraction of their income for room and board. It's the same percentage for everyone based on their pay to keep it fair. But to be honest, the way these kids eat, that money is just enough to keep groceries in the pantry."

"But they get so much more here than just room and board. They get you."

"I hope they see it that way. I missed so much while growing up in the foster system. I never learned how to get a job. I never learned any of the things that I'm trying to teach them. I had to learn everything the hard way. *Alone.* I don't want that for these kids. It's hard for them to catch a break. I want to be that break for them."

Saxon fell silent, but his brain wasn't idle even though he snuggled deeper into Cesar's lap, enjoying Cesar's fingers in his hair. Cesar waited in the quiet for him to continue. It wasn't a hardship.

"These kids are so remarkable." Saxon's eyes caught Cesar's. "I just want to help give them the skills to thrive."

Saxon closed his eyes to the gentle scalp massage, but Cesar knew he wasn't anywhere near falling asleep.

His eyes popped open as something came to him. "You should have seen them when they first came to Stonewall. They were shut down, defiant, angry, distrusting. And rightly so. The system failed them—failed to protect them. Now, they're blooming. They stand up and support each other. They're making the family they needed all along.

"Phoenix is enrolled in cosmetology school, Sophia is in community college, Oliver is working while deciding on a career, and Addi and James both found jobs.

"They're learning to navigate the world in a safe space, and I'm so damn honored to be here to watch them grow."

"Hey, Saxon?"

"Yeah?"

"Can I kiss you?"

"Why?"

By Saxon's teasing tone, he wanted a detailed explanation. Cesar grinned. If Saxon saw how incredibly gorgeous he was at that moment, he'd understand. And Cesar wasn't just talking about how he looked physically. Hearing him talk about Stonewall House, he might as well have been looking straight into Saxon's soul, and it was fucking beautiful there.

"I love how passionate you are about these kids. You light up. And it makes my heart happy hearing about it and I... I want to kiss you and touch a small part of that."

Saxon leaned up on one elbow. Cesar more than met him halfway. The kiss was tentative at first, more of a taste. But all it took was a taste for Cesar to take it deeper. Saxon hummed in the back of his throat, and that glorious sound went straight to Cesar's dick.

"Get up here," Cesar demanded.

Without hesitation, Saxon scrambled up and straddled Cesar's lap, wrapping his arms around Cesar's neck. Saxon was already hard. As hard as Cesar. They kissed and frotted. The delicious friction of their cocks rubbing together had Cesar leaking precum.

He reached down and took hold of Saxon's ass, squeezing the muscle in his hands. He knew Saxon wanted to take things slow, but man, what he wouldn't give to wrap his lips around Saxon's cock. If all Cesar could have that night was Saxon on his lap and the two of them grinding against each other like a couple of teenagers in the back seat of a car, he'd take it.

"How much time do you think we have?" Cesar broke the kiss long enough to ask.

Saxon leaned back enough to see Cesar's face, even as he continued to grind against him. Cesar's wanted to let his head fall back and enjoy what Saxon did to him, but he kept his focus on Saxon's beautiful face.

"Phoenix, Oliver, and Sophia all went to Under 21, so they probably won't be home until after one in the morning. James is sleeping over at his boyfriend's, and Addi should get off work at about eleven. Usually takes them about thirty minutes to get home on the bus."

Cesar glanced at his watch.

Saxon dropped his forehead to Cesar's shoulder. "Do I wanna to know what time it is?"

Cesar sighed, not wanting the night to end. "It's eleven-twenty."

Slowly and with great reluctance, Saxon slid off Cesar's lap and plopped down on the coffee table. "We should probably stop. Not that we're doing anything wrong, but these kids have already been through a lot, and I don't know if they'd survive the trauma of seeing their program director dry humping... I don't even know what to call you. After trying to suck each other's tonsils out, I think that would make us more than friends. But we're not —" Saxon shrugged at his lack of words.

"Boyfriends?"

"Yeah."

"How about you call me your friend you're trying to get to know better?"

"Yeah, nothing says *I'd like to get to know you better* than rubbing your dick against someone else's."

Cesar barked out a laugh. "In your case, I'm fine with that."

"Okay, then I don't think the kids want to see their program director dry humping my friend I want to get to know better. How's that?"

"Pretty accurate."

The front door opened, and even in the low light from the paused TV screen, Cesar saw the flash of red rush up Saxon's face.

Addi flipped on the den light as they walked inside. "Hey, Saxon. I'm home."

3

———

ADDI CLOSED THE FRONT DOOR AND STOPPED ABRUPTLY. THEIR eyes shifted between the two of them. "Um… hey?"

Even though Addi hadn't caught them in the middle of anything, it was still close enough to be obvious what they'd been up to. Saxon shifted to the couch beside Cesar and pointed to the TV screen. "We were just watching a movie."

Addi wasn't naive enough to fall for that, but it didn't keep the lie from falling from Saxon's lips. And really, was it that much of a lie when watching a movie had been what they'd intended to do?

"Yeah, sure." They glanced at the paused TV and back to Saxon, one perfectly plucked eyebrow raised at him. "I can see that."

Cesar stood and extended his hand. "I'm Cesar."

"Addi." They said it with unmitigated glee.

Addi hitched their thumb over their shoulder toward the stairs. "I'm going to bed. *Alone.* Though I'm glad at least one of us is getting some."

"*Addi.*" Saxon chastised them.

They giggled and ran up the stairs.

Saxon stood and shook his head. "Sorry about that. I feel like I'm back at my foster parent's house, trying to sneak my boyfriend out. Only it's too late."

"It's fine." And by the relaxed and amused grin on Cesar's face, Saxon could tell he spoke the truth. Unlike Aiden, who'd have secretly resented being interrupted and made Saxon pay for it later with unread texts and unanswered calls.

"I should probably get home. But... Thank you for tonight. I enjoyed it."

"Same."

Same?

Saxon wanted to slap himself upside the head. What an awkward response. Good gravy, no wonder Aiden cheated on him. Saxon had *zero* game.

Saxon walked Cesar to the door and held it open for him. Cesar crossed the threshold, turned back, and stepped into Saxon's personal space. He brushed the back of his knuckle down Saxon's cheek, which almost dissolved Saxon into a little, giddy puddle right there in the doorway.

Cesar brushed his lips against Saxon's, a barely-there kiss that had a very real impact.

He wanted to tell Cesar to forget about going home. He wanted to take his hand and drag him to his room. He wanted to throw Cesar on the bed and not let him leave until morning. Instead, he hummed involuntarily in the back of his throat and barely managed a "Thanks for coming."

"When can I see you again?"

Saxon blew out a wobbly breath. "I'm not sure?"

The smile faltered on Cesar's lips, and Saxon realized how that must've sounded—like Saxon didn't want to see him again when that was the farthest thing from the truth. "I mean, I want to see you, but I have plans to work on the upstairs all weekend, and then on Monday, I have—"

"I can help," Cesar said. "And I mean, *real* help this time. Not just bringing you pie and distracting you from your work the rest of the night. Let me come by tomorrow. Make up for tonight."

Saxon bit his lip, trying to hold back the grin. "Trust me. You have nothing to make up for. Though, I'll gladly accept another pair of hands." And then, before Saxon forgot his manners as he stared at Cesar's wide grin, he added, "Thank you."

"You're welcome."

Umpfh—what those two little, growly, whispered words did to him. At this rate, Saxon would be lucky to get to sleep before morning.

Cesar took a step away. "I'll bring breakfast."

"You don't have to do that. Money is tight here, but we can afford groceries. You don't have to keep feeding me."

Cesar fisted his hand in Saxon's shirt and tugged at it to get his attention. "Saxon?"

"Yeah?"

"Let me do this for you."

Saxon's heart skipped a beat, and his lungs refused to function for a second or two. How did he get so lucky to go from one extreme of a man to another?

It's just breakfast.

Sure, but Cesar also offered to help. He didn't try to make Saxon feel guilty for not dropping everything to spend time with him. *Be cool. Accept what he's offering.* "Thanks. I'd like that."

Even though it might have made him look over-eager, Saxon watched Cesar back out of the driveway, waving to him one last time as he shifted out of reverse and drove away.

Saxon patted his cheek as if that would help keep his head out of the clouds. If he wasn't careful, he could be totally gone for this man in a matter of moments.

What do you mean could be? Admit it. You're already falling.

Saxon closed the door and squeezed his eyes shut. No, he couldn't do that again. He couldn't fall for a man before he got to know him. His heart couldn't take it.

Even though he wasn't ready to rush back into another relationship, that didn't mean he was dead.

And even though he'd promised himself he'd never take another cold shower for as long as he lived after living that month at Stonewall House without hot water while he used the scarce funding he had to fix more important things, Saxon found himself climbing into the shower with only the cold water turned on.

The cold water didn't help.

The only thing that happened was that he came out of the shower with a rash of goosebumps all over his skin and a semi still dangling between his legs.

Good luck getting to sleep.

Despite his penile problem, he crawled between his clean, cool sheets, his eyes closing as soon as his head hit the pillow.

It wasn't the same kind of exhaustion he used to have when he was a counselor at the local high school. Working at Stonewall House was better in many ways, and he found it a hundred times more satisfying, yet his body ached from all the hard work that went into getting the program—and the house—up and running.

The last thing he heard before sleep took him was the *clump, clump* of Addi's feet as they walked around their bedroom, which happened to be above his.

He welcomed the sound. He liked hearing the kids above him, knowing he provided them a safe place to lay their heads at night.

Later, he awoke in the middle of the night to a herd of elephants storming through the front door. He bolted upright, rubbing the sleep from his eyes.

"Saxon!"

From the panicked sound of his name, adrenaline rushed through his veins, a flash of lightning blitzing his system. He stumbled to his feet, throwing on a shirt over his pajama bottoms as Phoenix and Sophia rushed into his room.

"Oliver—Oliver—" Phoenix gasped and couldn't catch her

breath. Almost as breathless, Sophia squeaked out, "Oliver has been arrested."

———

Saxon sat down at the kitchen table with a rattled Phoenix and Sophia. Addi had run down the stairs when they'd heard all the commotion. Saxon passed sodas out to each of them and popped the top on his own, wishing it was a beer. But from the sounds of it, he needed a clear head.

"Okay, slow down and tell me what happened."

Phoenix and Sophia glanced at each other. Neither one wanted to speak first. Phoenix had her wig in her hands, exposing her short, bright orange hair. Her black mascara left a streaky smudge down her cheeks from crying, and the neckline of her fabulous dress ripped at the neckline.

Finally, Phoenix said to Sophia, "You tell him."

Sophia wrapped her arm around Phoenix and pulled her to her side. "Everything was good."

"Really good," Phoenix added even though she'd told Sophia to tell the story.

"Until Braden Stahl showed up."

Where had Saxon heard that name before? Saxon snapped his fingers as the memory hit. "Isn't he the—"

"Mayor's son," Addi said. "He's a weasel, an asshole, on the fast track to becoming a rapist, too."

"That one girl from his college already accused him of assaulting her, but she took it all back," Sophia said.

Addi sneered. "Yeah, after they found a way to shut her up."

"What does this have to do with you two?" Saxon asked. "And Oliver getting arrested?"

A look passed between Phoenix and Sophia again, and Sophia continued, "Braden had been eyeing Phoenix all night. He tried buying her a drink, but Phoenix said no. We didn't want anything to do with him and tried to stay away. We stayed at Under 21 until closing to make sure he'd left."

Phoenix looked up at Saxon, tears filling her eyes again. She swiped at them, and Saxon handed her one of the napkins on the table to use as a tissue. "But he hadn't gone home. He was waiting for us when we left."

Sophia hugged Phoenix tighter. "He ambushed us before our ride-share could get there. He called Phoenix stuck up, a bitch, and every name you could think of, all because she didn't want him to buy her a drink. I mean, the club serves fucking soda. It wasn't like he could get her drunk."

Saxon squeezed his soda can tighter while trying to maintain an outer calm. It might have been easier pretending he was straight. Not that anyone would believe it at this point in his life.

He wanted to hop in his car, head straight to the mayor's house, and demand to speak to his little shit of a son.

"Then what happened?" Saxon braced for what she'd say next.

Sophia continued. "When Phoenix turned her back and walked away—instead of dotting his eye as she should have—he reached out and grabbed her hair."

Saxon's eyes dropped to the wig Phoenix had laid on the table. Before leaving for the night, she'd gathered the wig's box braids into a ponytail. It was nothing more than a tangled mess now.

Phoenix laughed through her tears.

Saxon came around the table and hugged her. "Hey, hey, now." She sobbed on his shoulder for a minute or two before breaking contact. "I'm so sorry, Phoenix. You didn't deserve that."

Sophia took Phoenix's hand, and Saxon returned to his seat.

"It only got worse. He couldn't handle being refused," Sophia said. "The slurs started flying. He grabbed the front of her dress. And, and—"

"That's when Oliver stepped in," Saxon said, knowing it to be true even as the words left his lips. That was the kind of young man Oliver was. He was protective. He was loyal. And even though he was skinny, and the Braden kid probably outweighed him by a good fifty pounds, Oliver wouldn't have let that stop him.

Phoenix nodded, and Sophia said, "Oliver went after him and shoved him into his group of friends. Oliver may be small, but—"

"That boy can bitch slap better than anyone I've ever seen," Phoenix said with a hint of a laugh.

"Braden must be used to getting into fights because he knows how to throw a punch. Oliver didn't stand a chance. We tried to break it up and pull Braden off him, but Braden's boys held us back. We heard the sirens. Someone called the cops, but instead of running, Braden shoved Oliver to the ground and just smiled."

"Did Braden get arrested as well?"

"You're kidding me, right?" Heat rushed up Sophia's cheeks as her voice rose. "Not even close. He told the cops how Oliver had been the one to attack him first, and his boys backed him up. One of them had been videotaping the whole thing, but he edited the video before showing the cops showed up, and it started with Oliver shoving Braden."

"There any other witnesses besides Braden's friends? Anybody else taking video?" Saxon asked.

"Maybe," Phoenix said, "but we weren't paying much attention to them. And the few people that had been there scattered as soon as they heard sirens."

"How is Oliver? Is he hurt?"

Sophia dented her soda can, again and again, her busy fingers releasing some of her pent-up anxiety. "He had a bloody nose and probably a bump on his head from where it hit the ground when Braden pushed him, but I don't know how bad it is."

"We gotta get him out of jail, Saxon." Phoenix's eyes welled up again, and Saxon handed her another napkin.

How could the cops take Braden's words over the others? What the fuck was wrong with the world? His thoughts jumbled in his head until finally the most important one surfaced. How the hell do you get somebody out of jail anyway?

"You don't know what to do, do you?" Addi asked.

Saxon shook his head and swallowed a mouthful of the soda he didn't want to give him a few seconds to think. Nothing brilliant came to mind.

"I've never even gotten a speeding ticket before," Saxon admitted. "The closest interaction I've ever had with the cops was having lunch with them after they presented the D.A.R.E program in middle school."

"Ohmygod." Sophia thumped her forehead on the table. "We're doomed."

"We're not doomed." Saxon injected his words with all the confidence he didn't feel. He was an adult. Even though he had no practical experience with the police, he could figure it out, right?

"I'll call the San Fernando Police Department. SFPD should be able to tell us what we need to do."

"They won't be able to help." Addi wasn't trying to be negative. They sounded like they were talking from experience. "He's going to have to go before a judge before he can ask for bail. It's Friday night. It'll probably be Monday morning before he can see a judge."

Phoenix stood as if she were going to march to the police department right then and yank Oliver out of the cell. "We've got to get him out. Oliver isn't like the rest of them. He's too sweet. They're going to eat him alive in there."

"Relax, Phoenix," Addi said, adding the confidence that Saxon lacked. "He's just going to be in a holding cell for the weekend. It's not like they're sending him straight to San Quinton."

Phoenix collapsed in her seat. "You're right. Still…"

Saxon pulled out his phone. "I'll see what we can do to get him out of there as fast as we can. Why don't the three of you go upstairs and get cleaned up and changed in case there's something we can do tonight."

Saxon hated giving them false hope. Addi was probably right about Oliver having to wait until Monday. But he couldn't take Addi's word for it without checking himself. He waited until the three of them had trudged upstairs before searching for the nonemergency number for SFPD.

After waiting on hold for what seemed like a couple of hours but in reality, the wait hadn't been more than ten minutes, Saxon got through to the police department.

He explained to the woman who answered the phone what had happened and who he was calling about. He heard the *tap tap tap* of her keyboard as she searched for the record.

Finally, she came back on the line. "I don't have anyone in the system under that name. In all likelihood, he hasn't made it through intake yet. It can take some time, especially on a busy Friday night. Just be glad it wasn't a full moon. Intake gets slammed when those nights fall on the weekend."

That wasn't much of an answer. "How much time are we talking about?"

"I can't say, sir. But—"

"I mean, are we talking minutes, hours, a day?" As much confidence he had in Oliver that he could manage the weekend in a holding cell without being too scathed, he needed Oliver home. Saxon had to tamp down on his growing frustration. He didn't want to start sounding angry. He just wanted answers.

"Sir, I wish I could give you a time, but I can't."

Saxon thanked her and hung up. He paced the small kitchen, but it was too small to pen him in, and he moved into the den. At least in there, he could pace laps around the coffee table. He couldn't let Oliver down. He couldn't let the girls and Addi down either. What good was he to them if he couldn't negotiate this hiccup?

Hiccup? Oliver has been arrested. That's a little more than a hiccup.

Saxon ignored his inner thoughts. He didn't need another half-panicked voice in his head.

Upstairs, the water ran in the shower. He knew he only had a limited time to put together an action plan before the three of them stomped downstairs, expecting him to know what to do.

You could call Cesar. He'd probably know what to do.

Saxon glanced at his watch. It was nearly two-thirty in the morning. He couldn't wake Cesar. Sure, they'd started becoming friends, but kissing and dry humping a guy didn't give Saxon carte blanche to call him in the middle of the night.

Who else can you call that isn't as clueless as you about this?

Fuck.

Aiden probably wouldn't help him even if he could.

If Aiden would even take his call. Not that he wanted to be beholden to his ex, that was for sure.

Which left Cesar.

Shit.

Okay. He could do this. For Oliver.

Saxon pulled up his contacts and called Cesar's number. On the third ring, Saxon went to end the call, deciding against the bad idea.

Then Cesar answered the phone. "What's wrong?"

Cesar sounded wide awake. Maybe Saxon hadn't woken him from a dead sleep. It certainly didn't sound like he had. "Did I wake you?"

"Yeah, but that's alright. What's wrong?"

"Look, maybe I shouldn't have—"

"*Saxon.*"

Fine. Saxon had already woken him up. He might as well ask his question. "How do you get a person out of jail?"

Maybe it was the type of work that Cesar did or the knowledge that Saxon wasn't the type of guy who says he wants to take something slowly and then rings him a few hours later for a booty call, but Cesar knew the second he saw Saxon's number flash across his screen that Saxon needed his help.

He swung his legs over the side of the bed and turned on the bedside lamp. "What happened? Who got arrested?"

"Oliver."

Saxon told him about the mayor's son, who, from what Cesar had previously heard on the streets, was in for a rude awakening when he pulled some stunt so egregious that even his daddy couldn't get his ass out of it. If you asked Cesar, it couldn't come soon enough.

He set his misgivings about the mayor's son aside for now. The first thing they had to do was find Oliver and see what, if anything, they could do for him before Monday rolled around. The kid needed a lawyer, which could cost Stonewall House a pretty penny.

"Okay. You and the kids sit tight." Cesar grabbed a pair of jeans and a Henley off the chair in the corner of the room and gave them a pre-emptive sniff before throwing them on. "Let me see what I can do, yeah?"

"Yeah, sure." Saxon's voice sounded small, unable to hide his uncertainty that Cesar could help. "I appreciate this. I owe you one."

Cesar merely grunted, his mind already turning to the people he needed to contact. Besides, he didn't keep score in situations like this. You helped. That's what friends were for.

He ended the call and went into the kitchen to brew coffee and make phone calls. His priority was to find out where the arresting officers had taken Oliver. He could be in a holding cell at intake, or the officers could have taken him to the hospital to be examined out of an abundance of caution.

As early as it was, he didn't hesitate to call the first person on his list. And if he were lucky, Bell would be on shift. Lucinda Bell answered on the first ring with an acerbic, "You know I ain't got enough money to post your bail. You need to talk to—"

"*Luce.*" He knew she was joking about the bail comment, but she didn't know how close to the truth she'd come.

"Oh, shit. Something's wrong. Did you and Mister Yummy have a falling out?"

"That *Mister Yummy* is my business partner, and he's engaged."

"Well, damn. Not that I had a shot anyway, but... you know." He heard the shrug in her voice. "What do you need, handsome?"

He and Lucinda went way back to middle school when she met the school bully under the bleachers and gave him a black eye for calling Cesar every slur in the book long before he realized he was gay. Lucinda had been a big Black girl back in middle school. She was more formidable now. Few people looked at her and thought they'd get away with anything.

In the past few years, she'd changed from patrol to night duty at the station to give her husband peace of mind. She still grumbled about that.

Her husband may or may not have breathed easier knowing

she wasn't patrolling the streets of the valley, but Cesar was sure anyone up to no good had a little party when they'd heard.

"I've got a friend. He's running that new place, Stonewall House for the kids—"

"I heard of it. There were grumblings in city hall when he bought the place. Neighbors were afraid he'd bring down their property values. He told the city that the property being a known crack house did more to decrease property values than a few kids would."

Cesar laughed. Sounded like something Saxon would say. "Well, looks like one of his kids got arrested tonight."

"Oh, lordy." Cesar heard typing in the background as if Lucinda were getting into the system. "Lemme guess, you want to know where he's at."

"Bingo. Always said you were too smart for law enforcement."

"Heh." The shortened laugh came with the requisite eye roll. He just couldn't see it. "What's this kid's name."

Cesar gave her all the particulars that Saxon had given him, and she searched the system. She hummed a tune in the background as the keys clacked and the mouse clicked. He heard voices of other officers in the background, but nothing he could make out.

"I can't find him," Lucinda said after returning to the line. "Let me check with some of the guys in the back."

While waiting on hold, he texted the next person on his list.

Cesar: *You up?*

It took several minutes for the return text to come in.

Kellon: *It's three in the morning. Why the fuck would I be up?*

Cesar didn't bother answering the question: *Since you're awake, can you do a little, teeny, tiny, itty-bitty favor for me?*

Kellon: *Grrrrrr.*

Cesar: …

Kellon: …

Cesar …

Kellon: *You're going to make me put on my pants, aren't you?*

Cesar: *Would it make you feel better if I lied and said no?*

"You still there?" Lucinda asked.

Cesar let the texts drop for now. He'd fill Kellon in once Lucinda finished with him. "I'm here."

"He's at Canyon Hospital."

"Wait, what?"

"He's okay, it sounds like. The ER is running tests to make sure he doesn't have anything serious going on."

Cesar swallowed down his heart which had rocketed into his throat. "Can Saxon go see him? He's the program director at Stonewall House. I don't think Oliver has any family who can be with him."

"You head on down there. I'll try to butter up the officers and see if they'll let Saxon talk to him. Oliver is still under arrest."

"Yeah. Thanks, Luce. Give Harold and the kids a hug for me."

After ending the call, he switched to his messages to see several lines of *???* from Kellon wanting to know what was happening.

Cesar gave Kellon a quick rundown on what was happening with Oliver.

Cesar: *The client is in the ER at Canyon Hospital. Can you meet us there?*

Kellon: *I'm not a lawyer anymore.*

Cesar: *Just because you left your firm doesn't mean you aren't still a lawyer. Derek told me you helped a client of his about six weeks ago.*

Kellon: *You're an asshole.*

Cesar: *Love you, too, buddy.*

Kellon: *Do they know my rates?*

Cesar: *LOL. Like you need the money.*

Kellon: *Christ. Why are we friends again?*

Chuckling, Cesar agreed to meet Kellon in the emergency room at Canyon. With luck, Oliver would be there when they arrived.

Cesar brushed his teeth, ran his fingers through his hair, stepped into his shoes, and ran out the door. He called Saxon as soon as he started his engine.

Saxon answered on the first ring. "Did you find him?"

"He's at Canyon Hospital," Cesar said as he backed out of his driveway. "I'll be at your place in twenty minutes."

"Is he okay?"

Cesar didn't want to give Saxon false information. It concerned him that the doctors thought it necessary to run tests, which meant he probably got beat up pretty bad. "I think so."

***

DESPITE THE EARLY HOUR, SAXON WAITED AT THE CURB FOR CESAR to arrive. He could have met Cesar at the hospital, but Stonewall House was on Cesar's way, and if Saxon were honest with himself, he wasn't exactly fit to drive.

Especially when Sophia, Phoenix, and Addi wanted to go with him. He wouldn't risk their safety with his addled brain behind the steering wheel.

In less time than Cesar had allotted, he pulled up in front of the house and rolled the passenger window down.

Saxon leaned through. "Do you mind if Phoenix, Sophia, and Addi come too?"

"They probably won't be allowed to see him, but I don't mind if—"

The car's rear door opened before Cesar could even finish his sentence, and Addi, Phoenix, and Sophia piled in. Where had they come from? He'd told them to wait in the house while he asked Cesar so he didn't feel obligated to take everyone.

Saxon settled into the front seat, noticing the wry smile on Cesar's lips.

"Told you he wouldn't mind if we came," Addi said from their seat behind Cesar.

Even though she was the tallest, Phoenix occupied the middle seat. "Thank you. Saxon is no help in a situation like this."

"*Hey*," Saxon protested. "At least give me credit for knowing when to ask for help."

"This may be a wasted trip," Cesar said as if trying to manage everyone's hopes. "We may not get to see Oliver. But I have a lawyer friend meeting us there. He might be able to help."

"Sounds expensive," Saxon said.

"Let me worry about that, okay? You've got enough things on your plate right now."

Saxon leaned back into the seat, some of the tension leaving his body as he rested his head on the headrest. It felt good to give up a fraction of control and let someone else take a portion of the load. He was so used to doing everything himself that just that mild relief made him feel like he wasn't in this alone.

Not that he could count on Cesar to be there all the time. Saxon didn't expect that and didn't want to put undue pressure on him to do more than he felt comfortable doing.

The last thing he wanted was to put too much stress on Cesar and push him away. Cesar was the first guy Saxon had been interested in that he felt like he could be honest about his wants, feelings, and desires without being made to feel needy.

His finger tapped the center console. Canyon Hospital wasn't far, and with minimal traffic, they made decent time, but that didn't calm his nerves.

Nerves about what the arrest would mean for Oliver.

Nerves about what the arrest would mean for Stonewall House.

He didn't need some asshole at city hall convincing the rest of the council that giving Saxon the license to run Stonewall House had been a mistake that needed to be reversed. If Saxon wanted to keep the doors open, the program needed to be seen as a net positive for the city.

Or, at the very least, not a negative.

Saxon's finger *tap, tap, tapped,* releasing his pent-up energy. Cesar slid his hand over and threaded his pinkie finger around Saxon's. Immediately, his finger stopped tapping. That slight, singular, supportive touch grounded him.

Saxon blew out a breath. Everything would be okay. He'd come too far, worked too hard for it not to.

"You know," Phoenix said, leaning forward until her head was between the two front seats. "You two can just hold hands. It's allowed. You don't have to be sneaky. It's not like we're five, and we'll be upset that mommy has a new boyfriend."

Cesar laughed, and Saxon groaned, but that didn't stop Saxon from turning over his hand and locking his fingers between Cesar's.

If the touch of that one finger had calmed his nerves, holding Cesar's hand and feeling his warmth and the comforting squeeze made Saxon nearly invincible.

Braking, Cesar pulled into the hospital and parked in the first available space near the emergency room. Saxon hoped his newfound calm wouldn't waver. Oliver needed support, not Saxon's unease.

The kids piled out as soon as Cesar threw the car into park, not even waiting for Cesar and Saxon to get out. They jogged for the bright light in front of the double sliding doors, giving Saxon and Cesar a few minutes to themselves.

"It's going to be okay," Cesar said, even though they both knew that he couldn't be a hundred percent certain about that but having someone there to support him meant everything.

While he loved that Stonewall House allowed his kids to forge lasting friendships and support systems, he realized how isolated he'd become while trying to build that for them.

Cesar brought their joined hands to his lips and kissed the back of Saxon's hand. The zap from the kiss went straight to Saxon's heart.

Damn.

Cesar was going to make Saxon fall for him without even trying.

Cesar dropped Saxon's hand. "Let's go see what we can do for Oliver."

"Thanks." Saxon's voice had nearly abandoned him. "Thanks for being there for me when I called."

Cesar smiled, "That's what friends who frot together are for."

Saxon laughed and loved that Cesar could make him do that when it was the last thing he thought he could do at a time like that.

They found Addi, Phoenix, and Sophia inside the emergency room, trying to talk their way to where they had taken Oliver. The nurse at the desk turned them away.

The three of them plopped into the chairs in the corner and started playing with the building blocks meant for the little kids.

Saxon and Cesar approached the desk, stopping when the double doors behind them slid open, and a man in a three-piece suit strode through with damp hair, his briefcase in his hand.

Cesar dropped Saxon's hand and met the man with a hug. "Thanks for doing this."

"I'm not sure if this will help," the man Saxon assumed was Cesar's friend Kellon said, "but we'll see what we can do."

The man had a slender frame, in his mid-thirties, maybe, with a reassuring smile that instantly instilled Saxon with confidence. The man might have been slight, but Saxon suspected he wouldn't be a push-over.

Cesar made the introductions, then the three of them approached the nurse's station. Other people dotted the waiting room, but for a Friday night, it seemed relatively quiet.

Kellon stepped up to the desk. "I'd like to see my client. Oliver Sims. He's in police custody."

The nurse glanced at the three men, then at Phoenix, Sophia, and Addi in the corner. "Your name?"

"Kellon Mathews. And Saxon Gray is his program director."

Saxon stepped up to the counter. "Oliver doesn't have any family. He recently aged out of the foster system."

The nurse sat down and pointed his finger at Saxon and Kellon. "Only you two." He sent Cesar a pointed look.

Cesar backed away with his hands in the air. "Sure thing."

The nurse directed them down the hall. "Through those doors, first door on your right. Bed eight. And if the doctors kick you out, then you're out."

"Yes, sir," Saxon said.

"Go," Cesar said when Saxon turned to him. As much as Saxon wanted Cesar to go with them, he knew that wouldn't happen. "I'll be here when you're done."

Saxon only nodded because hearing those words as if Cesar wouldn't have said anything else made his throat tight.

They walked through the double doors and into the first bay of the emergency room. There was a nurse's station with a bank of eight beds in front of them. Some of the beds had the curtains drawn closed, but they easily spotted Oliver's bed at the end. His curtain stood wide open with a bored-looking officer leaning against the nearby wall.

Kellon grinned as he walked beside Saxon and muttered, "I know that guy."

"Is that good or bad?"

Kellon chuckled the way one does when ready for a challenge. "I guess we're going to find out."

They stepped up to bed eight. Oliver smiled, and the officer frowned.

"Mathews." From the officer's tone, he didn't seem thrilled.

"Officer Henderson."

"I thought you retired."

"Mostly," was all Kellon said. "I'd like a few minutes to speak with my client."

The officer stood there for a moment, his forearms resting on his duty belt, before finally saying, "Five minutes. We're waiting on the discharge papers, and then I'm taking him in."

Henderson gestured to Kellon and raised his hands for a quick pat-down. When he finished, he turned to Saxon. "You, too."

Saxon stood there while the officer checked for weapons before allowing them alone with Oliver. Saxon didn't take offense. He was doing his job.

The officer moved out of earshot, and Saxon stepped up to Oliver's bed. Kellon drew the curtain closed behind him.

Oliver was sitting in bed, looking like he'd jumped out of a moving car. He had a road rash on his arms and face. A couple of black eyes and a shaved spot on the side of his head where he'd had stitches. He looked tired and scared, but at least he was coherent and in one piece.

Saxon hugged Oliver, and Oliver winced. Saxon let him go. "Are you okay?"

"I will be," Oliver said. He turned, exposing one of his sides with a bruise that looked suspiciously like a boot print. "This probably hurts more than my head or the black eyes. They said I have a mild concussion from when my head hit the pavement."

Then he smiled, though it looked more like a grimace as his eyes filled with tears. "I didn't think anyone would come."

Those words hit Saxon square in the solar plexus. "You're one of mine. Of course, I came."

He introduced Kellon, who went to the other side of the bed and shook the hand without the IV catheter.

"How's Phoenix?" Oliver asked.

"She's good. A little shook up. But she'll be fine. She and Addi, and Sophia are in the waiting room. They can't visit, but they wanted to be here."

The waterworks followed, and Oliver had to scrub away the tears with the heels of his hands. "What am I going to do now? Are they really taking me to jail? I didn't even start it."

Oliver's voice rose higher and higher. Kellon tapped the air with his palms trying to get Oliver to lower his voice so that Officer Henderson wouldn't overhear. Oliver took a calming breath. "I know Braden is the mayor's son, but he's the one who started it."

"Sophia said that one of his friends had a video," Saxon said.

Oliver slumped back against the raised head of the bed. "If that guy's lips are moving, he's lying. He's the one that should be going to jail, not me."

"What did you say to the officer who responded at the scene?"

"I wanted to tell him my side of the story. But they started questioning Braden first. Then the mayor pulled up in his car, and they stopped talking to his kid. I've seen videos on social media telling you not to talk to the police. When they let Braden get into the car with his dad, I realized they wouldn't believe anything I said, so I kept my mouth shut."

Kellon gave Oliver a fist bump. "Nice work, kid. Keep it that way. If they ask you questions, tell them you want to talk to your lawyer."

Kellon pulled a business card out of the inside pocket of his suit and handed it to him.

Oliver flipped it over in his fingers. "What happens now?"

"They'll take you back to the station, and you'll be processed into the system. You'll likely be stuck there for the weekend and brought before a judge on Monday. Just hang in there. We'll get you out."

"The officer said I could be charged with a felony. I mean, I gave the kid a bloody nose, but I'm the one who ended up in the hospital."

"A felony?" Saxon squeaked.

"I could get fired and—"

Kellon shook his head, and Oliver stopped talking. "Don't worry about the charges right now. That's for me to worry about. That's my job."

Officer Henderson slid the curtain back. He had a nurse with him with papers for Oliver to sign.

"Can I talk to you a minute?" Kellon asked Henderson. It wasn't a question—more of a command—even though Kellon had no authority over him.

Henderson glanced at the nurse, and the nurse said, "We'll be a few minutes. He's not going anywhere."

Henderson nodded his chin toward the door to the bay, and Saxon followed Kellon out. In the hall, Saxon stepped aside and stayed out of Kellon's way.

As soon as the bay doors closed, Kellon rounded on Henderson, his voice heated but low and steady. "A *felony*. Are you kidding me right now? "All Braden got was a bloody nose. My client has two black eyes, a possible concussion, and stomp marks on the skin over his kidneys. You going to believe that little shit over this kid? What assistant district attorney is going to prosecute that?"

"He's the mayor's son." Henderson glanced down at his boots and kicked at a scuff mark in the tile before meeting Kellon's eyes again. That sourness settled in Saxon's belly. He didn't think he would like what Henderson had to say next.

"The charges are coming from the chief of police."

"You've got to be fucking kidding me. You and I both know those orders aren't coming from the chief of police. The mayor is putting pressure on the chief."

Henderson's lips flattened. "You have proof of that? Because I have video evidence of that kid starting things with the mayor's son."

"You and I both know that video isn't the full story. It's the mayor's kid you should be taking in, not Oliver."

Henderson crossed his arms over his chest. "Wasn't my call."

"Unbelievable."

"We're done here." Henderson dropped his forearms to his duty belt.

Kellon stepped back, nodding as if those three words confirmed everything he thought was true. It was bad enough that Braden had beat the shit out of Oliver, but now Oliver was going to get fucked over by the mayor as well.

"See you in court on Monday," Kellon said. "Don't sleep in. You won't want to miss it."

Henderson spared them an anemic laugh and disappeared through the bay doors.

Saxon and Kellon headed for the waiting room, the knots in Saxon's stomach worse instead of better.

5

Cesar sat in a chair in the corner of the waiting room where Sophia, Addi, and Phoenix had been filling him in on what had happened at the nightclub. Saying that he was pissed would be an understatement.

"Here it is. Here it is," Addi said. They'd been scrolling through social media while Phoenix and Sophia told their story. "I found the video. One of Braden's friends posted it on YouTube. I should have gone there first. He posted it like an hour ago."

They handed Cesar the phone, and everyone crowded around to watch over his shoulder. The video started at the spot where Oliver called Braden a piece of shit and then shoved him.

It got worse. Much worse. They watched it over and over. Poor Oliver was lucky he was still breathing when the cops showed up. Cesar couldn't remember the last time he'd seen that level of brutality in someone so young.

On the third, fourth, and fifth runs through the video, Cesar looked past Braden's brutality and watched the people in the background of the video. More people stood watching than Sophia and Phoenix had remembered.

He took still shots of all the people in the background and

sent a copy of the photos and the video to his phone. One of those people had to have a video of the fight, and Cesar would make it his mission to find them, even if the cops didn't.

He scrolled through the still shots and zoomed in on the faces one by one. The parking lot wasn't very well lit, making the faces grainy and harder to recognize, but all he needed to identify was one person to start.

"Do you know any of these people?" Cesar asked the group.

Phoenix, Sophia, and Addi passed the phone around and scrutinized each face. Addi got the phone last. They flipped through the photos, stopped, then flipped back one.

"This one." Addi held the phone for Cesar to see. "I went to high school with him before I dropped out. His name is…" Addi stopped to think. "Johnathan Anderson. He was my lab partner in chemistry. He was an okay dude."

Cesar made a note on his phone. Phoenix took the phone and, not two minutes later, handed it back to Cesar. "Here's his Insta account, and he has a link to his Snap under his bio."

Cesar grinned. What he wouldn't have given to have that technology at the beginning of his career. The number of people he found through social media now astounded him. "Ever think about becoming a PI?"

Phoenix waved him off. "Nope. It sounds like it might involve running, and I'm not about that."

Cesar laughed. "Not often, but sometimes."

Shaking her head, Phoenix said, "I'll stick to cosmetology. There's no running in cosmetology."

The double doors to the emergency bays swung open, and Kellon and Saxon strode through. Cesar could already tell from their expressions that he wouldn't like what they had to say.

Everyone trailed behind him as he met Kellon and Saxon halfway. "How is he?"

"He'll live," Kellon said.

"Pretty beat up." Saxon gave them a quick rundown of his injuries. "It could have been way worse."

"We found the video," Addi said. "It's—"

Kellon perked up. "Send it to me."

Cesar sent him the video and the stills. "Addi identified one of the witnesses in the crowd. I'm going to try and track him down —" He glanced at his watch. Where had all the time gone? "Later today."

"There's nothing we can do for Oliver right now," Kellon said. "Everyone get some sleep. I'll visit him tomorrow and see how he's doing. Spending the weekend in jail won't be fun, but he'll be fine until he sees the judge on Monday."

Cesar clapped Kellon on the back. "I'll walk you to your car." Cesar handed Saxon his keys so they could wait for him there.

They parted ways, and Cesar waited until they were far enough away from the rest of the group so that he wouldn't be overheard. "What do you think?"

Even with Kellon's face shadowed, it wasn't dark enough to hide his concern. "That this kid will get screwed by the justice system if we don't fight hard. The mayor will try to distort the narrative any way he can to show his son is blameless. We'll have to show without a shadow of a doubt that Braden instigated all this."

Cesar grinned.

"What are you smiling about?"

"You kept saying *we*."

Kellon dropped his head between his shoulders and blew out a breath. "*Fuck.*"

"So, are you in? Are you going to take Oliver's case? I'll pay your fees. Just tell Saxon you're doing it pro bono. I don't—"

"Wait. You like this guy, don't you?"

It was too early in the relationship to confide in anyone about his feelings for Saxon. As it stood, Saxon could decide next week that even going slow would be too fast and call off whatever it was they'd started. "I just want to help."

Kellon cut him a look, evidently not believing the partial truth, but it was very late—or rather very early—and they'd both rather get home and get some sleep than delve into it any further.

"Send me your retainer fee, and I'll—"

Kellon laughed. The sound traveled in the quiet of the early morning. "I'm not charging you. It'll be a few hours' worth of work. Hopefully, the judge will dismiss the case on Monday, and we'll be done with it."

Cesar stuck out his hand, and they shook. "Thanks, I appreciate it."

"Any time."

Cesar returned to his car, the exhaustion and mild relief making it difficult to keep awake.

Saxon leaned over the center console and popped his door for him. He settled in his seat and turned so he could talk to everybody. "Kellon agreed to see this through with Oliver. Hopefully, it'll be over and done with come Monday."

"Do you think so?" Phoenix asked, her voice soft and small as if asking louder might affect what Cesar had said.

As bad as she had to feel about Oliver, Cesar had to be honest with her. "Probably not. But we'll work hard to resolve this as quickly as possible."

They drove back to Stonewall House mostly in silence, not waiting for Phoenix to give them her permission to hold hands over the console. Their hands just came together. It felt right. It felt natural.

It felt like he wanted to hold Saxon's hands like this for the rest of his life.

Cesar stomped on the brake as the realization hit. He quickly shifted his foot to the gas pedal again, but not before waking everyone in the backseat.

"What happened?" Sophia said, her voice groggy.

"Nothing. I thought I saw something on the road. Go back to sleep."

He watched in the rearview mirror as they settled back in for the ride. Saxon squeezed his hand. He'd been awake the whole time, fully aware there hadn't been anything on the road. He felt Saxon's eyes on him, so he glanced over and winked.

God… that sly fucking smile. It killed Cesar every time Saxon gifted him with it. He didn't dare mention it to Saxon. Cesar would scare him away for good if he did.

He pulled to the curb in front of Stonewall House. Everyone in the back seat roused, wiping the sleep out of their eyes. When Cesar and Saxon didn't open their doors to get out when the others did, Addi said to Saxon, "Are you going to ask him to stay?"

Cesar would have loved to hear a *yes* to that. Saxon's hand squeezed Cesar's. Had he meant to do that, or had Addi caught him off guard?

"No," Saxon said, staring out the windshield to avoid eye contact.

"He's totally bangable," Sophia said, "and I'm into girls."

"Totally," Addi and Phoenix added in.

Cesar laughed, and Saxon dropped Cesar's hand to cover his ears, but he had a grin. "La, la, la. I can't hear you. Now go to your rooms, all of you."

They all laughed. Saxon dropped his hands. Addi climbed out the driver's side, and Phoenix and Sophia slid out the other.

Saxon buzzed down his window, and Sophia leaned in. "You realize we're not toddlers? You can't send us to our rooms fa or timeout."

"Shame," Saxon managed with a straight face. "Now go. All of you."

They all started up the sidewalk. Phoenix stopped mid-way and returned, her face solemn when she said, "Thank you."

"You're welcome," Cesar said. "And Phoenix?"

"Yeah?"

"This isn't your fault. None of this is your fault."

In the dashboard's lights, Cesar saw the shine of tears flood Phoenix's eyes. She waved a perfectly manicured hand in front of her face trying to dry the tears before they fell. "Stop. You're gonna make me smear my mascara."

Saxon patted the hand she had on the sill. She squeezed his before turning and walking away.

Cesar wanted that invitation. They didn't have to have sex. That thought was the furthest thing from Cesar's mind. He just wanted to hold Saxon in his arms. Hold him tight, and let him know everything would be all right, that they would get through this.

He wouldn't ask. Saxon had already said no.

"Can I walk you to your door?"

Saxon's soft smile nearly did Cesar in. "I would love that."

Dawn lay around the corner. They met at the front of Cesar's car, Saxon reaching out for Cesar's hand. Slowly, they walked hand in hand to the door. At the door, Cesar leaned a shoulder against the jamb. "I'm going to find that guy in the photo, that Johnathan Anderson guy that Addi knows. I'll come by sometime later today and check on you. Does that sound alright?"

"You don't have to check on me. You have your own life. I didn't mean to suck you into all my drama."

"Too late."

Saxon pulled a face that said *I'm sorry* better than any words could have. Cesar reached up and wrapped his hand around the nape of Saxon's neck. "Hey, that's not a bad thing. I'm here because I want to be. Besides, I need a little drama in my life."

Saxon rolled his eyes but leaned in for a kiss.

"*Jesus Christ,*" Cesar muttered. He touched his forehead to Saxon's. "Your lips... I can't get enough."

"I want to invite you in. It's not that I don't. You know that, right?"

Cesar took both of Saxon's hands, brought them to his lips, and kissed Saxon's knuckles, his voice rough when he said, "I know. You have to do what's right for you. I'm okay with that."

Saxon blinked rapidly several times and, after swallowing hard, said, "Aiden was out of his mind to let you go. But I'm so fucking glad that he did."

SAXON HAD ALL THE WINDOWS OPEN ON THE THIRD FLOOR, TRYING to let the breeze in, except there wasn't one. The light traffic on the street in front of the house filtered in as the sweat ran down Saxon's back.

He screwed another screw into the sheet of drywall to hold it in place and stepped back to admire his work.

He hadn't managed to put up more than a couple of boards since Cesar had visited him the night before, even though Saxon had been upstairs a while.

After the stressful night before, they'd all slept in well past noon, fitfully, from the sounds of it. James was shocked at the news when he got home from his boyfriend's house. But he didn't have more than enough time to hear it and get showered and changed before he had to leave to go to work again.

Phoenix and Sophia had claimed the kitchen table after a rushed and haphazard lunch to study for upcoming tests the next week, and he didn't know where Addi had disappeared to.

Saxon had ventured up to the third floor intending to work on the drywall, but with only two drywall boards hung, it proved his mind and his heart weren't in it.

And the most disconcerting aspect was that while Oliver had been on his mind, his thoughts kept straying to Cesar. He'd done the right thing by sending Cesar home, even though it felt wrong.

Not hearing from Cesar yet that day made him wonder if

maybe he'd screwed things up. Cesar said he didn't mind taking things slow, but he had to have a limit.

You don't believe him when he says he's fine with going slow? You don't believe he has his own mind and agency and wouldn't tell you if that was a problem for him? Are you so jaded that you think all men are like Aiden?

Aiden hadn't cornered the market on bad boyfriend behavior, but in Saxon's dating life, a surprising number of them had.

It seemed that Cesar was too good to be true. Maybe Cesar had a fatal relationship-killing flaw that Saxon hadn't noticed. A red flag that he missed. With Saxon's track record, he'd already started doubting his instincts where men were concerned.

But… in this case… in Cesar's case, it sure didn't feel like his capabilities had failed him.

He heard the knock on the front door, and Addi called up the stairs. "Saxon. Your boyfriend is here."

Saxon face-planted into his palm. Cesar wasn't his boyfriend, even though the title gave Saxon a little thrill in his belly that only increased the closer he got to the ground floor.

He reached the ground floor and found the den empty.

"We're in here," Phoenix called out from the kitchen.

Saxon snagged his T-shirt off the banister and wrangled it over his sweaty torso. Cesar popped into the hall with a heavy plastic bag in each hand. His smile widened when he saw Saxon.

Cesar walked over and planted an unexpected, quick kiss on his lips. "Hello, handsome."

Saxon chuckled. He couldn't complain about the reception. He'd love it if every time he came downstairs, Cesar met him with a kiss.

Cesar held up the two bags. "I brought tacos."

He turned and headed into the kitchen, not waiting to see if Saxon followed. He did. Because right then, his three favorite things were in the kitchen. Tacos. His kids. And of course… Cesar.

"You don't have to keep buying us food. We can pay—"

"Yes, he does," Addi said. "Tacos are legit."

Phoenix and Sophia nodded as they unwrapped a taco and took a bite.

"*Mmmm.* So gooood," Sophia said, her words muffled by the food.

Cesar helped himself to a seat at the table as if he ate there all the time. "Sit. Eat. I've got good news."

Against everyone's protests, Cesar waited until Saxon got drinks for everyone and sat down with a taco in his hand before saying anything more.

"Tell us already," Addi said. "You're killing us."

"Okay, okay." Cesar wiped his mouth. "I found Johnathan Anderson."

Saxon stopped mid-chew. "Have you talked to him?"

"Not yet. I thought you might want to come with me."

Dropping his taco, Saxon stood. "Let's go."

Cesar waved him back into his seat, shaking his head at Sophia, Phoenix, and Addi, who all said they wanted to go, too. "We can't all go. I don't want to scare the guy."

"Besides," Saxon said, "don't you all have homework? Phoenix, I know you haven't finished your project and—"

"I don't have homework," Addi grinned. "And I don't have work until tomorrow, so I can totally go with."

Saxon hated to disappoint them, but Cesar was right. They didn't want Johnathan to feel ganged up on. "No. We're doing this Cesar's way. He's the expert here."

Addi grumbled. "You don't even know the guy. The only reason Cesar picked you is because he wants to get in your pants."

Jesusfuckingchrist. "*Addi.*"

Cesar choked his food, trying to keep from laughing. A *they're not completely wrong* look on his face.

"That's not the *only* reason." Cesar crumpled a taco wrapper and tossed it into one of the plastic bags. "He's the program director. He has a stake in how this plays out."

"So do we," the three of them said simultaneously, but they didn't press the issue, which Saxon appreciated.

As much as he called them his kids, they *weren't* kids. They were young adults, and they understood why everyone couldn't go.

They finished eating, and Saxon started cleaning up the mess when Cesar stopped him. "Why don't you grab a shower? We'll clean this up."

A part of him wanted to ask Cesar to join him even though Cesar wasn't smelly or sweaty. Saxon accidentally caught Addi's eye, and they grinned as if they knew exactly what he'd been thinking.

Saxon blanked his expression, but it was already too late. "I'll be quick."

6

WHILE CESAR WAITED FOR SAXON TO SHOWER, HE SPENT THE TIME talking to the three of them. Phoenix showed him the project she was working on comparing false lashes products. From Phoenix's own fabulous extra-long lashes, Cesar figured she was already a near expert.

Addi told him about their job at a local plastic manufacturing plant, while Sophia mostly ignored all the chatter and concentrated on math problems.

Cesar didn't have to wait long before Saxon returned wearing a pair of dark skinny jeans and an off-white Henley with the sleeves pushed up his forearms.

"I'm ready," Saxon said, his hair finger-combed and damp.

They said their goodbyes, and as soon as they were in the car, Cesar put his keys in the ignition and waited to start the engine.

"Is something wrong?" Saxon asked as he clicked his seatbelt.

Cesar leaned over the console, and Saxon met him in the middle. Their lips touched, and Cesar gave Saxon's bottom lip a playful tug with his teeth before letting go.

"What was that for?" Saxon asked. "Not that I'm complaining."

"This thing you have going. Stonewall House. It's a good

thing. A really good thing. And from what I've seen so far, the people here are amazing. I'm so proud of what you're doing."

Saxon sat back in his seat as if Cesar had stunned him.

"What?" Cesar reached for his hand and squeezed. "Did I say something wrong?"

Saxon swiped his sleeve across his eyes and gave Cesar a watery smile. "No. You didn't say anything wrong. I didn't expect you to make me cry as soon as I got in the car."

Cesar swiped one of the tears off Saxon's cheek that he'd missed. "I wasn't trying to make you cry. I just—"

"Just what?" Saxon's words came out choked.

"I wanted you to know what an incredible thing you are doing here and what an exceptional person I think you are."

"Stop," Saxon choked out. "You're gonna make me start blubbering again, and I'm going to be all red and blotchy."

Cesar kissed his cheek and started the car. "You're pretty damn adorable, red and blotchy or not."

"Now I know you're out of your mind." Saxon reached for Cesar's hand and rested their joined hands on his thigh. "But thank you. I know I'm making a difference, even if it's one person at a time, but it's nice to hear that other people see it as well."

Cesar maneuvered through the side streets until he got to the main thoroughfare. Being a Saturday, they wouldn't have to worry about rush hour traffic.

"Where are we going?"

"Johnathan works for the post office. From what his supervisor said when I talked to him, he should be back from his route within the hour. I wanted to be there when he got off work."

"How did you find out where he worked?"

"Addi had found him on social media. He had the postal service in his bio. It took me all morning to find out which branch he worked out of, but I eventually found it." Cesar chuckled. "Social media is a game-changer in the PI business."

"I can imagine. I just hope he'll help."

"If not him, maybe at least he can point us in the direction of someone who can."

"Will it matter? I mean, if the cops wouldn't take Phoenix and Sophia's side of the story into account because of who Braden is, do you think they'll listen to anyone else?"

"My goal is to find enough evidence to corroborate Sophia and Phoenix's story so that no matter who that asshole's father is, the judge will be compelled to do what's right."

"And if that doesn't work?"

"Then I have a reporter friend who'd love to get her hands on the story."

One thing Cesar couldn't stand was an abuse of power, especially when they'd been voted into that position to serve the community.

He pulled into the post office's parking lot a few blocks later. Several of the delivery vehicles pulled in and parked in the back.

From their vantage point, they had a full view of the employee parking lot and kept their eye on the people leaving for the day.

Saxon's phone buzzed with an incoming text. Cesar kept his eye on the parking lot until Saxon sucked in a breath. He glanced over, and Saxon had turned a shade of white that made him wonder if he should call 911.

"What? Is there a problem at the house? Do we need to go back?"

Cesar started the engine and had his hand on the gear lever when Saxon said, "No. Nothing like that."

Cutting the engine, Cesar said, "Then what is it? You're starting to worry me."

"It—It's my father. My father texted me." Saxon looked like he would have preferred a text from the mayor.

"Is that a bad thing? Are you two not close?"

Saxon huffed out a laugh, and some of his color returned to

his face. "He walked out on my mother when I was six. I haven't heard from him since."

Cesar sat back in his seat, taking in Saxon's unsettling history. "Like, not at all, or only a call on birthdays and Christmases?"

Saxon's hand shook as he rubbed it up and down his bouncing leg. "Like dropped-off-the-face-of-the-earth never."

Another text came in before Saxon could answer the first one. "He wants to meet."

Leaning his head back, Saxon stared at the car's ceiling. Then he rolled his head to the side to look at Cesar. "I don't even know how to respond to that."

"Are you sure it's him?"

"Positive."

Saxon held out the phone for Cesar to read the messages. The first one said, "Hello, Bean, it's your dad."

"Bean?" Cesar said.

"He used to always call me that. I have no idea why. But it's not like some random person would know that, right?"

From the corner of his eye, Cesar caught movement in time to see Johnathan walk out the side door of the post office and head for his car. Shit.

"Johnathan just came out. I can always come back if—"

Saxon shoved his phone into his pocket. "No. We don't have that kind of time. We need to talk to him now."

"Let's go see what he has to say then."

They stepped out of the car and approached Johnathan as he reversed out of his parking space. Cesar tapped on the guy's window, and he startled in his seat. Cesar motioned for him to roll down the window, and after hesitating, he did.

"What do you want?" Johnathon asked as he shifted into drive, ready to take off if he had to.

Cesar kept his toes clear of the tires if Johnathan decided to take off. "I'm Cesar Morales, and this is Saxon Gray. I'm a PI. We want to ask you a few questions. Is that all right?"

Johnathon looked right and left and checked his rearview mirror as if expecting someone else to be coming for him. "This is about last night."

It wasn't a question. It was almost as if he'd expected someone to come talk to him.

Saxon leaned in, putting his hands on the car's sill. "We're here on Oliver's behalf. The guy who—"

"I know who you're talking about," Johnathan said quickly as if he were afraid someone would overhear, but there was no one around. "Get in the car. I don't want anyone seeing me talking to you."

Johnathan returned to the parking space. Cesar slid the empty fast-food bags onto the floorboards and dropped into the passenger seat.

Saxon scrambled into the back, middle seat. "Thank you for agreeing to talk to us."

"Just ask your questions and go. If anyone finds out I talked to you, I could lose my job."

Johnathan appeared to be in his early twenties, with shaggy, dirty-blond hair, gauges in his ears, and a thirty-six-hour scruff.

"Why would you lose your job?" Cesar suspected he knew the answer. He wanted to see if Johnathan would verify it.

Johnathan shook his head as if Cesar had been born yesterday and didn't have a single clue as to how the world worked. "The mayor gets people fired all the time. At least anyone who dares to mess with his son."

"Are you friends with Braden then?" Saxon asked.

Johnathan laughed. It came out with a healthy dose of disdain. "I don't think anyone is Braden's friend. He has hangers-on. An entourage like a fucking rock star. I mean, sure, he has money, and his father is the mayor, but he thinks he's a bigger fucking deal than he is."

"How do you know him?" Cesar wanted to know where the

guy's loyalties lay so he could judge how much weight to give whatever information Johnathan told them.

"Around. You can't live in this town and not run into him and his lackeys. I rolled with them a year ago but distanced myself after I got tired of Braden's bullshit."

Cesar and Saxon exchanged glances, and Cesar saw the hope flash in Saxon's eyes.

"Did you witness the fight between Braden and Oliver last night?" Cesar asked.

"You wouldn't be here if you didn't know I was there."

Cesar smiled. "Okay. Can you tell us how it started?"

"Braden was being an asshole as usual. Was pissed that a girl didn't fall at his feet when he gave her attention like a lot of them do. Especially one as beautiful as she was. His over-inflated ego couldn't compute it."

"And then?" Cesar asked, not wanting to put any words into Johnathan's mouth.

"And then that Oliver kid stepped in. Braden started the whole thing. But he's going to get away with it because he always does."

"Not if you speak up. I'd like you to talk to Oliver's lawyer and—"

"Yeah. Hard pass." If Johnathan could have stepped back, he would have. As it was, he leaned against the door frame as if trying to get as far away from them as he could. Cesar didn't think Johnathan had made the move consciously.

"Oliver could use the help." Saxon played on his sympathies. "We don't want Braden to get away with this. Or for Oliver to have to pay for it."

"I need you to get out of my car."

"But—"

"Get out, Saxon," Cesar said. They both exited the car, but before Cesar closed his door, he leaned in and said, "Do you know anyone there who might talk to us? This is important."

"Cierra. Cierra Galloway."

"And where do I find Cierra?"

Johnathan shrugged. "She hangs at Under 21 a lot during the week. Sometimes she dances at the Spicy Parrot on the weekends for extra cash. But you didn't hear that from me."

"Thanks for the help," Cesar said, stepping back and closing the door as Johnathan started backing up.

He and Saxon watched as Johnathan drove away. Saxon sighed. "Is this how it always is, trying to get information from people? Are you constantly going from person to person to person, hoping to find someone willing to talk to you? If it is, it sounds exhausting."

Cesar laughed. "Sometimes it feels that way. And yes, it can be exhausting. Let's hope that Cierra's more willing to help."

On their return to Cesar's car, Saxon caught Cesar's pinkie with his own and held on. Cesar liked that. Liked that Saxon reached out. He didn't know what to expect from him, but he knew he wanted more.

Wanted to explore the pure chemistry between them.

And to say that he didn't want Saxon in his bed would be a lie because the man was so damn fuckable, but something more drew him to Saxon than the pure physical. Saxon also had the most phenomenal, caring, compassionate heart.

"Are you hungry?" Cesar asked after they'd buckled in.

"You have this inexplicable need to feed me, don't you?"

"Maybe. Plus, I'm starving. I only had toast for breakfast. And the kids attacked the tacos like a school of piranhas."

"They can eat." Saxon laughed. "I think I only had one taco. Not sure what I'm in the mood for. You pick."

"How about grilled cheese sandwiches at my place? We're only about fifteen minutes away."

"That sounds amazing."

"Great. You call the Spicy Parrot and find out when Cierra is scheduled to work."

After confirming Cierra was scheduled to work at the Spicy Parrot the next evening, Saxon followed Cesar into his quaint two-bedroom Craftsman-style bungalow. It sat on a quiet street in the shadow of the San Gabriel Mountains. He had a neatly trimmed lawn and a front porch that spanned the front of the house.

"This is nice." Saxon spun around to take in the entire street. It was the kind of neighborhood you expected to see young families holding onto the back of their kid's bikes as the kid learned to ride without training wheels.

"Wait until you see the view out the back. It's why I bought the place."

They walked inside directly into the living space. The living space, eating area, and kitchen were all open concept with another door at the back of the house. On the left was a short hallway Saxon assumed led to the bedrooms.

Cesar led him into the kitchen and went to the pantry to pull out the bread. "There's beer in the fridge. I also have soda and water, or I can start a pot of coffee if you like. Help yourself to whatever."

"Beer sounds really good."

"Agreed."

Saxon opened the fridge and pulled two beers out, twisting off the caps and handing one to Cesar.

They both took a long draw leaning against the counter as they decompressed for a few precious seconds.

"Tell me this is all going to be okay," Saxon said.

"It's all going to be okay."

"That was too easy. Now, tell me the truth."

Cesar put his beer on the counter and turned toward him. "If the world works as it should, Oliver shemould be home Monday."

"Except, it doesn't always work as it should."

"Not often enough."

Saxon took another swallow, but it didn't sit so easy on his stomach as the first pull had. "Thanks for the help. I don't know what I would've done without you."

Cesar looked away and fiddled with the label on his beer. "Why don't you save your thanks for when Oliver is home safe."

"Afraid to jinx it?"

"I'm afraid the mayor has more power and sway than he should. Besides, I'm happy to do what I can."

It was Saxon's turn not to know how to take the unexpected assistance. After all, Cesar didn't owe him a thing. To cover up his awkwardness, Saxon changed the subject. "Need help cooking?"

"It's more of a one-person job." Cesar patted the counter next to the stove. "Have a seat and keep me company."

Saxon boosted himself up. "I don't think I've sat on the counter since I was a kid. I'm thinking I need to do it more."

"I'm never opposed to a man sitting on my counter and watching me cook for him."

"You cook for counter-sitting men often?"

Cesar laughed, stepped between Saxon's legs, and ran his hands up Saxon's thighs. "No. You're my first."

It may have been prematurely possessive, but Saxon liked that answer a little too much. It wasn't like he expected Cesar to not have been with other men—after all, they shared an ex—but he liked that part of this was a new experience for them both.

Cesar went in for a kiss. It started as a brush of his lips against Saxon's, but a whimper slipped out.

That sounded way too needy.

Heat rushed up Saxon's cheeks. If Cesar noticed, he didn't comment on it.

"*Mmmm.*" Cesar went in for another kiss, and Saxon draped his arms over Cesar's shoulders, deepening the kiss. It wasn't rushed or feverish. It was slow and soft and sensual.

Saxon loved tasting the shared beer on his lips, smelling the faint hints of Cesar's spicy cologne. Cesar's hands found the hem of Saxon's shirt and slipped beneath, his fingertips exploring every inch of Saxon's torso and brushing over Saxon's nipples.

That simple touch sent a shot straight to Saxon's groin, and he whimpered again, but this time he couldn't be bothered to be embarrassed. He was too busy thinking of everything he wanted Cesar to do to him.

Maybe he wasn't so hungry after all.

At least not for grilled cheese.

"*Fuck*," Cesar muttered as he pulled away. "Sorry. I didn't invite you here to get into your pants. I did just want to feed you."

"It's okay." Saxon almost kicked himself for ever having told Cesar that he wanted to go slow. After all, he'd always been a jump first and ask questions later kind of guy—hence a house he was fumbling through renovating and a group of people coming to mean more to him than he'd ever thought remotely possible.

But jumping first and asking questions later was also why he had three failed relationships and multiple hookups with nothing to show for it except a few jagged scars on his heart.

When he wanted to say, *where's your bedroom?* Saxon said, "Maybe we should start cooking."

Cesar gave him a quick peck on the lips before backing away and retrieving the package of cheese from the fridge to slice. He melted butter in the pan and added the bread.

"Already smells amazing," Saxon said.

Cesar added the cheese and the other slices of bread on top, turning it to let the cheese melt and the other side brown.

With a coy, sideways glance, Cesar said, "Are you always so easy to please?"

And suddenly, they weren't talking about food anymore.

Saxon almost turned the burner off and showed Cesar exactly how easy he was to please. Instead, he said, "You'll have to wait and see."

That low, sexy chuckle of Cesar's nearly did Saxon in. He

needed a distraction. Something to get his mind off the fact that Cesar made him pop wood while sitting on the kitchen counter.

Cesar flipped the sandwiches and bumped his chin toward Saxon's phone. "Did you answer your father? Are you going to meet with him?"

Saxon pulled his phone out of his pocket and set it on the counter face down. "With what's going on with Oliver, I'm not sure I have the emotional bandwidth to deal with him right now, to be honest."

"Fair enough." Cesar turned the sandwiches again. The cheese had gotten all melty, and the bread had almost the perfect amount of brown. "It's been years since you've had any contact. A few more days or weeks to ensure you're in the right headspace is reasonable."

Clicking the burner off, Cesar plated the sandwiches and cut them diagonally with the spatula. Saxon hopped down, accepted the plate Cesar handed him, and took his plate and beer to the table.

Cesar grabbed a couple of bags of single-serving chips out of the pantry and joined Saxon at the table. "Do you remember much about him?"

Saxon shrugged more as an acknowledgment of hearing the question than that he didn't know. He took the first bite, chewing slowly to give him time to consider the question. He'd thought of his father a lot over the years, never seriously considering what *he'd* remembered compared to what his mother had told him.

"I was pretty young when he left. I remember he used to take me to the park at the end of the street. It had a big concrete basketball court that no one ever used, and he taught me how to ride a bike there. I would go around and around in circles until I was so tired he had to hold onto the handlebars on the way home so I didn't have to pedal."

Around a bite of food, Cesar said, "Sounds nice."

Again, the shrug. That memory didn't jibe with his memory of the last time he saw his father and what his mother had told him every day until the day she died. "Mom always told me he was a piece of shit. He was a lying bastard, not to trust him, and we were better off without him."

Cesar swallowed and washed it down with his beer. "Was it the truth, or was she rightfully bitter about him leaving her with a six-year-old to raise alone?"

"I've always wondered. Like did she tell me all that so I wouldn't want to go looking for him? Or was he bad news?"

"Did you ever try to find him?"

"The county did after my mom died, and they temporarily put me in the foster system. Eventually, I became a permanent foster. I never went looking for him because I figured if he was that hard to find, he must not want anything to do with me like my mom always told me."

As hungry as Saxon had been, he pushed his plate away, leaving half of his sandwich uneaten.

"I'm sorry." Cesar swallowed his last bite. "I didn't mean to put you off your food."

"Not your fault." Saxon appreciated how Cesar listened without judgment or tried to solve a life-long problem over grilled cheese. Sometimes, listening was the hardest part of the conversation. "I always thought my mom had kicked him out. In a way, I blamed her when he left."

"Did they fight a lot?"

"I guess that depends on your definition of a lot. They fought. When you're six and have no other frame of reference, you think whatever you're exposed to is normal. But, yeah, I would say so."

And because it was Cesar asking, and because Saxon didn't feel any judgment coming from him, he trusted it was safe to continue. "I've never told anyone this before. That last fight was on my birthday. I'd turned six, and he'd missed my birthday party. I knew before I found out that he'd left for good that that fight was different. And I couldn't even tell you how I knew. I just did."

"Kids have good intuition."

"All I remember was I was trying to sleep, and they kept getting louder and louder and louder. I crawled out of my room and down the hall, staying low so they wouldn't see me. I peeked into the den. On the coffee table, my dad unpacked stacks of money. I don't know where it came from. He must have taken it with him because I never saw the money or him again."

"Drugs? Gambling?" Cesar asked.

"No clue. I try not to think about it. It was a lifetime ago."

Outside, the sun started to set, casting a warm glow on the foothills of the San Gabriels visible through the windows into Cesar's backyard.

"Would you like to stay for a while?" Cesar asked. We could sit out on the back porch, drink more beer, see where the night takes us, or we could chill on the couch. Watch a movie."

Or maybe he could just curl up in Cesar's arms until that uneasy feeling the discussion brought up finally settled.

As worried as he was about Oliver, everyone back at the house had to be beside themselves, waiting for an update.

"Both sound amazing..."

"But?" Cesar quickly masked the flash of disappointment on his face and somehow managed to keep it from tainting that one word.

The last thing Saxon wanted was to leave. He wanted to disappoint Cesar even less, especially after all his efforts to help Oliver. *But* he had responsibilities he couldn't ignore.

Before Saxon could answer, Cesar said, "You need to get back to the house."

"I'm sorry."

"Never apologize for your responsibility to the kids. I've only known them briefly, and I get it. I would do the same thing in your shoes."

They both stood, and Saxon stepped closer to the Cesar. "I'm glad you're mine."

What did you just say?

The words caught Cesar off guard because his big, beautiful brown eyes snapped to Saxon's.

"I don't mean mine, I meant—I mean—"

Cesar eased closer, one thigh slipping between Saxon's as Cesar held the nape of Saxon's neck. "What *did* you mean?"

Cesar's voice sounded like liquid gold—thick and insanely rich. It did things to Saxon's will and control that he didn't think possible. Like making him want to ignore all of his responsibilities… at least until morning.

"I—"

Cesar kissed the soft spot under Saxon's jaw and worked his way to Saxon's ear.

Saxon's hands went to Cesar's hips to hold himself steady. "I meant that I like you in my life."

Cesar straightened. "I like you in my life, too. I wasn't looking for anything new. After Aiden, I'd sworn off dating for a while… until you called."

At the risk of sounding silly, Saxon said, "I'm honestly not sure what I thought would happen. That we would have coffee and vent about a manipulative asshole, maybe. I never expected I'd want more."

Saxon cringed. He hated being vulnerable. Hated that Aiden taught him to hate it. Yet, he'd come to trust Cesar implicitly in a very short period. Could that trust be misplaced? Absolutely. Though nothing Cesar did made Saxon think so.

He waited for Cesar's response.

Would Cesar laugh?

Would Cesar tell him that he only wanted casual sex?

If that was what he wanted, he could have gotten that off any of the apps without all the extra work of helping in a crisis.

That willingness to help didn't come across as someone who wanted a quick fuck.

Cesar pressed the barest, briefest, breathless kiss to his lips. "What *do* you want?"

"You." Saxon wanted to be as open and honest as he could. "But I'm scared of what that means. I'm scared to get hurt again. I'm scared that—"

Cesar's expression softened with each word that Saxon spoke. And the way his brown eyes regarded him—like Saxon made his world spin—shut him up.

But then Cesar nudged him, encouraging him to continue.

How would Saxon continue without making a fool of himself, especially if Cesar didn't feel the same?

The encouragement in those eyes had him talking again. "I'm scared you don't want me the way I want you."

"Fair enough," Cesar said, taking a step back as he considered Saxon's words. "Have I done anything to make you think I'm not interested? Anything to make you think you don't already matter to me?"

"No." If anything, Cesar's actions had shown he cared. Even if things between them were new. "Nothing."

"I'm already invested, Saxon. I'm scared, too. I'm scared of what might happen down the road. I'm scared of the feelings I'm feeling so soon. I'm scared that they're not real. Even if they're more real than anything I've felt before."

Cesar took both of Saxon's hands and held them to his chest. "What I'm inelegantly trying to say is that I want you, too, and not just in my bed. I meant what I said. I'm willing to wait as long as it takes until you're ready."

What the fuck are you waiting for, Gray? An engraved sign? One of those banners pulled behind an airplane on the beach that says, 'I promise not to hurt you?'

No one can promise that. Not one hundred percent.

Look at him. Did you hear the sincerity in his voice? Do you not see the integrity in his eyes? He's not Aiden. Cesar can't promise never to hurt you, but he won't hurt you with intention.

"I'm ready," Saxon said.

"Don't say that because you think it's what I want to hear." A smile came to Cesar's lips. "Why are you grinning like that?"

"Because I believe you, but you should have seen how your pupils dilated when I said I was ready."

Cesar flushed. "I'm not going to lie. There are so many things I want to share with you, do with you, but…"

Saxon knew exactly what Cesar would say and didn't like it one bit. He finished the sentence for him. "But I need to get back to the house."

Cesar pressed his forehead to Saxon's. "Yeah. I'm afraid to kiss you If I do, you won't be making it home tonight."

Saxon took the unwanted step back. This wasn't an end. It was a beginning. "Does this mean you're my boyfriend now?"

"Better believe it."

7

———

CESAR WOKE BEFORE THE SUN ROSE AND WENT ON A RUN TO CLEAR his head before showering and heading to the office. He hoped to find Derek there. But it was Sunday, and business had been slower the past couple of weeks, so he didn't expect him to be there. Now that Derek and Max were together, and he had the sexy tattoo artist warming his bed, Derek had a much better reason to stay home and sleep in on a Sunday.

He drove around to the parking spots at the back of the house that had been converted into their office space and parked next to Derek's Roadster, surprised and a little relieved to see him there.

Cesar and Derek had become good friends in the short time they'd joined forces as investigators, but not so close that he would call him up late at night to talk about personal stuff.

He walked in through the back door, which landed him directly into the old kitchen. They hadn't renovated the small space yet, but it was clean and more than serviceable for their office needs.

Derek had his back to him. He pulled a coffee mug out of the cabinet and turned around. "What are you doing here?"

"I could ask you the same thing." Cesar's eyes narrowed. "Why *are* you here? Why aren't you at home on a—"

"Max left for a week in Baja to visit his sister and help her with her tattooing."

"Sweet. She's doing well then?"

Derek and Max had gone on a mad hunt searching for Max's estranged sister when she'd disappeared one night. They'd found her safe in a small town in Baja, California, where she'd met a man and decided to stay.

Cesar had ended up in Baja briefly as backup, but Derek and Max had everything under control by the time he'd arrived.

Derek poured himself coffee. "Yeah. She is. And she invited Max to go down and visit, which was a first. He didn't waste time closing down the shop to go see her."

"Good for him," Cesar said.

With the coffee pot in hand, Derek said, "Want some?"

"I need the big mug."

Derek chuckled and pulled the extra-large coffee mug out of the upper cabinet. "Someone not get any sleep last night? Please tell me it was for a good reason."

Cesar took the filled mug from him and doctored it with cream and sugar just to give him something to do besides look Derek in the eye. "Saxon and I didn't have sex if that's what you're asking."

When Cesar finally looked up, Derek smiled. "But something happened between you two."

It didn't come out as a question because it wasn't one. Derek read people the way scholars read kindergarten primers. It was part of what made him an extraordinary investigator, though Cesar found it a little disconcerting having that intuition turned on him rather than someone they needed to question.

"What gave it away?"

"Even with your darker skin tone, I can tell you're blushing."

"I don't blush," Cesar said as his cheeks heated more.

"Whatever you say."

Derek moved past him to his office, and Cesar followed. They had a reception area at the front of the house with a comfortable couch and chairs, but they preferred to talk between themselves in either one of their offices.

Derek eased into his chair behind his desk, and Cesar plopped into the leather seat across from it, setting his untouched coffee on the desk.

"So, it looks like I have a boyfriend now."

Derek choked on his swallow of coffee, and for a second, Cesar thought he'd have a mess to clean up, but Derek managed to swallow it down without spitting it all over his desk.

Finally, Derek caught his breath, his voice weak when he said, "Say what?"

Cesar said it again. Stronger this time, even with Derek's raised brow aimed at him. The brow that said Derek thought Cesar had lost a screw or two. "Saxon is my boyfriend."

"That's… great." Derek tried to smile, but Cesar could tell he'd forced it. Derek wasn't the only one who could read people. But in this case, it wasn't a difficult read.

Already on the defensive, Cesar said, "What's the problem?"

"Isn't that a little soon?"

"Says the man who fell back in love with his ex in what, a week?"

Derek leaned back in this chair. He had his blinds open on the window to the street fronting the office. "We had a history. And I'd never stopped loving him."

That didn't invalidate what Cesar had already started to feel for Saxon. He may not know why he felt so close to Saxon already, but he did. He didn't need Derek's blessing *or* his permission. Cesar stood to leave.

"Wait." Cesar met Derek's eyes. His partner sighed and shook his head. "Sorry. That was a shitty thing to say. I'm happy for you. I just don't want to see you get hurt."

While Cesar understood and appreciated the sentiment, he realized he didn't want to play it safe anymore. At least not with his heart. Or Saxon. "I'd rather get hurt putting myself out there than risk never falling in love again."

"Brave." Derek's earlier skepticism morphed into respect.

Brave? Or foolhardy?

Either way, Cesar wouldn't change a thing that had happened between him and Saxon in the past couple of days. "Saxon and I had a history, too. In a way."

"Is a shared ex considered history?" This time when Derek said it, he had a sly grin.

"Well, a lot has happened since Friday evening, so…"

Derek perked up, sniffing a case. "What happened? Is this why you looked wrecked yesterday morning when we switched out the cars?"

While they'd exchanged cars and keys Saturday morning at Cesar's house, Derek had been in a hurry, and Cesar for too sleepy to go into what had happened the night before.

"Yeah." Cesar told him about Oliver, everything that happened at Under 21, his and Saxon's conversation with Johnathan, and the shitty kid the mayor had.

A pencil broke in Derek's hand. "I don't know how the fuck that guy got elected. He's the worse thing to happen to this town in years."

"Yeah, well, if we can't find anything compelling, his kid may go free while Oliver pays for it. Oliver doesn't deserve that."

"Nobody does. Do you need help?"

That's one of the many things Cesar had come to respect about his new business partner, his willingness to step in and help no matter what other cases he had working.

"I think I'm okay for now. I came in to research that Cierra Galloway girl that Johnathon told us about before I try to talk to her. She's working tonight at the Spicy Parrot. Anything I find,

I'm turning straight over to Kellon for Oliver's arraignment in the morning."

Derek's smiled. "How did you manage to talk Kellon into taking the case?"

"He wasn't too happy about it at first, but he hated what Braden did to Oliver and even more that the mayor will try to get his son out of it. That kid wouldn't know a consequence if it came up and bit him on the balls."

Laughing, Derek tossed the two broken halves of the pencil into his trash can. "No doubt."

Cesar picked up his coffee. He took a sip and grimaced. It was too sweet and now too cold to be palatable. He stood to leave. Then it hit him. Derek wouldn't be in the office on a Sunday if business were slow, even if Max had gone out of town. One of the reasons they had partnered up was for a better work/life balance.

"We have a new case, don't we?"

"I have a new case. You already have one you're working on."

"But my case is personal, not—"

"And me following Max into Mexico wasn't?" Derek's gaze didn't waver. "You handled things here while I had personal business. Now it's my turn."

"You're not even going to tell me what it is?"

Derek tapped his hands on the desk. "Don't you have work to do?"

Cesar laughed. "Fine. Don't tell me."

He turned to go when Derek stopped him. "About Saxon…"

It was Cesar's turn to raise a brow at Derek. He didn't want to fight about his new boyfriend, but he refused to stand there, wasting time and trying to justify why their decision felt right.

"… I'm happy for you two. From what I've heard, he seems like a really good guy."

Even though Derek had a good poker face and could lie his

way through many things that the job required, his sincerity hit hard. "Thanks. I appreciate it."

Cesar spent the next few hours delving into Cierra's social media accounts. It had taken him a good hour to find her profile. He'd had to wade through many more Cierra Galloways than he'd expected. He'd found her through a dating site linked to one of her social media accounts.

He went through her photos and posts one by one. It didn't take a PI genius to find Braden in one of her photos. "Sonofabitch," he muttered.

He must have been louder than he thought because he heard the creak of Derek's chair, and moments later, Derek stood in Cesar's doorway, his coffee cup in hand. "What did you find?"

"Cierra is Braden's girlfriend. Or at least she was. I found her on a dating site, but that could have been an old profile she never shut down." Cesar scrubbed his hands down his face.

"You don't think she'll be willing to talk to you, do you?"

"If she's his girlfriend, then no. Even if she isn't anymore, she may still be loyal to him."

"Or she's using those photos as a status symbol even if she has animosity toward him. She wouldn't be the first person to hang around someone because of their perceived power, even if they don't like them."

Cesar could only hope. "Agreed."

He held up his mug and asked for a refill. By the time Derek returned with his coffee, Cesar had fifteen different social media tabs open in his browser. He'd extended his search, going through the social media of friends of friends on Cierra and Braden's social media pages, trying to identify the other people in the background of the video Addi had found.

Lunchtime rolled around, and Cesar came up for air, his focus sorely tested. He wondered what Saxon was up to. He checked his phone, but he hadn't had any missed texts from Saxon.

He had his thumb over Saxon's name, about to text him, when

his phone rang in his hand. Kellon's name popped up on the screen.

"Hey, Kel. What's up?"

"I just left the jail. I talked with Oliver. I thought you might want an update."

"Saxon's going to want to hear this. Can we meet you for lunch?"

The hesitation on the other end of the line dragged on until Kellon's voice came over the phone again, a little sheepish. "I've got something I have to do, but you can meet me there."

Kellon gave him the address, and they set up a meeting time. He hung up, eager to hear what Kellon had to say and find out how Oliver was doing.

Though he couldn't deny that eagerness was bolstered by the knowledge that he'd get to see Saxon sooner than he'd thought.

He shut his computer down and picked up the tablet with the notes he'd taken. Before heading out, he popped his head into Derek's office to let him know he was leaving.

"You're going to see Saxon, aren't you?"

"Well yeah, but—"

Derek's laugh cut him off. "Oh, man. I can tell by your smile that you already have it bad for him."

"I'VE GOT IT," SAXON HOLLERED OUT FROM HIS BEDROOM OUT OF habit even though he hadn't heard anyone upstairs move to answer the knock at the front door.

They'd all had a late night, and everyone was probably upstairs taking a nap to catch up on their lost sleep.

Saxon glanced at himself in the hall mirror and swiped at a lock of wet hair sitting wonky on top of his head. He opened the door before Cesar could knock again.

"Hey," Saxon said, holding onto the door. Even in a casual pair of jeans and a form-fitting T-shirt, the sight of Cesar on his doorstep took his breath away.

"Hey, yourself." Cesar stepped closer, glancing up the stairs and around Saxon, ensuring they were alone. He kissed Saxon, then went back for another.

"I love that I can do that," Cesar said.

Saxon smiled. It probably looked a little goofy, though he did manage to stifle the giddy giggle. "I love that you do that."

Saxon went in for another kiss, when all Saxon wanted to do was drag Cesar into his room and lock the door, he broke the kiss. "Thanks for picking me up. I could have met you there."

"It was on my way."

Saxon eyed him. "It was fifteen minutes *out* of your way."

"Was it? I hadn't noticed." Cesar grinned. "Are you ready?"

"I just need to grab my keys and my wallet."

Saxon hurried to his room. The door closed behind Saxon, and he stopped at his dresser to find Cesar had followed him.

"Nice room." Cesar's gaze lingered on Saxon's cover-rumpled queen-sized bed before traveling around the rest of the room.

"I have a bed, a dresser, and a couple of nightstands. It's not much, but at least I don't have to share my bathroom."

"And you have a private entrance." Cesar walked to the far side of the room and looked out onto the outdoor patio.

The patio's folding bistro table and two chairs took up most of the space, but Saxon had never considered that he could sneak men in and out through his private entrance when he moved in.

But now that Cesar pointed it out…

Saxon stepped up behind him and looked out into the back-yard, a scraggly, weedy, more dirt-than-grass kind of situation. The large space would be a great place to hang out once he had the opportunity to fix it up. Until then, the rooms needed to come first.

"You okay?" Saxon asked.

Cesar turned, his eyes soft. "This place. You. It continues to amaze me what you're doing. I may not have earned the right to say this yet, but I'm so fucking proud of you."

Those words hit Saxon like a blunt force to the chest, his heart absorbing the soft, unexpected blow. It knocked the breath out of Saxon at the same time that it brought tears to his eyes.

A sucker one-two punch with all the feels. They may have been official for less than a day, but those words carried a lot of weight and had an enormous impact.

Saxon swiped at the wetness on his cheek. "Stop. You're making me fucking cry."

Cesar wrapped his arms around Saxon's neck and hauled him into his warm chest, Cesar's heart beating steady and true.

With a kiss on Saxon's forehead, Cesar leaned far enough away to see his face. "You good?"

Saxon blew out a hot breath and nodded. "Yeah."

Cesar took a step back and held his hand out for Saxon. "Come on. Let's go see what Kellon has to say."

Saxon let Cesar lead him out the door after a brief stop into the kitchen to leave a note letting everyone know where he went. He knew everyone had been worried sick about Oliver, and they'd be anxious to hear how he was doing.

In the car, Cesar reached across the center console, and Saxon threaded his fingers through his. Who would have thought something so exceptional would have started from the shit-show that was his relationship with Aiden?

But having Cesar in his life, having this novel, fresh beginning made all the heartache and the tears he'd shed over a man who never deserved them worth it.

Cesar followed his map app through the valley's Sunday traffic which for once wasn't all that bad. They'd managed to hit the slack time between everyone heading back through the valley to get to Los Angeles after a weekend away and the locals returning from the mountains and the beach.

Before long, Cesar pulled into a driveway and parked in front of a house that had been converted into a veterinary clinic. The sign outside said *Valley Vet.*

"Are you sure this is the right place?" Saxon asked.

"This is the address Kellon gave me." Cesar pointed to a car in the lot. "And there's Kellon's car."

They both got out and headed for the entrance. When they got to the door, they found it locked.

Before they could knock, a man came to the door with an aggrieved sigh and what looked like a sick puppy in his arms. He twirled the keys in the lock and opened the door. "You looking for Kellon?"

The man looked to be in his early forties. He had an epic beard, gauges in his ears, and a stethoscope around his neck. He would have been less intimidating and possibly more handsome if he hadn't met them at the door with a scowl.

"Yes," Cesar said.

"Come in, then," the man said. He didn't bother introducing himself before bumping his chin toward a door on Saxon's right. He locked up behind them. "Kellon's in the cat room. Make sure he locks the door when you leave."

The man didn't stick around. He vanished through a set of swinging double doors behind the reception desk.

Saxon leaned in as they walked toward the cat room. "Why are we meeting Kellon in a cat room at a vet clinic?"

Cesar shook his head. "Beats me."

They stepped to a door with Kellon's Cat Rescue painted on the glass.

"I guess that explains it," Saxon said as he opened the door.

"Watch—"

Cesar snagged a black kitten as it rounded the corner and tried to dart between his legs. Saxon scooped up the orange tabby running behind it before it could also escape.

"You made it," Kellon said.

They found Kellon wearing a pair of shorts and a rescue-branded T-shirt. He stood on a stool, cleaning one of the top cages in the bank of cages along one wall. An L-shaped bench seating took up the opposite wall beneath the windows.

"Good, you caught them," Kellon said, referring to the kittens. "Dr. McGrumpypants gets exponentially more grumpy when the kittens escape into the clinic area."

"Do they escape often?" The orange kitten settled in the crook of Saxon's arm, purring louder than a street packed with Harleys at Sturgis.

"You'd be surprised how sneaky they are. Especially the little ones." Kellon bobbed his chin toward the cat trees. "You can put them down there. I'm letting them run around while I clean cages."

Cesar and Saxon set the kittens on the first tier of the cat tree with the fluffy cat bed on it. The black kitten batted at a felt mouse hanging from the platform above it, while the orange kitten jumped down, scampered across the floor, and pounced on Saxon's leg. It started crawling up, meowing the indignities of being put down, its sharp little claws digging into Saxon's skin the entire way.

Kellon popped his head out of the cage to watch.

"Where are you going, buddy?" Saxon asked. Doggedly determined, the kitten climbed up Saxon's leg, up his chest, and curled in the crook of Saxon's neck, his sharp little claws kneading the muscle there.

Kellon laughed. "Looks like he picked his new person."

"Wait. No." Saxon tried to remove the kitten. It sunk all of its claws into Saxon's shirt and skin. "I—we can't—"

Saxon got one paw free only to have the kitten latch back on when he tried to get one of the other ones free.

"Face it," Cesar said, unable to keep from laughing as the kitten used all four of its murder mittens to stay on Saxon's shoulder, "he's yours now."

Saxon gave up trying to dislodge the kitten. It settled onto his shoulder. His purr box turned up to blast. "I can't—"

Wait. Saxon cut off his protest.

Why couldn't he?

After all, he made the rules at Stonewall House, didn't he?

Kellon did a piss-poor job hiding the knowing grin. But Saxon and Cesar hadn't agreed to meet at the clinic to look at a bunch of rescue cats.

Saxon sat on the bench and leaned against the wall, careful not to squish the kitten. The kitten closed his eyes, but the purr-factor upped several notches every time Saxon scratched under its little chin.

Cesar settled next to Saxon, and Kellen climbed off the step stool and sat on the adjacent seat. "I know you came here to see how Oliver was doing, not to pet the kittens."

"I'm not mad about the kittens, though," Saxon said. The kitten had already started growing on him. That contented purr did something to Saxon that he couldn't quite put his finger on. Spending so many years in foster care, he'd never had a pet of his own. Some of the foster homes he'd stayed in had pets, but none of those pets had ever been his.

Kellon rested his forearms on his knees, his hands clasped in front of him. "I finally got to see Oliver this morning. I hoped I could see him yesterday, but the timing didn't work out. Considering everything, he's doing well."

Saxon blew out a heavy breath that woke the kitten up. It sniffed Saxon and nibbled on his ear lobe before climbing down his chest. It stretched out along the length of Saxon's arm. At this rate, Saxon's skin would look like he'd gone ten rounds with a saber-toothed tiger by the time they left.

"Oliver was relieved to see me," Kellon said. "I can't get the look of surprise out of my head. Like he couldn't believe..." Kellon leveled his gaze on Saxon. "Even after talking to him at the hospital, he couldn't comprehend someone cared enough to send help."

Cesar patted Saxon's knee and squeezed it. Saxon swallowed hard. "That poor kid."

Saxon remembered what it felt like not having anyone in his corner. It's what drove him to start Stonewall House. He'd wanted to keep as many kids as possible from feeling like they were all alone in the world.

"You good?" Cesar asked Saxon. Cesar must have had questions for Kellen, but the fact that he took a moment to check in on Saxon meant a hell of a lot.

The lump in Saxon's throat grew. All he could do was nod. The kitten rolled to his back, his little front legs stretched over his head, exposing his little striped belly. Automatically, Saxon's fingers scratched through the kitten's fur. Instead of scratching and biting his hand, the kitten stretched out more and amplified his purr.

"Was Oliver able to tell you anything that we didn't already know?" Cesar asked.

"His story tracked with Phoenix and Sophia's. Which is good, but we need more to get this thing thrown out. And much more if we want Braden to pay for what he's done."

The black cat zoomed over and skidded into the wall with a tiny kitten-sized thud after putting on his brakes too late. Kellon scooped him up, but the kitten wiggled until he set him down again. They all watched the kitten scamper off.

"We're trying," Saxon said. "We found one of the witnesses. He wants nothing to do with anything concerning Braden, but he gave us a woman's name."

Kellon perked up. "What did she have to say?"

Cesar absently ran his hands down the kitten's tail spilling over Saxon's elbow, and the kitten slept right through it. "We're hoping to talk to her later. We have confirmation she's working at the Spicy Parrot tonight."

"I'm trying to stay positive." Kellon scooped up the little black kitten and put it back into the cage he'd cleaned, adding the full food and water bowls. "I'm confident we can get Oliver out tomorrow. Getting the charges dropped, and more importantly, finding enough evidence to get the prosecutor to file charges against Braden might be harder than convincing Dr. McGrumpy-pants to not kick the rescue out of the clinic to make room for more exam rooms.

Saxon took in the hunch in Kellon's shoulders, the exasperation in his voice, and the way he started frustration sweeping the cat room to mean that making Braden accountable would be nearly impossible.

"At this point, I just want Oliver out and his charges dropped. I don't want him having to pay for something he didn't start."

"Braden thought he'd be an easy target." Kellon picked up one of the disposable kitty litter trays from the stack in one of the corners while he spoke, putting cans of kitten food and a sample pack of dry kitten food in a *Kellon's Cat Rescue* branded bag. "But he's going to find out that Oliver has more people on his side than he expected. People that would love to see the little prick finally face the consequences of his actions."

Cesar stood, and Saxon did as well. He stroked his hand down the kitten's exposed belly. The kitten stirred and stretched in Saxon's arms.

Kellon handed Cesar the bag of food and the litter tray.

Cesar took it. "What's this for?"

Kellon bobbed his head at Saxon and reached for the broom again to sweep up the hair and bits of spilled kibble and litter. "So he can take the kitten."

"Wait. I can't—"

The kitten finished his stretch and pressed a paw to Saxon's protesting lips as if to shut him up.

"Why not?" Kellon had a way of making Saxon feel like he was the one guilty of a crime. Saxon didn't have an immediate answer because, in reality, nothing prevented him from adopting a cat. Kellon continued. "He picked you."

"Aren't there papers to sign or..." Saxon didn't even know what was involved in adopting an animal.

"There are papers that make it official. But why don't you take him home? Give him a few days. If it doesn't work out, I'll personally drive out to Stonewall House and pick him up myself. Besides, I don't have another place for all these cats if Dr. McGrumpypants makes me move the rescue. I need to find homes. It's been impossible to find an affordable place to house them."

"What do you think?" Saxon asked Cesar.

He chuckled. "Oh, no. This is your decision. I don't want to be blamed if it all goes wrong."

"Or you could be thanked when it all goes right." The suggestive way Kellon said *thanked* didn't make Saxon think he meant *thanked* with words.

Kellon continued sweeping while Saxon considered whether he'd take a chance on the kitten with the squishy belly, the cute pink nose, and the rings of white around his inquisitive blue eyes.

"What's the story with the hot vet? Are you and him..." Cesar didn't finish the sentence as if he were waiting for Kellon to fill in the rest.

Kellon had his back to the door, and he only stopped sweeping long enough to roll his eyes at Cesar.

He swept at some stubborn hair stuck to the floor in the corner between the wall and the bank of cat-occupied cages.

The door to the cat room opened, and a hot vet stepped into the room. He was about to say something when Kellon started talking. He was too absorbed with dislodging the stuck hair to notice they weren't the only ones in the room anymore.

"Trust me," Kellon said, his back still turned. "If we were the last two gays on earth, I wouldn't touch Dr. McGrumpypants even if he were hung like a horse and could suck better than a Dyson. He's—"

Saxon covered a laugh with a cough.

"Kellon," Cesar cautioned as the doctor leaned a shoulder against the wall and folded his arms across his chest, one hand stroking the length of his thick beard.

Kellon continued as if he hadn't heard the warning in Cesar's voice. "He's insufferable, egotistical…"

"*Kellon.*"

"… he's—"

"He's standing right behind you," Saxon said, unable to stand there and watch Kellon dig a hole so deep that neither he nor the kittens could climb out of.

Kellon jerked upright, bumping his head on the open door of the only empty cage.

"You were saying?" The doctor schooled his expression better than some of the street kids Saxon had run with after aging out of the system.

Kellon rubbed the top of his head. The tips of his ears turned crimson, and he tugged at the collar of his T-shirt.

The doctor straightened. "You left out opinionated, broke as fuck, and hanging onto this clinic by a microscopic thread."

"I—" Whatever Kellon thought about saying next, he swallowed it down.

The doctor took the broom out of Kellon's hand and leaned it against the wall, practically growling when he said, "And while I may not be hung like a horse, knowing how to pleasure a man—" His voice dropped impossibly deeper. "—*really* pleasure a man, and make him forget his name and his religion, takes a level of skill and expertise I don't think you're ready for or have the capacity to handle. Besides, you'd have to have more to offer than that fuckable ass for me to be interested."

The doctor spun on his heel and strode out of the cat room.

Seconds later, they heard the thunk of the lock in the front door slide into place, having never said what he'd come in there for.

Kellon's jaw lay on the floor with the wisps of swept-up cat hair.

That deep rumble the sexy vet had in his voice made Saxon have to adjust himself. "I don't know about you two, but I almost dropped to my knees and sucked him off right then."

Then Saxon remembered who stood next to him. He whipped his head toward Cesar. "No offense."

Cesar chuckled, and even the stunned Kellon managed a nervous, strangled laugh with him.

"None taken," Cesar said. "I totally get it. I would have gotten in line right behind you, but I don't want to step on Kellon's toes."

The playful dig sailed over Kellon's head. Then as if Kellon's rant-stalled brain flickered back online, he said, "He thinks I have a fuckable ass."

Saxon's bark of laughter startled the kitten. It jumped to his feet in Saxon's arms, its sharp nails digging into Saxon's skin. "He thinks you have a fuckable ass? *That's* your takeaway?"

Kellon swept the mess into the dustpan and dumped it into the trash can. "The sad thing is, that's the closest thing to any action I've had in a long time. I'll take it. Even from him."

"I don't believe you," Cesar said. "You should be killing it on the apps."

Kellon ignored Cesar's comment and turned his attention to the kitten in Saxon's hand. "What's it going to be? You taking the furball home with you?"

8

____

From ten miles away, a toddler could have seen that Saxon wanted the kitten. He hadn't put it down since it climbed onto his shoulder. But for some reason, he wouldn't permit himself to say yes.

"We can keep him at my place until you decide," Cesar said. "What do you think about that?"

The kitten claimed the spot on Saxon's shoulder and curled its tail around its feet, swiping its tongue on the underside of Saxon's jaw. Saxon scrunched his nose. So adorable. Saxon eyed the kitten before looking at Cesar again. By the _I can't leave him_ look in Saxon's eyes, Cesar knew he'd say yes before the words came out of his mouth.

"Okay. We'll take him," Saxon said.

Cesar liked the sound of _we_ more than he would willingly admit. It made it feel like they were a team, even in such a new relationship.

Kellon offered them a cardboard carrier, and Saxon placed the kitten inside. It immediately started meowing and clawing at the cutout air holes.

"*Awh.*" Saxon stuck a finger through one of the holes. "Poor baby."

Kellon chuckled as they left the room. He let them out, locked the clinic door behind them, and walked them to the car. After they settled into the car, Kellon rested his hands on the sill of the car and leaned down. "He'll be fine in the carrier until you get him home. Let me know what you find out tonight. I want the best chance of having Oliver's charges dropped tomorrow."

"It could be pretty late," Cesar said, especially if Cierra refused to talk to them until after her shift ended. "The club doesn't close until two in the morning."

"It doesn't matter the time. Call me."

"Will do."

After saying their goodbyes, Cesar pulled out of the parking lot. If they were going to do this kitten thing right, they needed more than a day's worth of food and a disposable litter box.

The cat howled and cried until Saxon couldn't take it any longer and let the kitten out. It scrambled out of the box and up Saxon's torso and settled on his shoulder again, perfectly quiet and perfectly content.

Cesar laughed. "That's awfully cute."

"Right?" Saxon had a smile on his face that made Cesar want to wrap him in a hug and never let him go.

"Going to be a lot less cute when he's nine pounds and doing that."

Saxon shrugged the way Cesar expected him to. "I'm willing to take that chance."

They finally made it back to Saxon's place after a pet store run where they spent *waaaay* too much money on a two-pound ball of fluff that they hadn't even signed the adoption papers for. Which didn't concern Cesar. He could tell by the mutual love-fest between the kitten and Saxon that the cat had already found its forever home.

Cesar pulled the keys from the ignition, and Saxon said, "I'll carry the kitten if you can get the bags."

"I thought he was staying at my place." Clearly, that would never happen unless Saxon came with the kitten. Which was fine with Cesar. He'd give a lot to have an uninterrupted evening alone with his—*gulp*—boyfriend.

"I—" The smile fell from Saxon's lips. "Yeah. Sure."

Cesar leaned in and wrapped his hand around Saxon's neck. The kitten batted at Cesar's fingers.

Cesar kissed Saxon, loving the way his boyfriend melted into the kiss. "If you want the kitten here, that's perfectly fine with me."

Saxon grinned, and it was at that moment that Cesar wanted to be the one to always bring that beaming smile to Saxon's face.

Tucking the kitten under his arm so it couldn't escape on the short walk to the front door, Saxon got out of the car. Cesar loaded up with more food, cat beds, and toys than any cat could ever need.

Saxon made it halfway up the walk before turning around. "Don't forget the cat tree in the trunk."

"I'll have to go back for it."

Arms loaded down, Cesar followed Saxon through the front door and made sure it closed solidly behind them.

They spent the next couple of hours or so setting everything up. The cat tree took the longest since the instructions were entirely unhelpful. Everyone was home, except Oliver, of course, and they all immediately fell in love, the same way Saxon had.

The kitten was friendly and playful with everyone, especially Phoenix. But when it got tired, even from Saxon's bedroom where they were setting up the litter box, they heard him meowing as he walked down the hall, searching for Saxon. For such a small thing, he had a healthy set of lungs.

"Your cat wants you."

"It's not just mine," Saxon said, even though the smile on his face said that Saxon loved that the kitten had already picked him to be its person.

"Yeah, well, tell that to the cat."

Saxon called out, "Kitty, kitty."

The kitten sprinted around the corner of the room, and Saxon scooped him up and held him to his chest as if he hadn't seen the kitten in a year instead of the five minutes they'd left it with Phoenix, Sophia, Addi, and James.

They pointed him toward the food and water bowls and showed him the litter box in the bathroom. After eating his fill, the kitten followed Saxon and Cesar into the bedroom.

"How long until we have to leave for the club?" Saxon picked the kitten up and sat on the bed with his back against the headboard.

"An hour or so. I want to get there early and hopefully catch her before she heads into the club. I don't mind waiting until two in the morning if that's what it takes, but I'd prefer not to have to."

Saxon patted the mattress beside him. "Come here."

Cesar didn't hesitate. He walked to the other side of the bed, kicked off his shoes, and stretched out beside Saxon. Saxon scooted down and rolled to face him. The kitten curled up in the dip in Saxon's waist and promptly fell asleep.

"He's had a big day," Cesar said. "He's out like a light."

"I could use a nap, too."

"Want me to leave? I can come back and—"

Saxon shut him up with a kiss that Cesar didn't dare deepen, not with the bedroom door open and everyone home. "Of course, I don't want you to leave." Saxon kissed him again and snuggled as close as he could without dislodging the kitten.

"What if someone walks in?"

"We're laying on top of the covers. There's nothing indecent about that. Besides, they're full-ass adults. I don't think they'd be scandalized to find my boyfriend on my bed."

Cesar couldn't find any reason to argue. Not that he wanted to. He couldn't think of anywhere he'd rather be than where he was. He'd hardly thought about Derek or his business in the past few days. He should feel guilty for letting Derek take the brunt of the workload, but he couldn't drum up the guilt.

He liked spending time with Saxon and almost dreaded what would happen when Saxon didn't need him anymore to help secure Oliver's release.

Not that he thought Saxon was using him. He wasn't that kind of guy.

He wasn't like Aiden.

He also couldn't expect Derek to do all the work forever, and Saxon had his own life. Cesar would have to enjoy this time with Saxon while he had it.

"Why the frown?" Saxon asked.

When Cesar glanced over, the concern in Saxon's eyes nearly stole Cesar's breath. When had anyone looked at him like that? Like he was needed. Like he *mattered?*

He cleared his voice. "Just thinking." He kissed Saxon because he'd rather not lay all of his insecurities at Saxon's feet, especially so early in the relationship.

"I'm sorry about what I said about Dr. McGrumpypants."

"I don't understand," Cesar asked. "What do you have to be sorry about?"

"You're my boyfriend. I shouldn't be looking at other men, and I definitely shouldn't be thinking about blowing them."

Cesar laughed. "You being my boyfriend didn't magically mean you no longer noticed hot guys or stopped thinking about what you would like to do with them. It doesn't work that way."

"But—"

"No *buts*. He was objectively hot. I get it."

Saxon still had that crease between his brows. "I'm not like Aiden. I would never—"

Cesar pressed his finger to Saxon's lips. "Stop. You don't have to remind me. Talking about other men and appreciating other men doesn't bother me. If we ever decide we want to open things up, that's a discussion we can have. In the meantime, keep telling me what you're thinking. I love hearing all your dirty thoughts."

"You do?"

"I definitely do."

Shifting the subject to something lighter, Cesar said, "Your cat needs a name."

"Mango." One quick word. No hesitation.

Cesar laughed. "That was easy. Mango, huh?"

"Yeah. He's orange and sweet."

"Perfect. Mango it is. Now get some sleep. We could have a long night ahead of us."

Cesar fluffed one of the pillows and rolled to his back. Saxon slowly shifted to his stomach, throwing an arm and a leg over Cesar and resting his head on Cesar's chest. Mango went with the roll and settled at the small of Saxon's back.

"Comfortable?" Cesar asked.

"*Mmmm hmmm,*" Saxon managed before his breathing evened out.

Cesar loved how natural it felt being in Saxon's bed and having Saxon in his arms.

If they didn't have to leave later, would Saxon let him stay?

———

WHEN CESAR'S ALARM CHIMED, HE SHUT IT OFF. SAXON GROANED, and Mango stretched and yawned wide as a lion.

"I was out." Saxon's voice came out thick with sleep. He lowered Mango to the floor, and the kitten scampered off for his food bowl. "I'm ready to find something that could help Oliver, but I could have slept through until morning."

Cesar rolled out of bed and gave Saxon a hand up. "You've had a stressful couple of days."

"Not nearly as bad as it's been for Oliver, I'm sure."

Cesar kissed him on the tip of his nose. Why did Saxon love it so much when he did that? "Then let's find evidence or a witness that can end this thing."

They spent a few minutes freshening up, alerted everyone that they were leaving, and brought them Mango to babysit. They drove across town and parked behind the Spicy Parrot in the employee parking lot, waiting for Cierra to show.

Turns out, they didn't have to wait long.

"Cierra?" Cesar asked as they walked across the parking lot to intercept Cierra before she disappeared through the club's rear entrance. Saxon did his best to keep up without breaking into a jog.

Cierra ignored him. Cesar called out again. She stopped and turned, crossing her arms over her chest. "Do I know you?"

Cesar and Saxon stopped a few feet away. They didn't want to frighten her. "We wanted to ask you about the fight the other night at Under 21," Saxon said.

"Yeah. No." Cierra turned, but Saxon jumped ahead and stood in front of the door.

"Look, dude. If you don't get out of my way, I'll have one of the bouncers come out here and teach you a few manners."

Saxon raised his hands and stepped away from the door. "I'm sorry. We just need a few minutes of your time."

She didn't agree to answer any questions but didn't reach for the door. Cesar took advantage of the tiny crack in the metaphorical door. "A guy is sitting in jail that shouldn't be there. Do you know that? You were there. All I'm asking is that you tell a judge—"

"You know I'm Braden's girlfriend, right? Why would I say anything against him?"

"Did you know he was hitting on another girl while you were there?"

"We aren't attached at the hip. He doesn't own me."

Saxon stepped closer. "But he thinks he does, doesn't he? He thinks you'll be waiting for him after he's had fun with other girls."

Damn. Where had that come from? If Saxon decided he wanted out of the group home thing, maybe Derek and Cesar needed a new partner.

He glanced over at Cesar, who seemed to be working overtime, keeping the pride off his face.

Some of the defiance melted from Cierra's expression. "You know I can't say anything, right?" She stepped away when somebody came out the door but otherwise paid the person little attention. "Braden has a temper. And no matter what he does, daddy dearest is there with a fresh mop and a gallon of sanitizer to clean up his messes. I'm just trying to live my life. I don't want to be caught up in any of his drama. And I don't want to do anything that might jeopardize my job. I need this money. You've got to understand that."

Saxon ducked his head. He couldn't fault her for protecting herself. "Are you okay? Do you need help getting away from him?"

Saxon may have been way off base, but he didn't think he was *too* far off.

Her eyes shifted to the ground before looking back up at them. "No. I'm alright. It's not really like that."

Not really like that. Definitely *not* a resounding endorsement for Braden.

Apparently, Cesar wasn't content to let the comment go. "In what way is it 'really not like that?'"

Cierra glanced over her shoulder at the Spicy Parrot's rear entrance as if looking for a way out. "Braden is controlling. Jealous. But it's not like he's violent."

Saxon raised a skeptical brow, and Cesar stifled what Saxon assumed was a sarcastic laugh. "The guy left Oliver black and blue, and you considered that non-violent?"

"Well, I mean, he's never been physical with me. Not in that way."

The back door to the club opened, and a woman stuck her head out. "Cierra, if you don't get in here, Marcus will fire your ass."

Cierra started backing away, looking relieved that one of her coworkers had come to the rescue.

Cesar reached into his wallet and pulled out his business card. "If something changes, or you just want to talk, give me a call."

"Yeah, sure." Cierra tossed the business card into her over-sized bag. It would be a miracle if she ever found that card, and Saxon lost all hope of ever hearing from her again.

9

———

THEY LEFT THE SPICY PARROT IN SILENCE, EACH OF THEM IN THEIR heads thinking about Oliver and Braden—and at least for Cesar —the unfairness of life sometimes.

Oliver didn't deserve to be targeted by a guy who thinks he's better than everyone else. Then again, if you had a father like the mayor who willingly covered up all the bad shit you did and never held you accountable, that bred a person like Braden.

A part of Cesar felt guilty that they couldn't dig up anything else about the fight in the short time they'd had.

Scratch that.

Maybe it wasn't so much that they *couldn't* find anything, as much as witnesses were afraid to talk. It wasn't like Braden was the *Godfather*, but he might as well have been.

They had to hope that Kellon could work his magic and get Oliver out of jail, at least until they could either find other evidence to corroborate Oliver's story or convince somebody to talk.

Cesar pulled into Stonewall House's driveway and got out with Saxon. Saxon came around the car and laid his hand in Cesar's when Cesar held it out to him.

"You don't have to walk me to the door."

"But I want to. Is that okay?"

The smile that slid across Saxon's face almost reached his eyes. Cesar missed Saxon's easy smiles and felt determined to put them back where they belonged.

"It's more than okay."

They walked up to the porch and stood under the light someone had left on.

"Do you want to come in?" Saxon asked.

Yeah. Definitely. He wanted to go in, wrap his arms around Saxon, and tell him everything would be all right. But he couldn't promise that. And more importantly, he knew that everyone inside would be just as worried about Oliver as Saxon, and he wanted to give Saxon uninterrupted time to spend with them.

Cesar cupped the back of Saxon's neck, sifting his fingers through the short, soft strands. The street was quiet except for the occasional dog barking. The leaves rustled in the breeze. The super sweet way Saxon's breath caught when he brushed his thumb over Saxon's lower lip nearly undid his resolve to go home.

What Cesar wouldn't do to spend the night kissing those lips. But he knew Saxon had other priorities, and he respected that.

Cesar kissed him. At first, it was nothing more than a touch of his lips against Saxon's, but the small squeak Saxon gave and how he melted into Cesar's body had him deepening the kiss. He held Saxon's head, loving how Saxon's tongue slid against his and imagining the pleasure that tongue would bring him to other parts of his body, and his to Saxon. He'd love to hear Saxon moan his name as he fell apart beneath him.

That would have to wait.

Saxon fell back against the door, and Cesar went with him. He slipped his thigh between Saxon's and ground against his hard-on. Cesar broke the kiss and leaned away to see Saxon's heavy-lidded gaze.

"I think we'd better stop here," Cesar said. "I'm not sure Kellon would be so generous of his time if your neighbors call the cops on us for lewd and lascivious acts."

Saxon blew out a breath with a laugh, his chest rising and falling as he caught up on his oxygen debt. "Maybe you're right."

The way he said it made Cesar think that Saxon didn't believe it for one minute. Cesar took a step back, and Saxon regained his footing.

The flush on Saxon's cheeks faded, and worry and sadness replaced the lust in his eyes. Cesar kissed him on the forehead. "Go," he said. "Spend time with your kids."

Saxon opened his mouth, probably to argue or maybe to ask him in again. Cesar took another step back and then another because he didn't know if he could tell Saxon no again if he asked him to stay.

"Good night, Saxon. Try to get some sleep. I'll meet you at the courthouse in the morning. Hug Mango for me."

Saxon chuckled as Cesar hoped he would. He stood on the sidewalk until Saxon opened the door and disappeared inside.

As Cesar drove home, all he wanted to do was make things better for Saxon. He thought about how he could do that. After he updated Kellon on what Cierra had told them, there wasn't anything else he could do on Oliver's case besides showing up at court the next day for moral support.

But maybe there was something else he could do for Saxon.

Even though it was getting late, he went to the office and parked in the back.

His legs took him inside, his fingers flipping on the light switches in the kitchen, the hallway, and the office as he walked to his desk and sat.

What he planned to do wouldn't help get Oliver out of jail or get Braden to stop being a complete dick, but maybe his efforts would bring a smile to Saxon's face.

Sometime later, Cesar clicked one more link with blurry,

gritty eyes. He must have been more tired than he thought because he hadn't even heard Derek come in through the back door until he turned the corner and leaned a shoulder into the door jam. "What are you doing here?"

"What are *you* doing here?" Derek's voice had that thick quality it always had when he had too much work and not enough sleep.

"You said we didn't have much work. Yet here you are at night."

"It's just the one job. And I've got it under control. Any news on the Oliver situation?"

Cesar scrubbed a hand down his face and leaned back in his chair. "Not anything that's going to help Kellon tomorrow. Everyone's afraid of this Braden kid because they know his father can make their lives miserable if they say anything."

"One of these days, that will catch up to the mayor."

"Not soon enough."

Instead of leaving, Derek came into the room, stepped around to Cesar's side of the desk, and bobbed his chin toward Cesar's computer screen. "What's all this?"

Cesar clicked to another screen, even though Derek had already seen what he'd been working on. "Nothing."

"Who's Melvin Davis?"

Maximizing his browser, Cesar showed his work on the screen and kicked his chair back so Derek could get close enough to see it. "Melvin Davis is Saxon's father. At least, I think he is. I'm still trying to verify with vital records to confirm, but I think this is him. Saxon hasn't seen him since he was a kid."

Derek crossed his arms in that way he had that told Cesar he wasn't going to like what came out of his mouth next. "Saxon ask you to do that?"

Derek wouldn't have asked that if he hadn't already known the answer.

"Well, no. But his father texted him yesterday. I was trying to do something nice for Saxon."

"You need to talk to him about this."

"It's fine," Cesar said even though he had that sinking feeling in his gut that Derek might be right. He pushed it aside.

Cesar *fixed* things.

That was his *job*.

And if he could bring a little happiness to Saxon's life, he wanted to do that. "Besides, I'm just checking into this guy in case Saxon decides he wants to meet up with him. Trust me. It is going to be a good thing. Just wait and see."

Derek grumbled, and Cesar decided he'd have to live with Derek's disapproval. What did Derek know anyway? He'd never even met Saxon before.

Instead of leaving him alone to get back to work, Derek plopped down in the chair opposite Cesar and stretched his long legs out in front of him. "You two are getting serious?"

Cesar squirmed under Derek's casually intense scrutiny. "No one has proposed if that's what you mean." Cesar left off the word *asshole* at the end of his answer, but his tone delivered a message. He got one of Derek's lopsided smiles for his effort. "Besides, I didn't know we were at the *reveal all* level of our friendship."

That time when Derek smiled, it was the kind of smile that told Cesar he'd royally fucked up. *How?* No doubt, Derek would tell him.

"So it was okay for you to be all up in my personal business when Max and I were rekindling our relationship, but suddenly it's all bets are off when we're talking about yours?"

All right, so maybe Cesar could see the hypocrisy there. It sure as hell had felt more like he'd been trying to help Derek than it did now when he sat on the other side of that question.

"We're…"

Why did it sound so good in Cesar's head to call Saxon his

boyfriend yet make him feel so exposed when he wanted to use that term for their relationship when he told Derek?

Derek raised an impatient brow.

Cesar picked up the thumb drive on his desk and fiddled with the tab that extended and retracted the USB drive. "We're boyfriends."

Derek straightened in his seat. *"Boyfriends?Already?"*

He didn't allow Derek to ask any other questions before he started spewing words to fill the void. "I mean, I know it's fast, and we both have gotten out of shitty relationships with the same guy, and I know we need to take it slow and figure out if this is what we want or if we're together somehow to shove it in Aiden's face even though he has no idea we are seeing each other and—"

"Whoa, whoa, whoa," Derek held up his hands, and Cesar swallowed down the rest of whatever nonsense would have come next. The heat rushed to his cheeks, and he could only sit in the awkwardness. "I'm not judging. I was… clarifying."

"I know it's too soon. I mean, we only met a couple of times before Friday, and it's only been—"

Derek chuckled. "Would you stop already?"

That flash of heat on Cesar's cheeks ignited as he waited for Derek to give him shit for jumping in with both feet without even considering if there was a safe place to land.

"I said I wasn't judging. Alright?"

"Yeah, sure."

"Is it soon? Maybe. Is it unexpected? Bet your ass. But is it wrong? No. Max and I dove right back in where we'd left off after all those years. It should have been a huge mistake, but it was the best thing I ever did. If it feels right, go with it."

Cesar's cheeks cooled, but his chest tightened. He appreciated Derek's support more than he would have ever expected. "Thanks."

"Not that you need my approval."

Cesar dipped his head but smiled. "No. But it's nice just the same."

Standing to leave, Derek's return smile faded. "I wish I could say the same about this father mission you're on. This has nothing but trouble written all over it."

Saxon arrived extra early Monday morning to bring clothes for Oliver to wear in court. It had been hours now. He pulled on his tie and slipped his fingers beneath the knot to unbutton the top button before it cut off his air. More sweat rolled down his back sitting in the courtroom than it had while hanging drywall on the un-airconditioned third floor during the heat of the day.

He leaned into Cesar sitting next to him. "Why do they have it so hot in here?"

"It's literally like sixty-nine degrees in here. Look at all the women who put on sweaters or blazers to keep warm."

Okay, so maybe Cesar was right, but that didn't do anything to soothe Saxon's nerves. They'd arrived at court early and had been sitting through other cases as they were brought before the judge, but since they didn't have a specific time for Oliver's arraignment, they had to sit through everything to ensure they were there for him.

Right then, they were between cases. The lawyer and client from the previous case left, and the judge, a middle-aged black woman with a preternatural bullshit detector and no time for courtroom shenanigans, flipped through paperwork as the bailiff called the next case.

The courtroom doors situated on the side of the room opened. The mayor walked in, and the judge pursed her lips. Saxon caught a flash of a frown before she schooled her expression.

"Mayor," her voice carried even though she'd turned her microphone off between cases. "Pleasure to see you in my courtroom."

She said it in such a way that Saxon thought she'd need a Clorox wipe to disinfect her eyeballs when court finished for the day.

A person behind them smothered their chuckle with a cough.

Across the room, Kellon sat with some of the other lawyers awaiting their cases to be called, and he smirked and glanced Saxon's way.

Kellon had texted that morning before court when he found out who the sitting judge would be, letting them know that Judge Jackson was one of the few judges who didn't allow the mayor's intimidation tactics to influence her.

Perhaps a little luck had fallen Oliver's way.

"Judge." The mayor nodded and claimed an empty seat close to the door.

Soon after, Braden and a woman Saxon assumed was one of the city's prosecutors entered. Braden sat next to his father. Kellon stood and shook the prosecutor's hand as she passed by with her briefcase. She took a seat at the prosecution table and got situated.

Cesar put a hand on Saxon's knee to keep it from jackhammering. He leaned in, his voice low and smooth when he said, "Relax, babe. Kellon knows what he's doing. Oliver's in good hands."

"Sorry. I just—" Saxon linked his fingers with Cesar's and glanced in the mayor's direction. The mayor caught his eye, and all Saxon wanted to do was go over there and wipe the smug ass smirk off the asshole's face.

Cesar tugged his hand as if he knew exactly the thought that had crossed Saxon's mind. "It's not worth it."

"How do you know what I'm thinking?"

"I don't. Not exactly. But the way you tensed up, I thought you were about to crawl over three rows of benches and blacken the mayor's eyes."

"I wouldn't do it." Although, in the months leading up to getting Stonewall House approved by the zoning commission under the watchful, disparaging eye of the mayor, he'd had some pretty vivid dreams about punching him in the face that had felt all too real when he'd woken up.

They waited nearly forty excruciating minutes before the bailiff called Oliver's case. "Ohmygod, there he is," Saxon exclaimed loud enough for the judge to look his way when Oliver came into the courtroom.

The bruising around his eyes had deepened, and he walked gingerly as if his torso were sore. If anything, he almost looked worse than when they'd seen him at the hospital right after the fight, but that was the nature of bruises. They looked worse before they looked better.

Ultimately, the contrast between how relatively unscathed Braden looked compared to Oliver might have influenced the judge's decision to release Oliver on his own recognizance. Unfortunately, Kellon wasn't able to get the case completely thrown out.

But Oliver was coming home until his court date rolled around.

The judge smacked her gavel down, and Braden and the mayor disappeared from the courtroom before the sound stopped resonating around the wood-paneled walls.

Cesar wrapped his arm around Saxon's shoulder, and he slumped against Cesar's warm body, absorbing his strength. He would have survived the arraignment without Cesar by his side. Barely. But he was glad he didn't have to.

Saxon's hands shook with the adrenaline coursing through his system with nowhere to go. His knees wobbled as they stood to leave the courtroom. With the relief Saxon felt, you would have thought Oliver had been acquitted of murder, not released pending a court appearance for battery.

Kellon met them outside the courtroom. "There's some paperwork that needs to be done, but they should release Oliver soon. You can pick him up downstairs."

Cesar shook Kellon's hand. "I appreciate all that you've done."

Instead of a handshake, Saxon went in for the hug. "Thank you, thank you." Saxon pulled back, and red bloomed on Kellon's cheeks.

"Don't thank me yet. We have a lot of work to do if we want to get these charges dropped." Kellon had addressed that line to Cesar, knowing full well that he would bear the brunt of the investigative work into finding something that could help prove that Oliver had been defending Phoenix.

"I know. But Oliver is coming home for now. I don't think the mayor was too happy that the judge let him go."

"Fuck the mayor," Kellon said. "I can't wait until the next election, and that asshole is voted out of office."

"We can hope," Cesar said, though he didn't sound like he believed it would happen.

Kellon rolled his eyes. "Don't get me started." He clapped Cesar on the back. "I'll be in touch. Let me know if you find anything new."

"Will do."

Saxon and Cesar found their way downstairs, and Saxon waited impatiently by the door where they'd release Oliver.

Cesar pressed a kiss to his cheek. "He's fine. You saw him."

"I know. But I won't believe it until I can touch him."

The door opened and closed several times, spitting out defendants from earlier that morning. After too much time passed for Saxon's liking, the door opened again, and Oliver stepped through. He swiped at the tears falling down his face. Saxon pulled him into a hug. They swayed side to side. That only made Oliver's tears fall faster.

Finally, Oliver broke the hug with an embarrassed laugh. "I bet you didn't think you signed up for this when you opened Stonewall House, did you?"

"I signed up for all of this. It's fine."

"If—" Oliver swallowed hard. "If you need me to move out, I'll understand."

"Wait. What? No." Saxon squeezed Oliver's shoulder until he glanced up at him, the tears falling harder. "You don't have to leave. You did nothing wrong. You were defending Phoenix. This isn't your fault."

Oliver gathered himself and blew out a breath, drying his face on the sleeves of the dress shirt they'd brought him. "Thank you."

Saxon hugged him again, then held him at arm's length. "Are you all right?"

"I will be," Oliver said. "I'll be even better once this is all over."

"You and me both, kid," Saxon said. They all turned and headed for the door.

Cesar shook Oliver's hand and introduced himself. "You hungry? Want to stop on the way home and get something to eat?"

"We can if you want, but I just want to get home and see everybody."

Saxon's stomach growled, he'd only picked at his food when the court had recessed for lunch, and now that Oliver was safely out of custody, his appetite came roaring back. "I can fix something at the house. How does that sound?"

"Amazing."

They'd taken separate cars to the courthouse. Cesar followed them home. Oliver was unusually quiet on the drive, but Saxon figured he was still processing everything that had happened over the last few days.

Saxon didn't even have a chance to put his car into park before James, Phoenix, Addi, and Sophia ran out of the house.

Phoenix held Mango in her arms, wearing the little harness and leash Cesar had bought him.

Phoenix gave the cat to Saxon before swallowing Oliver in a hug. The group hugged, laughed, swiped at tears, and pulled Oliver into the house, leaving Saxon and Cesar outside with Mango.

He held onto the leash, worried Mango might try to run off, but as soon as Phoenix handed him off, Mango climbed to Saxon's shoulder like a parrot and surveyed the world from his human perch.

"Do you want to come in?" Saxon asked. Cesar hesitated as if he wanted to but didn't want to intrude. "You know you're welcome here."

"I know. I think I'll take a rain check and let you all get reacquainted."

"You sure?" Saxon asked. As thrilled as Saxon was to have Oliver home, it felt like Cesar was taking a step back. Saxon narrowed his eyes at him. "Everything okay?"

"Sure. Why wouldn't it be?" Cesar didn't hesitate, but there was something concerning in his eyes.

Saxon didn't answer the rhetorical question. "Thanks for seeing us home. You didn't have to go out of the way to do that."

Cesar planted a chaste kiss on his lips. Saxon wanted more, but he wouldn't press the issue. "Yes, I did."

Mango's little paws started kneading Saxon's shoulder, and Saxon pulled Cesar into a one-arm hug so he wouldn't knock Mango off.

Cesar walked him to the door and shooed him in with a kiss and a tentative smile, leaving Saxon to wonder what was wrong with Cesar and what the hell that was all about.

10

INSTEAD OF DRIVING STRAIGHT HOME AS HE SHOULD HAVE, CESAR zipped through a fast-food joint and pulled into the office the same way he had the night before.

At least this time, Derek wasn't there to give him shit.

Saxon had asked him if anything was wrong, and while he hadn't lied when he'd said nothing was wrong, he had to admit at least to himself that he'd been thinking all day long about the warning that Derek had given him. And he'd taken some of Derek's words to heart.

If he was going to look into a man that wanted back into Saxon's life, Cesar wanted to make damn sure it wouldn't be a mistake Saxon regretted.

First, Cesar checked and double-checked that he'd found the right person. Then he started in on the background checks. For that, he went above and beyond his normal checks, but again and again, Melvin's background came up clean.

It was nearly eleven when he finally shut down the computer for the night and headed home. He should have felt better that he didn't find anything unusual on Melvin, but he still had a sick feeling in the pit of his stomach, like a hornet's nest that he'd unwittingly stirred up.

But maybe that was just the greasy cheeseburger he'd downed on the run.

Or maybe that was his body's way of encouraging him to make sure he'd done all of his homework before presenting the information to Saxon.

Once home, he stumbled into the shower, and not long after, he lay on top of his bed, the air conditioning trying to catch up after he'd turned the thermostat up for the day. Overhead, the ceiling fan whirled, the blade-whipping the air, drying all the spots he'd neglected while toweling off.

He tried to sleep but found himself staring at his text messages. He scrolled through his and Saxon's exchanges, reading them again. Most of it was innocent or low-key flirting.

Cesar missed him even though they'd spent the day together. He should have taken him up on the invitation to go inside. He could have helped Saxon make dinner for the horde, but he'd declined.

Why?

Maybe because deep down, you know Derek's right, and you should stop the nonsense with Saxon's father until you talk with Saxon and get his permission to proceed.

Maybe.

But Saxon had a lot of other things to deal with. He didn't need this decision dropped on his plate until Cesar had the full picture of who Melvin Davis was. When Cesar had all the pertinent information, he'd present Saxon with what he'd found, and Saxon could make an informed decision.

The phone buzzed in his hands.

Saxon: *You still up?*

Cesar: *Can't sleep.*

The three little dots appeared and disappeared before two little words popped onto his screen.

Saxon: *Come over.*

SAXON STARED AT HIS MESSAGES ON HIS PHONE AS HE LAY ON TOP of his covers with Mango sleeping in a ball on his pillow in the crook of his neck. Outside, crickets chirped rhythmically, counting the passing seconds with him.

He'd sent the 'come over' text about fifteen minutes before, and he couldn't take his eyes off it while waiting for the little bouncing dots to appear, telling him that Cesar was responding.

He kept waiting.

And waiting.

It *was* late. Maybe Cesar was trying to find a nice way to let him down. Or maybe he'd fallen asleep. Or—

A light tap came from his patio door.

Saxon extricated himself from the cat and tiptoed over. "Cesar?"

He kept his voice down in case it wasn't Cesar which was silly because if it were a burglar, they'd know he was there even if he'd whispered, which went to show that he wasn't thinking clearly.

He had the 'come over' text to back up that theory.

The knock came again, louder this time. "Saxon, it's me. Let me in."

Cesar came.

Saxon flipped on the patio light, twisted the lock, and yanked the door open. His heart did this weird stutter beat leaving him light-headed and breathless.

Then again, Cesar had a way of making him feel that way every time he saw him.

He stood on Saxon's patio with a bashful smile on his face. Saxon looked him up and down from his ratty tank top to his gym shorts to his... bare feet? "Where are your shoes?"

That bashful grin grew wider, and Cesar couldn't look him in the eye when he said, "Um… I was in a hurry."

"You never texted me back. I didn't think you were coming."

That bashful smile slid to a sexy one as Cesar leaned in and brushed a kiss against Saxon's lips. "Back to the 'I was in a hurry' comment. I guess I didn't consider the possibility that you'd think I *wouldn't* come."

"It *is* late."

"It's never that late."

Saxon fisted his hand in Cesar's tank top and hauled him into his room, locking the door and the chirping crickets outside.

Cesar backed Saxon against the door. "Please tell me you have a lock on your bedroom door."

"I do."

"Everyone doing okay? Oliver settled in?"

"He's doing better than expected. I think everyone piled into his room. They're sleeping on the floor like a tween's slumber party."

"They're great kids."

"They are. But I didn't call you over to talk about Oliver."

Cesar eased closer, dropping his voice even though no one could hear. "Why *did* you call me over?"

"I couldn't sleep. I couldn't stop thinking about you and wishing you were in my bed with Mango and me and—"

Cesar shut him up with a kiss that zoomed from zero to sixty faster than a Formula One car. He caught Saxon's wrists and held them above his head, keeping Saxon pinned against the door with a strategically placed leg between his thighs.

"Is that the *only* reason?" Cesar asked when he finally broke the kiss.

"That and I like the idea of a midnight booty call."

"*Mmmm.*" Cesar pressed his thigh into Saxon's hard-on. Saxon groaned, bringing a devilish smile to Cesar's face. "I'm a fan of your ideas."

Saxon loved the brush of Cesar's hairy legs on his inner thighs, the pressure on his hard dick, and the fact that Cesar couldn't wait to put on shoes before he made the twenty-minute drive in fifteen.

Saxon easily broke Cesar's grip on his wrists, pressed a hand to the center of Cesar's chest, and pushed him back until his calves hit the side of the bed. One playful shove and Cesar flopped onto the bed, catching Saxon's hand at the last second and pulling him down with him.

Their combined weight landing on the mattress launched Mango a couple of inches into the air, waking him up with a start. He stretched, hopped off the bed, and disappeared somewhere in the room.

Saxon didn't care where Mango went as long as he was off the bed. A queen bed was nice, but it didn't have enough room for two grown men, shenanigans, and a kitten.

"I think you're way overdressed." Saxon tugged on the hem of Cesar's shirt, drew it off, and tossed it somewhere in the room. They lay there in near darkness, the only illumination coming from the porch light streaming through the mini blinds.

"How's that?" Cesar asked, but Saxon was too busy running his hand up the length of Cesar's torso to answer.

Cesar had a bare chest that Saxon couldn't help running his fingers over. "Almost perfect."

With a chuckle, Cesar said, "*Almost?*"

"Almost perfect when it comes to your state of undress. You still have your shorts and underwear on and—"

"I'm not wearing underwear."

Saxon grinned. "Even better." He made a get-it-off motion with his hand, and Cesar's smile slipped. "What's wrong?"

When Cesar didn't respond, Saxon braced his weight on his hands. "Tell me."

He could barely see Cesar's face, but he heard the capitulation in his sigh. "I don't want you to be disappointed."

Disappointed? "Disappointed how?"

With Cesar's hesitation, Saxon was sure he'd have seen Cesar blush if there had been enough light. "Because *Black Stallion Studios* isn't beating down my door demanding I become one of their tops because of my gigantic dick."

"Thank God. I prefer big dicks on a screen, not in my ass."

Cesar chuckled.

Still, there were things they needed to clear up because along with the whole going slow thing that Saxon had instigated and quickly shot to hell—because who could resist a sexy PI who dropped everything to come to your aid?—they'd neglected part of a much-needed conversation as well.

Maybe Cesar didn't like to top.

"About the topping thing," Saxon said, "Is that what you want, or do you prefer to bottom or neither?"

Cesar brought him down for one of the gentlest, sweetest kisses anyone had ever given him. It made tears spring to his eyes, and his throat seized so fast that he might never get his words out.

When Cesar let him go, he said, "I can go either way. Right now, I want you any way I can have you."

11

—————

SAXON GRINNED AND COULDN'T WAIT TO EXPLORE THE WAYS THEY could bring each other pleasure. "Works for me. I'm vers, in the sense that I love both, not in the *I put* vers *on my HotDix profile because I bottomed once and hated it, but it still counts* kind of way."

He paused for a second, thinking about how that came out, and clarified, "Not that there's anything wrong with being a total top. I just prefer truth in advertising."

Cesar laughed. Saxon loved how the sound warmed his chest and made him want to do anything in his power to always hear that sound.

Pulling Saxon in for another kiss, Cesar said, "Good to know."

Saxon dug his fingers into Cesar's waistband, eyes on Cesar's the whole time. "May I?"

"Be my guest." Cesar lifted his hips, and Saxon slid Cesar's shorts down his legs. Cesar's dick bounced up, hitting Saxon in the chin as he pushed his shorts far enough down for Cesar to kick free.

"*Mmmm.*" Saxon took hold of Cesar's wonderfully, perfectly average-sized dick. "It's so. Fucking. Hard."

"You did that. I've been running around sporting a semi since—"

Saxon took him down, all the way to the back of his throat. Cesar made a noise as he arched up that sounded like he'd swallowed his tongue. Saxon pressed his hard-on into the mattress, needing that friction he left behind a slick spot of precum.

Cesar's hands went to the back of Saxon's head, gently holding him there. The joke was on Cesar because Saxon had no plans of going anywhere until Cesar's cum shot down his throat.

He worked the sensitive tip before taking Cesar deep again, loving the tremors and the moans and the hitches in Cesar's breath. The salty tang of Cesar's precum filled Saxon's mouth, and he couldn't get enough of it.

Saxon caressed Cesar's balls, felt his sack tighten against his body, and he knew that Cesar would blow any second.

"I'm gonna… gonna," Cesar said. His words came out delightfully strangled. Saxon adored the fact that he had that effect on Cesar, that he could make the man nearly lose his ability to speak.

Pulling off long enough to speak, Saxon said, "That's the point."

"Dork." Cesar laughed, but Saxon cut the laugh short with a swipe of his tongue along that glorious, glistening slit. *"Fuuuck,"* Cesar ground out.

"Come here." Cesar hauled Saxon up.

Saxon went with it, replacing his mouth with his hand as he stroked Cesar's cock. He rested on one forearm, half on and half off Cesar. "You want me to stop?"

"Not in this lifetime."

The tantalizing shadowed line of Cesar's jaw proved irresistible. Saxon rained a line of kisses over the lightly stubbled skin. "You have constructive criticism of my technique?"

"Not—"

Saxon skimmed his thumb through the slickness at the tip of

Cesar's cock. Cesar's hand came down on Saxon's, stopping him. "I can't talk when you do that."

"If you can talk, I'm doing it wrong."

Cesar shook his head. Saxon's dim light couldn't hide his smile. "It's your turn."

"There's plenty of time for that."

"Yeah, but—"

"I want to do this." That time, when Saxon started stroking him again, Cesar let him, thrusting into his hand. He kissed his way down Cesar's chest, found one of his flat nipples, and sucked it into a peak. "Let me do this."

"*Fuck.*" Cesar's head fell back as he gave in to the pleasure. That one strangled word had Saxon promising himself he'd attempt to launch the upcoming orgasm onto Cesar's top ten list. Top five if his luck held.

He slid down the bed, his own dick hard, needy, and leaking uncontrollably. He wanted Cesar's hands and mouth on him, and with the way Cesar writhed, he wouldn't have long to wait.

With his hands and mouth, Saxon worked Cesar's cock. Cesar's hands went to the back of Saxon's head, his fingers tightening in Saxon's hair, stopping just shy of painful.

Cesar arched off the bed, his muscles trembling, his breath coming in short, rapid hitches. Saxon swirled his tongue over the sensitive tip before taking him impossibly deep. Cesar's thrusts became erratic, and Saxon smiled at the first pulses of Cesar's orgasm.

Crying out, Cesar held tight to Saxon's head as he fell over that edge. Saxon glanced up at him with wonder and, yeah, a little bit of pride. He couldn't remember the last time he'd made someone climax so fast.

Cum shot down Saxon's throat, and he swallowed down every drop. He loved Cesar's taste. Loved pleasing him.

Saxon pulled off before Cesar got too sensitive, using his hand to gently stroke Cesar's softening cock.

"I'm dead." Cesar's voice lacked its usual vitality.

Releasing Cesar, Saxon crawled up Cesar's slick, sweaty body, braced himself on his hands above him, and kissed his lips. "Pretty sexy for the unalive. Maybe I have a new fetish I knew nothing about."

Cesar slapped him on the ass, too out of breath to speak. Then Cesar pulled Saxon into his chest and wrapped his arms around him. Saxon's nose pressed into the crook of Cesar's neck. He licked the crease, unable to get enough of his boyfriend's taste.

Cesar laughed. "You finished?"

Going in for another taste, Saxon said, "No. I could eat you up."

"You already did."

Saxon pulled away to see his face. "And I enjoyed every second of it. You're worse than heroin. One hit, I'm hooked."

The *for life* ending of that sentence, Saxon kept to himself. It was way too soon to say something like that. Cesar wasn't nearly as freaked out about taking things too fast the way Saxon had been, but that would have been too much even for someone like Cesar.

He didn't want to scare Cesar away.

Taking Saxon's face in his hands, Cesar said, "You're not going to find me complaining." Drawing Saxon into a kiss, Cesar immediately deepened it when Saxon opened his mouth.

"*Mmmph,*" Cesar said as he pulled back and immediately went back for more. "I fucking love how I taste in your mouth."

He rolled them without breaking the kiss and settled between Saxon's legs. He drew them up and spread them to give Cesar all the access he'd ever want or need. Saxon rutted against Cesar, the kiss making Saxon want and need a whole lot more.

Finally, Cesar broke the kiss. The way their tongues dueled and Cesar's sexy, satisfied groan could have made Saxon shoot off, given a little more time. But fuck, when Cesar braced above him, rolled Saxon onto his stomach, and lifted him to his knees, Saxon couldn't hide his excited, surprised squeak.

Ass in the air, face in the mattress, Saxon reached down and stroked himself, the precum spilling into his hand, providing more than enough lubrication to keep a racing engine from seizing.

From behind, Cesar settled between Saxon's legs, squeezing one of Saxon's ass cheeks before giving it a firm bite. *"Fuck.* This ass is everything."

He nibbled and bit and licked his way to Saxon's crack, and Saxon rocked back. His body knew exactly where it wanted Cesar. Saxon continued to jack himself, leaving both of Cesar's hands free to do as they please.

Which at the moment meant running a spit-slicked finger down the length of Saxon's crease. Cesar's finger came to rest against Saxon's hole, and his muscles spasmed against the pressure.

Cesar bit the meatiest part of Saxon's ass, the grunt of satisfaction going straight to Saxon's already straining dick. Then Cesar's tongue flicked across Saxon's hole, and Saxon muttered a strangled curse.

Cesar chuckled. It had a mischievous, delightfully evil quality that only made Saxon harder.

If that were even possible.

Saxon rocked back and whimpered as Cesar licked and sucked and tongue fucked him. His rhythmic rocking made Cesar's talented tongue go deeper and deeper.

"Fuck," Saxon managed.

"You like that?"

Guh! Saxon squeezed his dick to keep from coming. As much as he wanted to chase that orgasm, he didn't want it to end. "That feels so fucking good."

Cesar reached between Saxon's legs, gathering some of his

slickness on his fingers and dragging them ever so slowly to his waiting hole.

Saxon rocked back, easing one wet finger inside and taking Cesar to the last knuckle. "Another," Saxon ordered. One finger would never be enough. He needed that stretch, that fullness.

Cesar withdrew and returned with two spit-slicked fingers. The spit would do for now, but he'd have to reach for the lube if he added any more.

As it was, Saxon wouldn't last.

Cesar worked Saxon's ass, and Saxon worked his cock. His breath came hot and fast as Cesar covered Saxon's body with his, kissing and biting his sweat-slicked shoulder. Then Cesar curled his fingers, hitting Saxon's prostate with each glorious stroke.

Saxon shuddered, the base of his spine tingled, stars erupted in front of his eyes, his cock pulsed, and he shot his hot load into his hand.

"So tight," Cesar murmured in Saxon's ear. "I can't wait to be inside you and have you milk me dry."

Holy hell. Who would have thought Cesar liked a little dirty talking? Those intimately growled words would have shoved Saxon over the edge if he hadn't already unloaded into his hand.

Gently, Cesar pulled his fingers out and gave Saxon a light slap on the ass. "You're so sexy," he said as Saxon collapsed into the mattress, his muscles refusing to do any of his biddings. He didn't even care that he'd trapped his jizz-soaked hand beneath his body.

Cesar groaned as he collapsed and rolled on his back beside him. "I'm gonna sleep good tonight."

Mango made a running jump at the bed and used every single one of his ridiculously sharp baby claws to climb the side of the bed like Mt. Everest, meowing the whole trek up.

At least Mango had waited for them to finish.

The kitten galloped across the bed, up Saxon's torso, and slid to a stop on Saxon's shoulder with claws extended for added traction. Saxon sucked in a breath.

"*Mother f—*" Saxon cut himself off when Mango swiped his sandpaper tongue across his cheek. "I need to learn to trim those claws."

He turned to face Cesar as Mango scampered off to play with Cesar's wiggling fingers.

"I might need you to apply pressure to the wounds on my shoulder to keep me from bleeding out." Saxon was only half kidding. If nursing his wounded shoulder were left up to him, he'd die from blood loss because after that orgasm, call Saxon the Titanic because he was wrecked.

Cesar stretched across the top of Saxon and turned on the bedside lamp, casting the room in a warm light. He inspected Saxon's shoulder and found a few faint parallel pink lines scored across his boyfriend's skin. "I think you're going to live."

"You sure? No stitches required?"

Cesar chuckled. "I'm not a medical professional, but I passed first aid middle school." He pressed a kiss over the scratches on his overly dramatic boyfriend. "Better?"

"Lower," Saxon said.

Cesar moved down an inch and kissed him again.

"Lower."

Another kiss, this time to the small of Saxon's back. He knew exactly where this was heading.

"Almost there," Saxon muttered, sounding like he were already almost asleep. Almost asleep and they hadn't had a chance to shower and clean up.

Cesar smacked him on the ass. "Get up, or we'll stick to the comforter."

Saxon grunted but didn't move. Cesar rolled him until Saxon either had to get up or fall on the floor.

"You're pure evil. You know that?"

He crawled across the bed and followed Saxon into the shower. "You didn't think I was so bad a few minutes ago."

Saxon turned, gripping Cesar's chin in his clean hand, and peppered his lips with kisses between words. "You. Were. Fucking. Fantastic."

He grinned but shooed Saxon toward the shower before he had the chance to get hard again. It was late, and he needed to get to bed or else he'd be worthless at work in the morning.

They showered off without things going too much off course, but that was only through sheer willpower on Cesar's part because a sated, sexy, soapy Saxon proved nearly impossible to resist.

They toweled off, and Mango zoomed into the bathroom and skid to a stop in front of Saxon. The kitten meowed at him, and Saxon scooped him up before the kitten used those sharp claws to scale Saxon's naked body.

Mango meowed and meowed.

"Do you think he's hungry?" Cesar asked.

Saxon pointed with the kitten towards the corner where he'd set up the food and water bowls. "He has plenty in his bowl."

"Yeah, but you can see the bottom. If all those memes on social media can be trusted, you're about two seconds away from Mango calling and reporting you for abuse."

Saxon rolled his eyes but set Mango on the floor and poured more kibble into the bowl. Mango ran for the bowl and started eating as if he hadn't had a meal in decades.

"Told you so," Cesar said. "He's almost as dramatic as you."

Saxon narrowed his eyes, and it was all Cesar could do to keep from laughing. "Take that back."

"Make me."

Cesar sprinted for the bedroom, and Saxon tackled him on

the bed, sitting on his chest and pinning Cesar beneath him. Cesar could have wrestled his wrists free, but where would the fun be in that?

With Saxon sitting on Cesar's chest, Cesar had a tactical advantage. He stuck out his tongue and swiped it over the tip of Saxon's cock.

Saxon squeaked, then groaned. "You play dirty."

"Damn right I do. Don't you forget it."

Saxon leaned in and kissed him before shifting off. "As much as I'd love your mouth on me, I'm about to fall asleep sitting up."

Guess that was Cesar's cue to leave.

He eased off the opposite side of the bed as Saxon crawled beneath the sheets naked. Cesar found his shorts, slipped them on, and searched for his tank top. He might have to go home shirtless at the rate he was going.

"What are you doing?"

Cesar found Saxon propped up on his elbows, the sheet around his waist. He looked so damn fuckable with shower-damp hair and those sleepy, half-lidded eyes.

"Getting dressed. I'd prefer not to run to my car naked. They have laws about that sort of thing."

"Stay."

"*Saxon.*" Cesar straightened, unable to keep the pleading out of his voice, knowing that he'd used up all of his willpower in the shower to keep himself from taking Saxon against the tile wall. "I can't stay."

"Why."

Cesar glanced at the ceiling. "You know why."

"You can get up early and leave."

"I thought you wanted to take things slow." It was his last hail Mary. Not that Cesar didn't want to stay, but feared he'd never want to leave if he did, and he knew Saxon wasn't ready for that.

"You standing naked in my room after exchanging orgasms would indicate that we're past that, don't you think?"

Mango climbed up the side of the bed, ran over to where Cesar stood near the foot, and put his paw on Cesar's leg.

"If you don't want to stay for me, stay for Mango. He doesn't want you to leave."

"For the cat, huh?"

"For the cat," Saxon verified.

Shimmying out of his shorts, Cesar went to the other side of the bed and slipped under the cool sheets. Mango stayed at the foot of the bed, biting at his toes any time he twitched. Cesar turned on his side. Saxon turned off the light and scooted back until his back was to Cesar's chest.

Cesar pulled him close. He should have set the alarm on his phone, but he'd have to turn on the light to find out where he'd dropped it, and he just couldn't be bothered. Besides, Cesar was a naturally early riser. Getting up at the crack of dawn wouldn't be a problem.

Mango gave up on their toes and walked up Saxon's side from his legs, over Cesar's arm, and up to Saxon's shoulder and finally settled with his butt on the pillow and his body draped over Saxon's neck.

"Just be sure to leave before everyone gets up," Saxon muttered, his voice husky with sleep.

Cesar pressed a kiss to his shoulder. "Don't worry. I'll be out of here first thing."

12

———

THE THING ABOUT BEING TUCKED IN THE BACK BEDROOM ON THE first floor is that Saxon heard whenever someone walked around upstairs. And over the past few months, he'd learned to tell everyone's footsteps apart.

Addi had a way of sneaking downstairs with not even a squeak from the creakiest step and leaving for the day like a Ninja in training. Saxon never heard them coming or going. James sounded a lot like Sophia. Only his footsteps landed heavier, and then, of course, Phoenix had the *clackity-clack* of her high heels.

Saxon would never know how she hadn't broken her neck coming down the stairs in them.

And then... then there was sweet Oliver. He had this particular way of coming down the stairs, sort of a *clompity-clomp clomp, clompity-clomp clomp* that Saxon easily distinguished from all the others.

He smiled as those footsteps traipsed on the treads.

Oliver was home. Where he belonged.

Mango stirred. The kitten lay curled up under his chin, his purrs loud enough to rival his lion cousins.

An arm tightened around Saxon's waist and—

Saxon bolted upright. Mango ran, bounding into the bathroom. Light shined through his windows. And not that barely-there light of dawn, but actual sun up and beaming through the blinds as it climbed higher and higher into the sky.

What the hell time was it anyway?

Beside him, Cesar grumbled and tried to pull Saxon down. "Come back to bed. It's early. The alarm hasn't even gone off."

Saxon shook him. "Get up. It's late. You should have been gone already."

"Oh, shit." Jumping out of bed, Cesar scrounged for his shorts.

"Hey, Saxon," Oliver called out.

Saxon must have had an *oh shit* look on his face because as Cesar picked up his shorts, he said, "Relax, the door's locked, remember?"

"Saxon?" Oliver's voice came from the hall, and Saxon glanced at the doorknob to be sure.

It wasn't locked.

Cesar must have noticed at the same time because he sprinted for the door with his shorts in his hand.

The knock came on Saxon's door at the same time the knob turned, and Oliver opened the door. "Hey Saxon, there's a car in the driv—"

Cesar froze steps from the door, both hands holding his shorts in front of him, trying desperately to maintain at least the barest minimum of decency.

"Oliver, you can't just walk in."

"I knocked."

"Still, you can't—"

"Oh, hey," Oliver said as if he'd just noticed a nearly naked Cesar within arm's length of him. He gave Cesar a quick up and down. "Wow. Nice abs. What gym—"

"*Out,*" Saxon growled.

"Okay, okay. I guess that answers the car in the driveway

question." Mango ran out of the bathroom, and Oliver scooped him up. "I'll—" he hitched his thumb over his shoulder, "be out there."

He held his fist up for Cesar to bump, but Cesar had his hands full.

"*Oliver.*"

"All right already. I'm gone." Oliver turned to leave, and Cesar let go of one side of his shorts to close the door behind him, but Oliver stuck his head back into the room. "FYI, you two make a really cute couple."

Saxon groaned, and Cesar shut the door and twisted the lock.

"Shit. Shit. Shit." Cesar sat on the bed and buried his face in his hands. "I'm so sorry. I usually don't oversleep like that, and I prom—"

Unable to control his laughter, Saxon let the belly laugh roll through him. Even with Cesar's browner skin, he'd never seen that shade of red on a person before.

Saxon crawled to Cesar at the end of the bed and collapsed on his back, trying to catch his breath between hiccuping laughs.

The clear relief on Cesar's face had Saxon pulling him down for a quick kiss.

When Cesar broke it, the smile widened on his face. "You're not mad?"

Saxon shifted to his belly and wiped the laughter tears from his eyes. "No. I'm not mad."

"But you didn't want them knowing."

No. That hadn't been it at all.

Saxon sobered and sat on the bed beside Cesar, wanting him to see the truth in his eyes. "I have zero problems with them knowing you and I are together. Did I want them to find you in my bed, especially this early on? Not particularly. Only because we're pretty new, *and* it's not very professional."

"I get it." Cesar put his arm around Saxon and kissed his

temple. "I am sorry, though. I gave you my word, and I let you down. It's important to me that you can trust—"

Saxon shut him up with a kiss. "I do trust you. I don't know what it is, but Aiden always had me on pins and needles, not trusting what he did or said, but even though this is new, it's completely different. I *do* trust you, Cesar. And I'm running with it."

Cesar ducked his head, and that blush rose to his cheeks before he met Saxon's eyes. The stark vulnerability and peace Saxon saw in them nearly brought real tears to his eyes.

"I can't express how much that means to me." Cesar lifted Saxon's chin and kissed him—all giving and no taking. It turned on the waterworks.

Cesar pulled away and brushed a tear off Saxon's cheek. "I know this is new—"

With a finger to Cesar's lips, Saxon silenced him. "I think we should stop putting a qualifier on this relationship. It's new, sure, but we feel what we feel, and we shouldn't have to qualify that or make excuses for it. It feels right. At least to me it does, and I want to go with it."

Cesar's soft smile had Saxon swiping at his cheeks. Since when had he become such a sap? Cesar kissed his forehead. "I love the way you think. My boyfriend's a genius."

Love.

Saxon loved the way that word sounded falling from Cesar's lips. Despite what he'd said to Cesar mere moments before, it was probably too early for them to talk about the L-word in any capacity that included their relationship.

Right? Even if the words *God, I fucking love you* almost came out of Saxon's mouth on several occasions already. And some of them had nothing to do with the intoxicating orgasm Cesar had given him.

They stood. Saxon took Cesar's hand and led him into the bathroom. They couldn't stay naked in his room all day.

Pity.

AFTER A QUICK SHOWER, CESAR AND SAXON MET UP WITH OLIVER in the kitchen. He'd already brewed a pot of coffee and was drinking it at the table while scrolling through one of his social media accounts.

"Where is everybody?" Saxon asked.

Oliver shrugged as he continued scrolling. "They were gone by the time I got up."

"Were you able to get hold of your boss?" Saxon asked.

Oliver put his phone down, and his eyes immediately rimmed with red. "He said to take the week off to recover and start back next week. He said what happened was bullshit and that he would pay me for the shifts I missed."

"Wow," Cesar helped himself to some coffee and poured one for Saxon. "You don't often hear about employers taking care of their people like that."

"Right? I thought I'd get fired."

"Have you eaten?" Saxon asked Oliver.

"I figured you'd want to make me breakfast on my first day home."

Saxon laughed and got out the frying pan. "Just this once. I don't want you to make a habit of getting arrested, so I'll cook you breakfast."

"Deal," Oliver said.

Cesar's stomach growled on cue. "Can I help?"

"There's sausage and eggs in the fridge and a purple onion if you want to get them out and chop up the onion. We should have some tortillas to make breakfast tacos."

Thirty minutes later, Cesar pushed his plate away. He'd already devoured three tacos, and as much as he wanted another, his stomach would burst if he ate it.

Meanwhile, even though Oliver had a slight build, he'd already put away four and reached for the remaining one on the serving plate.

"Anyone mind?" Oliver asked.

"All yours," Saxon said, "unless Cesar wanted it."

Cesar held up his hands. "All yours."

The front door opened, and someone called out. "Hello. Where is everyone?"

While Stonewall House was a residence for some, Saxon had explained to Cesar that it also offered other services to the young adult LGBTQ community, so they were open for shortened business hours during the week and a few hours on the weekends, which meant it wasn't unusual for people to walk in during the day.

"Hey, Grant," Saxon called out. "We're in the kitchen."

Cesar glanced down at his ratty, thrown-on-last-minute-for-a-booty-call tank top and old gym shorts, feeling underdressed for visitors, even if Saxon knew the person. At least Saxon had put on presentable clothes.

Saxon started clearing the table, and when the man entered the kitchen, Cesar stood and stuck out his hand. "Cesar Morales. I'm—"

Turning away from the sink, Saxon said with a saucy grin, "He's mine, and I'm not sharing. At least not yet."

Grant laughed.

Grant Hardy laughed.

Grant Hardy, who had been one of Black Stallion Studios' hottest performers not long ago. And yes, Cesar had seen and jacked off to some of his videos because… he was human.

And horny.

Grant had a famously open relationship with his fiancé Sebastian, the nephew of Black Stallion Studios' owner. And yes, maybe Cesar had at one point spent too much time on social media that talked about the couple. But he loved how open they were about their lives and didn't give two shits what anyone else in the world thought about them or how they'd constructed their relationship. It worked for them, and he admired that.

"Grant Hardy," Grant said, shaking Cesar's hand.

Cesar went with the traditional 'nice to meet you' line instead of 'I know.'

Bobbing his chin at Oliver, Grant said, "How's it going, O?"

Oliver smiled. He had the sweetest, nerdiest smile that the right boy would flip over one of these days. "I'm better now."

Saxon gestured toward the table. "Have a seat and a cup of coffee."

"I can't stay. I came to ask you a huge favor."

Leaning against the counter, Saxon said, "Anything." Then for Cesar's benefit, Saxon said, "Grant runs The Cory Center. It's an LGBTQ youth center in town."

Oliver went to refill everyone's coffee mugs, then returned to his seat, one ear on the conversation and the rest of his attention on his phone.

Cesar nodded his thanks to Oliver. Cesar knew about the Center. You couldn't follow Grant and Sebastian and not know about Grant's work. "I've heard good things about it."

"Thanks. Anyway," Grant looked a little sheepish, and Cesar glanced at Saxon's open, expectant expression. "I've got a kid just turning eighteen who needs a soft place to land, and all of my other contacts haven't been able to help."

"I'd love to help," Saxon said, "But we're at capacity. I won't have the third floor done until…" Saxon grimaced. "I don't even know. It could be a month. Maybe two. Could be longer. It's not going as fast as I would like. Certainly someone—"

"There's no one. At least not for him."

Cesar narrowed his eyes. "Why. What's up?"

Grant leaned against the wall as if the explanation would take a while. "He's… got a bit of a past," he said as if trying to put as good of a spin on it as he could. "He's had a few run-ins with the law."

"That's okay," Oliver said, "we're all a bunch of felons here."

Saxon rolled his eyes.

"Well, some of us are," Oliver elaborated, his sarcasm didn't go unnoticed, "and by *some of us*, I mean me."

Laughing, Saxon said, "Let him talk." He turned his attention back to Grant. "You were saying?"

"Yeah, well, he's not a bad kid. Things haven't gone his way until he showed up at Pigments."

"Isn't your son apprenticing there?"

"Tavi? Yeah. Well, this kid's got talent, and he and Tavi have hit it off. Except Kai aged out. Today. And his foster parents kicked him out."

Wait. What? "It's his fucking birthday, and his foster parents kicked him out?" Cesar's hands drew into fists. He'd love to find the asshole that deserved an introduction to all ten of his knuckles.

"It happens more than you'd think," Saxon said. "Even to the foster kids that aren't LGBTQ or getting into trouble with the law. But that doesn't magically give me the extra space. I have strict capacity guidelines I have to follow."

Grant stared at the floor and blew out his breath, the disappointment something Cesar could almost see and touch. Grant nodded and looked up. "Yeah. I understand. I had to try, though."

"As soon as something opens up..." Saxon let the end of the sentence fall off.

"Wait." Oliver turned to Saxon. "He could have your room."

Saxon scratched the light scruff on his jaw, considering the option as Grant got his hopes up way too high. "I guess I could sleep on the couch in the den. I'd have to check, but I don't think there are rules about me doing that. I think I just can't put a group member on a couch."

"You can't sleep on the couch for two or three or more months," Cesar said.

"What else do you expect me to do?" Saxon's voice rose with his frustration. Not aimed at Cesar, he knew, but the situation putting a vulnerable person out on the streets. In reality, Stonewall House had limitations on how many people it could help at one time.

"You can stay at my place." Cesar stood. He didn't know why. It felt like it was important that he did. "You already said that you don't have to live here. Give him your room, and you come stay with me."

Saxon laughed, but it was kind of an uncomfortable laugh. Grant grinned as if the situation had been resolved. Oliver looked particularly proud of himself. Mango ran in from wherever he'd been playing and scaled Saxon like a tree.

"I can't come live with you."

"I have a guest room," Cesar said, even though that wasn't where he wanted Saxon. He wanted Saxon in his bed every night, but if he could only have him down the hall, he'd take it. "It's a hell of a lot comfier than the couch."

Saxon hesitated.

"It would only be until you finish the third floor. You said so yourself, and if you want, I'll help you finish it to speed it along."

"You don't have to do that."

"I want to." The words were out of Cesar's mouth before he thought about it, but they were the truth. And sure, he liked the excuse of having Saxon in his space, but it went beyond that. He saw how hard people like Saxon and Grant worked to make life better for others and wanted to be a part of that.

"You don't know what you're doing." Saxon shook his head, not as if he wouldn't go through with it, but as if he couldn't believe that he was.

13

For a moment, Cesar had stunned Saxon into silence. He knew Cesar was a good man, but when Cesar had agreed to be his boyfriend, he hadn't signed up to be dragged into the messy realities of the community work Saxon did.

Then again, with the way he'd jumped in to help with Oliver, maybe he knew exactly what he'd signed up for and was fine with it.

Aiden would never have made the offer, even though he had two spare rooms.

Saxon grimaced. He had to stop doing that. He had to stop comparing Cesar to Aiden. Cesar was the only good thing that Aiden had brought into Saxon's life, making that whole shitty situation worth it.

From here on out, he refused to give Aiden free rent in his head.

"Well?" Cesar came around the table and took Saxon's hand. Mango scampered to the shoulder closest to Cesar.

Saxon couldn't refuse.

And as much as he wanted to make the move all about Kai, deep down, Saxon admitted the truth. He *wanted* to go. And Kai gave him an excuse to do what he wanted without questioning the timing.

"Let's do it." Cesar smacked a kiss on Saxon's cheek.

Grant gave Oliver a fist bump. "Let's do this."

"I'll let Kai know." The smile on Grant's face alone made the decision worth it. "I think Tavi said he'll be at the shop until this afternoon. I'll bring him by when he gets off."

"I'll be here."

Grant turned to leave and then turned back. "Just… don't let his first or maybe even his second impression put you off. He's worth the trouble. I promise."

Saxon and Cesar exchanged glances after Grant saw himself out. "Am I not thinking this through?"

Cesar took Mango, who'd perched on the end of Saxon's shoulder, ready to make the jump over to Cesar. "I'm sure it's not anything you can't handle."

"Plus, you have us." Oliver got up. "I'll help get your room ready for him, but I'm not washing the sheets."

Oliver left the kitchen with a smug grin on his face. Saxon laughed and bonked his forehead onto Cesar's shoulder. "Oh, my *gaaawd*. I was hoping he'd forgotten about that."

"Same." Cesar kissed the top of his head, and Saxon straightened.

"To be fair, though…" Saxon ran his hand under the hem of Cesar's tank and across Cesar's stomach. "You do have amazing abs."

Cesar trapped Saxon's hand under his shirt. "Don't start something you can't finish."

Saxon stepped closer, already sporting a semi just thinking about the night before. He kissed Cesar. It started sweet with a little spice to get Cesar's blood pumping to all right areas. The next thing Saxon knew, Cesar had Saxon backed against the counter, his hard-on pressed to Saxon's hip.

Saxon had to break the kiss or risk passing out from oxygen deprivation.

"Tonight," Cesar practically growled.

A warning.

And a promise.

"Tonight," Saxon said.

They parted, adjusted themselves, and headed into Saxon's bedroom to pack.

Turns out, it didn't take long to get the loads of laundry started and pack his clothes into some boxes he'd stored on the third floor.

His room had two closets, so Saxon emptied one as well as the dresser to give Kai room for his things. Then he packed his toiletries.

He had a small box on the unmade bed. He opened the bedside table drawer and retrieved his lube and supply of condoms. He figured Cesar had some at his house, but he wanted to be prepared.

He dug into the back of the drawer and took out his purple dildo about the time that Cesar walked back into the room from taking a box to his car.

Saxon shoved the dildo into the box, the heat rushing to his cheeks as he closed the flaps and reached for the packing tape dispenser.

"What was that?" Cesar asked with a grin that said he knew *exactly* what it was.

"Nothing."

"Oh, it was *something*." Cesar came over to his side of the bed, flipped the flaps open, and looked inside.

Even though Cesar had had his mouth and hands all over Saxon the night before, even though Saxon knew how Cesar tasted, how he sounded, how he looked when he came, Saxon couldn't keep the blush from burning brighter.

At this rate, they'd need to get the fire extinguisher to keep him from spontaneously combusting.

Cesar took hold of Saxon's chin, forcing Saxon to look at him. "You are so fucking adorable." He pressed a chaste kiss to his lips and let him go.

"Maybe I should leave this here."

"Ab-so-fucking-lutely not." He took the box from Saxon and sealed it.

"I mean, I would hide it in my office. It's not like I'm going to leave it here in the drawer for Kai to find."

Cesar turned to face him, his voice dipping low when he said, "I already have plans for you and your purple penis."

Saxon grinned and had to reach down to readjust. Cesar followed the movement. "Fuck." He shoved the box into Saxon's hands. "Do something with this before I decide to use it now."

Saxon almost called Cesar out on his… threat? Promise? *Whatever.* But then Mango bounded into the room with Oliver on his heels.

"Do you need help carrying stuff to the car?"

Saxon handed him the box to get rid of the temptation. "This can go. I think all I have left to pack are Mango's things."

"Leave his stuff here," Cesar said. "I'll pick up a few things on the way home. That way, you'll have food and bowls and whatnot in both places."

"Want me to put his cat tree in the den and the litter box in the laundry room?" Oliver asked.

Why was Saxon hesitating? It wasn't a big deal. Though, for some reason, it felt like one. The reality was that if things didn't work out with Cesar, he could always move back and sleep on the couch. He'd done enough couch surfing in his early days to learn to be comfortable almost anywhere.

He had to stop thinking that just because his other relationships had never worked out didn't mean this one wouldn't. "That would be great. Thanks."

Cesar glanced from Saxon to Oliver, watching him leave with the box and cat tree before pinning Saxon with a look that usually meant Saxon was in trouble.

"What?" Saxon asked, even though he didn't want to hear the answer. Was this where Cesar told Saxon he had second thoughts?

"Are you okay?" Cesar asked Saxon.

They stood in Saxon's room, more barren after the packing they'd done. Outside, the shadows nearly disappeared as the sun rose high in the sky. In the backyard, the grass had grown knee-high, Saxon too busy with his other responsibilities to take proper care of it.

Cesar had no doubt the lawn would get sorted, but they had Kai to worry about getting settled first. And he couldn't help but think he'd pushed Saxon into something he didn't want to do because he'd felt out of options. Cesar would find another place for Saxon to stay if he needed to.

When Saxon didn't answer, Cesar took his hand and sat beside him on the edge of the bed.

"You having second thoughts?" they both asked at the same time.

Cesar chuckled. "Not a one. You?"

Saxon took a deep breath before blowing it out. He looked so unguarded. Cesar wanted to wrap him in his arms and never let him go. "You don't have to do this."

"I wouldn't have offered if I didn't want to."

"It's so soo—"

"Stop." Cesar put a little force behind the word to squash that line of thinking. "We already talked about the *too-soon* thing. We're not moving in together. You're moving in to make temporary space for someone who needs help. Don't read too much into it."

"You're right. I'm overthinking."

Cesar squeezed his hand. "Let's get the last of the stuff in my car. I've got to make an appearance at work before Derek starts looking for another business partner."

After leaving Saxon's, Cesar borrowed a pair of Saxon's flip-flops from one of the boxes in his car and ran by the pet store before going to the office. He still wore the clothes he'd run to Saxon's in the night before. Luckily, since there were times that either he or Derek had to spend the night in the spare room at the office, they both kept extra clothes there. Cesar could change into something more work-appropriate and save time running home to change.

Fortunately, Derek wasn't at work when Cesar showed up to raise a brow at his questionable attire. He changed into some chinos, a button-down dress shirt that he rolled the sleeves up his forearms, and settled for the old pair of running shoes he'd left in the closet for emergencies.

While he'd been out, Derek had left a file on his desk, and Cesar promptly got to work on it. It was a worker's compensation job that Derek had accepted. The insurance company had gotten wind that the injured man may not be as injured as he claimed.

Those investigations weren't very interesting or took a lot of brainpower, which was good because between Saxon moving in, volunteering to help with the renovations, and making sure he did his due diligence where Melvin Davis was concerned, Cesar already had a full plate.

But it was time Cesar carried some of the weight Derek had been shouldering the past few days.

He spent the next couple of hours working on the insurance case, getting up to speed with the file and determining how and when he wanted to get eyes on the guy.

From some of the supplied information, it had been reported

that the man had been seen coming and going out of a certain gym in the afternoons.

Cesar picked up one of their cameras with the telephoto lens, checked to make sure it had an empty media card, and climbed into his car. At the gym, he parked out of the way, cracked his windows, got his camera ready, and waited.

At some point, Cesar shook himself awake. More than an hour had passed since he'd parked. Sweat trickled down his back, and his stomach complained that he hadn't fed it since the breakfast tacos that morning.

He'd probably missed the guy altogether. He ran inside to check but didn't see the man inside. It wasn't until he saw the billboard as he left the gym parking lot that he turned right instead of left.

As soon as he parked at his new location, his cell rang. Cesar jumped in his seat. *Derek.*

"What are you doing?" Did Derek's tone sound mildly accusatory, or was it Cesar sitting across the street from Melvin Davis's used car lot that made Cesar feel like he was doing something wrong?

"I just left that guy's gym. The one with the disputed insurance claim. Never saw him, though."

It wasn't a lie. And Cesar tried not to feel guilty about hedging the truth. Not that he worried Derek would get mad at him for falling asleep outside the gym. They'd both been there before. It wasn't a big deal. If Cesar didn't run into the guy today, there was always tomorrow. He didn't want to admit where he'd ended up after because Derek would have a strong opinion about it, and he wasn't in the mood to defend his actions.

"Did you need something?"

"No. I'm heading home early," Derek said. "Just wanted to let you know not to expect me at the office later. You need anything from me?"

"I'm good," came Cesar's quick reply, wanting to get off the phone before Derek asked any probing questions.

The hesitation on the other end of the line made Cesar hold his breath and brace for a question about his research into Saxon's father that he didn't want to answer.

"You thought any more about our conversation?"

He blew out his breath. "We've had many. You'll have to be more specific." And where the fuck had that snarky, teenager-esque tone materialized from?

Cesar waited for Derek's biting reply but only got a feeble chuckle. "Don't play me."

"I'm…" Cesar didn't know quite how to respond. "I'm digging deeper. I want to be sure before I say anything to Saxon."

"You should say something to Saxon before wasting your time."

"If this guy turns out to be a bad bet, I'll drop it, and Saxon never needs to know. Look, I don't want to talk about it."

"You don't want to talk about it because you know you're doing something you shouldn't. Just talk to him."

"Saxon's got a lot going on right now. He doesn't need to deal with this as well."

Was that a groan? That was a groan. "You can tell yourself whatever you need to justify it, but don't say I didn't warn you."

Cesar waited out Derek's long pause. He had more to say, and as much as Cesar didn't want to hear it right now, he might as well hear Derek out so they didn't have to continue the conversation later.

"Do me a favor," Derek finally said.

"What's that?"

"Ask yourself why you're doing this. The *real* why."

"I told you—"

"No. You told me what you thought would get me off your back."

Because it was true, Cesar didn't correct him. "See you tomorrow?"

Even over the phone, Cesar heard Derek's sigh. When Derek spoke again, he'd dropped the big-brother-knows-best tone. "Yeah. I'll be in early."

They hung up, and Cesar stared at the used car lot across the street. He could turn around and drop the whole thing, but then he thought back to Derek's question about Cesar's motivation.

And he sat there in the car and interrogated that motivation. First, he wanted to make Saxon happy, and if that meant he could do that by making sure that Saxon's father wasn't a walking, talking red flag, he would. Maybe his father had been shut out of Saxon's life. Maybe it hadn't been his choice. It happens. Maybe Saxon's father would be a great addition to his life.

But Cesar wasn't naive enough to believe it couldn't all go wrong.

That instinctual need of his to protect people had him pushing the boundaries of his normal background checks and the reason why he'd parked across the street from Melvin Davis's used car lot.

The background check had come back clean, besides a few parking tickets, he'd taken a little longer than most to pay.

However, not having a criminal history did not make him a good person, and Cesar didn't want anything negative walking into Saxon's life. And even though times had changed, they hadn't changed enough. If Melvin Davis was a homophobic asshole, Saxon didn't need that.

But shouldn't Saxon be the one to decide that?

Yes. And Cesar would let him—as soon as he found out what kind of man Melvin Davis was.

14

———

AFTER CESAR LEFT, SAXON HAD GONE UPSTAIRS TO WORK ON THE third floor before Kai arrived that evening.

He grabbed an old rag, wiped the sweat and drywall dust from his face, and took a long drag from his water bottle, the ice cubes had long since melted, and the water gone warm.

As much as he hated the heat, he'd miss not having to pay for the extra air conditioning once installed. To keep costs down, he wouldn't turn the air on until they at least got to the wall painting stage. And although he prided himself on how far he'd come in a short time, he *was* only one man.

Though, at his current pace, he might be able to start taping the drywall in a couple of weeks.

Sure Cesar had offered to help—which was generous—but Saxon had to keep in mind that Cesar had work of his own and couldn't spend every minute spare minute working on renovations.

A light breeze blew through the windows, and Saxon went to the open window and leaned out, closing his eyes and taking in as much of the delicious breeze as possible. If he used his imagination, he could pick up the slightest hint of the salty Pacific Ocean in the air.

Or was that all the salt in his sweat he smelled?

The roar of a motorcycle had him opening his eyes. A Harley with a sidecar turned at the end of the street. He watched in fascination as the driver pulled into the driveway and cut the engine.

Two teenage-looking kids got off the bike. One out of the sidecar, and one off the back of the motorcycle, allowing one very large man whose size could have been the inspiration for all those books about trolls living under bridges to dismount.

Though from the third floor, he seemed more yummy than troll-y.

All three pulled off their helmets, and Saxon rubbed as much sweat off his face, neck, and chest as he could with the rag and pulled on his T-shirt. He ignored the grittiness of the dust on his skin as he pulled the shirt down and brushed a hand through his hair. Drywall dust rained down. Not much he could do about that. He started down the two flights of stairs to answer the doorbell, even though it wasn't locked.

That happened more often than not because Stonewall House still looked very much like a private residence and less like a place of business.

"Coming," Saxon said as the doorbell rang for the second time.

He scooped Mango up on the second story when he ran out of Phoenix's open door. Mango hadn't yet learned to navigate the stairs well enough not to roll down a couple if he didn't take his time.

Saxon held Mango to his chest and answered the door. "Can I help you?"

The big man put a hand on the shoulder of the teen with the backpack. Not a shove, more of a gentle encouragement, which Saxon found endearing in such a large man.

The tall, thin, Asian teen stepped forward, tossing his head to get the long dark bangs out of his eyes. He had pink gauges in both ears big enough to put a dime through and a black stud in the dent beneath his bottom lip.

"Um, I'm… I'm Kai," the teen said. "Mr. Grant said I could come here."

"Of course," Saxon opened the door wide to let everybody in. "I thought he was bringing you himself."

"He got tied up," the bear of a man said. "I said I could bring him after the shop closed." He stuck out his hand for Saxon to shake. "Truman."

Where had Saxon heard that name before? Then it clicked into place. "You own Pigments."

"That's me." For a man as big as he was, Saxon was thankful he didn't feel the need to prove his strength when he shook Saxon's hand. They both knew Truman could probably crush him with a hard look.

Truman's open smile didn't make him look like he routinely went around pulverizing people for the hell of it.

"*Meow.*" Mango struggled in his hands, and Saxon closed the door and let him run around. Without hesitation, he climbed Truman, perched on his shoulder, and started licking a paw.

"Sorry about that." Saxon reached for the kitten.

"It's fine," Truman said. "Cats seem to like me."

"That's because you feed, like, twenty of them behind the shop every morning." That from the other teen. He had the long hair going on, and Saxon liked the sass.

"And if you tell Cat, I'm going to bust you back down to baby apprentice, and you'll be mopping the floor with a toothbrush for a week," Truman said.

Truman might have sounded scary, but his lips twitched at the corners, and the teen rolled his eyes and scoffed.

Saxon turned his attention to him. "You must be Grant's son, Tavi."

"Guilty," Tavi said. "Where's Kai gonna stay? I was going to help him unpack."

A single backpack wouldn't take two people to unpack, but Saxon didn't point that out. He directed them to the back of the house. "On the right, past the kitchen."

Mango slid down Truman's torso to follow the boys. Truman caught him and set him on the floor. The orange menace ran after the boys, its little paws sounding like a galloping miniature horse on the old hardwood floor.

"I appreciate you bringing him," Saxon said. "I could have picked him up if I'd known Grant couldn't do it."

"It's not a problem." Truman glanced down the hall as if making sure Kai was out of earshot. "And I wanted to talk to you about Kai."

"Grant already told me he has a history with law enforcement."

"He does, but that's not what I wanted to talk to you about."

This should be interesting.

Saxon glanced down the hall as well and braced for the worst.

Truman glanced down, scuffing the toe of his motorcycle boot on the floor as he gathered his thoughts. "It's just that, Kai…" Truman met Saxon's eyes. "He's not as tough as he makes out. He's had it rough. Tavi knows more about it than I do, but that's not Tavi's story to tell, so I don't press."

"I get that," Saxon said. "It's nice that Kai has someone he can confide in. And his new house-mates are the best. Plus, we have access to mental health services if that's something he needs."

Truman visibly relaxed. "He might. I'm not the best judge of that. The world has treated him dirty. He's put up high walls. But in the little time he's been at the shop, he's starting to lower his defenses, and I've caught glimpses of the thoughtful, kind, compassionate person on the other side."

"You're worried about him."

Truman nodded, his tongue toying with the ring through his

bottom lip. "I've seen what happens when people like him fall through the cracks. I don't want that to be Kai."

"Me either," Saxon said. "I've been on the other side of those cracks, wondering how I fell through." Not wanting to elaborate further, he added, "It's not a good place to be."

Truman worked his lip ring before he said, "Thanks. Let me or Grant know if you have any problems."

"I don't expect to run into anything I can't handle."

Truman stuck out his hand, and when Saxon took it, Truman gave him a friendly clap on the shoulder. Somehow, Saxon managed not to take a step back to catch his balance.

"Tavi," Truman called out. "Gotta go. Your grandmother is expecting you for dinner."

"Coming," Tavi called from Kai's room.

A few moments later, Tavi emerged without Kai. The three said their goodbyes, and Saxon closed the door behind them. Still no sign of Kai.

He found Kai on the floor with his head resting against the wall, his eyes closed, and Mango on his lap. Saxon almost left him there, but he saw Kai's fingers working through the kitten's fur.

"All settled?"

Kai startled and jumped to his feet. Mango scampered off and disappeared around the corner.

"Sorry," Saxon said. "I didn't mean to scare you."

On the outside, Kai quickly composed himself, but on the inside, his heart must have been hammering in his chest. His chin went up. "You didn't scare me."

Saxon didn't argue. "There's food in the kitchen if you want a sandwich or something." He didn't want Kai to have any insecurities about food. He walked over to the bedside table and pulled out the drawer. "I put some snacks in here, too. Let me know if you want something specific, and I can get it for you."

Kai nodded.

"And if you need any toiletries, deodorant, toothbrush,

anything like that, I've got a bunch of stuff in the office to choose from."

Kai nodded again.

Saxon noticed the backpack on the bed, still full of whatever possessions he had. He hadn't unpacked at all. "We have other things as well. Clothes. Underwear. Socks. If you need them."

Kai eyed the door. Saxon didn't even think Kai knew that he'd done it. "I have everything I need."

When Kai finally looked back at Saxon, Saxon bobbed his chin toward the patio door. "Don't run."

Kai slid down the wall, sat on the floor, and mumbled, "Not like I have anywhere to run. Besides, this… it's different."

"Different, how?"

"You actually act like you *want* me here."

Those words stole Saxon's breath. "That's because I do."

Mango chose that moment to zoom in. He scaled the side of the bed and stretched out on Kai's backpack, his belly in the air, his head back, and his front paws stretched out. It couldn't be comfortable, but Kai would have to risk waking the kitten if he wanted to high-tail it out the patio door.

"I'll be in the office if you need anything. It's next to the kitchen."

Kai didn't answer, and Saxon didn't hang around waiting for one. He understood that Kai needed time to process. The stress of being kicked out without a place to go was a lot to take in. And while ending up at Stonewall House had to be a relief, the whiplash of his housing situation being ripped out from beneath him and finding something new took an adjustment.

If Kai needed space, Saxon would give it to him.

CESAR WAS *JUST* GOING TO TALK TO MELVIN DAVIS. RIGHT? Nothing wrong with a little conversation, and if it went horribly wrong, then Cesar could warn Saxon off if he ever decided to answer Melvin's text.

But what if it all went right?

What if Saxon got a parent back? What if they could rebuild a shattered relationship? What if Saxon was no longer alone in the world?

He has you.

Yeah. Not the same thing, though.

And if he could help give this gift of family to Saxon, he wanted to be the one who could do that for him.

What that said about Cesar and his own issues, he didn't know. But a lot of good could come from this.

At least that's what he kept telling himself as he walked across the street to the used car lot and pulled open the door.

The interior could have used a new paint job, but the floors were clean, the lights bright. There were only three cubicles along the back wall with the half solid wall with plexiglass partitions on top that didn't reach the ceiling.

A man came out of the back room after hearing the ding of the door chime and pasted on one of those smiles that said he'd rather be somewhere else.

"Can I help you?" the man asked. He couldn't have been older than his early thirties and clearly not the man Cesar came to see.

"I'm looking for a new car," Cesar said, "I had a friend recommend I talk to Melvin Davis."

The man's smile dipped when he realized he wouldn't get a sale. Cesar wanted to tell him it was okay because Melvin wouldn't get one either. "Of course. One minute. I will get him for you."

Cesar wandered the showroom, which wasn't much of a showroom because it didn't have those big sliding doors that let you display cars inside. Instead, there were car posters tacked up on the walls. High in one corner, a silent TV broadcasted some car race going on somewhere. He paid little attention.

Hearing a door close, Cesar turned, and for a fleeting second, his breath hung in his chest as he caught a glimpse into the future at what Saxon might look like in twenty or thirty years.

Look at you, already settled into the Happily Ever After when you know that your relationship history shows that you would be lucky to make it twenty weeks with Saxon, much less twenty years.

No lie.

But this thing with Saxon felt different than any other relationship he'd ever had. Just him thinking about a life with Saxon proved that.

A hand waved in front of Cesar's face, and the heat rushed into his cheeks as he returned to himself. "Uh, sorry. I'm Cesar. My friend said if I needed a new car, I needed to come talk to you."

The man beamed. Melvin had Saxon's smile. Or rather, Saxon had his. The man kept his hair shorter, more of a buzz cut than the brown locks that had grown a little over the ears because Saxon was too busy with Stonewall House to think about getting his hair cut.

After introductions, Melvin asked, "Who is your friend?"

Cesar didn't hesitate. He tossed out a made-up name as if he'd spent every day of the last ten years with this friend. "Harper James."

He had to hand it to old Melvin, his eyes lit, and his smile widened as if he knew the fictional person Cesar had mentioned.

"Oh, yes," Melvin said, "I enjoyed working with her. I do hope she's happy with her car."

"Very much so." Cesar put Melvin's seemingly innate ability to lie on his mental *Yellow Flag* list. He didn't exactly see it as a red flag since he lied just as well as Melvin did. The man was trying to make a living, and was a little white lie that big of a deal? "Very happy."

Melvin didn't waste much time with small talk before ushering Cesar outside to show him what he had in the lot.

"Is there anything particular that interested you?"

"A minivan." Cesar got a bright idea as soon Melvin asked the question and went with it.

Melvin's brows went up.

"You know, for the kids."

"Of course, of course. Would your wife—"

"Husband," Cesar corrected.

"Husband. Sure. Sorry," Melvin corrected without any indication he had an issue with that. Cesar liked that he was quick to apologize and move on. Melvin could have been faking it the same way he had about Harper James, but Cesar didn't think so. "And how many children."

"Two right now, but we have another on the way."

Without skipping a beat, Melvin steered him from one of the smaller mini-vans to one of the larger ones. At the hood of the van, he said, "This one may be better, especially if you decide to have more."

Cesar almost shuddered. He wasn't opposed to having kids someday, though the thought of wrangling more than three of them at the same time made sweat bead on his upper lip.

Or maybe it was just the southern California sun.

Despite Cesar's talking skills, Melvin's were better, and Cesar didn't leave the lot without taking a test drive and promising to call the next day. At least he managed to get out of there without having a credit check done.

It was close, though.

As Cesar drove home, he had to admit that meeting Saxon's father had gone as well as he could have imagined. Melvin even seemed likable. Not that you could get to know someone well over a fake car deal, but Cesar still left the dealership hopeful.

And determined to tell Saxon what he'd been up to.

15

SAXON SHOULD HAVE BEEN WORKING ON THE THIRD FLOOR WHILE he had the chance, but he wanted to stay close in case Kai had any questions. He expected Phoenix, Oliver, Addi, James, and Sophia to start coming home soon, though he didn't know exactly when. Besides, he had a lot of paperwork he'd neglected while dealing with all things Oliver.

And Cesar.

Who was the best distraction ever.

Sometime later, Mango ran into the office, scrambled up his leg, and slid across the desktop, sending papers flying before jumping off again and running out the door.

Talk about whiplash.

He bent to pick up the papers and came face to foot with Kai's shoes. The shoes were clean enough where shoes were concerned, but the sole had started peeling away from the toes exposing the sock beneath. Saxon would have to fix that.

Kai picked up some of the scattered papers around his feet and handed them over.

"Thanks," Saxon said.

Kai stuffed his hands in the front pockets of his jeans. "Why are you doing this?"

"The paperwork or Stonewall House?"

Kai waved a hand around as if indicating Stonewall House. It's what Saxon had thought he meant, but he didn't want to delve that deep if the question didn't require it.

Saxon knew by the steady way Kai scrutinized him that he couldn't go with the standard *because I want to help people* that usually satisfied the question.

Saxon recognized the distrust in Kai's eyes. The system had let him down. What made him think that Stonewall House—and Saxon—wouldn't as well?

Saxon leaned back in his chair and gave Kai enough of the truth without dredging up too many bad memories. Some might think that after all this time, Saxon would be over his childhood traumas by now, but they'd be wrong.

"I was you not too many years ago. I've run away. I've been kicked out. I've walked the streets, not knowing where I would spend the night. I've been hungry without knowing when I would eat next, wondering if I could make it one more day without having to sell myself for a greasy cheeseburger and stale fries."

Saxon stopped talking because his throat had tightened, and he didn't want it to crack. This conversation wasn't about him, but he wanted Kai to know that he'd walked miles in Kai's battered shoes.

Kai nodded as if he got it, and some of the defiance melted away. He hitched his thumb over his shoulder. "Mind if I fix myself something to eat?"

"Help yourself. If a package has a name on it, it belongs to one of your housemates, but there's plenty that is fair game."

Saxon's phone rang, and Kai disappeared into the kitchen. "Hello?"

"Hello, *boyfriend.*" Cesar's voice came out as this low grumble that went straight to Saxon's dick. He slid the pocket door on his office closed even though it made him a little claustrophobic.

"Hey, you." It hadn't been all that long since Cesar had left with Saxon's things, yet it felt like an eternity.

"You sound tired."

"I guess I am."

"You still want me to come over tonight and help with the reno?"

Saxon blew out a breath. He should ask Cesar to come over. Anything to make the work go faster. The heat up there had been exhausting, and his short conversation with Kai had taken more out of Saxon than the drywall had.

"I think I just want to come home," Saxon said instead, not even realizing what came out of his mouth until silence met him on the other end of the phone, and he had to think back to what he'd said.

Saxon blew out a breath and rolled a pen on the desk between his fingers. "Wait. That came out wr—"

"Home." Cesar's voice had more of a purr to it than Mango's. "I like the way that sounds. You going to be much longer?"

"Probably not much. I want to wait until someone else gets here. I'd hate to leave Kai alone on his first night."

"How is he?"

Saxon appreciated that Cesar thought to ask. "A little shell shocked, I think. He'll do fine, I'm sure. He has friends and people who care about him. That goes a long way."

Before Saxon could overthink the *home* comment, Cesar said, "That's good. What you're doing is important. Take all the time you need. You don't have to rush. I'll wait up."

Que the tears.

Saxon didn't quite know what set him off. His life had had a few emotional ups and downs over the past five days with limited sleep, and it was just so fucking nice to have someone steady that didn't throw a fit if he ran late. Someone who built him up instead of tearing him down.

Someone who believed… *in him.*

He let the tears fall and allowed himself to feel those feelings. To feel like he wasn't alone. That he was wanted.

And not a burden.

A soft knock sounded on his door jamb, which was only a couple of feet from Saxon's head. Kai could have spoken, but he must have heard him snuffling in his office.

"Um… you okay?"

Saxon dried his cheeks with the heels of his hands, tacked on a smile, and slid the door open. "I am. These are happy tears." He didn't want to think about his abandonment or relationship issues or whatever the hell it was that made him cry because his boyfriend wasn't a dick to him. "At least I think they are."

Kai shifted, looking like he wanted to run from anything that remotely resembled a feeling. But he stood his ground anyway. "You said you had some things I could have."

Saxon jumped out of his chair, bumping his head on an open cabinet above his desk. He rubbed his head and pushed his chair out of the way to get to the lower shelves with the bins of donated supplies.

He kneeled and invited Kai into the cramped space. "What do you need?"

Bin by bin, he found toiletries for Kia, new socks, and a few pairs of underwear. As well as two gently used designer T-shirts Saxon had picked up from one of the local discount shops a month or two back.

"It's not much," Saxon said, "But that should help until we can get to a store."

"Store?" Kai looked confused.

"I'm taking you shopping if that's okay with you. Get you other things you might need."

Kai glanced at the stuff in his arms. "I have what I need."

"How about what you want?" Stonewall House didn't have it in the budget to go on a shopping spree for everyone who came to stay. Until then, Saxon used his own money for each of them after arriving. He wanted them to have more things than they could fit in a backpack and to know they weren't going anywhere. At least not until they were ready.

It was Kai's turn to tear up. "Look what you made me do."

Saxon wanted to wrap him up and tell him everything would be okay, but Kai might not be comfortable with that. "Is it okay if I give you a hug?"

Kai thought about it for a second before he nodded, and Saxon pulled him in. Letting him cry on his shoulder until Mango found them and jumped up on their shoulders and walked around meowing as if Saxon were purposefully starving him.

Kai laughed and sat back on his heels. Mango jumped off Saxon's shoulder and settled in the space between Kai's legs, turning his purr box up to maximum.

The front door opened and closed. "Where is everybody?"

Saxon clapped Kai's shoulder. "Come on. I'll introduce you to your housemates."

<hr>

CESAR DIDN'T MIND THE WAIT. NOT FOR SAXON. HE SAT ON THE couch in his den, his laptop propped on his thighs as he worked on a few background checks for potential new hires for a local company they frequently worked with. He had pasta sauce on a low simmer on the stove, a pot of water ready to boil, and the oven pre-heating for the garlic bread.

He took a sip of beer, compiled a report on one of the candidates, and moved on to the next one. Headlights flashed across his front window, and a car door closed shortly afterward. He set his work aside and went to open the door for Saxon.

"Hey, baby," Cesar said as if he greeted Saxon at the door after work every evening. Funny thing was, it wasn't the least bit awkward.

After a quick kiss, Cesar stole the kitten out of Saxon's arms, closed the door, and set Mango loose to explore.

Saxon leaned against the closed door, his hair adorably mussed. All Cesar wanted was to eat him up.

"Hey there yourself," Saxon said in that lower register that made Cesar's dick come alive. "Smells good in here. What did you have for dinner?"

"I waited for you. It's jar spaghetti with a few spices I threw in for good measure."

"You didn't have to wait."

Cesar moved closer and nuzzled his neck, tasting the salt on his skin from his work on the third floor. "I wanted to."

Saxon's head fell back and thumped the door as his eyes fell closed. Cesar leaned away to see his face. "You look exhausted. What do you want to do? Do you want to eat or—"

"I think I'd rather unpack your car first so I don't have to do it later."

"I already unpacked."

Saxon's eyes opened, and he must have taken in the den for the first time. "And you got Mango a cat tree for the house."

"And I got him a litter box, and food bowls, and a couple of cat toys to keep him busy."

Saxon wrapped his arms around Cesar's neck and kissed him. "Thank you."

And because it looked like Saxon could fall asleep against the door, he peeled Saxon's arms off his shoulders, took him by the hand, and led him through the den. Cesar had a small, two-bedroom bungalow. The house tour wouldn't take more than a minute.

At the first room on the right, he stopped. Mango zoomed in, disappeared under the bed, and zoomed out again. "Here's the guest room. It's not much."

Saxon stepped in and spun in a tight circle, taking in the full-sized bed, the unmatched bedside tables, and the small dresser on the wall opposite the foot of the bed. Saxon sat on the end of the bed. "This is great. Thanks for letting me stay."

"What's wrong?" Cesar stepped into the room. He watched the wheels turn in Saxon's head, and before Saxon could come up with a lie, Cesar said, "Tell me the truth."

"I thought that maybe..." Saxon hesitated, then continued, "But no, that was presumptuous of me to think—"

"*Saxon.*"

Saxon met his eyes. "I thought maybe I would be with you."

Cesar grinned. "Follow me."

He showed Saxon the single bathroom at the end of the hall and then turned into his bedroom. It was significantly bigger than the guest room. At some point, one of the owners must have expanded the room, taking a chunk of the back porch with it. At least it gave him room for a king bed, double closets, and a dresser big enough for both of their clothes.

Cesar went to the first closet and opened the door. All of Saxon's clothes hung in there. "I put your clothes in here because I wanted you in here. Presumptuous. But we can move them to the guest room if—"

Saxon shut him up with a kiss that left the top of Cesar's head steaming and his toes curling. *Guh.* All the naughty, sexy things he wanted to do to this man or have Saxon do to him. The list kept getting longer as the kiss went on.

Cesar finally had to break it to get air, and Saxon's blossoming smile told him he'd done the right thing. "I definitely want to keep my clothes in here."

Yep. *Slow* was definitely a thing of the past.

Cesar no longer cared what people might say or what the

established relationship norms were. Nothing prevented them from going at whatever speed felt right for them.

And after one night sleeping with his arms wrapped around an inspiring, thoughtful, compassionate, sexy as fuck man, Cesar wanted to spend every night like that one.

Saxon must have found a hidden reserve because the exhausted man who'd walked through Cesar's door not five minutes ago had enough energy for them both.

With his hands on Cesar's chest, Saxon walked him back until Cesar's legs hit the side of the bed, and he fell crossways onto the mattress with his head toward the door. He scooted, making room for Saxon. Saxon followed, bracing himself on his hands and knees above him.

That look in Saxon's eye said Cesar might want to turn off the oven and stove. "I thought you were hungry."

"I am." Saxon stretched out on top of him, raining kisses down Cesar's neck, nipping at his earlobes, and drawing the neediest moans from Cesar's mouth. "But I want you more."

Cesar was perfectly willing to starve if it meant having Saxon now. The food would be there when they finished.

Cesar ran his hands down Saxon's sides. If he didn't want to burn the place down, he had to stop him now. "Let me up. I need to turn off the stove and oven."

The end of Cesar's nose got a kiss, and Saxon popped up. "I'll get it." He turned down the hall, his hand caught on the jamb, and he stuck his head back in. "Don't go anywhere."

Cesar chuckled. Like he would actually leave. "I'll be here."

He heard the crunch of kibble coming from the kitchen. Mango must have found his food bowl. Maybe Cesar should have felt guilty for not showing Mango where all of his stuff was, and he might have to clean up a mess if Mango didn't find the litter box that Cesar had put in the laundry room, but he didn't. Not one tiny, little nano-bit.

It wouldn't take long for Saxon to return, so Cesar ditched his clothes, kicking them off the bed. He settled on his back, head over the edge, looking at the door, impatiently waiting for Saxon to return. What the hell was taking so long?

Then he heard Saxon's feet on the floor, and Cesar's mind immediately referenced that long list of things he wanted to do with his man. He couldn't wait to get another taste of Saxon.

Cesar's hand went to his dick, not surprised to find the tip slick with precum. He rubbed it over the head and down the shaft as Saxon rounded the corner.

"*Oof.*" Saxon stopped at the threshold. "You're so fucking sexy like that."

With his head tilted back, Cesar looked at upside-down Saxon. But upside-down Saxon was just as remarkable as the upright version of him. "You have entirely too many clothes on. Get in here, strip, and shut that door before we have a teeny, tiny audience."

Saxon grinned, shutting the door and going straight for his belt. Cesar loved a man who followed orders and had his priorities straight.

After shucking every stitch of clothing, Cesar rolled onto his stomach. "You're beautiful," he said, his voice soft and full of wonder, like someone seeing one of the great wonders of the world in person for the first time. Saxon wasn't built like a Greek god. He had a trim, athletic build, more like a swimmer than a powerlifter. The light smattering of hair across his chest and the slightly darker trail arrowing down from his belly button made Cesar's mouth water.

Then there was Saxon's cock.

If Cesar had the tiniest poetic bone in his body, he'd write whole sonnets or plays about Saxon's cock. But the most remarkable, beautiful thing about it was that it was hard.

For Cesar.

Saxon went to walk around the bed, and Cesar shook his

head. He didn't even have to say anything because Saxon watched him closely.

"What's wrong?" Saxon asked.

Cesar smiled. "Absolutely nothing. I have a naked man in my room who has come to matter quite a bit. A naked man that I can't wait to get my mouth on."

Saxon's brows rose. He brushed the hair out of his eyes and gripped his dick, biting his lip before he said, "Where do you want me then?"

Cesar loved that he'd left the room's overhead light on. That way, he could see every emotion that passed over Saxon's handsome face in the span of a few seconds—the shyness, the eagerness, the lust, the vulnerability.

Rolling to his back again, Cesar hung his head over the edge of the bed, his arms reaching out for Saxon. "I want you down my throat."

16

I WANT YOU DOWN MY THROAT.

Saxon loved a direct man. A man who wasn't afraid to ask for what he wanted. It was a hell of a rush.

And that *that* man wanted *him*… well, Saxon wasn't going to delve into his insecurities right then. As far as his insecurities went, they could take a fucking hike and fuck the fuck right off.

He stroked himself as he stepped toward Cesar, his dick leaking precum like a 1950's faucet. One of Cesar's hands snaked around Saxon's thigh and pulled him within reach of his mouth.

The first hot, dick-melting stroke of Cesar's tongue on the underside of Saxon's cock had his head falling back and a soft moan escaping his throat.

Cesar pulled him closer, and Saxon went willingly. "Fuck," he muttered.

Saxon's legs shook, and his hands went to Cesar's chest to steady himself. Cesar's chuckle sent a delightful vibration up Saxon's dick. As Cesar took him deep, again and again, coming up for air only when needed, Saxon knew he wouldn't last.

Not with the glorious way Cesar's warm mouth and wet

tongue worked Saxon over. The sensations made Saxon's skin pebble and his spine tingle with his impending orgasm.

As much as he loved Cesar's mouth on him, he wanted to come with Cesar deep inside him. To do that, he would have to pull Cesar off. But Saxon couldn't make himself do it. It felt too damn good.

He had about decided that he could always have Cesar fuck him after he came when Cesar released him, his mouth making a loud *pop* sound and his hand replacing his mouth as he continued to stroke Saxon.

Saxon's eyes rolled to the back of his head for a second before he could manage to look down at Cesar. "I love your mouth on me."

Cesar grinned. The type of grin that did things to Saxon's heart. Like, make him believe that *this*—whatever the hell this relationship was—that this could last. That years from now, Saxon would be looking down at that same grin, but Cesar would have gray in his stubble and crow's feet at the corners of his eyes.

Cesar rested his head on Saxon's outstretched hand for support. "You taste amazing."

Before Cesar used that mouth again and made Saxon forget what he wanted, he bent down and kissed Cesar. It was the sweetest, awkward-est upside-down kiss, and it made Saxon's heart hurt.

"*Mmmm.*" He kissed Cesar again. "That talented mouth."

"*Fuck yeah*," Cesar muttered, holding the back of Saxon's head, keeping him close enough to devour his mouth as he continued stroking Saxon's dick.

Saxon's knees wanted to buckle. Cesar's fingers worked Saxon's shaft, his thumb sliding over the sensitive head and across Saxon's slick slit over and over again.

"You slay me," Saxon kissed Cesar again, with tongue and nips and more upside-down awkwardness. "And as much as I love what you're doing to me, I want you to fuck me."

Cesar's hand stilled and his heavy breath caught in his lungs. It spilled out with a loud rush that made Saxon second guess himself.

Fuck. Maybe Cesar didn't want that. Maybe all he wanted was oral or some mutual masturbation. Nothing wrong with that, but…

"We don't have to do that," Cesar said.

"Unless you don't want—" Saxon blurted on top of Cesar's words.

Cesar grinned and rolled to his stomach, locking eyes with Saxon. "Oh, I *want*."

He took Saxon's hands and pulled him onto the bed between his legs as he rolled to his back. "You sure that's what you want? We don't have to do it if you think that's what I want to hear. Because as much as I would love to be inside you, there are so many other things we can do that we would both enjoy."

They were still new at this boyfriend thing. Still figuring out what each of them liked and how they fit together in bed. Saxon appreciated that Cesar took the time to clarify wants, needs, and expectations. And with them being vers, maybe next time, it would switch it up.

Saxon ground against Cesar, the friction of their dicks rubbing against each other made Saxon's head spin. "I wouldn't have asked if it wasn't what I wanted."

Cesar's raised brow made him look skeptical.

"Really," Saxon said. "I want you to fuck me until your name is the only word I remember. Until I come so hard, I forget every other man I've been with. Until—"

With a finger pressed to Saxon's lips, Cesar shut him up. "The pressure." The smile said Cesar was joking. Mostly. "I don't want you to get your hopes up so high that all I'll do is disappoint."

Saxon reached down and took Cesar in his hand. Cesar hissed in a breath and held it as Saxon stroked him. "Trust me. You couldn't disappoint me. But don't worry about all that. I want you in me. Now."

Cesar spun them around, and Saxon cried out and laughed as his back hit the mattress. The anticipation built, and he thrust upward, hunting that friction.

Angling over Saxon's body, Cesar reached into his bedside table and retrieved a fresh bottle of lube and a box of condoms with the wrapper still on the box.

Cesar handed him the lube. "Take the seal off the top while I get this wrapper off."

"Did you just buy these?"

With his teeth on the corner of the large box of condoms, Cesar muttered, "Yes."

The caution in his voice made Saxon smile, and before he could ask what the problem was, Cesar blurted, "I tossed everything out after…"

He didn't have to finish that sentence for Saxon to know what 'after' referred to.

Not what… *who*.

Before Saxon responded, Cesar rattled on with his unnecessary explanation. "But I didn't get them because I expected us to end up here. Especially on your first night. I mean, I'm not complaining, but I wouldn't have minded if we didn't get here right away or ever."

Cesar shook his head as if frustrated with the words flowing out of his mouth. "I'm not making any sense. I want you. I wanted to be ready in case…" he waved his hand between them, indicating their current state of undress. "*This.* But I didn't expect—"

Saxon pulled him down and kissed him until Cesar gave up trying to talk and gave into him, and the kisses and the attention Saxon lavished on the underside of Cesar's jaw. The stubble pricked Saxon's lips, which only made him want more.

When he finally let Cesar go, Saxon said, "You don't have to explain. It's not like you lured me here with the promise of a place to stay to get into my pants."

Cesar ran his hands down Saxon's chest and flicked his thumbs across his flat nipples, quickly teasing them into hard peaks, his grin evil. Deliciously, mischievously, delightfully evil. "Or did I?"

Saxon laughed. It was one of those carefree, joyous laughs that he heard from other people but had been rare coming from him. That Cesar had the capacity to gift him that or pull that from somewhere deep within him—however, the hell that worked—said something incredible about the man hovering above him. "I don't think I care anymore how I we got here. Do with me what you will."

CESAR COULD GET USED TO LOOKING DOWN AT THE MAN WHO looked up at him as if he'd hung the moon, swept the stars up into the sky, and caused the universe to expand. It was heady stuff, and Cesar couldn't get enough.

He fumbled with the condom box while Saxon chewed the seal off the top of the lube, leaving little tooth marks on the bottle's threads. Saxon replaced the lid and swiped the condom packet from Cesar. A hand in the center of Cesar's chest had him sitting back on his haunches.

All the pre-sex prep had done nothing to make Cesar's dick flag. It made him harder. The anticipation of pushing inside Saxon had Cesar leaking into the condom as Saxon rolled it down his shaft.

He had to take hold of Saxon's wrists and put himself when Saxon finished to keep him from coming early. "You'll have to keep your hands to yourself and give me a minute."

Saxon pouted, fighting a smile. Cesar kissed him on the end

of the nose before releasing his hands. "I promise I'll make it up to you."

"You'd better."

It was a challenge that Cesar would do his best to exceed expectations. Those little niggling thoughts intruded into his head. The ones that said his ex would never have cheated on him if he'd been good enough in bed.

He shoved those thoughts as far out of his mind as he could. Saxon wouldn't judge him. That wasn't the kind of man he was. And this wasn't a performance. This was the two of them coming together, sharing their bodies and their desires.

Saxon flipped the top on the lube and squirted the contents into Cesar's hand. He used it liberally on his dick before putting more on his fingers.

Saxon's eyes drifted closed as Cesar stroked one slick finger along Saxon's crack and teased the tight ring of muscle.

One thing about Saxon was that he wasn't afraid to go after what he wanted, and Cesar appreciated that. Saxon groaned as he pressed against Cesar's finger, his back arching. Cesar started with one finger, but Saxon opened his eyes and looked up at him. "Give me two."

Cesar opened his mouth, but Saxon must have known what he would say next because he said, "You saw the purple people eater." Cesar laughed, remembering the purple dildo that Saxon had packed to take with him. "I can take two fingers easily."

With Saxon's legs spread out before him, Cesar nipped at the tender flesh on the inside of Saxon's thighs. He gently pressed two fingers inside and scraped Saxon's thigh with his teeth. Saxon was tight at first, but he relaxed around Cesar's fingers as Cesar eased his way inside.

Saxon didn't wait for Cesar to set the pace. He set it himself, riding Cesar's fingers.

Cesar took that beautiful cock to the back of his throat, and

Saxon fucked himself on Cesar's fingers at the same time he fucked Cesar's mouth.

"So. Fucking. Good," Saxon ground out with each thrust, the gravel in his voice going straight to Cesar's dick, spilling precum into the condom. At this rate, the condom would be full before they fucked.

He couldn't wait any longer to be inside Saxon, and the way Saxon pulled at Cesar told him Saxon couldn't wait either. He removed his fingers, Saxon's hand going to the back of Cesar's head, threading through his hair and fisting there. The tight hold Saxon had on the strands should have been on the verge of painful, but it only revved Cesar more.

"Come up here," Saxon said, his words barely there as he gently pulled Cesar up by his hair.

Cesar went willingly. Crawling up Saxon's body, kissing his way from the sexy treasure trail, up the midline of his abdomen, to the gentle rise of his pecs, to his neck, and finally to his kissable lips. Cesar's cock rested against Saxon's balls, nudging his taint and sliding between his slick cheeks.

Saxon broke the kiss, breathing hard, the sweat breaking out along his hairline. He reached between them and lined Cesar up with his hole, making his wants clear.

"You ready for me, baby?" The endearment fell from Cesar's lips as if he'd been calling Saxon that for years and not for the first time.

Saxon's kiss nearly sucked every last molecule of air out of him. "Fuck me already."

Cesar grinned and canted his hips, and even though Saxon grabbed his ass and pulled him closer, Cesar eased inside. The tight grip Saxon's ass had on his cock nearly made Cesar's eyes cross. It felt so fucking good.

"*Ooof*," Saxon groaned, holding Cesar in place when he bottomed out. "Don't move. I'm barely hanging on here."

Letting his head drop between his shoulders, Cesar glanced at

Saxon's straining dick and the way his own disappeared in Saxon's ass. Saxon flexed. The ensuing tightness around Cesar's cock ripped a hiss out of his throat.

He wasn't going to last, and that was okay.

Hopefully, there will be many more times. Times when they could make it last if they wanted, but tonight wasn't one of them.

Cesar dropped to his forearms, burying his face into the crook of Saxon's shoulder as he pulled out and thrust in again. The grip, the slip, the slide made Cesar's blood heat and sweat slick his skin. He nipped the soft spot where Saxon's shoulder met his neck and tasted the salt there. He breathed in Saxon's scent. An intoxicating mix of fresh air and drywall dust.

Cesar pumped faster, egged on by Saxon's firm grip on his ass, directing the speed and depth. The base of his spine tingled. He didn't want to come before Saxon, but as soon as he thought that, Saxon reached between them. Cesar rose to his hands to give Saxon room to jack himself.

The moans, the slap of flesh on flesh, the way the pleasure danced on Saxon's face had Cesar's orgasm exploding through him. Every muscle shook, every nerve tingled, every breath a fight for much-needed oxygen.

Saxon threw his head back and stiffened beneath him, his hand working his cock as he shot his second load of the night over his hands and abdomen.

As Saxon returned to himself, he opened his eyes and smiled at Cesar with the sweetest, shyest, sultriest smile.

"What are you thinking in that devious head of yours." As Cesar started to go soft, he couldn't help flexing his hips one last time before pulling out.

The flush rushed into Saxon's cheeks, and Cesar knew he'd love whatever came out of Saxon's mouth next. "I love the way you fuck me."

Jesusfuckingchrist. This man...

Cesar leaned down and kissed Saxon, his arms shaking from

his exertion. He barely kept the *I love you too* from falling out of his mouth. The need to say those words hit so strong. It took Cesar a moment to interrogate that thought.

Did he love Saxon? Could he this soon?

The smile slipped from Saxon's face. "Are you okay? Did I say something wrong?"

Maybe the *I love you* popped into Cesar's head because it was the unvarnished truth. He hadn't had to think about it. It was just… *there.*

Saxon's hands went to Cesar's hips and gave him a little shake that brought him out of his head. "You're scaring me."

With a kiss meant to convey the enormity of Cesar's heart, he left them both breathless again. "I love being with you, too."

Saxon smiled, but something in the way Saxon looked at him told him that Saxon knew he'd held something back. He hated that he'd made Saxon doubt what they'd just shared. He should have just told him the truth, but as some of the light left Saxon's eyes, Cesar knew that he'd lost the moment.

A plaintive cry came at the bedroom door. The perfect distraction. Little paws slipped under the door, yanking on it as if Mango could pull himself through the thin space.

He opened the door on the way to dispose of the condom. Mango scampered in with another exasperated complaint and scaled the side of the bed. Saxon hopped up before Mango could get to him, needing to get cleaned up before he held the little orange gremlin.

Saxon followed Cesar into the bathroom with Mango on his heels. They took a quick shower together. Mango scaled the towels he and Saxon had laid across the toilet seat and watched from his perch on top. By the time they dried off and dressed enough to return to the kitchen, heat the sauce, and boil water for the noodles, Saxon had returned to his normal self.

One day, Cesar would tell him exactly how he felt, but he didn't want to scare Saxon off by admitting how deep his feelings had grown so quickly, especially when he didn't want Saxon to feel obligated to feel—or *say* he felt—the same.

Their relationship didn't need that kind of pressure. The right time would come.

While they ate, Cesar wanted to tell Saxon about his research on Melvin but didn't quite know how to broach the subject. And he'd be lying if he said some of the caution that Derek had beat into his head didn't affect his view on what he'd done. But he'd done it, and he couldn't *unknow* what he'd found. He understood Saxon would be cautious meeting with his father, but so far, Cesar hadn't found anything that would be a huge red flag.

Saxon scarfed down dinner while Mango sat on his lap and tried sneaking his paw onto Saxon's plate. Saxon kept pushing his plate away until it was out of reach of the little furry paws.

What was the best way to broach the subject of Saxon's father without looking like he knew something that he shouldn't? Or maybe Cesar should let the subject drop. It wasn't like Saxon had brought up his father after the texts had come in.

And if Saxon had no plans to answer the texts and reconnect with his father, then Cesar could forget about his unsolicited background check and quit feeling guilty about going behind Saxon's back.

Besides, it wasn't like he'd meant any harm by it. He'd just been trying to protect Saxon and help bring him happiness.

Which he never asked you to do. He's not a child. If he wanted your help, he would have asked for it.

Cesar hated having this potentially explosive secret and needed to get it off his chest without blowing up their relation-ship the first night Saxon moved in.

It weighed heavy on him.

Cesar ripped the corner off a piece of garlic bread and sopped up some of the remaining sauce on his plate. Around the bite, he asked, "Have you heard anything more from your father?"

Saxon dropped his fork onto his empty plate and scooped up

Mango into his arms. "I haven't responded. I know that's pretty shitty of me, but—"

"You don't owe him anything. You don't have to respond now, tomorrow, or ever."

"I know that in here." Saxon pointed to his head. "But in my heart…" He shook his head and rubbed his chin against Mango's little face, making the furball purr even louder. How could such a small creature make so much noise? "In my heart, I feel like I need to give him a second chance. But I haven't decided what to do about it yet."

"There's no rush. You have a lot going on. Besides, for all your father knows, he could have texted the wrong number."

Did that sound like a supportive boyfriend, or did that sound like a man who wanted to potentially stay out of the doghouse?

Cesar cleared their plates and started loading the dishwasher while Saxon put the leftovers away. If he still felt the need to fess up in the morning, Cesar would.

17

———

IT HAD BEEN SEVERAL WEEKS, AND EVERYTHING ABOUT SAXON being in Cesar's space was better than he hoped it would be. Having him there surpassed anything imaginable.

Of course, the sex continued to be wondrous. Still, he hadn't realized how much he'd come to look forward to arriving home from work and finding Saxon there or meeting Saxon at Stonewall House and them both falling asleep at their home later in a tangle of arms and legs and fuzzy tails, exhausted after several hours spent finishing hanging the drywall and taping and mudding the joints.

It was a huge job, but day by day, he and Saxon were getting it done. One day, the third floor would be finished, Kai could move out of Saxon's room, and they'd have to decide if Saxon would stay with Cesar or if he would reclaim his room at the house.

Cesar didn't like thinking about that.

As he parked across the street from Melvin Davis's used car lot, he tried to put the thought of Saxon leaving out of his mind.

As usual, the sun rose on another beautiful southern California day, the breeze light. Cesar rolled down his car window and shut off his engine to save gas.

It would probably take more than all of his fingers and toes to count the number of times he'd parked across the street from the used car lot. He didn't know what he'd expected to find, but he kept pulling in when he had ten, fifteen, or even thirty minutes to spare if he were in the area.

And he hadn't seen anything.

Well, that wasn't completely true. He'd noticed that in the time he'd been watching the lot, the change over in inventory was… minimal. It wasn't that it didn't change at all. It was just that it didn't seem to change fast enough to support Melvin and what appeared to be his two sales associates.

But—

"What are you doing?"

Cesar jumped in his seat. He'd been up in his head and hadn't noticed Melvin Davis walking up from behind him.

He had a grocery bag in one of his hands which he leaned on the sill of Cesar's car. Before Cesar arrived, he must have walked to the grocery store to get some drinks or a snack.

"Nothing." Cesar sounded exactly like someone who had definitely been doing *something*.

"Wanna try that again? You've been watching my place for several weeks now. I'd like to know why."

Fuck. He hadn't thought he'd been that obvious. Plus, he'd always remained in his car, his vehicle was pretty nondescript, and it wasn't like Cesar always parked in the same spot.

But he'd be lying to himself if he'd said he'd approached his mini stakeouts with the same kind of professionalism and attention to detail as he used with his clientele.

Maybe Freud could figure out why. Cesar couldn't. Especially while Melvin waited for an answer. "Get in. We can talk."

Cesar reached over and popped the passenger door in invitation. Melvin walked around and dropped down into the seat beside him.

Melvin dug inside the grocery bag, hauled out two Gatorades, and held one out to Cesar.

Cesar picked the red one leaving Melvin with the blue. "Thanks."

The fact that Melvin hadn't completely lost his temper over finding Cesar watching the lot went far in Cesar's dog-eared book.

Which made him feel more guilty for having kept what information he had from Saxon. Maybe if he told Saxon what he'd found, it would make Saxon's decision to contact his father easier.

Cesar gulped half his bottle before setting it in the cup holder between them. Part of that was because he was thirsty, but the vast majority of it was a stall tactic. Did he plan on playing it straight with Melvin and coming clean, or did he try to lie his way out of it?

Though the problem with lying was if Saxon ever resumed a relationship with his father, he'd be caught.

"Now, do you want to tell me what the hell is going on?" Melvin asked, his bottle open, even though he hadn't taken a sip.

Cesar stared out the windshield at the passing cars on the street in front of them. He had plans later to take Saxon with him to see Cierra, but he had plenty of time before he had to be at Stonewall House. "I'm trying to figure out if you're the man you appear to be."

Melvin raised his hands and held them out in a gesture that said, 'well?'

A bit of the blue Gatorade spilled onto his slacks, but they were blue and hid the stain, not that Melvin seemed to care. "What did you find?"

"It seems that you are." Cesar met Melvin's eyes, keeping his opinion open. "So far."

"And who wants to know that?"

It made sense that Melvin would make the leap that Cesar

worked for someone. He didn't seem nervous to find that out, as a person might if they had a secret to hide from the world. Another plus in the *Melvin Might Be Okay* column.

Maybe Melvin was exactly who he seemed to be.

Cesar had to take a leap of faith that what they said would stay between them, at least until Cesar had a chance to come clean with Saxon. "Your son."

Melvin sucked in a long breath between his teeth that made a whistling sound. "He hire you?"

"No."

Taking that in, Melvin nodded with the news. Cesar appreciated how the man rolled with the punch.

"What is he to you?"

That question Cesar hadn't seen coming. He hesitated, trying to decide between *he's a friend* and *someone who matters to me*. But it wasn't Cesar's place to out Saxon to his estranged father. If Saxon met with him, and *if* Saxon wanted to tell his father, he would.

Before Cesar could come up with a believable lie, Melvin said, "You're with him, aren't you?"

The slight emphasis Melvin placed on the word *with* told Cesar that Melvin had already guessed the truth.

"It's not my place to say."

Melvin laughed. Not cruel, just astute. "You don't have to. It's written all over your face."

On instinct, Cesar rubbed his cheek as if the truth were mustard that he could wipe off his skin. Cesar groaned to himself and took note. Looked like he wasn't as good at this PI thing as he thought… at least when it involved his personal life.

Or maybe when it came to Saxon, Cesar couldn't hide what the man meant to him.

Melvin narrowed his eyes. "Hell, son. You haven't even told him you're watching me, have you?"

Who was this guy? The next psychic sensation?

"I'm going to."

The laugh that rolled out of Melvin's chest sounded so much like Saxon when Cesar had done something foolish that it made Cesar chuckle along with him even as nerves rolled through him. He *really* needed to have that talk with Saxon.

"Don't wait so long that you fuck it up." Melvin took a sip of his drink and replaced the lid as if about to get out of the car.

"You're not going to tell him?"

"I haven't heard from him. I reached out. The ball is in his court." Melvin pushed the car door open with his foot and climbed out, closing the door behind him.

Cesar buzzed his window down. "Hey, Melvin." Cesar waited for the man to turn around before asking his question because he wanted to see Melvin's face when he answered.

Melvin leaned in the door. "Yeah?"

He had one more question he needed answered before things went any further. "About Saxon and me... Do—"

"If you're trying to ask if I have a problem that my son is gay or bi or just into dudes or whatever, the answer is no."

Cesar nodded, weirdly choked up about Melvin's answer, and it wasn't even his father. He cleared his throat. "Thanks."

"One more thing."

"Yeah?"

"You need to come clean with Saxon."

Without waiting for an answer, Melvin thumped the door with his open palm and turned toward the lot, braving a middle-of-the-street crossing instead of walking to a crosswalk.

Cesar rolled up the windows, started the car, and cranked up the air conditioning. If he were only the PI digging up information, why did sweat run down his backbone when it wasn't that hot out?

Maybe because you're not going to tell Saxon anything?

That wasn't true.

Cesar pulled into traffic. A car he didn't see coming swerved and honked its horn. He earned a long, drawn-out middle finger for it as well.

He'd tell Saxon everything. One day. Soon. But that was a problem for future Cesar. Because if Saxon never contacted his father, was it an issue?

"He's in the backyard," Saxon heard James say through the open window overlooking the backyard, where he had a close eye on Mango as the kitten leaped through the high weeds in the backyard's overgrown and long-neglected raised flower beds.

Kai wiped the sweat off his face with the T-shirt he'd taken off long ago and looked through the window. "Looks like your boyfriend is here." Kai's tone had a sing-song quality, and he made kissing noises.

Saxon laughed. "*Enough.*"

Kai smiled once more before returning to the push mower someone had donated. It was one of those people-powered mowers with curved blades. A job and a half for the grass that had morphed into more of a petrified forest from the neglect.

Saxon's throat tightened, not because the teasing hurt his feelings, but because shy Kai felt comfortable enough that he would tease him. And even though Kai had smiled more in the past few days than he had over the previous weeks combined, Saxon knew that he still had to watch for signs that Kai was having problems adjusting.

Stonewall House was a great place, but he'd be naive to think there might not be a time when Kai had trouble processing his trauma, and he wanted to be a person Kai felt comfortable coming to when that happened.

But right then, all seemed good.

"Wow." Cesar stepped into the backyard. "This place looks amazing." He turned his gaze to Kai. "Did you do this?"

A self-deprecating smile immediately followed Kai's shy shrug. "There's still a lot to do."

"Don't sell yourself short," Cesar said. "That's really hard work."

Cesar's eye caught on the flat of flowers and kitchen herbs that Saxon couldn't help buying when Kai's eyes had lit up at the lawn and garden store that morning. Sure he'd spent more than he'd needed on the yard, especially since he was trying to finish the upstairs, but witnessing the joy on Kai's face had been worth every cent a hundred times over.

"Where are you putting these?" Cesar asked about the new plants.

Kai pointed to the old, raised flower bed where Mango was trying to scale a scrubby weed that had grown nearly three feet tall. "Over there. It should be perfect if we can keep Mango out of it after I finish weeding."

"That's going to be beautiful."

Beaming, Kai said, "After tattoos, plants are kind of my thing." He stuck the earbuds Saxon had let bought him and started pushing the mower, slowly chewing his way through the overgrowth.

Saxon stepped over and greeted Cesar with a chaste kiss. He lowered his voice even though Kai couldn't hear him over the music streaming through the earbuds and the awful racket the push mover made as it crunched the weeds. "Thank you for that. You made his day."

"I only said it because it was true. Plus, I thought he needed to hear it from someone who wasn't you."

"I know that. But not everyone would have recognized that. So, thank you."

Cesar kissed him again but pulled away before he made Saxon moan and want to find a quiet corner in the house. Cesar hadn't come to turn him on. Cesar was taking him to see Cierra.

He put Mango in the house, gave him some kibble, and

followed Cesar to his car. He had some exciting news to tell Cesar, and Saxon couldn't wait to hear his thoughts.

They buckled their seat belts and pulled out of the driveway. "I texted my father today."

Cesar's foot slammed on the brake before letting off again. Luckily, with the light traffic, no cars were on their bumper. "You what?"

Though there was no way Cesar hadn't heard him correctly, Saxon repeated himself, "I texted my father back. I decided to meet up with him."

Cesar hesitated the slightest bit before he smiled. "That's terrific."

Uh, oh. "What's the matter?"

"Why would something be the matter?" Cesar had to have been trying his utmost to sound casual, but he hadn't managed to loosen his grip on the steering wheel or make the smile travel all the way to his eyes.

Saxon looked him up and down. Why was Cesar being weird about this? He thought he'd be more excited. "I don't know. You tell me."

Instead of answering the question, Cesar asked one of his own. "When did this happen?"

"Right before you came."

Had Cesar gone pale, or was that the effect of the light as they turned the corner onto the next street? And why wasn't Cesar looking at him? Like not even a glance like you normally do while talking and driving. Cesar stared out the windshield as if he were driving through a blizzard and couldn't see the road ahead of them. "What did he say?"

"He said he was glad to hear from me and wanted to meet me."

"Is that all?"

Why did this suddenly feel like an interrogation? "What is going on with you?"

Cesar stopped at a light behind a long line of cars. The sigh he expelled dropped a weight in Saxon's belly so heavy that it made him nauseous. What? Did Cesar know something that he didn't?

Finally, Cesar looked over at him, a mix of emotions rolling across his face so fast that Saxon couldn't begin to decipher them. "When we're done with Cierra… we need to talk."

"Now you're scaring me."

Cesar took Saxon's hand and kissed the back of it, letting it drop as he accelerated to follow the cars through the light.

Saxon folded his hands in his lap. Cesar reached across and squeezed his thigh, and the gesture did nothing to keep the bile from rising in the back of his throat.

"It's not like that," Cesar said, not sounding reassuring if that was how he'd intended the words to come across. "I just—We need to talk."

18

—————

THE MOOD IN THE CAR CHANGED FROM THE EXUBERANCE OF Saxon's cautious excitement to…well, Cesar didn't know quite how to describe it. It made Cesar second guess everything Saxon said since they got into the car. He nearly turned into a parking lot, but what he had to admit to Saxon he couldn't do quickly in a box store parking lot.

Saxon deserved Cesar's full attention.

If Cesar were honest, he wanted to wait to tell Saxon at home where he didn't fear Saxon would get out of the car and not stop walking until he made it back to Stonewall House and then send a car to Cesar's to get his things.

What the actual fuck had Cesar been thinking?

Derek had warned him—Melvin had warned him—and he had been too stubborn to listen. This had disaster written all over it.

From Saxon's demeanor, Melvin hadn't said anything about their interaction earlier that day. *That didn't mean it* wouldn't *come up or that any second now, Saxon's phone might ping with a text that said, 'Hey, your boyfriend has been stalking me.'*

No, Cesar had to get ahead of this before it completely blew up in his face.

They arrived at the Spicy Parrot, and he pulled into the back parking lot. He put his personal problem on the back burner and hoped like hell Saxon didn't get a revealing text from his father in the meantime.

He drove past the row of cars and saw Cierra's car.

"I think she's already inside."

Cesar pulled through to the customer parking lot and claimed a space. "Looks like we'll have to go in if we want to talk to her without waiting until closing."

"We could come back another time."

"I haven't checked on her in a week. I hate to put it off any longer. Kellon has been laying on the pressure. He still has a chance of getting Oliver's charges dropped if we can bring him other evidence, and I think she's our best option."

"Let's go then. I've never had a woman give me a lap dance before."

Cesar laughed as they got out of the car and beeped the alarm behind them. "And how many men have given you a lap dance?"

Saxon's sly grin gave Cesar a chubby at the worst possible moment, but he fucking loved that all it took was one suggestive side-eye from Saxon to turn him on.

"Stop that," Cesar muttered under his breath as he opened the door for Saxon, "or I'm going to haul you into the bathroom when we get inside and have my wicked way with you."

"Wouldn't be the first time."

Cesar barked out a laugh. By Saxon's saucy look, it might have been more of a challenge than a response. He stepped behind Saxon to adjust himself.

They paid their entry fee and found a table near the back, the room dark enough that they could ignore the patrons at the other tables around them. For it being not much later than the dinner crowd, the Parrot was rocking.

They each ordered a beer and glanced around, searching for Cierra. The music ended, and the woman on stage collected her money and disappeared behind the curtain. The music changed, and another woman came on.

"Over there," Saxon nodded toward the door to the back room. Cierra strode out in a thong and a bikini top that barely covered her nipples.

She worked her way around the floor, not realizing they were there until she walked near their table. She probably hadn't recognized them in the dark with the oversized pair of sunglasses she wore. You know, the kind of sunglasses the famous actresses wore when they didn't want to be recognized, only Cierra wasn't famous and not a paparazzi photographer was in sight.

Cierra stepped back when she saw them. Crossing her arms over her chest, she said, "Go away."

She turned to leave, and Cesar took her wrist. She stopped and stared at the spot where he had his hand on her. Saxon tapped Cesar's foot under the table, and Cesar glanced up to see one of the bouncers striding their way.

Dropping her wrist, Cesar held his hands up in surrender, but the bouncer didn't stop until Cierra waved him off.

She rounded on them. "You've got five seconds. I don't want anyone seeing me talking to you."

From his wallet, Cesar pulled out two hundred-dollar bills and handed them to her. When she didn't immediately take them, he dropped them on the table. She adjusted her sunglasses and took the crisp bills. "Follow me."

Cesar stood and started after her. She turned to Saxon, still in his seat. "You, too."

He scrambled to follow, not catching up until they squeezed past the crowd of people surrounding the bar.

They passed the bouncer that had been coming to Cierra's rescue, and he stared them down the entire way.

"You alright?" the bouncer asked Cierra as she walked by.

"I'm fine."

He didn't argue with her, but his mouth flattened, and his bunched fists looked like they could single-handedly demolish a concrete building. If Cesar had been more easily intimidated, he might have changed his mind and turned back.

Cierra escorted them into the back hall. Private rooms branched off on either side, the entrances covered with heavy curtains. A couple of rooms had the curtains drawn, and they walked past them to an empty one.

The door behind them opened and closed, and he glanced back to see the bouncer standing at the door, clocking which space Cierra led them.

No doubt, if Cierra made a single questionable sound, the man would be in the room faster than Cesar could say, *Don't kill me.* But he and Saxon weren't there to harm her, just to see if she had anything more to tell them.

And now… to see what was up with those sunglasses.

Instead of sitting in the chair, Cesar held it out for her. She sat and blew out a breath. She dropped one of her high heels off her foot and started rubbing her instep.

"Why do you keep bugging me? I'm not saying anything against Braden."

Saxon bobbed his chin toward her face. "What's with the sunglasses?"

"Guys like a mysterious girl."

Cesar chuckled. "Want to try that again?"

Saxon squatted, getting eye-level with her so he didn't appear intimidating. Not that Saxon was that scary, but she relaxed a little, so it must have helped. "Sweetheart, give me the glasses."

When Saxon said *sweetheart*, it didn't come out sounding like a straight man who only wanted to get into her pants. He sounded like her gay best friend at an intervention that only wanted what was best for her.

He held out his hand as if he expected her to hand over the

sunglasses. To Cesar's surprise, she took them off. She didn't hand them to him. Then again, she didn't have to.

"What the hell happened to your eye?" That may have come out harsher and louder than Cesar had meant because Saxon spun around and mouthed *What the fuck?* before glancing past him to the curtain as if he expected the bouncer to come boiling through, looking to make mincemeat out of them.

"Sorry." Cesar put his hand on Saxon's shoulder and let him continue without any more of his outbursts. But damn. He hadn't seen that big of a shiner on anyone that hadn't come out of a boxing ring.

"Tell me what happened." When Saxon spoke, his voice had that soothing, soft tone. It made you want to tell him all your secrets and let him make them all better. Cesar didn't question it. He just stood there in awe as she responded to Saxon's kindness.

She glanced at Cesar, but Saxon drew her attention, and she said, "I think you know what happened."

Saxon stiffened. Cierra didn't notice as she wiped away the tears that welled up and spilled over her cheeks. As difficult as it was, Cesar kept his mouth shut. There were so many things he wanted to ask all at once, and even though he was usually good at keeping calm and his temper in check, knowing what Braden had done to her and that he'd likely get away with it made him see red and every other color in the visible spectrum.

"Have you contacted the police?"

Cierra met Saxon's valid question with a wobbly, watery laugh. "I think you know the answer to that one, too."

"Are you going to leave him?" Cesar had better control of himself now. Enough that it didn't sound as if his anger was directed at her and not the asshole who deserved it.

She pointed to her eye. "That's how I got this. He didn't want me. He's cheated on me more times than I can count, but his ego couldn't take it when someone dumped him. His ex warned me. I should have listened."

"He's done this before?" Cesar asked. "Gotten violent when someone breaks up with him?"

Saxon stood and took Cesar's hand, allowing him to ask the questions now that she was talking.

"I thought his ex was jealous and wanted to scare me away so she could have him back. I was *so* wrong."

"He's a manipulative, charming, dreadful bully," Saxon said.

"Correction," Cierra said, "he's a *single*, manipulative, charming, dreadful bully."

Saxon laughed, and she bumped his fist when he held it out to her. "But seriously, are you okay?"

The tears came again. She managed to sniff them back and wipe them away before they fell. "Totally worth the black eye if it means he's out of my life for good."

"You should file a report." Cesar wanted the asshole to face some kind of accountability, even if it wouldn't be for Oliver.

"Right now, he's out of my life. He's moved on to the next shiny thing that caught his eye. I want to move on and forget I ever met him."

She looked tired. More than that, she looked exhausted. Cesar didn't have the heart to hammer her with other questions. Not tonight.

"I'm sorry this happened to you, but I'm glad you're away from him." He took a step back, ignoring Saxon's double-take. Clearly, he hadn't expected him to pull back from the questioning. But Cierra needed space right now, which was more important than any damning information on Braden he might get out of her. "We'll let you get back to work."

Squeezing Saxon's hand, they turned to leave. He had the curtain parted when she said, "Turn on your AirDrop."

He turned around. "It's on."

"Wait here."

She hid her black eye behind her sunglasses before leaving them in the room. Through the gap in the curtain, he watched her disappear through the door marked *Employees Only*. The bouncer hadn't left his post. Cesar gave him a nod. He liked knowing that those guys took their jobs seriously.

Not long after, his phone chimed, and he checked his AirDrop and found a video waiting for him. A blurry neon number 21 on the screen told him exactly what it was.

The fight video.

Saxon sucked in an audible breath. "Holy shit."

In this day and age, when everyone had video equipment in their pockets, he'd known there had to be other footage of the fight out there.

He couldn't wait to watch it, though the back room at the Spicy Parrot wasn't the place.

"Let's go," he said to Saxon, whose jaw still lay on the floor.

Cesar yanked the curtain open and headed toward the bouncer. He didn't expect to see Cierra again that night, or she would have returned to the room with her phone and sent him the video from there. The bouncer moved aside and held open the door for them, clearly eager to get them away from her.

The *Employees Only* door on their left opened before they stepped through it, and Cierra held out the two hundred-dollar bills. "Take it."

"That's yours," Cesar said.

She put it in Saxon's hand because Cesar refused it. "I don't want your money. Not for this."

Cesar gave her a nod as the bouncer said, "Time to go, gentlemen."

The man dogged their heels until they exited into the parking lot and stood in the open doorway until they reached their car and drove away.

"This could be Oliver's ticket," Saxon said. "The kid could use a break."

"Hopefully, it's what we think it is, and Kellon can use it to get the charges dropped. I'm afraid to get my hopes up. Braden is more slippery than a snail in a bowl of slime."

———

As much as Saxon wanted to watch the video, he wanted Cesar to watch it with him, so he waited until Cesar parked in the lot of a grocery store, both too eager to wait until they got home.

Home.

Funny how in the short time since Saxon had moved in with Cesar, his humble home had become more of a home to Saxon than the months he'd lived at Stonewall House.

As soon as Cesar shifted into park, he unlocked his phone, set it on the holder on the dash, and played the video. Saxon grabbed Cesar's hand, his grip getting tighter and tighter as the video played.

"Ouch." Cesar tapped Saxon's hand to get some relief.

"Sorry." Saxon loosened his hold, never taking his eyes off the screen until it ended.

"Well," Cesar said, "It's pretty much what Phoenix and Sophia claimed from the start."

"It wasn't that I didn't believe them but seeing the video… it just shows how unhinged Braden gets when things don't go his way. I mean, I knew it was true. But knowing it and seeing it is eye-opening."

Cesar immediately sent the video to Kellon. "Fingers crossed, this will do exactly what we hope it will."

Leaning back in his seat, Saxon blew out a breath. "I'm wrung out. I can't even imagine how stressful it is for Oliver, though he's managed to hide it fairly well. I can't wait to tell him we have the video."

"I don't think we should do that yet." Cesar shifted into reverse and drove around the lot until he could find an exit and pull into traffic. Rush hour had ended, and the sun had set on another picture-perfect southern California day.

Made even more perfect after uncovering a two-and-a-half-minute video that could change the course of two young men's lives.

Cesar should have looked as relieved as Saxon felt, but something else was up with him that they'd have to deal with later.

"Why can't we tell them?"

"I hate to burst your happy bubble, but we need to protect Cierra as the source of the video for as long as possible. Everyone at the house knows we went to talk to her tonight. If word unintentionally gets out that Cierra has that video before Kellon can convince her to talk to the authorities, there's no telling what Braden will do."

Cesar was right. Even if Saxon hated that Braden had the power to intimidate Cierra, or worse.

"Of all the people Oliver could have gotten into a fight with, he had to do it with one of the few guys in town who's untouchable."

"No one is untouchable. Even the mayor's son."

Saxon wouldn't believe it until he saw it. "Yeah, well, I sure would like the world to prove me wrong."

Cesar patted Saxon's thigh. They swooped into Stonewall House to pick up Mango for the night. Cesar stayed in the car and kept it running.

At home, Saxon offered to make them dinner, but Cesar looked like he could throw up any minute and declined. Saxon fixed himself soup and a sandwich.

Cesar sat at the table across from him, which was odd. Cesar didn't say anything, so Saxon propped his phone against the napkin holder and started reading a book on his phone.

"*Fuck*," Cesar muttered, then sighed.

What the hell was up with him? Saxon glanced up from his book.

"Saxon, we need to talk."

His attention had already returned to his book. Saxon slurped a spoonful of the chicken noodle soup. He was in the middle of a good part. "Uh, huh."

"It's important."

Saxon swiped his finger across the screen and changed the page, nearly at the end of the chapter.

Cesar took the phone out of his hand and set it face down on the table.

"What the hell? I was reading that."

"About that talk…"

Saxon sat back and wiped his mouth with his napkin. "Who died?"

"Wait. What? No one died."

"Then why do you look like you're heading to your own wake?"

Now that Cesar had Saxon's full attention, Saxon noted the stress lines on Cesar's brow and the flatness of his lips. If someone hadn't died, then it had to be nearly as bad.

"I don't—I just—" Cesar stumbled over his words, expelling his frustration on a hot breath. "It's about you."

Mango scaled Saxon's leg as if sensing the tension—or was he after the cheese spilling out of his sandwich? Saxon boosted the kitten onto his shoulder before Mango could put tiny holes in his shirt.

Saxon couldn't remember a time that he'd given Cesar a reason to believe that he couldn't talk to him about anything. And that *It's about you* statement had Saxon starting to sweat.

Had he done something wrong?

Had Cesar decided he no longer wanted Saxon at his house?

Had he changed his mind about everything?

Knock it the fuck off. Don't let your insecurities derail you before he says anything.

But it couldn't be anything good, right? Cautiously, Saxon said, "Spit it out. I won't bite."

Cesar huffed out a laugh, but he didn't seem the least bit amused. Or relieved. "Don't make promises you can't keep."

"*Cesar.*"

"It's about your father."

That was the last thing Saxon expected Cesar to say.

Saxon crossed his arms, already not liking where this was going, not when Cesar said it with such a serious tone. Was Cesar going to tell him not to meet with his father?

Saxon decided to beat Cesar to the point. "You're my boyfriend, but you haven't yet earned the right to tell me who I should or shouldn't let back into my life."

If Saxon sounded defensive, it was because he was. And it wasn't until then that Saxon realized how much he *wanted* to meet with his father. He had so many unanswered questions. He didn't think he could ignore the chance to get answers to some of them.

Cesar raised his hands. "I'm not trying to tell you what to do. If you want to meet with him, that's entirely up to you. It sounds like you do."

Uncrossing his arms, Saxon softened his voice and admitted, "Yeah, I do."

"Yeah. Okay. Great." Cesar swiped a hand across his forehead, and he wiped away the dampness.

"Why are you sweating? Are you sick?" Saxon came around the table and squatted beside Cesar's chair, placing a hand on his forehead like parents do when their kid isn't feeling well. "Why are you clammy?"

Saxon narrowed his eyes and scrutinized Cesar. "Your color is off, too. Do I need to take you to Urgent Care?"

Cesar took hold of Saxon's wrist and removed Saxon's hand from his forehead. "I'm not sick."

Oh, no. If Cesar wasn't sick... Saxon's mind jumped to the worst-case scenario, and he plopped his ass on the floor, his voice a fraction of what it should be. But he didn't have the air in his lungs to speak any louder. "Are you breaking up with me?"

"What? No. Baby, that's not..." Cesar pushed his chair back and sat on the floor with Saxon. He took Saxon's hands and spread his legs so that Saxon sat between them. "I said it was about your father."

"Right. Sorry," Saxon finally managed, the heat rushing up his face. "My therapist did say I might have abandonment issues."

"Might?"

Saxon laughed. "Fair point." He scrubbed his hands over his face and pulled himself together. "Okay. I'm sorry. What was it you wanted to say about my father?"

"After your father texted you that first time, I went to the office on my way home, and I might have done a background check on him."

Saxon stilled and pulled his hands away from Cesar's. "I didn't ask you to do that."

"I understand that."

"Then why did you do it?"

"I wanted this for you, but I also wanted to protect you."

"To protect you. In case he was as bad as your mother said."

Saxon scooted back. It wasn't a conscious move, and he hadn't realized he'd done it until he had. That cautious optimism he'd felt about meeting his father soured in his gut. He found himself looking through the fingers of the hand he put over his face. "What did you find?"

Cesar shrugged. "Nothing. A few parking tickets. No criminal record."

Saxon dropped his hand, taking a full breath for the first time in minutes. He nodded, more to himself than Cesar, when a realization hit. A realization that made his heart rate jump and him question the trust he'd blindly given Cesar. Would Saxon ever fucking learn that not everyone could be trusted? "You weren't going to tell me, were you?"

"I was… eventually."

Eventually? Why now, then?

Saxon scrambled to his feet and hugged his arms around himself, needing the space and comfort. "What changed? Why did you decide to tell me now?"

Cesar stood, his arms out to his sides as if he didn't want to startle Saxon with a sudden move. Saxon wasn't a fucking deer. He wasn't going to bolt.

At least he didn't think he was.

"I might have gone further than executing a routine background check."

"*Might?* How far?"

"Your father owns a used car dealership. I went in, pretending to be a customer."

Saxon spun away as the words struck. He paced to the front door and back again, but considering the size of Cesar's house, it wasn't far enough to relieve any of the tension. "You *met* him? You met him and didn't tell me? When?"

19

———

That one question had the potential to blow up the entire conversation as if it weren't already a tinder box of volatile emotions ready to explode.

If Derek were here right now, he'd be saying he told you so. Because he did. Multiple times.

Yeah, and now Cesar's unwise, stubborn ass had to find a way out without triggering any emotional land mines. "It's been a few weeks."

"A few weeks?" Saxon repeated everything as if he couldn't trust his ears. "And you didn't think I should know this? Or maybe ask if I minded if you went behind my back and—"

"I didn't go behind your back."

Saxon's raised brow told Cesar how silly he sounded. Had Cesar ever seen Saxon that pissed? Nope. "Not on purpose anyway. I was trying—"

"To protect me. Yeah. You already said that. But here's the thing. I'm a grown man. I'm not a child. I don't need your protection. I need your honesty."

Saxon's words hit like an ax, cleaving Cesar open and spilling his blood. He'd done the background check with the best intentions, but he'd had no right to do that. Not without Saxon's blessing.

Saxon tilted his head and must have seen something in Cesar's expression because he said, "Fuck. There's more, isn't there?"

If Cesar had been more scared in his life, he couldn't remember when, including when one of the people he'd been hired to follow had pulled a knife on him in a dark alley.

"Hear me out." Cesar stepped closer, but Saxon retreated the same number of steps until he stood in the middle of the den. Mango crawled up his cat tree and eyed them from a safe, wary distance. "After I went to the car lot, I had no plans to approach him again, but on days when I was near and had spare time, I'd park across the street from his car lot and watch the building to make sure there wasn't anything obvious going on that didn't show up on a background check."

Saxon looked like he had questions, but he held his tongue and let Cesar continue. "Today was one of those days."

Cesar told him about Melvin recognizing him. About the conversation they had. He couldn't tell if he'd dug the hole deeper and Saxon was about to take the shovel and bury him or if he'd say *fuck it* and walk out the door and leave him to figure out how to get himself out.

"Let me get this straight. You *stalked* my father. You *met* him. And when he made you, you *outed* me to him."

"Not exact—"

But yeah, it *was* exactly like that, minus a few inconsequential details.

"You don't think that maybe I might want to tell him myself?" Saxon's voice rose the more he talked. "Or maybe not want to tell him at all?"

As much as Cesar hated that Saxon had stepped away, the way Saxon stalked toward him made *him* take the step back.

If Saxon decked him, he'd earned it.

Saxon got in his face. "You had no right to do that."

"You're absolutely right." Cesar chanced taking Saxon's hand, and to his surprise, Saxon didn't pull away. "I fucked up, royally."

"Yeah, like having-to-leave-the-country-you-once-ruled royally, not like wearing the wrong color hat to a tea party royally."

Cesar laughed, amazed that Saxon managed a joke at a time like that because, by all indications, he was still pissed.

"It won't happen again."

The vow was the most solemn words Cesar had ever spoken. Saxon must have heard the truth in them because he closed his eyes and blew out a breath. When he opened them, some of the anger had died out.

"I trusted you."

And Cesar had broken that trust.

Saxon had been clear from that first day when they'd groped each other in the unfinished space on the third floor that, for Saxon, honesty was paramount.

And Cesar hadn't been honest.

Whatever reasons he'd told himself that justified his actions, they weren't valid.

Cesar's knees went weak, and he sat on the arm of the sofa so Saxon wouldn't see his legs shake. "If—" Christ, his throat had gone so tight the word squeaked out. "If you want to break up…"

Cesar let the rest of the sentence drop because he didn't know how to finish that sentence. He wanted to give Saxon a way out, and the only person he'd have to blame if Saxon did want that out was himself.

Saxon stood quiet for so long that he figured Saxon was considering his words thoroughly. Saxon walked over to the cat tree and scooped up Mango, gently bumping Mango's forehead with his own.

When he turned back to Cesar, he said, "I don't want to break up. But I'm going to need a little space."

The relief that washed through him felt like that first gentle gust of wind before a much-needed cleansing rain. "Anything."

He watched as Saxon disappeared down the hall, returned with a pillow and a blanket, and put them on the couch. "What are you doing?"

The anger had drained from Saxon's face, but none of his stubbornness had. "What does it look like I'm doing?"

"We have a guest room. You don't need to sleep on the sofa."

Saxon tossed the blanket and then the pillow onto the cushions. Mango looked down his cute little pink nose at Cesar from his perch on Saxon's shoulder. "Who said these were for me? And I know we have a guest room, but I think this gets my point across better."

Cesar only nodded. There was nothing to say to that.

"Good night," Saxon said. He turned on his heel, slapped the den and hall lights off as he headed for the bedroom, and closed the door behind him.

"Motherfucker," Cesar muttered as he fell back onto the sofa, relieved beyond belief that Saxon hadn't taken the cat and walked out the front door. "You're one lucky son of a bitch, Morales."

The light in the kitchen remained on, and Cesar was too emotionally exhausted to give two fucks. He yanked the pillow out from behind his back, held it tight against his body, and stared up at the ceiling, the fight swirling around in his head on a vicious repeat.

If sleep came, it would be a damn miracle.

Saxon followed a hungry Mango into the kitchen the next morning and drew up short at Cesar sitting at the table in nothing but his shirt and a pair of boxer briefs, a half-empty cup of coffee in front of him.

His hair sat at odd angles to his head, he had dark bags under his eyes, and from the pillow and blanket still on the couch, it looked like Cesar had indeed spent the night out there.

Saxon should have felt bad about kicking the man out of his bed, but he didn't.

He dumped kibble into Mango's food bowl, poured himself a cup of coffee, and sat across from Cesar. "You look like shit." It was more of an observation than an insult.

"That's a few steps up from how I feel."

Saxon grunted. He knew he'd eventually forgive Cesar. But he wasn't above letting him stew a bit.

"I really am sorry," Cesar said.

Not only did he look sorry… he looked miserable. Saxon thought it had less to do with the uncomfortable couch and more with coming to terms with what he'd done. Good intentioned or not.

"I need support, Cesar. Not protection."

"I get that now."

Did he? "I need to know I can trust you. Something like this can't happen again."

Cesar swallowed hard. "I get that, too."

Saxon nodded once. He didn't want to talk about it anymore, and if Cesar took one look in the mirror, he'd see how hard it would be for anyone to stay mad at him when he looked so torn up over what he'd done.

Putting his coffee down, Saxon stood and held out his hand to him. Cesar scrambled to his feet, nearly knocking over his mug to get to him.

Saxon wrapped him in a hug, or was it the other way around?

They held each other tight, rocking back and forth in the compact kitchen.

Cesar buried his face in the crook of Saxon's shoulder, and just when he thought Cesar would break the embrace, he held on tighter. "I fucking love you."

Saxon stilled, and Cesar pulled back, placing his hands on either side of Saxon's face. "Maybe it's too soon to say that, but… you wanted honesty."

Cesar's shy smile almost undid Saxon. He didn't know if he felt the same. All he knew was that ever since he'd moved in and they'd been playing at the domestication thing, it felt right. It had felt like he belonged there from the minute he put his boxers in the drawer, set his toothbrush in the holder suctioned to the mirror, and slid the purple people eater into the bedside table.

He wanted to say those same words to Cesar, but he held back. Instead, he said, with a smile he had trouble schooling, "I appreciate the honesty."

If he'd disappointed Cesar by not telling him that he loved him too, Cesar did a good job of hiding it. Cesar pressed closer, his hands going to Saxon's ass and squeezing. "I missed you last night."

And if Saxon demanded honesty from Cesar, he owed the same in return. "I missed you, too. Mango didn't. He stole your spot and didn't feel one bit bad about it."

"The little brat."

Mango meowed on cue at their feet. Cesar picked him up before the kitten could scale his bare legs. Then he must have noticed what Saxon was wearing. "Why are you so dressed up this morning? I thought we were working on the renovation today."

Saxon hesitated but didn't know quite why. "I'm supposed to meet Melvin for coffee this morning." He glanced at his watch. He'd have to leave soon if he didn't want to be late.

Cesar's brows rose. "So soon?"

"He has a hard out this morning at nine. We figured that would keep the first meeting from getting too awkward if one of us wanted an excuse to end it."

"Like meeting a HotDix hookup in public to decide if you vibe first."

Saxon laughed. "Not quite, but a little."

Mango struggled in Cesar's arms, and he set the kitten down. Mango scampered out of the kitchen, sliding as he took the corner too fast, and bonked into the wall.

"That's better," Cesar said as he used Saxon's belt loops for leverage, pulled Saxon against him, and went in for a kiss.

It started gentle, Cesar's hand going to the back of Saxon's skull as he deepened the kiss. Cesar tasted of coffee, creamer, and remorse. Saxon wrapped his arms around Cesar's waist, Cesar's hard cock rubbing against his own.

Saxon's hands went into the waistband of Cesar's boxers, a finger skimming along Cesar's crack. Cesar grunted, breaking the kiss and resting his forehead on Saxon's shoulder as he pressed back against Saxon's finger.

"Fuck," Cesar said, his eyes blazing when he looked up at Saxon. He backed Saxon into the table and aligned their hard cocks. "I want you in me. Right now."

Saxon's finger found Cesar's hole. It twitched beneath his touch. It wouldn't take much to strip Cesar naked and—

"Do we have time for makeup sex?" Cesar asked.

Saxon groaned. For a moment, he'd completely forgotten about meeting his father. He glanced at his watch again. "I really do have to go. You'll have to take a rain check."

Cesar stepped away, which was a good thing because if Cesar had pushed it, Saxon didn't think he would have walked away. "Tonight then."

"That's a promise." Saxon reached down and adjusted himself. "Meet you at Stonewall after coffee?"

"Sounds good."

Cesar followed Saxon to the front door, and before he could leave, Cesar said, "Good luck with the meeting. I hope it's everything you've wanted."

Hearing the sincerity in Cesar's voice hit Saxon right in the heart. Saxon pecked his cheek when he wanted to kiss him until nightfall. "Thanks."

20

———

THE BUTTERFLIES IN SAXON'S BELLY GREW TO THE SIZE OF Hercules moths and then into pterodactyls the closer he got to Biscuits and Beans—the same coffee shop he'd met Cesar that first time.

As he pulled into a parking spot, he didn't even think he'd be able to take a sip of coffee without it coming right back up.

"Here goes nothing," Saxon said, trying to psych himself up as he got out and closed his car door. The sun had barely peaked above the San Gabriels, and a cool breeze swirled leaves and bits of trash in a mini tornado against the curb.

He'd worn chinos and a blue plaid button-up with the sleeves rolled up his forearms. He'd considered a tie, but that seemed like overcompensation, and he'd nixed that right away. And as much as he tried to tell himself he didn't have to impress Melvin, it was hard to keep that thought in mind.

As soon as he stepped through Beans' door, he spotted his father. He hadn't seen a recent photo of him, but he would have recognized him even after all those years.

Melvin glanced up when the bell on the door chimed, and the

instant smile on his face grounded the pterodactyls. Melvin stood as Saxon approached, and instead of taking Saxon's outstretched hand, he pulled him in for a hug.

Saxon hugged him with a series of awkward back pats. When they parted, they both swiped a hand under their eyes. It was the greeting Saxon had always hoped for but never expected.

"Um… hi," Saxon said.

Could you be more awkward?

"Look at you." His father clapped him on the shoulder. "All grown up."

Yeah, that's what happens when you disappear for twenty-some-odd years.

Saxon caught himself before his negative thoughts and suppressed anger spiraled. His father deciding to reach out had been a good thing. At least he thought it was. And he had to give the man a chance to tell his side of the story before passing judgment.

They sat, and a waitress came over to take their order. His father had Saxon's eyes. Actually, it was the other way around. They had similar builds, though his father was thicker through the shoulders and middle.

When the waitress left, Melvin said, "You didn't want to order anything to eat? It's on me."

"Coffee is fine." Saxon didn't even know if he could choke that down, much less anything more solid. Especially when what he had to say, or rather ask, could end this little reunion before it started.

"Cesar said you know about me. About *us?*"

The smile slipped from his father's face, and the pterodactyls took flight. "He told me."

Saxon's brows drew together, trying to decide what he wanted to say next, but his father reached out and laid a hand on his forearm. He leaned in and said, "It doesn't matter to me if you're gay if that's what you're asking. You're my son. That's all that matters."

Melvin patted his arm, and Saxon had to grab one of the napkins off the table because the tears welled and spilled too fast to blink away.

And why the hell did he care what a man he didn't even know thought about him?

Because even though he left, he's still your father.

Melvin put an arm around him and squeezed his shoulder before releasing him. The coffees arrived, and Saxon warmed his hands on the mug as he got his emotions under control. He had a feeling they might need more napkins on the table before their conversation ended.

"I was mad," Saxon said, "when Cesar told me he'd checked into you. That he'd told you about us."

Melvin blew on his coffee and took a slow sip as if giving himself time to figure out how to respond. He put his mug down, clasped Saxon's fingers on the table, and released them. "I can see where that was wrong, but..."

He rubbed a hand over his jaw as if unsure how Saxon would take what else he had to say.

"Just say it."

"But I can also see where he was trying to look out for you. I kind of admire that about him."

"What?"

"Well, not the secrecy part, but putting in the effort to make sure you were safe. That man, he cares about you a whole lot."

"He said he loved me." Why was Saxon spilling his guts to a man he didn't know?

"I'm not surprised." His father took another sip, and Saxon could only stir his with the spoon. Saxon didn't think he could get the cup to his mouth without his shaking hand spilling the hot liquid down the front of him. "And while you have the absolute right to feel the way you feel about what he did, maybe don't be too hard on him."

"Wait. You're taking his side?"

"I'm not taking anyone's side. I'm saying that someone can do something with the best intentions and still have it be wrong."

Saxon narrowed his eyes and really looked at Melvin. Something in his father's eyes told Saxon that he might have had some experience in that area. "I'll take that under advisement."

Melvin chuckled and clapped him on the shoulder. "That's my boy."

And while Saxon wanted to bristle and the term *my boy*, especially when Melvin hadn't been in his life to earn that right, Saxon weirdly clung to it. His stomach settled out, and Saxon took his first sip of coffee. It wasn't hot, but it wasn't cold yet either.

"I suppose you have a lot of questions for me. I'm an open book. Ask me anything."

"How long have you known where I was?"

"A year or so, maybe." Melvin pulled the wrapper off the chocolate chip muffin he'd ordered and tore off a piece.

Saxon had a ton more questions but held them in to allow Melvin to finish. He snuck a glance at his watch. They couldn't cover all the ground they needed to in one short meet over coffee.

After Melvin swallowed, he continued. "I moved back to town around then. I wasn't sure if you were using my last name or your mother's. I read the paper one morning and saw your picture in that article about you fighting city hall to get your zoning for that house thing you wanted. I thought that was you, but I had to be sure, so I went to one of the council meetings."

Saxon nearly choked on the coffee he was in the middle of swallowing. He coughed and wiped his mouth. "You went to one of the meetings?"

Melvin nodded. "Knew it was you as soon as I saw you. You have your mother's smile… and determination."

Saxon didn't say anything because his father had struck him speechless. To hear that his father had taken the time to go to the meeting took his breath away. And then to hear him mention his mother. He couldn't remember the last time anyone had said anything about her to him. His aunt and uncle, who'd briefly taken him in after she'd died, hadn't wanted him and blamed her for what happened. They definitely didn't have anything complimentary to say.

"The state looked for you when she died."

Melvin ducked his head, and Saxon might have seen a flicker of regret when he looked up at him. Then again, he didn't know this man well enough to read his emotions.

"I didn't know she died until I moved back and ran into an old high school friend of hers at the grocery store."

"Would you have come back if you'd known?" That was a question Saxon needed an answer to. A question that had haunted him all those years in the foster system and even after he'd aged out. If his father had known, would he have cared enough to come back?

"In a heartbeat."

It might have been words that Melvin thought Saxon wanted to hear. Easy to lie when you know the words wouldn't change the past. However, the way Melvin reached for a napkin to dab at his eyes made Saxon believe he meant every word.

"Why now? Why not contact me when you found out I was in town? Why not stop me that night at the city council meeting?"

Melvin turned his head away and stared out the front window. There were plenty of open seats in the coffee shop. Most of the people who came in bought their coffees to go.

When he turned back, a flush had infused his cheeks with red. "I haven't had the easiest life, son. That's on me. When I first found you, I barely had a pot to piss in. I had nothing to offer you."

"I don't want your money."

"I didn't think you would. But I didn't want to come to you as a failure. I wanted to come to you as someone who could make you proud."

All Saxon wanted was family. People who loved him without condition. Isn't that what *everyone* wanted? "That wasn't necessary."

Melvin held Saxon's gaze as he thought about his son's words. It should have been uncomfortable, but it wasn't. His father's eyes softened as if he'd come to some sort of realization. "Maybe for you it wasn't, but for me... I needed that."

Saxon nodded. It wasn't up to him to decide what his father needed to feel worthy. "I'm glad you found what you needed."

"Thanks. I feel like I'm finally on the right track." Saxon watched as Melvin's eye lit, and the shine brightened the more he talked. "Business was slow at first, I expected that, but sales are starting to go up each month. I was able to hire two sales staff. It's not some big fancy dealership catering to the rich and famous, but that's okay. I sell quality used cars at a good price that people can afford. I think that's something to be proud of."

"That's great." And it was. Maybe that meant that Melvin would stick around long enough for them to develop some kind of relationship.

"But we're not here to talk about my car lot."

"It's fine. We're just here to talk. To get to know each other."

"You have to have more questions." Melvin glanced at his watch, which made Saxon check his. They probably had about five more minutes before Melvin had to leave for his meeting. "Want to ask any more before I have to go?"

As well as the first meeting had gone, Saxon had the feeling they would be seeing each other again and have more time for questions, but with as many questions as he had, he didn't want every time they saw each other for it to be an informal interrogation. That wouldn't be good for either of them.

However, he had a question he'd been asking himself since his father left. "You disappeared. Why didn't you ever call? Or write?"

Melvin's face went slack. "You didn't get my letters?"

"What letters."

"I called. For weeks. Months even, and your mother wouldn't let me talk to you."

The news hit Saxon in the gut, and he had to push the coffee away because the smell made his stomach queasy. "You called?"

Melvin nodded, the slack expression turning more into total frustration. "She told me that I could write you. That if I stopped calling, she'd make sure you got the letters. I agreed. I thought that would be better than nothing."

"I never got a letter."

"I should have realized that. But I had this voice inside my head that kept telling me that it was reasonable that a kid wouldn't want any contact with a loser like me. Back then, I went from job to job, unable to keep anything steady. After a year or two without a response, I quit writing. Hell, at that point, I wasn't even in the state. For all I knew, your mother had moved, and the letters weren't getting delivered."

"We were there. In that house. You could have come back."

Melvin's head dropped between his shoulders. He shook it and blew out a shaky breath. "By that time, I was two states away panhandling on street corners in Albuquerque. I couldn't have come back if I'd wanted to."

That explained a lot. Saxon wanted to blame his mother, but he had no idea what she'd been dealing with at the time. Maybe she'd thought it would be best for him to keep Melvin out of his life, or maybe she'd been so bitter after he'd left that she wanted to do the only thing she could think of to hurt Melvin, and that was keeping him away from his son.

But his mother was dead. It wasn't like Saxon could ask her what the hell she'd been thinking.

"I'm sorry, son." Melvin's hand went to Saxon's shoulder again and squeezed. "I should have tried harder."

At that moment, Saxon had a bit of clarity, or maybe it was maturity talking, but he realized that Melvin had done the best he could, and Saxon couldn't fault him for that.

Saxon leaned back in his chair, his throat tight. He didn't care if Melvin knew that his emotions were raw. He'd have to not have any for them not to be. "You'd better get going, or you're going to be late," he managed.

Melvin stood, and Saxon stood along with him. Melvin went for his wallet, but Saxon waved him off. "You go. I'll get this."

"Thank you." Melvin smiled and nodded at the table. Though Saxon knew the gesture was about more than just picking up the tab.

"And thank you for your candor."

Melvin had one of those sappy, sad smiles. "You deserved answers. Can we do this again?"

"Yeah," Saxon said. "Soon."

Melvin went in for a parting hug. "I'd really like that."

CESAR STOOD ON THE RENTED SCAFFOLD, SWEATING HIS EVER-loving ass off on the third floor of Stonewall House, applying mud to the drywall joints in the ceiling. His shoulders screamed at him. He couldn't remember the last time—if ever—that he worked so long at something over his head.

Chances were, he wouldn't be able to lift his arms above his waist come morning. It was worth it, though. The space was coming along, and before Saxon knew it, he could take in more people aging out.

Stonewall House wouldn't save the world.

But it would help a few of the people in it.

And that Cesar could be a small part of that—even if he lost every single electrolyte in his body through his pores—made his efforts worthwhile.

Especially when Saxon walked through the door with an amazed smile.

"Wow." Saxon spun around. "Have you considered giving up your day job to work construction?"

Cesar squatted as Saxon stepped over and gave him a quick kiss through the safety bars of the scaffold. He wanted to take the kiss deeper, but his knees would give out before his need for Saxon's mouth ever would. "You're the only man I'll tape ceilings for."

Saxon laughed. "How do you make that sound so romantic?"

Cesar grinned. Since when had he become such a sap?

Since you fell in love with a sexy man with an even sexier, selfless heart.

"I see you found the change of clothes I brought you."

Saxon smoothed down the front of his T-shirt. "Yeah. Thanks. I don't know what I was thinking when I left without anything to change into."

Cesar gave him one more kiss before standing and looking down at him from above. "You were thinking about seeing your father, who you hadn't seen in many years. I would have been surprised if your mind wasn't more focused on that than working here after."

"True." Saxon picked up the drywall knife and filled a pan with mud. He could work on the lower joints on the walls that wouldn't require the scaffold.

Cesar went back to mudding and taping the ceiling. "How did it go?"

By the smile on Saxon's face when he'd climbed up to the third floor, Cesar imagined it had gone well. But after all the time he'd spent checking into Melvin's background, he felt he had a vested interest that went beyond being Saxon's boyfriend and wanting it to be a good experience.

"It went so much better than I'd ever hoped." Saxon kept mudding and taping as he talked. "I got to ask him some of my biggest questions, and it was hard and validating at the same time. There's still so much to talk about, but he'd seemed genuine and happy to reconnect. I won't pretend to know everything that happened between him and my mother, but as I'd come to suspect, there's more than one side to the story."

Cesar stopped to give his shoulders and neck a break. As he'd found many times in his investigations, rarely was one person's version of a story the whole truth. Everyone came into a situation with their own lived experience and bias. "Your father wasn't the monster your mother had made him out to be?"

"I don't know," Saxon allowed. He stopped mudding to look at Cesar. "He could be a totally different man than he was back then. I don't think so, though. At least that's not the impression I got. At least not where it counts. I appreciated his candor, even if it didn't always paint him in the most complimentary light."

He swiped at the joint in front of him a couple of times before continuing. "My mother could have said what she said, thinking she was protecting me somehow. Or maybe she only wanted to hurt him, and keeping him from seeing me was the best and easiest way for her to do that."

"Could be both." Cesar set the mud pan down so he could descend the scaffold and reposition it.

Saxon shrugged as if conceding the point. His concentration was so focused on the joint in front of him that he didn't hear Cesar walking up behind him. "We're going to try to see each other again soon."

Cesar wrapped his arms around Saxon's waist from behind. As much as he'd like to drag him back home to have the makeup sex Saxon had promised, he just needed the contact, needed Saxon in his arms, even if he were a ball of sweat.

"Ew." Saxon chuckled. Turning around, he lifted his full hands over Cesar's head to rest his arms on Cesar's shoulders. "You're all sweaty."

He nuzzled Saxon's neck, where he'd also gone damp from the heat. "I thought you liked me all sweaty."

"That's different." Saxon tilted his head back, which with the hold he had around Cesar's neck, pulled Cesar even closer. He shifted to align their growing erections. Apparently, Cesar's shirt being nearly soaked with sweat wasn't enough of a deterrent for him to pull away.

Cesar chose that moment to ask one of the burning questions he had. It might not have been the best time to ask it. Then again, was there ever a perfect time to ask a question about homophobia?

"What did he think about us?" From Cesar's interaction with Melvin in the car, he thought the man would be fine with his son being gay. Hearing about it and sitting across the table from the truth could have hit Melvin differently.

"That's where the problem is."

Even though the smile got wider on Saxon's face, Cesar stilled. Would Saxon want to put the brakes on their relationship while navigating his new relationship with his father?

Cesar didn't want to take any steps back. He liked the path they'd taken, but he would back off for a while if Saxon demanded it.

Please don't demand it.

Cesar was afraid to ask. "What was the problem?"

"He made it clear that he was on your side." When Cesar merely raised his brows at Saxon, he continued. "He said I should give you a break on the whole thing about you checking him out behind my back."

Saxon had a grumble in his voice and a fake pout on his lips. "He's my father, and he's already on your side. Maybe I shouldn't see him anymore."

Cesar laughed. After all these years, he figured it would take much more than Melvin agreeing with Cesar to make Saxon not want to continue building the relationship.

He kissed the end of Saxon's nose. "I think I like your father already."

"Brat," Saxon said as he stepped back. They needed to get back to work if they wanted to finish the third floor, and standing in each other's arms and letting the mud in their pans dry wouldn't help.

They split apart. Saxon started on his wall again, and Cesar repositioned the scaffold.

"To answer your question, he seems to be fine with it. It didn't sound like he'd always had the easiest time over the years. He moved around a lot, chasing jobs until he found a venture that worked for him. This car lot seems to be it."

"That's good to hear." Cesar climbed up the scaffolding and went back to work.

"From what he'd said, he'd known I was here. He went to one of the city council meetings a while back when I was trying to change the zoning for Stonewall House."

Saxon filled Cesar in on Melvin's reasonings for not contacting Saxon sooner. Saxon would never have made his father feel inferior or held it against him for not having his life sorted. Unfortunately, Melvin wouldn't have known that.

As they mudded, and worked, and shifted the scaffold, Saxon told Cesar everything they'd talked about at the coffee shop. He loved hearing the excitement in Saxon's voice. Almost giddy at times as the hope for developing a relationship bubbled to the surface.

Cesar's heart swelled as he listened. Even after Oliver's arrest, Saxon had been optimistic, but the man mudding beside him seemed fundamentally changed. Like now, *anything* was possible, and no matter what he found out from his father later, reconnecting had been the best thing that had happened to him in a long time.

His and Saxon's relationship, hopefully notwithstanding.

And that hope, that feeling of endless possibilities Saxon had, was contagious, and Cesar's chest nearly overflowed with it.

21

BY THE TIME THEY'D FINISHED TAPING AND MUDDING THE ENTIRE third floor, the sun had started to set, the breeze had cooled a fraction making the heat on the third floor nearly bearable, and Saxon's parched throat made it difficult to swallow.

They'd gone downstairs and taken a snack and water break at mid-afternoon. That had been a while ago. They'd been so close to finishing in the last hour or so that neither of them had wanted to take a break to run downstairs for water.

With a rubber mallet, Cesar tapped the lid down on the five-gallon bucket of mud, and Saxon wiped their tools clean in a bucket of dirty water. Right now, even with the bits of dried mud floating in the water, clouding it to an opaque gray, he almost reached in and brought a cupped hand full of water to his mouth.

"Don't do it," Cesar warned from the other side of the room. "We're almost done, then we can drink all the water we want. And maybe a few beers as well."

Damn. Beer sounded better than sex right then. It had been a long day, and all Saxon wanted to do was shower off all the sticky sweat, get into a clean change of clothes, and chill on the couch with the man he loved.

Because how could he not love a man who supported him and his dreams with every ounce of his blood, sweat, and tears. Okay, maybe not blood because drywalling wasn't that dangerous. And no one burst into tears when Cesar tapped the lid on the bucket, but that was the gist.

Cesar loved him and went out of his way every day to prove that he did. And yeah, as much as Saxon hated that Cesar had gone behind his back and investigated Melvin without his permission, he'd done it with the best of intentions because Saxon mattered to him.

He couldn't fault the guy for that.

Or stay mad at him.

They heard hollow footsteps coming up the stairs and Mango's plaintive meow a second before the door to the third floor opened. Kai came in with two water bottles in one hand and Mango in the other.

Mango scampered to Saxon, leaving little paw prints on the dusty wood floor. Saxon scooped him into his arms and scratched under the kitten's chin, where Mango loved it the most.

Kai passed out the waters, and Cesar twisted the lid off one and handed it to Saxon. Saxon guzzled half the bottle the same way Cesar did without coming up for air.

"How much longer until you're done?" Kai asked.

"You tired of being in my old room?" Saxon asked.

"It's actually pretty dope. But I feel bad kicking you out of your room."

Sliding over, Cesar put his arm around Saxon's waist and pasted a chaste kiss on Saxon's cheek. "I'm not."

They all laughed.

"Still…" Kai let the rest of the sentence drift off.

He understood how Kai felt. When Saxon was in foster care, some of his foster parents had made it seem like they deserved a medal if they provided the bare minimum in accommodations or had to go out of their way for Saxon. Over the years, he'd learned to not ask for much… and always felt guilty when he got it.

Which probably helped explain why it had taken him so long to figure out that Aiden was a shitty boyfriend. Saxon had never believed that he'd deserved better.

And here Cesar was every day proving that Saxon deserved more.

"A month or so," Cesar said. "It feels like we made a lot of progress today."

Mango jumped down and started investigating the room. He'd no doubt leave covered in dust, but that had never stopped him before.

"Where is everyone?" Saxon asked as he went to close the windows for the night.

Kai shrugged and said, "Dunno. Out I guess."

Saxon turned. In the past, the kids had been good about including the newcomer in activities, especially if they were going out on the town. "You didn't want to go with them?"

"I'd rather stay here."

"And cat sit?" Cesar asked.

Kai shrugged again, but he had a shy smile turning his lips. "I don't mind. He's a lot of fun. Besides, I'm more of a homebody. At least I am now."

From some of Kai's stories, Saxon had come to find out how often Kai had been sneaking out and staying gone until well into the next day at previous foster homes.

Kai hadn't come right out and said *Thank you, Saxon, for making me feel safe.* But him preferring to stay at Stonewall instead of going out when he had the chance pretty much said it for him.

"Cesar and I were heading home, but if you'd rather, we can get cleaned up here, and I can order us a pizza or something."

"You don't have to babysit me."

"I know, but—"

"You afraid to leave me here alone?"

Saxon jumped on that before Kai could take it the wrong way. "I didn't say that. More importantly, I don't think it either."

Nodding, Kai said, "You were in foster care. You know how rare it is to get a place to yourself, even for a few hours. I'm actually looking forward to it."

Saxon scooped up Mango and handed the kitten to Kai. "Here. Take Mango for the night. He'll keep you company."

Mango licked Kai's jaw, and Kai scrunched up his nose at the roughness of Mango's tongue. "You sure?"

Even though Kai had asked, he looked like he wanted to take Mango and run away with him. "I'm sure. There's kitten food in the pantry. It's getting close to his dinner time, too."

At the mention of dinner, Cesar's stomach grumbled. Saxon needed to get Cesar home and fed, especially after all the hard work he'd put in. He owed him that much.

They headed downstairs and said their goodbyes at the door. As much as Saxon wanted to bring Mango with him, especially since he had hardly seen him all day, he knew Kai needed him more.

On the way to their cars, Cesar's stomach growled again, and Saxon pulled Cesar up short. "Why don't we swing through a drive-through on the way home? That way, we can save a little time, and you'll have your strength back by the time we get home."

"I thought I was done working." Cesar's flirty grin told Saxon he knew exactly what Saxon had meant but wanted him to have to explain himself.

Saxon took hold of the front of Cesar's shirt—not even caring that the neighbor down the street was out walking their dog—and yanked Cesar closer, pressing a kiss to Cesar's lips that left them both breathless and their neighbor getting an eyeful. "Sweetheart, we haven't even started."

Cesar didn't mind that Saxon had left Mango with Kai because when they walked through the door, they didn't have to waste precious seconds feeding the kitten and making sure he was settled before Cesar hauled Saxon into their bedroom and had his wicked way with him.

Or Saxon had his wicked way with Cesar.

Either way worked.

It was hard to tell who dragged who toward the bedroom, but he barely managed to kick the front door closed before Saxon yanked Cesar's shirt over his head and started tugging down his athletic shorts in the hallway.

Cesar stumbled as he kicked his sweat-dampened shorts and underwear down the hall, the cool air conditioning on his over-heated skin raising goosebumps.

Or the goosebumps could have been from how Saxon skimmed his curious hands down Cesar's flanks as Saxon's hand headed farther south. He batted Saxon's hand away to keep Saxon from taking hold of the semi he already sported because if Saxon got hold of him now, they'd never make it to the shower.

Cesar had to lock Saxon's wrists in one hand to keep Saxon's exploring hands away, though Saxon could have broken the hold any time he wanted. It wasn't like Cesar had huge hands.

He turned on the water in the shower, leaving it on the cool side. It would feel good after so many hours sweating their asses off.

"Behave." Cesar gave Saxon the eye.

Saxon didn't utter any promises, but when Cesar dropped his wrists, Saxon kept his hands to himself long enough for Cesar to strip Saxon naked.

They both stood in a bathroom barely large enough for the two to turn around without bumping into the counter or the toilet.

With his hands on Saxon's shoulders, he guided him into the shower. Saxon hissed as the cool water hit his overheated skin. The water took Cesar's breath away, but it also felt so damn good.

Saxon commandeered the soap first, sudsing up his hands and going after Cesar. Like he knew Saxon would, Saxon went straight for Cesar's dick, lathering up his cock and balls probably better than Cesar had ever done so himself.

Cesar appreciated Saxon's attention to detail as his head fell back, and Saxon worked his shaft, sliding from root to tip and back again.

It took all of his willpower to reach down and take hold of Saxon's wrists again.

"What's the matter?" Saxon asked, though, by the self-satisfied smile on his face, he knew exactly what the *matter* was.

"I want your ass, Mr. Gray. That's not going to happen if you keep doing that." He backed Saxon against the tile wall, their hard cocks aligning as he ground into him.

"What if I want yours, Mr. Morales?"

Cesar's breath caught. Saxon knew Cesar was vers, but up to that point, Cesar had been topping. Not because Cesar didn't want to feel Saxon deep inside him, but because he couldn't get enough of the feel of Saxon's sweet ass wrapped around him and the way Saxon groaned Cesar's name when he came deep inside him.

Wanting to ditch the condoms, they'd gone and got tested a few days before but had only gotten the results the day before.

"My ass is all yours," Cesar said. "Don't just stand there. Get cleaned up and take me already."

Saxon laughed and took the soap when Cesar handed it to him. "Yes, sir."

"*Fuuuck,*" Cesar groaned as he watched Saxon wash, unable to keep from leaning in and stealing a kiss that almost made him forget their goals. "I love the way those two words sound coming out of that dirty little mouth of yours."

Saxon's pupils dilated, and his nostrils flared, and the way he looked at Cesar, all stormy and sexy, they may not make it to the bed after all.

Somehow, they managed to get somewhat clean without Cesar taking Saxon in the shower. It would have been fine if they'd had more room, but Cesar's cramped shower wouldn't cut it. They probably both would have slipped and ended up in the ER with broken hips. Try explaining *that* to the attending doctor.

They cut the water and dried off with a few quick licks from the towels, leaving a trail of water from the bathroom to their bedroom. Cesar jumped on the bed, turning mid-air to land on his back.

Saxon pounced and prowled up his body on all fours. He stopped and straddled Cesar's hips. The hallway provided ambient light in the dark room. They'd been in too much of a hurry to turn on the bedroom light.

"I've got you right where I've wanted you," Saxon said.

A thrill went through him, goosebumps rode in waves over this damp skin, and his breathing kicked up a notch. How often had he laid in bed, fantasizing about this very thing? But as he reached down and took Saxon's ample dick in his hand, he got nervous.

He'd bottomed with Aiden numerous times, but he hadn't done it since they'd broken up. "As much as I want you in me, you'll have to take it slow. It's been a while. And unlike you, I don't have a ginormous purple dildo to keep me ready at a moment's notice."

"It would be a ton of fun remedying that," Saxon said. "Until then, I've got you."

Whatever amount of apprehension Cesar had vanished with those simple, reassuring words. *I've got you.* Cesar liked the sound of that.

Saxon shifted between Cesar's legs and hitched them over Saxon's shoulders. It made him feel vulnerable and completely exposed, and Cesar loved it. Loved giving Saxon that power, knowing he'd more than earned it.

Saxon kissed along the creases on the inside of Cesar's legs, his tongue painting a wet trail to his balls. Saxon sucked one into his mouth and then the other, the suction stopping short of painful.

His hands went to Saxon's hair, fisting the strands between his fingers. Saxon grunted at the pressure, but that only made him lick and suck harder.

Cesar's other hand went to his dick. He could have easily come from the combination of the stroking and sucking if he'd wanted, but he wanted to feel Saxon inside him when he came more.

Then Saxon tipped him back, exposing Cesar's hungry hole. The first swipe of Saxon's tongue on the puckered ring nearly had Cesar blowing his load. He grunted and clamped his hand around his dick hard enough to distract him from the attention Saxon lavished on his ass.

The vibration from Saxon's dark chuckle went straight to Cesar's dick and made the base of his spine tingle. Saxon's tongue breached his hole, and Cesar pressed against him, fucking himself on Saxon's tongue.

It was too much, and Cesar was too close. "Stop."

Saxon immediately came up for air, his finger tussled hair, and the knowing raised brow that looked down at him made Cesar's heart skip in his chest, and his brain slip a gear because instead of *You're going to make me come* falling from his lips, he said, "I fucking love you."

He'd said it before, and maybe when his boyfriend was eating out his ass wasn't the most appropriate time to say it again, but damn... he couldn't help the feelings that overwhelmed him.

Saxon let Cesar's legs drop to the mattress, and he wiped his face on the sheet before bracing himself above Cesar, their pelvises aligned. Instead of the mischievous expression Cesar expected, Saxon's face softened, and he kissed his way along Cesar's jaw before dropping his full weight on Cesar and nibbling his earlobe.

"I fucking love you, too," Saxon whispered the words as if afraid to let anyone else hear.

Like it was something precious and only for them to share.

Those five words made Cesar feel weightless, even with Saxon lying on top of him. He pushed Saxon up to see his face. "You know you don't have to say—"

Saxon shut him up with a kiss. "I didn't say I love you because I had to. I said it because it's true, and I wanted to. I love you, Cesar. I love the man that you are. I love how you love me. I love the way we fit together, and I'm not just talking about in bed."

"Though, for clarity's sake, that's pretty damn good."

Saxon laughed. He had the most amazing, infectious laugh that made Cesar want to hear it every day. "Yeah. Pretty damn good."

Cesar pulled him down for a kiss. He smelled of musk and soap. A more intoxicating mixture than any alcohol Cesar had ever swallowed. The kiss went on and on, their tongues meeting and mating, their bodies grinding. The ceiling fan couldn't keep up with the heat they generated, and a thin layer of sweat covered their bodies.

Cesar hardly noticed the heat as he reached between them and took both cocks into his hand. Saxon stroked into his palm and against Cesar's cock. He swallowed Saxon's throaty groan.

Saxon came up for air, burying his face in the crook of Cesar's neck. He wrapped an arm around Saxon's head, holding him close as he brought them closer and closer to the brink.

"Jesus. *Fuck.* I want you." Saxon pulled away and braced himself on his arms. The way Saxon looked at Cesar made him wonder if he'd ever been loved like that before. Like he was the sun, the moon, and the stars. Even if that were true, Saxon didn't know that he was the center of Cesar's universe. It started and ended with him.

Saxon shuddered as he continued stroking into Cesar's hand. And by the soft *umph* he uttered, it became clear how difficult it had been for Saxon to break the contact and reach into the bedside table for the lube.

Cesar had never been so glad they'd agreed to ditch the condoms. He'd never gone bare before. Even with Aiden, there had always been something in the back of his mind telling Cesar that Aiden couldn't be trusted with his safety. No surprise that he'd been right.

Saxon was different. Cesar trusted him one hundred percent. He didn't have to protect his body… or his heart from him.

And that felt so fucking freeing.

He hadn't even realized until then the relief he'd feel, knowing Saxon would do everything in his power to keep him safe.

Getting to his knees, Saxon flicked the lid on the lube, squirted some into his hand, and slicked up his dick before pouring more onto his fingers.

Saxon braced himself on one hand and leaned in to kiss Cesar, his tongue exploring Cesar's mouth as his slick fingers eased between Cesar's cheeks.

"Right there," Cesar muttered as Saxon ran his fingers over his entrance. Not that he had to give Saxon direction, he knew what he was doing.

With gentle pressure, Saxon breached the tight ring of muscle, and Cesar's head fell back as he blew out a breath.

"I can take more," he said as he arched and pressed against Saxon's finger. Saxon added another, and Cesar forced himself to relax.

The stretch and the slide made his dick rock hard. He usually didn't stay hard while he was fucked, but that didn't make it any less enjoyable. He took Saxon as deep as he could, ready for those fingers to be replaced with Saxon's beautiful cock.

"I'm ready," Cesar said, unable to wait any longer.

Saxon chuckled and nipped at Cesar's chin. "Impatient thing, aren't you?"

He locked eyes with Saxon. "I want your dick. Now."

"*Fuuuck*," Saxon groaned as he took Cesar's mouth and didn't relinquish control until they both lost their breath. "I love that bossy mouth of yours."

Saxon withdrew his hand, and Cesar couldn't wait to have Saxon inside him. He reached down and aligned Saxon with his hole. He expected Saxon to bat his hand away, but he shifted into position, locking his gaze on what Cesar was doing to him.

The heat and fire blazed in Saxon's eyes, and he didn't waste a moment when Cesar released him. He positioned Cesar's legs over his shoulders again and pressed inside.

The stretch and the fullness had Cesar's head falling back.

"Eyes on me," Saxon said. "I want you to know who's fucking you."

Cesar chuckled, but Saxon silenced him as he slowly buried himself to his balls.

"Trust me," Cesar said after adjusting. "I know."

They'd brought up the possibility of some degree of openness early on in their relationship, though at that moment, Cesar couldn't think of anyone he'd rather have over him, and in him, and bringing him closer and closer to the brink.

Saxon's strokes grew faster and harder, and it took every fiber, every ounce of control Cesar had to keep his eyes locked on Saxon and not have them roll up into the back of his head with the pleasure.

Cesar shuddered. A rash of goosebumps erupted and ran across his skin. The punishing position Saxon had him in was also the perfect angle to brush across his prostate.

"Right there," Cesar's voice nearly abandoned him, but by the taunting grin on Saxon's face, he knew that already. Saxon hit his prostate again, and Cesar's head fell back, and he could do nothing about it. Saxon had complete control of Cesar's body and his pleasure.

He started jacking himself and arched up. "I'm so close."

Saxon dropped Cesar's legs from his shoulders and braced his hands on either side of Cesar's head. He set a beautifully brutal pace that stole Cesar's breath and made his heart race in his chest.

He barely heard Saxon's breathless, "I'm coming," over the *whoosh* of blood rushing past his ears. He tightened his grip on his dick, working the shaft and concentrating on the sensitive head.

Saxon stiffened, his strokes stalling as he came. Cesar felt every pulse as the heat of Saxon's cum flooded into him, throwing Cesar over the edge after him.

He spasmed around Saxon's thick cock, loving the fullness. Saxon collapsed on top of him, hugging him close as Saxon fucked him through his orgasm.

Saxon grunted. "You're so tight."

He kept up a slow, sated rhythm until his dick softened and the cum on Cesar's chest started dripping over his ribs.

Cesar couldn't even drum up a fuck to give. Saxon shifted to get off him, but he held Saxon in place. "You're not going anywhere."

Even as Saxon softened, Cesar didn't want him to pull out. If he had a choice, he didn't want to ever break the connection. Never in his life had he felt so safe with a partner. Never had he felt like he could be himself and not fear that he would be judged and found lacking.

Their breathing slowed, and eventually, Saxon slipped out. Cesar held him tighter. "You're stunning."

Saxon kissed Cesar's neck. "You aren't so bad yourself."

Saxon rose, their skin stretched, sticky with cum and sweat. On his knees, Saxon swiped a finger through it and fed it to him.

He licked Saxon's finger clean, and though he hadn't recovered from his last orgasm, his dick thought about getting hard again. Leaning in, Saxon swept his tongue into Cesar's mouth, getting a taste for himself.

"I wanted you to see why I can't get enough of your taste," Saxon said.

Cesar drew him in again. He couldn't imagine a time when he'd ever have enough of this man. "I love you."

This time when Saxon said it, the words came without reservation or hesitation. "I love you, too."

22

———

CESAR DIDN'T KNOW IF IT WAS BECAUSE THEY WERE HEADING INTO summer or what that caused the number of cases coming to their firm to multiply exponentially.

They had to turn clients away that they otherwise would have accepted and sent others to PI colleagues they knew would treat their clients well.

He had appreciated the time off work Derek had supported while he had the chance because, for the past few weeks, Cesar had rarely seen Saxon awake. He would arrive home late at night and kiss Saxon on the cheek when he found him asleep in their bed.

Now and again, he'd get lucky and get to leave a little later in the morning and have breakfast with Saxon, or if he was *really* lucky, they stole some time for a quick romp.

Not seeing each other sucked, but they texted during the day as best they could. At least they were living together. Otherwise, with their busy schedules, he probably wouldn't have had a chance to see Saxon at all.

And he felt guilty as hell that he'd promised Saxon he'd help with the third floor and hadn't had a chance since they'd finished mudding.

At least Saxon had been able to meet his father multiple times, usually for lunch. Cesar had been invited, but he hadn't been able to make that happen.

Tonight… tonight was different. He'd managed to sneak out of the office a little early and planned on surprising Saxon with dinner out at his favorite sushi place.

He pulled into his driveway, pleased to find Saxon's car there. To say that he loved seeing that vehicle in his driveway would be an understatement, and he loved the man who drove it even more. He hadn't realized how much he enjoyed coming home when he knew Saxon would be there to greet him.

"I'm home," Cesar called out as he walked through the front door. Saxon wasn't in the kitchen or the den. He called out again. "Saxon?"

"Coming!" Saxon's reply came from the bedroom.

He smiled. Maybe them both *coming* would be a great way to whet their appetite for said sushi. Cesar strode down the hall toward the bedroom, unbuttoning the top button on his dress shirt and unfastening his cuffs.

The bedroom door opened, and Mango zoomed through Cesar's legs.

Saxon wore a nice pair of slacks and a fitted mint-green dress shirt that made Cesar want to reach for him and tear it all off. "Hey, beautiful."

"Hey, there. I wasn't expecting you this early." Saxon pecked him on the cheek and followed Mango into the kitchen, where the kitten meowed plaintively as if he hadn't eaten in days instead of hours.

Cesar trailed behind Saxon, the whiff of his cologne making him want to start kissing that neck and work his way down from there. But clearly, that wasn't on the menu tonight. At least not at the moment.

He leaned against the counter as Saxon dug into the container with the kitten kibble and poured Mango a healthy scoop. "Why are you all dressed up?"

"Dad called. He had an extra ticket to the community play and invited me." The smile dropped from his face. "If I'd known you were coming home early, I—"

Dad? Since when had Saxon started calling Melvin dad? Cesar waved Saxon off. "No. It's fine."

Cesar no more got those words out than Saxon went on with unrestrained excitement. "After the play, we're going to that sushi place on Hampton. He said I could pick, and I haven't had sushi in so long, and I can almost taste the salmon sashimi now. And—"

Saxon stopped mid-sentence. "Do you want to meet us for dinner after?"

A good boyfriend would have said yes. Especially one that had come home early for that purpose. Call it sour grapes if you wanted to, but Cesar didn't want to be the third wheel in Saxon's and Melvin's night.

"I have… work," Cesar decided on because he didn't have a reason not to meet them there other than he didn't want to. Besides, he'd see Saxon when he got home, right?

Cesar followed Saxon into the den. Saxon sat on the ottoman and slipped on his dress shoes. "You and Melvin are spending a lot of time together."

It may have sounded accusatory, even though he tried to hide it. He chalked it up to his disappointment in coming home to find Saxon had other plans, even though he never expected Saxon to sit at home alone pining for Cesar to come home from work. He should be glad that Saxon had other things going on.

And he was.

Really…

Saxon grinned with that childlike exuberance as if Saxon had asked his father to play outside with him, and his father had said yes. "We have a lot of time to make up for."

Saxon's smile dimmed, and he stood, wrapping his arms around Cesar's waist and pressing a tentative kiss to his lips. "You okay with this?"

The last thing he ever wanted was for Saxon to think he had a problem with him reconnecting with his father. That would be a shitty thing to do. He stuffed whatever ambivalence he had to the back of his mind and buried it deep. Saxon never needed to know about his reservations.

Cesar smiled and kissed that soft spot under Saxon's jaw that he couldn't get enough of. "Why wouldn't I be?"

Saxon extricated himself from the kiss and held Cesar at arm's length, scrutinizing him. Afraid of what he might see, Cesar distracted him with a question. "So, *Dad*, huh?"

That fucking boyish, heart-stopping grin returned. "I know, so unexpected, right? Have you seen my wallet?"

Saxon let Cesar go and searched for his wallet that he could never remember to unload into the bowl on the entryway table. He raised his voice, so Cesar heard him while he searched. "Calling him dad just came out the other day, and it felt right and —fuck, where did I put my wallet?"

Saxon brushed by Cesar on his way into the kitchen, opened the refrigerator, and found his wallet next to the milk. He shoved it into his back pocket and went hunting for his keys. "And Dad seemed to like it as well. I never thought I'd feel comfortable calling him that a month ago, but yeah... Oh, here they are." Saxon had that triumphant tone as if he'd conquered Rome and not just found his car keys.

Saxon checked his watch. "Ack, I'm running late." He kissed Cesar's cheek and waved to him over his shoulder as he headed for the door. "See ya tonight."

"See ya," Cesar parroted, but the door had already closed, and he doubted Saxon heard.

But he was happy for Saxon. Really.

Fuck.

He went to the fridge for a beer but nixed the idea in favor of something stronger. He poured himself three fingers of scotch and headed for the back porch to watch the sunset. Mango ran out with him into the fenced yard. Luckily, the furball hadn't learned to climb trees or fences yet.

As Cesar sat, his phone rang. He didn't even look at the screen before answering with an annoyed, gruff, "Yeah?"

"Whoa." Derek chuckled. "I know this is the first night you've had alone with Saxon in a long time. I'll make it quick."

"Sorry." Cesar slugged a mouthful of scotch, making him wince. Derek hadn't deserved that kind of greeting. He'd been more supportive and understanding than Cesar had expected regarding the time off to spend with Saxon. "And you're not disturbing me. What's up?"

"Did you email the Edwards file to me? Max closed the shop tonight to do a tattoo on a celeb, so I figured I'd get started on it."

"Max has been getting more of those lately," Cesar said, pleased for how well Max's fledgling tattoo shop was going. "Word must be getting around Hollywood."

"Tell me about it. It's the second time this month that he's closed the shop for a VIP. You know… never mind about the file. I have other stuff to work on. You can send it later when you get back from dinner. I don't want to disturb—"

"It's fine. We're not going out. Saxon had a thing."

"Oh…" The silence on Derek's end of the phone dragged on until Cesar started feeling sorry for himself. It was just dinner. It wasn't like they couldn't do it another night. "Everything okay?"

One thing about Derek is that he didn't miss anything.

"Fine. Give me a few minutes to boot up my laptop, and I'll send the file over."

"Doesn't sound fine. You want to talk about it?"

Abso-fucking-lutely not. Besides, his reservations about Saxon's father had to be grounded in some sort of fucked up jealousy, right? Like Cesar wanting Saxon all to himself or something. That's not how life works in a healthy relationship.

He threw back the second—and last—swallow of scotch and set his empty glass on the patio table. "I don't think I'm in the mood for you to get on my case. Thanks, though."

"Now I have to know."

"I'll need another drink for that."

Derek chuckled. "I've got nothing but time."

Cesar left his phone on the patio table as he returned for the bottle of scotch to save on the number of trips he'd likely have to make for refills. He latched the screen door behind him as he came out and located Mango stalking through clumps of weeds in his flower beds that he needed to pull before they took over the backyard.

Cesar plopped into his chair, put the phone on speaker, and turned the volume up so he wouldn't have to hold it. "I'm back."

"I got a drink too. I wouldn't want you to have to drink alone."

Cesar laughed. "I appreciate that. And to be fair, I'm not sure what my problem is. I mean, sure, I'm disappointed Saxon wasn't available for dinner, but me coming home early was a last-minute thing that he didn't even know about, so I couldn't expect him to drop everything."

"Seems reasonable." Derek's tone said he'd put his judgment on reserve until Cesar laid everything out.

Cesar told him about the play, dinner with Melvin afterward, and about declining to meet them. After all, Derek couldn't make a fair assessment if he didn't have all the facts.

"He's even calling Melvin *dad* now."

There came another long pause on the other end. Was Derek taking a sip of his drink, or was he contemplating how to respond? Maybe both.

"*Dad?* That seems…"

"Fast. Right?"

"A bit," Derek conceded, "but I guess it isn't up to us to

armchair quarterback their relationship. If it feels right to them, who are we to judge?"

"Yeah, I get that." That was what he'd told himself before this conversation started. "But here's the thing… I can't get past my gut feeling. You know, like those people you hear about who start dating and they love-bomb their new person with attention and presents and pressure them into a relationship faster than normal. What's happening with Saxon and Melvin reminds me of that. It would be a red flag for a romantic relationship, but… fuck, I don't know what to think of it."

"Even if it *is* fast, that doesn't mean there's anything wrong with it. Look at you and Saxon. Your relationship went from zero to one hundred, and it's good and solid."

Derek had a point. Maybe Cesar's baseline level of paranoia had spiraled a little out of control. "Still…"

He let the sentence drop. They sat in comfortable silence for a minute or so. Mango curled up in a pool of fading sunlight, pawing at a seed head that dangled above him. Birds chirped, and even in the early evening, the road noise buzzed at a minimum. Yet Cesar's gut churned with unease.

Or was that because of the two glasses of scotch on an empty stomach?

"Cesar…" Derek's voice held a note of warning.

"I'm not going to do anything."

"That's great. Remember what happened the last time you stuck your nose into Saxon's business without his blessing? You can't make that mistake again."

Cesar knew that. "I promised him I wouldn't."

"Uh, huh. Don't forget it either. You've got a good thing going with him, and I'd hate you see you fuck it up because you can't leave well enough alone."

I F SAXON NEVER DID ANOTHER RENOVATION IN HIS LIFE, IT WOULD be too soon. What he'd thought would only take a couple of months had dragged on way longer than he'd expected. At least now, he was starting to see the light.

Once he finished the final coat of paint, he could hang the new light fixtures, install the sink, cabinet, and toilet in the bathroom, and then he could look at furnishing the place.

The renovation money had nearly run out, but he had about ten thousand he'd squirreled away from selling his house when he bought Stonewall. He could always pay himself back later. He hated to make Kai wait. Kai was anxious to get settled in his new space, and Saxon was eager for the program to be able to help more people.

Finally, all of his professional plans were coming to fruition, and his personal life… well, he couldn't remember when his personal life had been any better. He had a man he loved with everything that he was, and having his dad back in his life—in his corner, even—was more than he could have hoped for.

He was so damn lucky.

"Which wall do you want me to paint next?" his dad asked.

Melvin had given up his free evening to help Saxon. And it wasn't even the first time.

Saxon had the shit job of painting the ceiling. He was nearly covered in paint splatter and drips. He could barely see through his paint-smudged goggles when he looked at his dad. "Start in the bathroom if you don't mind. That way, I can work in there the first chance I get. I can't wait to get the toilet installed up here. I'm tired of traipsing downstairs every time I have to pee."

His dad chuckled. "Not gonna lie. I could do without having to go up and down the stairs so much."

Melvin poured paint into a pan and headed into the bathroom with his brush as footsteps sounded on the stairs.

The door to the third floor opened, and Cesar entered with a cup of coffee in each hand from Saxon's favorite coffee shop.

"Hey, stranger." Saxon grinned as he took the offered coffee and pecked Cesar on his cheek. "This is a nice surprise. What are you doing here?"

Cesar gave him a funny look. "I told you I'd be here. Sorry, I'm late. I had to write up a report for the case I closed. But I've got the best news."

Saxon slapped a hand to his forehead. "I forgot you were coming."

"Oh, hey, Cesar." His dad came out of the bathroom. "I didn't know you were going to be here. What's the news?"

Cesar and his dad had met briefly since Saxon had reconnected with Melvin, but with everyone's busy schedules, it had only been in passing. A scowl line formed in the middle of Cesar's brow, but the smile looked genuine enough as Cesar moved his cup to the other hand and accepted Melvin's outstretched hand.

Saxon looked between the two men who meant the most to him in his life, trying to figure out where the tension emanated from. Had his dad not gotten over Cesar checking into his background?

No. That didn't seem right. His dad had been the one to tell Saxon to cut Cesar some slack. Was it Cesar who—

"You said you had news?" his dad asked again.

Oh, yeah, news!

Saxon schooled his excitement. He'd learned through his dealings with Stonewall House that he had to keep his expectations in check. It seemed like three bad things always followed something good. "What is it?"

The wattage on Cesar's smile nearly blinded him, and Saxon's heart soared in his chest. So much for not getting his hopes up too high.

"Kellon called me on the way over. The DA dropped the charges against Oliver. All because of Cierra's video. The cops persuaded Cierra to give a statement."

"Ohmyfucking*gawd*." Saxon threw his arms around Cesar's neck and planted a loud smacking kiss on his lips. "This requires a… celebration."

He pulled Cesar closer, moving to deepen the kiss or climb him like a tree or strip him naked and have his way with him even though most everyone was downstairs.

Behind him, his dad cleared his throat.

Oops. He'd completely forgotten they weren't alone.

"Should I leave?" his dad asked with an indulgent smile.

"No. Stay." Saxon let Cesar go but took his hand. "Come with us to tell Oliver the good news."

"Alrighty, then."

Saxon nearly ran down the stairs. He let go of Cesar's hand because he wasn't moving nearly fast enough for Saxon's liking.

"Everyone downstairs," Saxon called out as he hit the second floor's landing and clomped down the stairs.

In the kitchen, Saxon couldn't control his smile as he waited for everyone to come to the table. He bounced on the balls of his feet, and Cesar took his hand and squeezed. Phoenix came in from the den with a sleep-drunk Mango in her hand, looking equally as sleep mussed with her eyeliner and mascara smudged and her cotton sheath dress wrinkled. James arrived next, followed by Oliver and Addi.

"Is that everyone?" Saxon asked.

"Kai's working late at Pigments tonight," James said.

Addi wedged their chair in next to Oliver. "And I think Sophia has a group study session tonight."

Saxon hated that they weren't all there, but trying to get that many people in the same room at the same time had gotten harder and harder. Besides, Oliver was present, and that's what mattered most.

"What is it?" Oliver asked as if afraid the news would have nothing to do with him. After all, the fight had happened weeks and weeks ago, and Saxon knew he feared the charges would stick.

"The charges were dropped," Saxon said, barely able to keep from jumping up and down as he said it.

"What?" Oliver's utter disbelief made Saxon's eyes swim with tears. "My charges. They were dropped?"

"One hundred percent dropped," Cesar said as if that validated what Saxon had said.

Oliver burst out of his seat, nearly sending Addi to the floor, hollering, "Ohmygod, ohmygod, ohmygod."

He ran to Saxon and hugged him, then yanked Cesar in for a messy, jumping group hug.

Mental note: jumping group hugs only work when everyone involved also jumps. Saxon would have to fill Cesar in on that tidbit later.

Oliver let them go, swiping the tears from his face, but they fell so fast he couldn't keep up. James, Addi, and Phoenix scrambled to hug him, and Saxon's dad scooped up Mango in his arms to keep the kitten out of the fray.

Melvin leaned against the wall, the kitten in his arms. He caught Saxon's eye and mouthed, "I'm proud of you."

Being the sap he was, Saxon started ugly crying. It was all too much emotion in one kitchen. Cesar wrapped an arm around his shoulders and tugged him in tight. Saxon happy cried onto Cesar's shoulder for a minute before regaining his composure.

Not that it mattered that he was crying.

Everyone had to wipe their eyes. Even his dad had turned his back to everyone to dry his eyes on the sleeves of his shirt before clearing his throat and turning around.

"I'm almost afraid to ask," Oliver said, "but what about Braden? Anything going to happen to him?"

Everyone retook their seats, and Addi laid their arm across Oliver's shoulder in solidarity.

Cesar leaned against the counter, his hands gripping the

Formica on either side. Saxon stood beside him and picked up Mango to hold after his dad had released him.

"Kellon doesn't know yet. The DA knows what Braden's done. It's one thing to drop the charges, but I'm not sure the DA is brave enough to file charges against the mayor's son."

"What the fuck?" Addi said, their face turning red as their indignant anger rose.

"It's shitty," Phoenix said, "but people rarely get any kind of justice. I'm taking the charges being dropped as a win."

"Seriously?" James crossed his arms and shook his head. The frown on his face said exactly how he felt about Braden likely getting off.

Phoenix raised her hands. "But hey, if I ever find that DA, he's going to have six-foot-two inches of a pissed-off trans girl in his face telling him exactly what I think about his little bitty yellow-bellied balls."

The group laughed. Fuck, these kids amazed him.

"How did this happen?" Oliver asked.

Saxon knew Cesar wouldn't go into all the details to keep Cierra as anonymous as possible for as long as possible. It was in everyone's best interest to keep speculation about sources off social media to keep her safe.

"We found a video that showed the whole fight. You'd have to be blind—"

"Or corrupt," Addi added.

"Or spineless," Phoenix pointed out.

Phoenix and Addi bumped fists, and Cesar commanded the floor again. "Anyway, with the addition of the videographer's statement, there's a chance charges will be brought."

Oliver rolled his eyes. "I'm not holding my breath."

Probably for the best.

"You know what I think?" Saxon had a brilliant idea. A chorus of *whats* reverberated around the room. "I think this calls for a celebration. What do you think? Party? Here?

Saturday night? Everyone should be off work by seven, right?"

They all looked around, nodding to each other. His dad nodded when Saxon glanced his way, and Cesar pressed a kiss to Saxon's temple and said, "I'll make sure I'm there."

Phoenix said, "And I'll make sure Sophia doesn't schedule a study session. It would be just like her to study on a Saturday night instead of having fun."

"Can..." James hesitated. "Hamish and I had a date on Saturday."

"He's invited," Oliver said, then glanced Saxon's way to make sure he hadn't overstepped.

"Of course, your boyfriend can come."

"Cool, cool."

"We'll have a lot to plan, but that can wait until tomorrow," Saxon said. "We have paint drying on the third floor."

Everyone dispersed, and they spent the next couple of hours finishing the primer coat on the walls. By the time they finished, Saxon had a headache from the fumes even though they'd had fans blowing out the window.

On the drive home, Saxon kept his windows down, hoping the fresh air would help. It did. By the time they'd gotten out of the shower, and he followed Cesar's cute ass into the bedroom to find clothes, he decided he'd give Cesar the proper thanks he deserved.

If it hadn't been for Cesar's determination, none of this would have happened, and Oliver might be looking at doing time.

"No, you don't." Saxon came up behind Cesar and ripped the pair of boxer briefs out of his hand. He dropped them in the drawer and shoved it closed. With a kiss on Cesar's shoulder, he rubbed his semi against Cesar's warm ass. "Where we're going, you don't need those."

Cesar turned in Saxon's arms, his hands going to Saxon's ass and squeezing. "And where are we going?"

Saxon spun them around and backed Cesar into the bed until his legs folded and Cesar fell back. Saxon followed him down to the mattress, his knees straddling Cesar's hips.

He nibbled Cesar's earlobe and whispered. "I want to personally thank you for all your hard work getting Oliver's case dismissed."

Cesar laughed. His hands went to Saxon's ass, and he ran a finger up Saxon's crease. Saxon sucked in a ragged breath. *Fuck.* It wouldn't be easy, but this was about Cesar, not him.

"I don't need sexual favors to do my job," Cesar said, though he didn't take his hands off Saxon's ass, and that finger continued to explore, making it hard for Saxon to think.

He brought his mouth to Cesar's, his tongue demonstrating exactly what he wanted to do. When he broke the kiss, they both had to catch their breath before they could talk. "I know you don't *need* sexual favors, but *sexual* favors are the best kind of favor."

Cesar chuckled, that low sound going straight to his dick like an earthquake reverberating through his entire body. "I can't argue with that. Except, if you want to thank someone, you should be thanking Kellon. He's the one who convinced the DA to drop Oliver's charges."

"Should we call him and have that three-way we'd talked about? Do you think he'd be into that sort of thing?"

Cesar flipped them, pinning Saxon to the mattress. Cesar gave him a little thrill every time he did that. With gravel in his voice, Cesar said, "I know we talked about having a degree of openness, but right now, all I want is you."

Saxon grinned. He loved Cesar's possessiveness, especially since Saxon knew that that 'right now' qualifier meant his possessiveness wasn't rooted in misguided jealousy.

"Cesar?"

Cesar kissed his way down Saxon's neck. He let his head fall back and enjoyed the concentrated attention. Cesar finally broke away. "Yeah?"

The way Cesar said *yeah,* made Saxon's heart race like a greyhound, flooding blood into Saxon's dick.

Cesar waited for Saxon's reply with a grin, knowing he'd be into whatever Saxon said next.

Saxon grinned back. He loved Cesar's playful side. "I think you should have your way with me."

23

Saturday night, and Saxon was exhausted. Exhausted but so fucking happy. Saxon meandered to the corner of the yard and sat on the edge of the raised flowerbed to rest his sore feet and watch everyone having fun.

They were already three hours into the party celebrating Kellon getting Oliver's charges dropped. Cesar had his phone bluetoothed into the speaker Kellon had brought, his choice of music an eclectic mix that everyone enjoyed.

Grant had brought his fiancé Sebastian, and their adopted son, Tavi, along with a cake big enough to feed all of them several times over. Having a porn star at the party raised a few smiles, but Grant was more than his public body of work, and he soon had everyone in stitches over some of the mishaps on set.

Sebastian, being the party planner he was, had arranged for tables and chairs to be loaned for the night, and supplied hamburgers and hot dogs for grilling.

Watching his dad getting along with all the important people in his life, well… it couldn't get any better.

Cesar sauntered over with a beer in his hand.

Saxon took it from him and stole a swallow and a kiss. "How are you doing?"

"Great party. I can't believe you threw this together on such short notice."

"Everyone helped, so it wasn't just me. And Kai stepped it up with the backyard. Without his work, we would have been packed inside the house like sardines instead of out here on this beautiful night."

"The neighbors complain about the noise yet?"

"I got a text from the house catty-corner to our backyard. But I'm pretty sure they won't call the cops on us. Besides, we aren't being that loud."

Cesar's phone buzzed, and he checked it. "It's Derek. I'd better take this. He wouldn't be calling tonight if it weren't important."

Saxon deflated, but he also knew how demanding Cesar's work life could be. Cesar bent and kissed him. "I'm not leaving." And to make himself clear, he raised Saxon's chin with a finger. "If it can't be handled over the phone, Derek will have to find someone else to help tonight. Okay?"

Saxon nodded, that tightening in his belly he always got when Derek called loosened. "Okay."

He must not have taken his eyes off Cesar as he walked away because the next thing he knew, his dad sat down on the edge of the flower bed beside him.

His dad had a beer in each hand. He opened one and handed it to Saxon. Even though Saxon had already had plenty to drink, he accepted it. "Quite the party, son."

He took a sip of the beer he didn't want. It wasn't exactly peer pressure, but somehow it was. He wanted to be cool. *Like his dad?* Jesus. Where had that come from?

"You enjoying yourself?" Saxon asked.

He didn't know what else to say. While they got along, and his dad had been great helping with the third-floor reno, it was easier to talk across the room with a paintbrush or screwdriver in his hand than a one-on-one with nothing to distract them.

It would get better. It would take some time, is all.

Melvin absently picked at the label on his bottle with his thumb and stared off into the near distance, a sigh escaping.

"What's the matter?" Saxon asked.

"It's nothing."

But clearly, it was *something*. He didn't know his dad well, but he did know him well enough to tell when something weighed on him. Saxon's stomach knotted. They may not be at a point in their relationship where they told each other everything or most things, but something was bothering him, and if he hadn't wanted to tell Saxon, he never would have sought him out.

"What's going on? Is there something I can do to help?"

His dad's chin fell to his chest, and he turned his head away from Saxon. When he spoke, Saxon had to lean in to hear him.

"I'm in a bit of a pickle," his dad said.

"What? How?"

His dad stood and shook his head, the furrow between his brows deep when he said, "No, this is wrong. I should never have—"

His dad cut the sentence off and turned to go. Saxon grabbed his arm and ordered him to sit. Saxon couldn't remember when he'd had to work this hard to get someone to confide in him. He had one of those faces that made people feel comfortable around him, and it usually didn't take much prodding for near strangers to open up.

"Tell me." Saxon used his program director's voice. The one he'd used to convince the city council to approve his zoning for Stonewall House. If it worked on men with sticks up their asses, surely it would work on his dad.

Melvin set his beer down and scraped his hand down his face. "There's been a delay with some financing on a lot of cars I was going to buy from the auction house. It's the best deal I've found in a long time. I was hoping it could boost my business to the next level. But a document was missing, and I had to resubmit all the paperwork. That means it could take another week before they can release the funds."

That twist in Saxon's belly should have gotten better. Instead, it worsened. He set his beer down, not caring if it got warm. "Let me guess. You need money for the sale before then."

"I need to wire them the money before the close of business on Wednesday."

How many times had Saxon been exactly where Melvin was with money promised but delayed? He was in that same situation right now, waiting on his remaining funds to finish out the renovation.

Melvin waved him off before Saxon could figure out a game plan.

"Wait. Stop," his dad said when Saxon opened his mouth, unsure what to say. "Forget I mentioned it. After everything I put you through, it's shitty of me to come to you with my hand out. There'll be other deals. My plans for the business may be on hold, but there's always another auction. I'll find another deal. I have to remind myself to be patient."

Melvin clapped Saxon on the back. "Thanks for listening to the ramblings of an old man."

Before Melvin stepped away, Saxon said, "Dad. Sit."

The tightness in his belly eased as soon as those words left Saxon's mouth. He was doing the right thing.

His dad sat. "Look, son..."

"How much do you need?"

Melvin pursed his lips, then said, "Fifteen grand. It's a lot. I don't—"

"No. Listen." Saxon met his dad's uneasy gaze. "I can float you ten grand for a few days if you can come up with the other five."

Sure he'd planned on using some of his savings to help finance the remaining renovations and purchase the much-needed furnishings, but what was another week? It wasn't like Kai didn't have a place to stay.

And Saxon wasn't in any hurry to move out of Cesar's place. He loved the life he, Cesar, and Mango were building, and he already started dreading moving back.

"That's too much. Really. Forget I said anything."

"You need it, right?"

Melvin sighed and nodded. "But not at the cost of our relationship. We're building a good thing here. At least, I think we are. It's not worth jeopardizing—"

"You plan on paying me back?"

"Of course, I do."

"Then you're not jeopardizing anything. Family helps family."

Saxon didn't realize how those prophetic words would affect him until they were out. The sting came to the back of his eyes and the party playing out in front of him started to blur.

Family.

For a kid who'd spent half his young life in the system, he'd never thought that one day he'd have people in his life he considered family. And to now have his *dad* be a part of that family, well...

Fuck.

His dad pulled Saxon into his chest, and Saxon held on tight and took everything the man gave. They both pulled away, sniffing and swiping at their eyes.

Melvin glanced at his watch and patted Saxon's shoulder again. "I'd best be heading home. I've got to be up early tomorrow to figure out how to make room at the lot for all the new vehicles."

"Sure," Saxon said. "Thanks for coming. I'll walk you out."

IN THE DARKNESS IN FRONT OF STONEWALL HOUSE, CESAR approached Saxon from behind as Melvin's taillights disappeared down the street. The light traffic noise and normal sounds of the city seemed muted under the sparse cloud cover and intermittent stars. From the backyard, the music drifted over the fence, not loud enough for neighbors to complain but soft enough for him to hear himself breathe.

"Hey, beautiful." Cesar wrapped his arms around Saxon's waist.

Saxon leaned against him, covering Cesar's hands with his own. "Hey, yourself."

The wistfulness in Saxon's voice had Cesar resting his chin on Saxon's shoulder. While the party was fun, getting to know the kids better and spending more time with Kellon, standing out front with his boyfriend in his arms, topped it. "You okay?"

Saxon turned in his arms. "Couldn't be better."

"You and your dad have a good talk?"

By the way Saxon hesitated and stiffened in Cesar's arms before relaxing against him again, made something inside Cesar wake up and take notice. What was that about?

"We did."

Cesar pulled back to see Saxon's face. There was enough light from the streetlight one house down that he could see Saxon's expression clearly enough, and he didn't like what he saw. "What aren't you telling me?"

"There's nothing to tell."

Saxon couldn't lie. The crease between his brows deepened, and the way his eyes went wider than normal was Saxon's tell. Cesar wanted to know what was going on, but Saxon wasn't obligated to tell him every single thing. It wasn't like his right to privacy was nullified under sub-clause one, section two of the boyfriend contract. Saxon was allowed to keep things to himself.

"If you don't want to tell me, you don't have to lie. You're allowed to say that you'd rather not say."

"Sorry." Saxon stared at nothing over Cesar's shoulder. He looked sheepish when he met Cesar's eyes again. "I'd rather not say."

He kissed the tip of Saxon's nose. And as hard as it was to let it go, he said, "See? That wasn't so hard."

"Asshole." Saxon's sexy, little shy smile made Cesar want to toss him over his shoulder and steal him away from the party, even if Saxon was the host. With everyone having such a good time, they might not notice.

Saxon gave him a playful shove and started up the sidewalk. "Stop that."

"Stop what?" He fell into step beside him and pulled Saxon into his side.

"Stop looking at me like that. It makes me want to ditch my party, take you home, and let you have your wicked way with me."

Cesar waggled his brows. "I'm in."

"We can't ditch the party."

"Shame."

He dropped his hand from around Saxon's waist and took his hand. At the front door, Saxon pulled him to a stop and faced him. "Dad asked to borrow money."

The words fell out of Saxon's mouth more like a confession than a statement. That those words didn't come as a surprise only made Cesar's concern about how fast Saxon and his father's relationship had progressed intensify.

Is that why Melvin had latched on to Saxon so fast? Because he needed money? He bit back every caution he wanted to throw out.

Saxon's chin came up as if bracing for what he would say, or maybe *should* say. He tried to hold his tongue but staying quiet wasn't his forté.

"How much?" His question came out quietly. His stomach knotted, waiting for Saxon's answer.

"Fifteen thousand."

Cesar felt his eyes go wide, and in that instant, he was relieved he wasn't on a sensitive case where his facial expression would have given his true feelings away.

Saxon quickly added, "Obviously, I don't have that much. I did tell him I could spot him 10k. He expects his financing to come through in a week, and it's not like that will put the renovations back much. And Kai can stay in my room for a little longer. It won't kill him, and if this is going to help Dad's business, then I want to be able to—"

Cesar shut him up with a kiss. He let it linger until he'd silenced Saxon's word explosion. He pulled back and let Saxon catch his breath.

After Saxon took a deep breath, draining much of his frenetic energy, he said, "You think it's a bad idea. Don't you?"

Hell yeah.

It was the worst idea in the history of ideas.

But he couldn't say that. Instead—with a neutrality he didn't feel—he said, "It's your money. You can do whatever you want with it. You don't need my approval. There's no need to justify it to me."

Saxon sagged against the door as if he'd feared a fight. "You're right."

"When does he need the money?"

"Wednesday at the latest."

Cesar stepped closer, cupping Saxon's cheek. "Do me a favor, though, would you?"

"What's that?"

"At least give yourself until Tuesday to think about it. Don't run down to the bank first thing on Monday. Make sure this is really what you want to do, and I'll support you on it."

"Come here." Saxon brushed his lips against his. As soon as his tongue brushed against Saxon's lips, he wanted to sink into Saxon and pretend the last ten minutes never happened.

"I love you," Saxon said.

"I love you, too."

They rejoined the party, though it had started breaking up. Cesar would be lying if he said he wasn't very concerned about Saxon lending money to his father. If he were wrong about Melvin, he'd parade down Sepulveda Boulevard in a neon jock strap in the middle of rush hour, but he didn't feel the need to shave his nuts and break out his credit card just yet.

24

CESAR RETURNED FROM THE SHOWER TO FIND SAXON NAKED AND asleep on the bed, the covers kicked to the foot of the bed. He smiled to himself. So much for a little post-party sex.

Cesar pulled on a mostly clean pair of sweats from the chair in the corner of the room, drew the covers over Saxon, and kissed his temple. Saxon didn't stir. Saxon had worked so hard on the renovations all week and prepping for the party that he'd driven himself to exhaustion.

On the other hand, Cesar was too wired to sleep. He couldn't get it out of his head that Melvin had asked Saxon for money. For *a lot* of money. Money that Saxon had squirreled away for a rainy day, not to dig his father out of a financial mess.

It's not your money. You don't have a say in how Saxon spends it.

He flicked on the den light and plopped on the couch, his eyes dropping to his laptop on the coffee table. Normally, if he had work, he preferred doing it at the office. If he were home alone, he'd have thrown on a T-shirt and driven in. The office wasn't far.

Having Saxon in the next room stopped him. He didn't want Saxon waking up in the middle of the night to find him gone and have him asking questions because what he needed to do, he needed to keep to himself if at all possible. And outright lying to Saxon wasn't something he would do.

But *fuck*.

Had he missed something on Melvin's background check? He settled his laptop across his legs, typing *Melvin Davis* into the search bar after it booted.

He sat there, his cursor blinking, waiting for him to hit *enter*.

He'd made a promise to Saxon that he wouldn't do anything like a background check on Melvin without talking to Saxon first.

Cesar debated with himself. Saxon already knew Cesar had researched Melvin. He'd broken that rule from the beginning.

How much could it hurt if he bent it a bit more?

Besides, hadn't the man brought it on himself by asking to borrow every last cent Saxon had in savings?

His finger hovered over the enter key. Saxon never needed to find out Cesar had dug deeper.

Then Cesar remembered a conversation he and Saxon had about the last time Saxon had seen Melvin before the man had disappeared from Saxon's life.

The fight his mother and father had.

The money on the coffee table.

Where had the money come from? Cesar could only think of a couple of ways you could get your hands on stacks of cash seemingly overnight. Drugs. Gambling. Or bank robbery.

He hit enter, hoping it wasn't the biggest mistake of his life.

Hours later, the bedroom door opened. Cesar sat hunched over his computer. The early rays of dawn seeped through the blinds, and Saxon shuffled across the hall to the bathroom, still half asleep.

Cesar had worked through the night. He stretched the stiffness out of his spine, saved the work folder onto an encrypted part of his hard drive, and cleared his search history. Saxon had never used Cesar's computer without permission, but with the information Cesar had found, he wasn't taking any chances that Saxon would find his new research before Cesar was ready for him to see it.

By the time Saxon entered the kitchen, Cesar had brewed a much need pot of coffee.

"Oh, hey," Cesar said as Saxon came up behind him and wrapped him in a hug from behind, pressing his half-hard cock into the crease of Cesar's ass. He pressed back against him and kissed Saxon over his shoulder. "You're up early for a Sunday."

"I rolled over, and you weren't there. What are you doing up?" Saxon released him and pulled two mugs out of the cabinet. His hair was still mussed, and his voice had that sleepy, deep timber that went straight to Cesar's dick.

"I had some work," Cesar said cryptically, hoping Saxon's brain wasn't online enough to ask more pointed questions. "The night got away from me."

"You get it all done?"

"Enough. For now." Cesar gripped Saxon's hips. "Jump up."

Saxon allowed Cesar to boost him onto the counter, keeping his legs wide for Cesar to step between. Though drained and bleary-eyed, all he wanted to do was get lost in Saxon and forget about the Melvin Davis-sized rabbit hole he'd fallen into the night before. He practically had bruises on his ass from kicking himself for not finding it before.

"You going to Stonewall House this morning?" Cesar trailed kisses down Saxon's neck and flicked his tongue over one of Saxon's flat nipples. The groan he earned had him sliding over to the other one and sucking it into his mouth.

Saxon's head knocked against the cabinet with a dull thump, his hands fisting in Cesar's hair. "I should go in for a bit. I've got the party clean-up and want to work on the reno. I may not stay long. I'd rather spend the day here with you."

"You want company? We can get things done twice as fast and get home early."

"I like the sound of that."

Cesar didn't think he could wait until that afternoon to get his hands on Saxon. He'd need a little something to tide him over. Especially when he had Saxon's hard dick within reach, stretching Saxon's underwear to the limit.

He hooked his thumbs beneath the waistband of Saxon's briefs. "Up."

As he did, Saxon asked, "What are you doing?"

"What's it look like I'm doing?" Cesar worked Saxon's briefs down his legs and tossed them aside. "Giving you something to remember me by."

Saxon grinned. "You're coming with me."

"Then it'll give you something to think about every time I look at you." Being an eager, intelligent man, Saxon put his hands on Cesar's shoulders and gave downward pressure. Not that Cesar needed any encouragement.

Hooking his hands under Saxon's legs, he scooted him to the edge of the counter to give Cesar easy access to Saxon's balls. He dipped his head, giving the tip of Saxon's cock a slow, warm lick.

"*Ungh*," Saxon groaned, or something equally unintelligible, which only encouraged Cesar to take Saxon deep.

He loved to make Saxon forget how words worked, loved his salty taste, and loved how Saxon wrapped his legs around his waist, pulling him close.

Saxon's hands tightened in Cesar's hair, his hips pumping, chasing the suction. Cesar took him to the back of his throat, stopped short of choking, and pulled off.

"Don't stop."

Cesar chuckled, replacing his mouth with his hand and dipping down to his knees to suck one of Saxon's balls into his mouth and then the other. Saxon's precum spilled freely, keeping his dick slick beneath Cesar's hand.

Finally, he came up for air. Saxon's eyes closed, his hips working erratically, needing something to fuck. A beautiful sight, watching Saxon start to unravel. Cesar kept stroking Saxon's cock, his own already dampening the front of his sweatpants.

"Get down here," Cesar said, breaking his hold on Saxon long enough for him to hop down and for Cesar to strip off his sweats.

Saxon's eyes went dark as Cesar dropped to his knees in front of him and sucked him down to the back of his throat. With his hands on Saxon's hips, he encouraged him to take what he wanted. What he needed. Saxon caught on quick, his hand going to the sides of Cesar's face holding him in place so he could fuck his face.

Cesar palmed his leaking cock, jacking himself as Saxon stroked into his mouth. He couldn't get enough. Couldn't get Saxon deep enough.

Saxon's thrusts became erratic, and Cesar worked himself harder, the base of his spine tingling. So close. So damn close. Saxon's eyes slammed closed as he palmed the back of Cesar's head, pushing to the back of Cesar's throat and holding him there, briefly cutting off Cesar's air.

Cesar enjoyed that moment of pure bliss.

The tingling at the base of Cesar's spine exploded throughout his body. His cock pulsed, and he came in his hand. Saxon stiffened, loosening his grip on the back of Cesar's head, allowing him to breathe and swallow down everything Saxon gave him.

Saxon collapsed against the counter, his legs shaking as he helped Cesar to his feet. Saxon stroked a lazy hand down Cesar's spent cock. He pulled away before he got too sensitive, still tasting Saxon on his tongue as Saxon pulled him in for a kiss.

"*Mmmm*," Saxon said. "I love the way you suck cock."

Though they were too spent for their bodies to respond, Cesar ground against Saxon, loving how their bodies fit together. Loving Saxon's warm skin on his own.

Cesar pulled him in for a hug, burying his face in the crook of

Saxon's shoulder, and released him with a playful nip. "I love sucking cock. Most especially yours."

Even though they'd both had their mouths and dicks every possible place on each other, even though they'd shared and given so much, red effused Saxon's cheeks.

So. Fucking. Adorable.

Cesar kissed the ball of each cheek. "And I love that I can still make you blush."

SAXON FIGURED CESAR WOULD HAVE TO GIVE HIM CREDIT. SAXON had done what he'd asked. He'd spent Sunday, Monday, and most of Tuesday seriously considering the offer he'd made to his dad. After all, ten thousand dollars was a *ten thousand dollars.*

Not that Saxon wanted to lose it, but even *if* he did, he still had Stonewall House and his income from that. It wasn't like he'd be out on the streets. It would just mean he wouldn't have a financial cushion until he could build his savings up again.

Was it worth the risk?

Saxon weighed everything he knew about his dad. He'd been nothing but kind since they'd reunited. They'd shared meals. His dad had spent many hours on the hot third floor helping with the renovations. Would he have done all that, made all that effort, just to play Saxon?

If Melvin had, it was a hell of a long con, and frankly, the more he got to know his dad, he couldn't see him doing that. The money loan was on the up and up.

It *had* to be.

"It's done," Chuck said as Saxon pressed send on the wire transfer to his dad's bank account.

Chuck stood in the doorway of Saxon's office, wiping his dirty hands on a rag he'd tugged from his back pocket. Chuck was the guy who'd agreed to install the third-floor air conditioning at a discount if he could install it when his schedule opened up. Luckily, Saxon had ear-marked the installation money long ago to keep the renovations from eating into it. So even as his money whisked its way out of his account, at least he could pay Chuck for his hard work.

"You're amazing." Saxon pulled out Stonewall House's checkbook and filled in the agreed amount. "Thank you so much for doing that."

"Happy to do it. I left it running. A lot of heat has built up there. It may take a while to cool down. After that, it should maintain the temperature with ease."

"*Saxon?*" Cesar called out as he entered the house, the front door slamming behind him.

"In the office," Saxon hollered back.

He handed Chuck the check. The big man pocketed it and shook Saxon's hand as Cesar stepped up behind him. Cesar's wild look made Saxon's adrenaline sizzle in his veins. Cesar was usually the calm, cool, collected one. What the hell had happened?

"Thanks again," Saxon managed, dismissing Chuck.

"Sure." Chuck acknowledged Cesar as he stepped back. "I'll see myself out."

The front door opened and closed, and still, Cesar hadn't said anything. Words caught in Saxon's throat. He didn't want to know what happened. He wasn't built for drama. "Want to go into the den and have a seat?"

"No," Cesar said. "But maybe you should sit down."

Saxon braced a hand on his desk, wanting to take the news standing, but with his shaky legs, it may not be up to him whether he sits or stands. "What is it?"

Instead of answering the question, Cesar said, "Have you sent the money?"

He didn't have to ask *what* money. "I did. Just."

Cesar glanced at his watch. "It's a little bit before five. You can call the bank. Maybe you can cancel the transfer."

"Why would I want to do that?"

Cesar fisted his hands on his hips, his gaze falling away.

"*Cesar. What. Have. You. Done?*"

When Cesar locked eyes with Saxon's, all of Cesar's frantic energy slammed into him, stealing his breath. Heat infused his veins. His heart rate kicked up, and Saxon had the urge to run.

Physically, he wasn't in danger, so why did it feel like he was?

"Just make the call while you can, and I'll explain later."

As realization dawned, Saxon dropped his voice, the warning in his voice ringing loud and clear. "*Tell me.*"

Cesar scrubbed his hand through his already disheveled hair. It only made it worse. Saxon waited Cesar out. He had a pretty damn good idea what Cesar had done, and the urge to run turned into an urge to fight.

He held tight to his emotional reins, waiting for Cesar to speak and verify Saxon's suspicions before making any accusations he couldn't take back. Saxon tasted his lunch at the back of his throat and swallowed the vile, sour taste.

Cesar's expression softened. And why the fuck did that make Saxon want to cry?

"Don't send the money, babe. Your father is a crook."

Saxon white-knuckled the corner of the desk to keep himself upright. Maybe he *should* sit down. "What are you talking about?"

Cesar stepped closer. "Make the call, babe."

"Not until you tell me."

Stalemate. Cesar wouldn't tell him before Saxon called the bank, and Saxon wouldn't call the bank until Cesar gave him a reason.

Cesar reached out. Saxon pulled away. Cesar's touch could make him lose all objectivity.

Cesar's touch tended to do that to him.

"Can we at least sit?"

Saxon folded his arm over his chest. "Quit stalling."

"After Saturday night, I did more digging."

Saxon knew it.

He *fucking* knew it.

His throat tightened, and he couldn't keep the vibration out of his voice, but fuck it. Cesar deserved to know how much he'd pissed him off. "We talked about this."

"I know, but—"

"No *buts.* You *promised.*"

Cesar's chin went up. "Will you listen?"

Saxon grumbled. He didn't shut Cesar down, so that was as much of a go-ahead as he could give. The front door opened and closed, and Oliver popped his head into the office before Saxon could slide the pocket doors closed.

"Oh…" It took him a couple of seconds to take in Saxon's crossed arms, uncommon scowl, and the sweat forming on Cesar's forehead. "*Ooooh,* um… I have a… um… thing."

Oliver disappeared, his big feet stomping up the stairs, the door to his room closing loud enough that they'd know he hadn't stopped to eavesdrop.

"You scared him off," Cesar said.

"*You're* scaring *me.*"

Cesar drew in a lungful of air as if he were going to try to get what he had to say out in one long breath. Saxon's heart rate kicked into a gear usually reserved for running up the stairs of the Empire State Building or being chased by a monster.

"I know I should have said something to you earlier," Cesar said, pausing as if waiting for Saxon's reaction. All Saxon gave him was a raised brow because the brewing anger would make it too difficult to talk without shouting. Cesar better have a quick and efficient way to excavate himself out of whatever crater-sized hole he'd dug. "But I figured if I were wrong, none of this would matter."

This felt like the same story different chapter. Hadn't Saxon made it clear he didn't want Cesar going behind his back about things that concerned him?

Saxon let Cesar sit in the weighty silence until he finally continued.

"I didn't have much to go on. Then I remembered your story about your parents fighting the night your father left. About the stacks of money you saw on the coffee ta—"

"Wait. You took something that I'd never shared with *anyone* else, and you used *that*—"

Cesar stepped closer and raised his voice over Saxon's. "I used that information to find out that your father and two other men were likely involved in a string of bank robberies in Orange County around that time."

What the actual fuck?

It took everything in Saxon not to flat-out call Cesar a liar to his face. *Keep it together. Keep it together.* "You have proof?"

"No. No one was ever charged, but—"

Saxon scoffed. But what possible motivation could Cesar have for dragging his father's name through the mud?

Cesar didn't let Saxon's doubt sway him. "There was a robbery the same night as your birthday. The same night he showed up at your house with the money. The same night he left. And you know what else I found out about that string of robberies?"

Saxon didn't say anything because, with the head of steam Cesar had built, it wouldn't have slowed him down.

"Those robberies stopped after that night. The night your father left. Don't you see?"

As hard as it was to ignore the plea in Cesar's voice, Saxon managed to pull it off. Maybe it had something to do with Saxon's rising level of pissed-off-ed-ness.

If that word wasn't in the Old English Dictionary, then it should be.

"What I *don't* see is why you're doing this."

"Why? You don't see *why?*" The way Cesar's voice rose, it probably didn't matter that Oliver had closed his door to give them privacy. "I love you. That's why."

He said it like the answer should have been obvious. But it wasn't. "Then why does your love feel so much like betrayal?"

Saxon waited a beat while Cesar's mouth gaped. "I *confided* in you. I laid my trust in your hands, and you threw it away. You let me down, Cesar. *Again.*"

"No. I—"

"You need to leave."

Cesar held up his hands. "Wait. What are you going to do?"

Saxon opened the door and brushed past him. He didn't know where he was going. He just knew that he couldn't be there. "That's not any of your business anymore."

He made it as far as the entryway before Cesar caught up and pulled him to a stop with a hand on his forearm. "Melvin also embezzled funds from the dealership he worked for in New Mexico. It would likely be enough to have helped him start the dealership he has now."

Saxon shook his arm free. He wasn't the kind of man to throw punches, but he was closer now than ever before.

"It's all there in my report," Cesar said, his lungs billowing as if he'd been running from that monster as well. "It should already be in your inbox."

Saxon vibrated, his voice shaking as much as the rest of him. "You. Wrote. A. Fucking. Report? Like I'm a client or something?"

Cesar opened his mouth to answer and then closed it again.

Just as well.

Saxon turned to leave, and Cesar stopped him again with a hand on the door by Saxon's head. "We're still good, right?"

Are you fucking kidding me?

When Saxon went to open the door, Cesar dropped his hand, and Saxon said, "I don't know what we are anymore."

25

SAXON DROVE AROUND THE CITY WITH NO DIRECTION IN MIND. IT allowed him time to think. Time to be alone with his thoughts and figure out what the hell he would do next.

At some point, he pulled out onto an overlook up one of the roads to the San Gabriels, got out of his car, and watched the sunset over the valley. Cars passed by below in miniature. He sat there long enough to watch the rush-hour traffic ebb and flow. Darkness fell by the time he braved pulling out his phone and checking his email.

He clicked Cesar's report and opened it. It held all the damning information. Everything Cesar had told him and more. Everything in the report validated what Saxon's mother had told him.

If everything in that file were true, his father wasn't a good person.

But the man in that file and the man who'd reached out to him, the man who'd given his time to help with the renovations, was not the same man in that report.

At least Saxon didn't feel like he was.

And after all that driving around, he hadn't decided what to do about Cesar. He still loved him. That hadn't changed. Probably always would. But could he be with him? Wondering what else he would do without his consent?

Did Cesar look at him like he was a child that needed saving?

Fuck that.

He'd been powerless enough times in his life that he wouldn't stand for someone taking that away from him.

Even if that man were Cesar.

But Saxon would be a fool if he ignored the report completely.

He thumbed over to his contact list and pulled up his dad's number before realizing what he needed to ask his father he needed to ask him in person.

He pocketed his phone, climbed into his car, and dropped into the valley. He needed to have a conversation with his dad sooner rather than later.

In the valley, he skirted the main roads to avoid the last of the rush-hour traffic and rolled by the car lot.

The non-confrontational part of Saxon wanted to drive by and talk to his dad in the morning. Unfortunately, the matter of his money couldn't wait.

He parked in front of the entrance. The overhead lights had been turned off, leaving only the interior security lights on in the showroom but Melvin's car in the parking lot.

Saxon got out and knocked on the locked door. It took a few times knocking for his dad to come out of his office to investigate.

Seeing Saxon, he rushed over, turned his keys in the lock, and opened the door. "Son, what are you doing here?" The smile dropped from his dad's face as he took in Saxon's dishevelment. He pulled Saxon into the dealership and locked the door behind them.

"What's wrong? Is everyone okay? Oliver? Cesar?"

"Everyone's fine." Except for maybe Cesar. The devastation on his face as Saxon walked out the door of Stonewall House nearly had Saxon second-guessing the whole shitty situation.

Right then, Saxon didn't have the bandwidth to think about that. "We need to talk."

Melvin didn't ask any questions. He ushered Saxon to his office, offered him a seat, and settled behind his desk. He picked up a pen and started rolling it between his fingers. He looked concerned, not guilty.

Saxon took a deep breath and went for it. "The night you left... where did the stacks of money on the table come from?"

His dad's eyes widened, all that white offsetting his cool, blue eyes. The pen dropped from his fingers, and he leaned back in his chair. He took a moment. To gather his thoughts? To conjure a lie?

"You wouldn't be asking if you didn't know the answer." Melvin appeared more resigned than angry. There could have been a little bit of relief mixed in there too, but Saxon didn't know him well enough to be certain.

And maybe you didn't know him well enough to give him ten grand either.

"Cesar told you?"

Saxon couldn't and wouldn't deny it. Besides, it didn't matter how he'd found out. It mattered that he had. "You robbed banks."

Melvin nodded. That he didn't offer an excuse helped on some level. "I lost everything that night. Your mother. You. If it matters any, I never robbed another bank."

Saxon didn't know how to feel about that, so he laid that aside to analyze later... or not.

"But that wasn't the last time you stole money." Saxon didn't raise his voice at the end the way he would if he were asking a question because he wasn't asking a question.

Melvin grimaced. "I suppose you know the answer to that one as well. I'll give it to your boyfriend. He does a thorough job."

Boyfriend.

Were he and Cesar boyfriends anymore? Or were they ex's now?

"That dealership in New Mexico had promised me a bonus for sourcing the used cars for them. They reneged on the deal. I only took what they owed me. No more. No less. Was it right?" Melvin tilted his head from side to side. "It is what it is. Not so much an excuse as an explanation."

Did that make it any better?

At least it gave Saxon more insight into the man who'd fathered him. Saxon massaged his temples to stave off a headache that might take a full bottle of pain relievers to tackle.

"Look." Melvin leaned forward and clasped his hands on the desk. A few files and miscellaneous pieces of paper dotted the surface. "I haven't always lived on the right side of the law. But this car lot..." Melvin held his arms wide as if he could encircle the whole business in his embrace. "It's on the up and up. I'm legit now, and I'm damn proud of that."

"About my mon—"

"If you want it back, I can wire it to your bank first thing in the morning. If I miss this deal, there's bound to be another down the road."

Would a crook offer to give money back?

Saxon's nerves started to settle. "You've changed. Is that what you're telling me?"

"It happens," Melvin said. "Am I perfect? Far from it. But I'm trying hard not to slide back into that man I want to forget I ever was."

Though Saxon didn't ask for it, Melvin picked up one of the pieces of paper on his desk and slid it over to Saxon. He stared at it for a few seconds before picking it up. It was an invoice from a car auction house with the amount Melvin had quoted him on Saturday.

Could Melvin have faked the invoice? Yeah. But he'd had no idea Saxon would come by and need to see it.

"It's legit," his dad said. "I don't want your money if you have any doubts. Son..."

His dad waited until Saxon's eyes locked on his. "I don't want to jeopardize our relationship. It means too much to me. Correct me if I'm wrong, but I think it means a lot to you, too."

Saxon's throat constricted. It felt like it had closed completely, but Saxon hadn't passed out yet, so a few hapless molecules of oxygen must be getting through.

Either Melvin was one hell of a con man, or he was telling the truth. The only way to know for sure was to take a leap of faith.

Are you sure you want to do that? You gave your trust to Cesar. Twice. And you saw how that went.

Fuck. Saxon was either a fool, gullible or a sucker for a sob story. And he needed his dad to be much more than he'd ever been.

Melvin walked around the desk and hitched a leg over the corner. "What's it going to be, son? Up to you. No pressure."

No pressure.

Melvin could say that. It didn't make the pressure disappear. In his head, Saxon heard Cesar's warning.

Or maybe that was Saxon's voice of reason talking.

"Okay," Saxon finally said. He couldn't tell if that made the knots in his belly better or worse.

"Okay?" As good as his dad had been about saying the choice to lend him the money or take it back was entirely Saxon's, the pure joy on his dad's face when Saxon agreed to let the transfer stand hit somewhere in Saxon's chest that only that six-year-old boy who wanted nothing more than his dad's approval would fully understand.

Saxon nodded, and his dad clapped him on the shoulder. "That's my boy. I won't let you down. Promise."

Promise. He'd heard that word too many times. And too many times, all it leads to is disappointment.

Saxon left the dealership and headed for Cesar's house.

Cesar's house? What happened to thinking of it as home? What happened to wanting to talk to Cesar about not moving back into Stonewall House after he completed the reno?

So much had happened that Saxon couldn't process everything, and he couldn't shake the feeling that he was screwing everything up.

The problem was that he couldn't tell *what* he was screwing up.

And now…

Now he considered himself lucky he had a place to go besides Cesar's. A place to go to. To think. To consider his options.

Fuck. Fuck. Fuck. He knew things with Cesar had been too good to last. If living in the foster system had taught him anything, it was how fast situations could change and how he could find out that people—even people he thought he knew well—might not be who he thought they were.

People let him down.

Lesson learned… the hard way.

How had Saxon forgotten so easily?

Cesar's gut churned as he sat on the couch in his den, trying to distract himself with work. Who was he kidding, though? He hadn't completed the simplest tasks in the hours Saxon had walked out the door.

He knew he'd hurt Saxon, but it wasn't anything they couldn't get past. Right? After all, he'd done what he'd done to protect Saxon. He was looking out for Saxon the best way he knew how.

By going behind his back?

Again?

Yeah, that's totally *going to make him feel safe around you.*

Would allowing Melvin to fleece Saxon of every last cent he had been better? Saxon had worked too hard to lose what little money he had left.

The minute Saxon's car pulled into the driveway, Mango ran to the front door, meowed, and looked back at Cesar as if to say, *don't just sit there, open this thing.*

The knock caught him by surprise.

The door wasn't locked. He picked Mango up and opened the door for Saxon. He pulled him into a one-armed hug, careful not to crush Mango between them. "Why did you knock?"

Saxon stiffened, and Cesar realized Saxon wasn't hugging him back. That twist in his gut threatened to squeeze every last ounce of blood out of it.

He broke the hug, and closed the door, setting Mango on the floor. "What's wrong?"

Besides the whole going behind Saxon's back to investigate his father. Because Saxon didn't look angry, he looked wrecked. Like everything he knew that was right with the world had been wrong.

Saxon scoffed and bumped Cesar's shoulder on the way to the bedroom, not even turning around when he said, "You seriously have to ask that?"

So it *was* because of what Cesar had done.

Not that that wasn't more than enough. At least something else terrible hadn't happened. The twist in his gut loosened a fraction and still nearly doubled Cesar over with the pain of it.

"I know you think what I did was wrong," Cesar started.

Saxon tossed his backpack onto the bed and rounded on Cesar. "I don't *think* what you did was wrong. It *was* wrong."

Fuck. Raising his hands, Cesar said, "I'm sorry."

Saxon turned away, opening drawers and tossing a change of

clothes into his backpack. He shouldered past Cesar again to get to the bathroom to retrieve his toothbrush and deodorant. "Not sorry enough to stop pulling this shit."

"Would you stop packing and talk to me?" Cesar grabbed Saxon's arm and spun him around. Cesar couldn't remember a time when Saxon looked like he would deck someone… until now.

Cesar let go. "Talk to me."

"The time to talk was before you continued your investigation. Not now."

"I know I screwed up. I prom—"

"*Don't*. Don't you dare. Your promises don't mean anything. You've proven that by that stunt of yours. And honestly, I'm not convinced you think you messed up. I think you understand what you did upset me, but I think you think the end justified the means."

"He robbed banks. He embezzled money."

Saxon didn't argue. He just shook his head, and Cesar couldn't remember a time when someone's blatant disappointment in him burned so brutally.

Saxon finished filling his backpack, slung it over one shoulder, and turned to go down the hall.

"He embezzled funds from a dealership." Cesar followed a few steps behind. If only he could get Saxon to understand the risk he'd taken with his money. He might as well have thrown the cash in the trash and lit it on fire.

"I know." Saxon strode straight for the door.

"Saxon, wait," Cesar said.

Saxon already had his hand on the doorknob. Mango ran into the kitchen the way he always did, the little thump telling Cesar he still couldn't negotiate corners at speed without sliding into the cabinets.

Saxon sighed and turned around. His shoulders slumped

before he gathered himself and straightened as if preparing to meet whatever nonsense Cesar planned to spout.

"I love you," Cesar said. He poured as much of himself into those three little words as he could, but words could only say so much. Saxon was starting to understand that now.

"Do you?" Saxon said at last. "Because if that's your version of love, where you don't treat me as an equal, as a partner, as someone who can make decisions on my own, I'm not sure I want any part of that."

"I—" Cesar couldn't dispute Saxon. He couldn't dispute the truth. "Is this it…" Cesar had to take a breath to steady his voice. "…for us?"

Saxon's gaze dropped to the ground. "I don't know what this is." He cleared his throat. "It isn't the Happily Ever After that had started playing out in my head."

They stared at each other. Cesar wanted to ask him to stay, but he didn't think Saxon would. Clearly, Saxon needed space. The fact that that space was from *him* made his fucking heart break.

Holding up a finger, Cesar said, "Wait one second."

As Saxon didn't open the door, Cesar went into the kitchen and picked up Mango, half expecting Saxon to be gone when he returned. He wasn't. He stood beside the door, his chin dropped to his chest as if utterly defeated.

Cesar had done that.

Would he ever forgive himself for that?

Would Saxon?

"Here." Cesar held Mango out. "I'm pretty sure he'd rather be with you. You were always his favorite."

Saxon's face softened. He took the kitten and hugged him against his chest. "Thanks. I'll come by and get the rest of my things tomorrow."

The *when you're gone* part, he didn't say out loud. He didn't have to.

Saxon left without a backward glance. If he checked his rearview mirror as he drove down the street to see Cesar standing on the stoop, wondering how everything had gone to shit so fast, Cesar would never know.

He just hoped this was more of a bump in the road of their relationship and not the place where it crashed and burned.

Fuck. Fuck. Fuck.

What had he done?

26

———

It was about time for the renovations to be done, and Saxon woke early on a Monday morning, determined to install the flooring so he could finally finish.

He'd done it.

He'd finished the renovation, not on time, but at least within his thin budget, and now with the air conditioning up and running, it was almost pleasant working up there.

"You want me to start opening these boxes of laminate?" his dad asked from across the room.

While laying the floor could be a one-person job, it would certainly be faster with an extra person. He counted himself lucky that his dad had taken the time away on a workday to help.

"That would be great. It'll keep us from slowing down whenever we get to the bottom of another box."

From the stairwell came the sound of footsteps on the treads. It was much easier to hear someone coming up now that he didn't have to keep the third-floor door closed to prevent the cool air from escaping.

The smile slipped from Saxon's face as he glanced across the room to see Cesar cresting the top of the stairs. He stood. "What are you doing here?"

"I promised I'd help you with the floor. Here I am."

Saxon hadn't told Cesar he'd planned on working on the floor that morning. He hadn't spoken to Cesar in the almost two weeks since he'd walked out Cesar's door. He hadn't known what else to say, so he hadn't said anything at all.

Cesar had sent texts, of course, and Saxon had let his calls roll to voicemail. He hadn't had the nerve to listen to any of them.

Why? Because you're afraid you might cave? Afraid you'll admit that every minute of every day is filled with what he said, what you said, and the ugly mess you both made of something good?

If it was *so* good, why did Cesar feel the need to do things on his own instead of talking to him like an adult?

Saxon didn't want to think about who ratted him out and texted Cesar to let him know he was working on the floors that morning, even though it had to be one of the kids. They probably figured if they got him and Cesar together, all would be forgiven, but that's where they were wrong. He'd deal with that matter later and remind them that his and Cesar's relationship was none of their business.

"Okaaay," Saxon allowed. "So, it's only *some* promises you break. Got it."

Saxon dropped to his knees, pulled one of the laminate strips out of the box beside him, and started laying the first row.

Behind him, Cesar said, "Could you give us a minute?"

"No, he can't." The question had been aimed at his dad. Didn't keep Saxon from answering. His voice rose an octave at the thought of being left alone with Cesar, even for a minute. He had floors to lay, and the last thing he needed was to think about another failed relationship.

"Fine." Cesar moved to the middle of the room. Saxon kept his head down and looked at Cesar upside down in the space between his arm and his side like a kid not wanting to be caught looking at something he shouldn't. "What do you want me to do first?"

Saxon closed his eyes and pressed his lips together until the urge to say, *Come over here and hug me,* passed. "You can clear the stuff out of that first room. Should be enough space on the landing if you lean the air mattress against the wall at the top of the stairs. I need all that out so I can lay the floors in there."

A cell phone went off, and Melvin answered it. When he ended the call, Saxon knew what his dad would say before he said it. Didn't make it any easier to hear. "That was Chris at the lot. A customer refuses to deal with him and won't leave until I talk to him."

"That's fine," Saxon flat-out lied. He wanted to say *Please don't leave me here alone with Cesar.* Luckily, he had better self-control than that. "I appreciate you coming."

Cesar and Melvin exchanged some sort of awkward handshake before Melvin left. Saxon shoved it out of his mind as he reached for another laminate strip.

By the time Saxon had reached the far wall with the first row of laminate and marked a piece of laminate for cutting, Cesar had finished emptying the room Saxon had been camping in since he'd returned to Stonewall. It wasn't the Ritz or even Cesar's comfy bed, but it wasn't a park bench on the shady side of town or a hook-up's place either, so Saxon couldn't complain.

He handed the laminate to Cesar to cut.

"You could have stayed in the guest room," Cesar said, his voice soft, and was that a little bit of guilt layered beneath it? "You didn't have to sleep on a fucking air mattress."

"I've slept on worse."

"That's not the point."

Saxon sat back on his heels. "What *is* the point?"

Cesar looked like he had a lot he wanted to say, and to be honest, Saxon didn't want to hear a word of it, no matter that he'd spent countless nights on that leaky air mattress wanting to hear so much from him.

Starting with an apology.

But not an apology that started off invalidating Saxon's feelings like the one Cesar had thrown out the night of their fight.

"Can we not do this?" Saxon asked. "I want to get these floors done."

"There's no furniture in here. Or any furniture waiting in boxes downstairs."

And if Saxon didn't want to talk about not sleeping in Cesar's guest room, he really didn't want to talk about the reason why he hadn't bought any furniture to finish out the third floor.

Saxon held out his hand. "Hand me that laminate back if you aren't going to cut it."

Cesar took the laminate to the makeshift cutting stand Melvin had made out of the empty boxes. "You don't have the money for the furniture, do you? Melvin hasn't paid you back."

What part of *can we not do this* did Cesar not understand? But if Saxon didn't answer, Cesar would never let it drop, and they'd never get the floor finished.

"It's barely been a week past when he said he'd get me the money." Saxon forced pure optimism into his voice. He still believed he'd get the money back. Mostly. "Sometimes, these things take longer to go through the banks than you expect. It's out of his hands."

Cesar cut the laminate to size, holding onto it when he handed it back, waiting until Saxon met his gaze. "I can spot you the money for furniture. You know, just until Melvin pays you back."

That last part cost Cesar to say because, from his tone, he didn't expect Saxon to ever see that money again.

And why the fuck Cesar's offer made Saxon's eyes tear up, he'd never know.

He turned to lay the strip of laminate before Cesar witnessed the waterworks. Cesar put a hand on Saxon's shoulder and squeezed, making the whole eyes watering situation worse.

Saxon's chest tightened. He might as well be breathing out of a straw.

He had laid part of the next row of laminate before the lump cleared out of his throat enough to speak. "The renovation has already taken months. A day or two more sleeping up here on an air mattress won't matter one way or the other."

"Yeah," Cesar said. "Sure."

By the fourth row, they developed a rhythm, and the work went by quickly. They only spoke enough to get the job done. Saxon had to bite his tongue the whole time, swallowing down his uncertainty. He'd made the loan to his father with his eyes wide open.

At least, he thought he had.

He'd known it was possible that he'd never see the money again. But he hadn't been willing to seriously consider that possibility. Because, you know, it was his *dad*. But as each day wore on and each day his dad said he'd have the money to him the next day, and he didn't, the more Saxon started feeling like he'd been played.

Or conned.

Maybe if you hadn't let your pride get the better of you, you would have considered the consequences of lending Melvin the money, and you would have realized it was a poor decision. Ten thousand dollars.

Ten.

Thousand.

Dollars.

If you'd put your pride aside, would you have given Melvin the money to prove to Cesar that you were right and he was wrong?

Fuck if he knew.

It was late afternoon when the alarm on his phone chimed, interrupting them as they started moving Saxon's belongings back into the finished bedroom.

"Hot date?" Cesar asked. He was joking, mostly.

"Hot date with a certain grumpy vet."

Cesar dropped his end of the air mattress. "Mango, okay?"

"He's fine. It's time for his last round of vaccinations."

Cesar hitched a thumb over his shoulder. "I guess I should go ahead and get out of here."

He didn't sound like he wanted to go anywhere. At least not without Saxon.

And there went Saxon's eyes, stinging again. And Cesar got all blurry. And Saxon's nose got all stuffy. And he couldn't hate the situation more.

"Oh, baby," Cesar whispered as he wrapped his arms around him.

Instead of stiffening, Saxon's body revolted and melted into Cesar's. Cesar held on to him, his steady heartbeat a calming metronome beneath Saxon's ear. When the snooze on Saxon's alarm sounded again, he silenced it. Cesar broke the embrace and pressed his forehead to Saxon's. "I don't like this. This isn't where we should be."

Saxon couldn't disagree. But he couldn't see a path back to where they once were. "I need to go."

Cesar wrapped an arm around Saxon's neck and kissed the side of his head. "I love you," he said before letting go.

"Yeah," Saxon squeaked out. That's why it fucking hurt so damn bad.

Saxon booked it down the stairs, grabbing Mango on the way, who let out a surprised meow. Saxon didn't wait for Cesar to follow him down the stairs before leaving. Cesar knew the way. He could show himself out.

SAXON HIT THE STEERING WHEEL AS MANGO MEOWED WITH indignant rage from the carrier on the passenger seat beside him. Whenever he drove, Saxon always put Mango in the carrier to cut down on the chance the kitten could cause an accident. Mango had yet to learn to appreciate Saxon's take on safety.

"We're getting closer." Saxon stuck his finger through the holes of the door. At the rate they were going, they might not get there until the clinic closed. They had the last appointment of the day, but they were cutting it close.

As much as Saxon loved California, sometimes he would give his left nut to be able to drive across town without having to worry about rush-hour traffic snarling the roads.

The light turned red again before Saxon made it more than a couple of car lengths. He pulled out his phone and called the clinic, letting them know he may be running late. The receptionist told him the doctor had an emergency and was running behind on appointments. Saxon may have to wait to be seen, but at least he didn't have to worry about the clinic closing before he got there.

Thirty minutes and a lot of cussing and meowing later, Saxon arrived at the vet clinic ten minutes after the official closing time.

"Sorry, sorry," he said as he stepped up to the reception desk. "Mango is here for his appointment."

The receptionist checked them in. "The doctor is with the appointment before yours. It might be a short wait if you want to have a seat."

"Sure. No problem."

Saxon turned to find a seat as the door to Kellon's rescue opened. "I thought I heard you out here. Everything okay?"

"Just getting his boosters."

"I've got the adoption paperwork right here if you want to go ahead and sign them."

"Oh, jeez, my bad. Sorry." Saxon picked up the carrier and hurried through the door as Kellon held it open.

"It's fine. I wasn't worried about you stealing the cat."

Saxon sat the carrier on the bench beside him, and Kellon bent to look at Mango. "Wow. He's gotten so big."

"He won't stop eating. Or growing."

Kellon laughed. "The kittens tend to do that."

From a folder Kellon had on top of a stack of empty crates, Kellon pulled out the adoption paperwork and handed Saxon the paper and a pen.

Saxon filled it out and handed it over as well as cash for the adoption fee.

"Thanks." Kellon took the paper, checking through the information. He pointed at the top of the sheet. "You can put Cesar's name here if you both want to be on the paperwork."

Saxon glanced down at Mango, sticking his fingers through the door again. Mango rubbed his face on his finger. "No. It's just me."

"Wait. What?" Kellon dropped onto the bench on the other side of Mango. "What's going on?"

"Cesar didn't tell you?"

"He didn't tell me anything. I was at his office last week discussing a case with Derek, and he basically ignored me. I thought he was in the middle of something and couldn't break away to catch up."

"We broke up." Saxon thought back to earlier that day and the *I love you* that spilled from Cesar's lips even though Saxon had packed up his things and left. "I think we did. It's complicated."

"What did he do?"

Saxon chuckled even though his wreck of a relationship wasn't a laughing matter. "Why do you think it's something he did?"

"History has a way of repeating itself."

Saxon raised a brow. "How so?"

Kellon's hand went to the back of his neck as if considering what he could tell Saxon without breaking a confidence.

Saxon didn't want to put him in the middle. "You don't have to say anything. It's okay."

"Let's just say Cesar has a bit of a savior complex. He tends to jump in and try to save the day when no one asks him to. Is that even close?"

"He definitely has boundary issues."

"If it helps, his actions come from the heart. He means well, especially when it's someone he cares about."

"I get that. But sometimes it's still too much." Saxon didn't quite know how to put it into words. He decided he needed to try, though. "I don't need a white knight to slay my dragons. I need someone who will stand by me and hand me a new sword each time one breaks."

"*Oof.*" A rush of air escaped Kellon's lungs, and his hand went to his chest. "That hits right here."

The receptionist stuck her head into the room. "Dr. Graves can see you now."

"Thank you." Saxon picked up the carrier.

"I'm not choosing sides here," Kellon said, "but maybe Cesar deserves a second chance."

Clearly, Kellon didn't have any of the details, and the words sliced Saxon's chest, the pain sharp as if Kellon had been the one wielding a sword. "That's the problem. He's already used up his second chance."

The crooked grimace on Kellon's face could have been pity, or maybe it was resignation. He'd obviously watched Cesar go through something similar before. And it hurt like hell that Cesar hadn't learned his lesson before now. Because as hurt, and angry, and betrayed as Saxon felt, a part of him wanted nothing more than to pull into Cesar's driveway with a car he still hadn't unpacked and try again.

But if he did, would anything change? What would happen the next time Cesar felt like Saxon suffered an injustice? It was bound to happen. And Saxon couldn't go through this again.

He said his goodbyes to Kellon as he headed for the open exam room on the other side of reception.

"Have a nice evening," the receptionist and another scrubs-clad person said as they left and locked the door behind them.

It was well past normal office hours now. The reception area was quiet, and the only sound came from dogs barking in the kennel in the back. Dr. Graves stood in the doorway and motioned Saxon inside.

"Sorry about the wait," the doctor said, "It's been a hectic day."

"No, I appreciate you staying to see us."

"You're a friend of Kellon's. Call me Gideon."

Saxon nodded. "Gideon, then."

Saxon closed the door and set Mango's carrier on the exam table. He pulled Mango out, and the doctor put the carrier on the floor.

"How's Mango been doing? Any problems I need to be aware of?"

Problems? Did catching Mango staring at Stonewall's front door multiple times a day as if waiting for Cesar to walk through the door warrant a problem that needed to be mentioned?

If there were a medication that could help Saxon get over Cesar, he'd be scarfing them like Tic-Tacs.

"No. He's been great."

Mango jumped on the doctor's shoulder, and it took the two of them to unhinge all of his claws and pull him off. Gideon started the exam while Saxon did his best to keep Mango from jumping on him again. Saxon learned he had subpar animal wrangling skills that would probably have gotten him fired if he'd been working there.

A knock came at the door, and when Gideon answered, Kellon opened it.

"Here, let me help."

Saxon let Kellon take over, and the doctor finished his exam.

"Something I can do for you?" Gideon asked, his smile brittle at the corners, and Saxon figured there would have been a lot more aggravation in his tone if Saxon hadn't been standing there.

Kellon tore his attention away from Mango and met the man's eyes. They maintained eye contact for so long that Saxon had to swallow his urge to clear his throat.

The doctor's eyes dropped to Kellon's mouth and flicked back up when he realized what he'd been doing. So it was like *that* between them, was it?

Saxon smothered his grin. And was it just him, or did the temperature in the room rise a degree or two?

Mango meowed, tired of being confined, breaking whatever was going on between the two of them. Gideon picked up the vaccinations on the counter behind him.

"Almost done," Kellon said to Mango, adjusting his hold. "Has everyone else gone home? I have a celebrity coming any minute to look at that litter of kittens I got in last week, and he'd prefer to fly in under the radar."

Mango's eyes widened, and he squirmed as he got the vaccinations. Kellon let Mango go as soon they were done. Mango made the two-foot leap into Saxon's arms with an eye on Kellon as if Mango had been the one betrayed. Saxon quickly stuffed him into the carrier before he got any other ideas.

"It's just us," Gideon said. "I let everyone go home."

"Great." Kellon's eyes raked up and down the doctor's body.

Gideon crossed his arms and raised a brow. "Anything else?"

"Um… yeah… no. Um… thanks."

Kellon hurried out the door like a scalded cat, and Saxon watched as Gideon watched him leave. Gideon's eyes locked on the last spot he'd seen Kellon, an appraising smile teasing his lips.

That time, Saxon cleared his throat, and Gideon frowned as if remembering Saxon was still there.

He reached behind him and opened the door to the treatment area. "Hang on. I'll get your bill."

Saxon managed to contain his smile. "Sure."

While Saxon waited, he heard a knock on the glass door. A few seconds later, Kellon's keys turned in the lock as he let the celebrity in. Saxon heard their murmured voices until they disappeared into the rescue. From Saxon's angle, he couldn't see the front door and hadn't wanted to stick his head into the hall to see who it was.

A few minutes later, Gideon returned with the bill. To make things easy, Saxon paid with cash. Gideon's attention drifted to the last spot he'd seen Kellon.

Interesting. Very, very, interesting.

"You know," Saxon said, "you could skip all the eye fucking and just go ahead and jump to the real thing."

Gideon stared at him for a second, and Saxon thought he'd have to look for another vet after going waaaay outside his lane.

Then Gideon grumbled and shook his head. "It's not that simple."

When Saxon just looked at him with raised brows that said *Sometimes it is that easy*, Gideon added, "Just because he might be fun to have in my bed doesn't mean he'll fit into my life."

Saxon grinned. "I didn't say you had to marry him. I said you should fuck him."

That got a rumbling, begrudging chuckle from Gideon, bringing pink to his cheeks. "Yeah… not going to happen."

"Pity," Saxon said.

Gideon changed the subject. Probably the absolute last thing Gideon wanted was to have this conversation with a client, especially a client trying to play matchmaker with their friend. "Kellon let you take Mango before he was neutered. You'll want to get that done in the next few months."

"I'll call tomorrow when your staff's in and set up a time."

"Thanks. That would make things easier. My computers are all shut down for the night. Here, let me unlock the door for you."

Saxon picked up Mango's carrier and followed Gideon to the exit. Gideon held the door open. On the other side of the threshold, Saxon stopped and turned back. He should have walked out the door and kept on going, but even if he and Cesar had a tenuous future, he couldn't sit by while Kellon and the Gideon circled each other with neither of them willing to make the first move. "Oh, and doc?"

"Yeah?"

"Um… I'm having a party at Stonewall House Saturday night. Stonewall House is—"

"I'm familiar with Stonewall House. Kellon told me all about it and what you're doing there. Pretty cool stuff."

Saxon grinned and couldn't help the swell of pride in his chest. As much as he hadn't opened Stonewall House for praise, he had to admit he didn't hate it. "We're celebrating the completion of the renovations. You should come."

When Gideon looked like he was searching for a polite way to back out of the invitation, Saxon said, "It's at seven. Kellon will be there."

Gideon just shook his head. "Good night, Saxon."

27

———

It was Friday afternoon, and Derek knocked on the door jamb of Cesar's office. And because Cesar thought he knew exactly why Derek stood there, he didn't look up. "I'm right in the middle of something. Can it wait until Monday?"

"I don't know," Derek said. "Do you think you'll have pulled your head out of your ass by then?"

Cesar grunted as if Derek's kick in the ass had been physical instead of mental. He glanced up, still pretending he was busy even though he'd been staring at the blank Google page for an hour. "Go away."

There. Cesar couldn't be any clearer than that. Talking to Derek about his relationship with Saxon was off the table. He'd known it had been a mistake telling Derek he thought they'd broken up, and he'd been right. Derek had been trying to have this conversation ever since.

Cesar not having the guts to call or text Saxon and ask if he'd called things off for good, said a lot. He was afraid if he pushed for an answer, that answer would be a resounding *yes*.

He couldn't face that possibility and had hoped that by giving

Saxon time, they'd have an opportunity to talk later and iron things out.

That he'd be able to apologize *again*.

Hell, he would apologize daily—for the rest of his life—if he thought it would help.

Derek ignored him and plopped in the chair across from Cesar's desk. Cesar leaned back. Derek held that level, steady gaze on him. The one that made people talk to him when they didn't want to.

Cesar didn't know how Derek did it, and it pissed him off that he knew what Derek was doing, and he still couldn't stop himself from talking. "It has taken everything I have to not drive down to Melvin's lot and find out where the hell Saxon's money is."

"But you haven't."

Cesar couldn't tell if that was a question or a statement. "No. I haven't."

Derek nodded. "I suppose that's growth. The Cesar I knew a few weeks ago would have done it anyway even if it wasn't what Saxon wanted."

"See? I can change."

"I'm not the one you have to convince."

"I still think that putting a little pressure on Melvin might give him the impetus he needs to stop stressing out his kid and give him his money back. I can't imagine what Saxon is going through. He has to be wondering if he'll ever see that money again. How does their relationship recover from that? They had only recently reconnected, and Saxon had this glow about him every time he talked about his dad, and now..."

Cesar didn't know how to finish that sentence, so he didn't. He appreciated that Derek didn't jump right in and try to fix it, that he let Cesar vent and figure his shit out. No doubt Derek would give him advice or help if Cesar asked, but Cesar hadn't.

Just like Cesar should have been there for Saxon without

taking any decisions out of his hands without first asking if he even wanted help.

Motherfucker.

Cesar had screwed up. Royally.

The revelation must have shown on Cesar's face because when he glanced up at Derek, his friend had the smuggest fucking smile.

"Knock, knock," came Kellon's voice from the reception. Cesar had been so engrossed in his own mess that he hadn't heard the door open.

Derek called out, "We're in Cesar's office."

A few moments later, Kellon turned the corner with a smile. It fell once he laid his eyes on Cesar. "*Dude*, you look like roadkill."

Cesar scrubbed his hands through his hair, but he doubted that it improved his appearance. Not only might he look like roadkill, he felt like it. "What are you doing here, and why are you so dressed up? You going to the clubs?"

Kellon laughed and handed Derek the file in his hand. "Here's that paperwork on the Blacksmith case you needed. After you talk to them, you can see if they still want to go to the police and file for that restraining order."

Derek took the file. "Thanks."

Turning his attention to Cesar, Kellon said, "And I'm too old for the club scene. I'm headed to the party at Stonewall House."

"Party? What party?" It was all Cesar could do to keep his voice casual. By the way, Kellon tilted his head, he hadn't pulled it off.

"You and Saxon still aren't talking?"

"You told me I looked like roadkill. What do you think?"

Cesar expected a quick quip, but Kellon took a second before he said, "I think you should go to the party. I think you need to talk to him."

"What if he doesn't want to talk to me?"

Kellon glanced at Derek as if expecting him to add his opinion.

"Don't look at me," Derek said, "I've been trying to get him to talk to Saxon all week. I'm tired of him moping around all day every day."

"I'm not moping." Cesar ignored that maddening brow of Derek's that called his statement into question. "I was there on Monday. I helped him finish laying the floor. Trust me. He didn't even want me there. I was lucky that he needed the help, or I think he would have kicked me out as soon as I arrived. I don't want to show up there when he's trying to celebrate and make everything worse."

"I don't think you can make it worse," Derek said.

Kellon fist bumped Derek. "Agreed."

"I'm not going."

Kellon raised his hands and started backing out of the room. "Call me if you change your mind. In the meantime, I have a party to get to. See you boys later."

Derek stood to leave as well. He'd have asked Derek to go with him to the party as moral support, only he didn't want more witnesses there to watch Saxon humiliate him when he threw him out.

"Do you want my advice?" Derek asked. By the disgruntled look on his face, Derek expected Cesar to shoot him down.

Cesar took a moment to consider the question. Whatever the hell Cesar thought he was doing wasn't working. Maybe it was time to take the advice of friends. "What?"

"Go to the party. The worse that can happen is Saxon won't want to talk to you and ask you to leave. But maybe he won't. Maybe he'll listen."

Shaking his head, Cesar said, "I don't even know what to say. What to do."

Derek gave him one of those smiles parents give their kids

when they're proud of them. Cesar wasn't sure he deserved that. It could all blow up in his face. "That's easy. Grovel."

SAXON ARRIVED AT STONEWALL HOUSE FRIDAY EVENING WITH about an hour to spare before guests would start arriving, his arms weighed down with paper goods and odds and ends for the party.

The event had turned into a potluck party since money was tight, but no one seemed to care that they needed to bring something, and Saxon tried to put out of his mind the reason he couldn't afford another simple party.

He also had to stomp down on the self-recriminations.

What was done was done. He'd have to live with the decisions he made. Maybe learning not to trust so easily was worth the ten-thousand-dollar price tag.

With his hands full, he nudged the door open with his foot. All his kids were sitting in the den. His smile spread across his face. "Look at all of you together." He dropped the bags at his feet and grabbed for the phone in his front pocket. "Don't move. I want to get a picture."

He glanced at them again. His smile faded as he took in their serious faces one by one. His stomach knotted. Did something happen to one of them? He counted heads. Everyone was there.

His stomach settled out until Addi pushed his office chair toward him. "What's this?"

"An intervention," Phoenix said as he caught the rolling chair and sat, "because you've done lost your mind."

This ought to be good. "I don't know what you're talking about."

You don't think they're that unobservant, do you?

Mango jumped off Kai's shoulder and into Saxon's lap. At least now, Mango could jump up instead of clawing his way up.

Saxon mindlessly scratched under Mango's chin. The kitten started a loud, throaty purr that even with six sets of eyes assessing Saxon, his heart rate settled into a lower gear.

"You've been moping," James said, flipping his long bangs out of his eyes, "and you've hardly smiled for over two weeks."

"You trudge around every day as if you're going to a funeral," Sophia added from the corner of the couch across from him."

"I don't *trudge*," Saxon said.

Sophia abandoned her seat and mimicked how he walked, slumping her shoulders and dangling dead arms at her sides. She combined the posture with heavy foot stomps and added a few sad sighs for dramatic effect.

Everyone laughed, and Saxon slapped a hand over his eyes and peeked through his fingers. He did *not* walk like that. Mostly.

Sophia looked at Oliver after sitting down as if the group had a previously agreed-upon order to list their grievances.

Oliver picked up the cue and spoke next. "And usually, you're the optimistic one we can go to with our problems."

Saxon's heart did a pirouette in his chest, making breathing hard. "You can always come to me."

"Yeah, well…" Kai stared at the floor, and everyone waited him out. He didn't like to speak up in a crowd, preferring to stay out of the limelight, but not tonight. "We don't want to bring you our problems when you're dealing with your own."

"Badly," Addi added as if that extra information was helpful.

It wasn't.

Had they needed him, and he hadn't been there for them? How had he not seen how his problems affected everyone in the house?

"Is this true?" He glanced from person to person. They all had similar versions of a sympathetic smile on their lips, but they all nodded in turn.

Fuck. Saxon blew out a breath. "I'm sorry if I've let you all down. I thought I had my personal stuff under control and had kept it from affecting you. Clearly, I was wrong. I'll do better."

"You can try… or… you could get back together with Cesar," Addi said. "I'm sure that would help."

James shifted on the couch, tucking his legs beneath him. "Besides, we miss having him around."

A lump immediately clogged Saxon's throat, and he had to swallow a few times to reduce it to a manageable size. "It's not that easy."

"He's a good man," Oliver said.

"I never said he wasn't." If these kids were trying to make him cry, they were about two seconds away from accomplishing their goal. He gave Mango extra scrunches while he collected himself. "I'm not going to get into all the details, but he breached my trust, and I'm not sure we can come back from that."

"Bullshit." Sophia cringed at her outburst. "Respectfully."

That got a round of chuckles, and even Saxon couldn't stop a hint of a smile.

"Did he mean to?" James asked.

Addi couldn't keep from speaking their mind. "Yeah, like was he *trying* to hurt you?"

"Well… no. He was trying to protect me." The words came out of Saxon's mouth without thought, and his gaze swept over the group. They looked as stunned as they looked unimpressed.

"I can see why that would be disqualifying," Kai said. Saxon would need a sharp putty knife to scrape off the layers of sarcasm, and Kai's epic eye roll earned him a fist bump from Phoenix. "Yeah, I hate it when people close to me don't want to see me get hurt."

Saxon shook his head. They didn't get it…

Or maybe… they did.

He glanced at his watch. He didn't want to drag their intervention out any longer than necessary. People would arrive soon, and they needed to finish setting up the tables in the backyard and start the fire in the grill.

"If I promise to talk to Cesar, will that get the lot of you off my back?"

There came a round of *yeses* and *definitelies,* and at least one muttered *About damn time,* but he couldn't pinpoint who said it.

"Okay then." Saxon stood, and Mango jumped to the floor and ran up the stairs. For what, Saxon had no clue. "As hard as it was to hear all that, I appreciate you caring enough to confront me." His voice thickened, and he had to clear it to speak. "You all are the best."

Phoenix wiped tears from her eyes, her mascara already starting to smear. She'd be mad about that, but she pulled him in for a hug. "We're in this together, right?"

"Right," a chorus of voices rang out, and one, *Damn straight.*

Kia muttered, but it came out loud enough for everyone to hear. "That's the only thing *straight* about any of this."

Laughs rolled around the room, and Saxon swiped at his eyes. He loved watching Kai blossom into his own. He was a shy kid around people he didn't know well, but he was a different person around his housemates.

Phoenix stepped back, grumbling about having to fix her makeup, and disappeared upstairs. One by one, the rest hugged Saxon before heading to the backyard to finish getting ready until only Kai stood there awkwardly as if not knowing if he was expected to hug Saxon like the others.

"You don't have to hug me," Saxon said, not wanting to put Kai on the spot. He held out a fist for a bump, but Kai left him hanging.

"I could hug you," Kai said.

Saxon pulled him tight to his chest and whispered, "Thanks for being here for me."

Kai didn't immediately let Saxon go the way he thought Kai

would, and when Kai finally broke away, his eyes swam with tears. "You were here for me."

Kai followed the others outside. Saxon took a few moments to collect himself before heading out there.

Not long after, almost everyone who'd been invited to the party had arrived. Like the last party, they had music playing on the outdoor speakers and plenty of food on the table. Truman had arrived shortly after Grant, Sebastian, and Tavi. He immediately took over the grilling duties, which was just as well because, as forgetful as Saxon had been since the breakup, he'd likely burn everything.

He picked at his hamburger patty, having peeled off the bun. He wasn't that hungry, but he had to eat something, and at least the burger would give him some much-needed protein.

A laugh caught his attention, and he scanned the backyard and found Grant and Sebastian talking to Tavi and Kai. He couldn't remember Kai smiling so much or looking so relaxed. Day by day, he became less of the rebellious teen and more of the caring, thoughtful man he would one day grow to be. Saxon loved being a small part of that.

In a grassy area far from the grill, Phoenix sat on James's shoulders while Addi sat on Oliver's, both with pool noodles in their hands while they jousted. Sophia refereed and kept score.

This is what he'd wanted so desperately to build. A place for people who had no one and nowhere to belong. A community. A home. A family.

And he'd done it.

But not alone.

That Cesar had been a part of that. He deserved to celebrate with the rest of them.

He pulled his phone out of his pocket to tell Cesar and tell him that, then dropped it back into his pocket without calling. When would he stop taking out his phone to share something with Cesar, only to realize that Cesar was probably the last person who wanted to hear from him?

Sure Cesar had helped out with the flooring at the beginning of the week, but he'd shown up out of obligation, nothing else.

Kellon walked over with a beer and an easy smile on his face. "You should be really proud of what you've done here."

Saxon ducked his head, and the heat rushed up to his cheeks. He didn't know how to take compliments graciously, and after an awkward beat, he decided to own it. "Thanks. I am."

Kellon gestured to the phone in Saxon's pocket. "You going to invite Cesar?"

"I don't think he'd want to be here."

"I don't know about that," Kellon said. "He put hours of hot, sweaty work into the renovations. Why wouldn't he want to be here?"

Barely, Saxon managed to rein in the eye roll. "I'm the last person he wants to see."

"That's not what Cesar said." Kellon had an expression on his face that Saxon couldn't quite read, and he couldn't tell if Kellon was telling the truth or making shit up.

"When did you see Cesar?"

Kellon's casual shrug seemed calculated along with his nonchalance. "I stopped by his office earlier this evening. He looks like you."

Like me? "What do you mean?"

"I mean, he looks like shit. I mean, he looks like a man who fucked up, knows he fucked up, but hasn't a clue how to fix it or if it's even fixable."

Stuffing his hands deep into his pockets because Saxon didn't quite know what to do with them, he said, "Oh."

"Oh?" Kellon asked. "That's all you've got? *Jesus Christ.* You two are perfect for each other."

"I don't know what else to say." That he missed Cesar and might have made the biggest mistake of his life packing up his things and moving back into Stonewall House? If that sit-down the kids had with him before the party was any indication, they thought so, too.

Since his mother had died, he hadn't had a real home. Not until he'd inadvertently moved in with Cesar.

The sliders at the back of the house slid open, and Saxon glanced up, his heart in his throat as if he'd actually expected Cesar to step over the threshold. Which was impossible. Saxon had never told him about the party.

Kellon's gaze followed Saxon's to the man with the thick beard and the permanent furrow between his brows.

"Oh, looky." Saxon nudged Kellon even though Kellon was already staring at the man. "It's Grumpy McGrump-face."

Kellon chuckled, then the smile fell when the good doctor locked eyes with Kellon. Instead of coming over to say hello, he broke eye contact and bee-lined for the food. Maybe he was really hungry. Saving furry lives would undoubtedly do that to a person.

"What is he doing here?" Kellon asked, his voice lacking its usual confidence.

"I invited him. He likes your ass."

Kellon swung around and burst into laughter. "And how would you know that?"

Saxon grinned. "Because he said so, and he couldn't stop looking at it when you left the exam room the other day."

"Oh, yeah?"

"Yeah."

Kellon dropped his gaze to the ground and kicked at the dandelion that dared to grow in the middle of the grass that Kai was quickly transforming into a beautiful lawn. "Doesn't matter. It would never work between us."

"Who says it has to work forever? Maybe it only needs to work for one night?"

The heat ran up Kellon's cheeks. Gideon glanced over, his

brow raised as if curious as to what the hell they'd been talking about. But since Saxon and Kellon were looking directly at him when he'd turned, he probably had a good idea.

"Go," Saxon said. "They don't come much dreamier than that."

Unless it's Cesar.

"Only if you promise me you'll call Cesar."

"Okay, okay. Now go so that I can make that call."

Kellon patted Saxon on the shoulder and walked away, on a direct path to intercept Gideon.

Saxon turned his back to the others to give himself a modicum of privacy and took out his cell phone. Mentally, he blocked out the noise, the lively conversation, the laughs, the music and typed into the message box.

Saxon: Party. My place. You should be here.

His thumb hovered over the send button before erasing it and replacing his previous message with *There's a party at Stonewall. You belong here. Please come.*

Behind him, he vaguely became aware that the chatter had stopped, but he was too focused on the knots in his belly as he hurried to send the message before he could tack on an ill-advised *I miss you.*

28

—————

AS SOON AS CESAR OPENED THE SLIDING DOORS INTO THE backyard, he knew it would get awkward with a yard full of witnesses. He didn't care. He didn't even blush when everyone stopped talking and stared at him.

Not that they could see him blush with the helmet's visor covering his face.

He couldn't see much through the rectangular eye holes of the visor. He found Kellon first. He was easy to spot with his back against the fence, the doctor caging him in with one arm on the wood boards by his face.

Kellon jerked his head. Cesar followed the direction and found Saxon standing alone near one corner of the yard, his back to everybody. Cesar passed a few people with their mouths dropped open. Others stifled their laughter.

He still didn't care.

He was there for one reason and one reason alone.

Saxon.

Cesar's phone chimed in the pocket of his jeans. It was the chime he'd set weeks ago reserved for Saxon. He would have reached for it, however, encased in full-body armor, his phone wasn't exactly accessible.

Saxon spun on his heel as soon as he heard the chime. His hand flew to his mouth, but the gasp slipped through before he could stop it.

"What are you doing here?" Saxon looked him up and down. "And why are you wearing that armor?"

Cesar pushed up the visor blocking his vision. It was getting stuffy inside the metal, and he wanted to see Saxon's face.

"First off..." Cesar glanced around, and, yep, everyone was watching. Heat pricked at the back of his neck. He ignored it. "I came here to grovel. And secondly..."

Cesar took Saxon's arm and led him farther out of earshot. He wasn't afraid of making a fool of himself. If he had been, he never would have shown up dressed as he did.

But this... what he wanted to say was for Saxon and Saxon only.

Cesar handed Saxon the white carnation he'd taped to his chest since there wasn't such a thing as a white suit of armor. At least not one he could get his hands on at the last minute. He was lucky that his cosplay friend had been home when he'd gotten his bright idea after the conversation he had with Kellon after leaving work.

He took Saxon's hands in his and got down on one knee because that was the only way he knew how to grovel. The long plastic sword he had tied to his waist with a string got in the way, and Cesar had to yank it free to get down on his knee.

His friend had lent his metal sword to another friend, so Cesar had settled for his friend's son's play sword. It had a yellow grip, a brilliant blue guard, and a bright red blade. It wasn't ideal, but it worked.

When he finally settled on one knee with the sword balanced across it, he retook Saxon's hand. "A little bird told me you don't need a white knight to fight your battles. You need someone beside you to hand you a sword when yours breaks."

Cesar laid the sword in Saxon's hands. "Here is that sword. I want to be the man who hands it to you time and time again."

Saxon gulped, and his eyes swam with tears as he stared at the dark sky. Cesar held his breath, and while they had stepped away from the crowd, it seemed as if they held their collective breaths as well.

Cesar stood, and Saxon leveled the most adoring gaze at him. He drank it in, drawing on it to give him the strength to say what he had to.

"Forgive me. Please. I can't promise to never fuck up again, but I can promise to be the one who has your back or stands beside you no matter the fight."

A sob ripped from the back of Saxon's throat. He wrapped his arms around Cesar's neck and pressed a salty kiss to his lips. It was awkward in the suit of armor, and when Cesar lowered his head to take the kiss deeper, the visor fell closed.

Carefully, Saxon helped him remove the helmet, but the suit's chest plate kept them from getting close enough. "Is that a yes?" Cesar asked. "You forgive me?"

"Y-yes. I forgive you."

A round of applause went up, and they both laughed. Cesar waved them off. With the drama over, everyone returned to what they were doing before Cesar had interrupted.

"Help me out of this," Cesar said, "I need you closer."

Saxon scrambled to undo all the buckles and remove the pieces one by one. It took a few minutes. It might have been faster if Saxon's hands hadn't been shaking.

Finally, Cesar stepped out of the last leg, laid it on the grass beside him, and pulled Saxon into his arms. Saxon held on tight, but Cesar held on tighter.

He'd been so close to losing him. He never wanted to go

through that again. Maybe one day, he'd learn not to be a dumbass.

Cesar buried his face in Saxon's neck, taking in his scent and stealing every bit of warmth he could. Saxon broke the embrace and took a half step back. Cesar wiped at the moisture on his cheeks and thumbed a couple of drops off Saxon's.

"You were right," Saxon said.

Really? Cesar locked his fingers behind Saxon's waist. If he had his way, he'd never let Saxon go again. "Right about what?"

"My father. He still hasn't repaid me. I guess you can say you told me so now."

Cesar pressed a kiss to Saxon's lips. He'd missed those lips and the pleasure they brought both of them. He rested his forehead on Saxon's. "I never wanted to be right. I'm sorry, if that helps. I wish he'd been the man you'd wanted him to be."

Saxon blew out a breath. "I can't believe I gave him money."

Cesar straightened so he could see Saxon's face. "Why did you do it then? Was it a test?"

"You mean like to see if I could trust him?"

Cesar shrugged. "Yeah, I guess."

Saxon's eyes dropped as he considered Cesar's question. Finally, he glanced up. "Yes. No. I mean, I never thought of it like that, but maybe? Not consciously, though. As much as I need that money, it's not *about* the money. But I'm not going to lie. It's put me in a bind."

"If you need mon—"

Saxon held a finger to Cesar's lips. "No. But thank you for the offer."

"If you won't take my money, would you allow me to go with you to confront your father to see if we can get your money back?"

Saxon thought about that before kissing Cesar again. Cesar wanted to deepen it, but that kiss wasn't about that. "I think I'd like that."

Stepping back, Cesar glanced at his watch. "The lot is open late on Friday nights. If we hurry, we can—"

Saxon caught Cesar's arm before he could leave. "Not tonight. Tonight we celebrate. Are you hungry?"

Cesar's stomach growled at the mention of food. He hadn't had an appetite since Saxon had packed up and walked out his door. The extra notch in his belt corroborated that.

They joined everyone around the food table. They both ate until Cesar thought they'd explode. Looks like he hadn't been the only one unable to eat.

They laughed and joked, and everyone seemed to have a good time. Even the grumpy doctor. The crevasse between his brows didn't seem as deep, and he cracked a sly smile or two. Mostly at something Kellon said.

The moon rose high in the sky, and the guests began leaving one by one until only the kids and Truman remained. The kids started putting away the leftover food, taking it into the house, and loading it into the refrigerator. A ton of food remained, but with all the hungry mouths in the house, Cesar doubted it would last more than a few days.

Saxon walked over to where Truman was scrubbing the grill. "Stop." Saxon took the scrubber away from him and closed the lid. "Go home. You don't have to cook *and* clean."

"I don't mind."

Saxon took him by the arm and led him toward the door. "Go. I know the shop opens early on Saturdays. Thanks so much for coming and for cooking."

Truman let Saxon pull him into a hug even though Truman struck Cesar as more of the fist bump type guy.

And to prove that, Kai came over and bumped Truman's fist. "See you in the morning?"

"Don't be late, or you'll be fired."

Kai laughed. "Keep telling yourself that. No one can mop a floor like I can."

To Cesar and Saxon, Truman said, "He's not wrong."

They both saw Truman out and returned to the backyard. Saxon glanced around. "Did you see where Kellon and Doctor Dreamy went?"

Cesar growled, and Saxon laughed.

"I have no clue where they are," Cesar said. "They probably snuck out when no one was looking."

"Together?" Saxon asked, dropping his voice even though no one was around to hear.

Snugging Saxon against him, Cesar said, "They were eye-fucking each other over the apple pie."

"Speaking of fucking…" The way Saxon grabbed Cesar's hand as if they needed to be somewhere else five minutes ago made Cesar's dick fill and begin to strain against the front of his jeans. Not that it had taken much. He'd been sporting a semi since Saxon came up behind him as he scooped their ice cream and pressed his hard-on to Cesar's ass.

"Where are you taking me?"

"Shhhh." Saxon dragged him toward the far side of the house.

It wasn't Saxon's bed, but it would at least give them a few private moments out of sight of the kids for the first time in way too long. That side of the house had a security light, but the old, yellowed plastic housing blocked so much light it barely reached the ground.

Plus, the fence was high, and the neighbors didn't have a window overlooking that side. It wouldn't be private, but it would do… for now.

Saxon and Cesar rounded the corner and heard a muffled *fuuuck* and a hollow sound as if something had hit the house's side. Saxon drew up short. The dim light couldn't hide the wide grin on his face.

Cesar squinted and saw the outline of a man standing behind the newly installed air conditioning unit, visible from the waist up, leaning against the house, his head thrown back.

"Oops," Saxon said, his voice carrying in the night now that the guests were gone and the music was off.

The head turned toward them, and they saw the whites of the man's eyes. "Oh, shit," the man—no. *Doctor Dreamy*—said.

Before Cesar could pull Saxon away, a head popped up from behind the air conditioner and snickered. Kellon wiped the side of his mouth with the back of his hand and waved as the doctor stuffed himself into his pants.

"I told you this was a bad idea," the doctor said as Kellon pulled the man further into the shadows.

Right before they heard the clank of the gate latch, they overheard Kellon say, "It wasn't a bad idea. It was the best idea, and..."

Kellon's voice drifted off, and the heavy spring on the gate slammed it closed behind them. Cesar chuckled and tugged Saxon against him. His thigh went between Saxon's legs and snugged against Saxon's hard cock.

Saxon hissed in a breath, and Cesar drew him into a kiss. A deep one this time. One with tongue and tenderness, groans and forgiveness.

Both of their breaths sawed in and out of their chests by the time they broke apart. Saxon tipped his head toward the spot Kellon and the doctor had vacated. "We could—"

"Nope." Cesar reached down and squeezed Saxon's ass. "What I want to do to you we can't do behind the air conditioning unit."

"Oh, yeah?" Saxon had that sexy, saucy tone in his voice that Cesar had always found addictively seductive. "Where would you suggest?"

"My bed, for starters. We can move on to the shower after that. Maybe the couch. The counter is never a bad option."

Instead of answering, Saxon gripped Cesar's wrist and marched him toward the back door.

"Where are you two going?" Addi asked as they tied up one of the garbage bags.

"Home," Saxon said. "Leave the rest. We'll finish cleaning up in the morning."

Cesar cleared his throat, and Saxon glanced back at him. "How about late afternoon?"

Addi laughed. "Don't worry about it. We've got this."

The smile on Saxon's face nearly made the backs of Cesar's eyes sting again. It was a mixture of appreciation and gratitude, and maybe a little bit of proud papa thrown in there.

"Goodnight," Cesar said as he guided Saxon into the house.

They waved at Kai, James, and Oliver, who were already digging into the ice cream again. Phoenix came down the stairs with Mango in her arms. She took in their hurried pace and covered Mango's ears with her hand. "We'll keep him here tonight. We wouldn't want him scarred for life."

Saxon rolled his eyes but wrapped her in a one-arm hug, careful not to squish the cat. "Thank you."

Phoenix fist-bumped Cesar as he passed, and they were out the door and in Cesar's car without looking back.

Cesar started the engine and glanced at Saxon in the seat beside him. He must have had a funny look because Saxon said, "What?"

"I..." Why did his throat always revolt when he needed his voice the most? He cleared his throat, but it sounded like gravel crunching. "When I showed up here tonight, I never thought... I mean, I had hoped, but...*fuck.*"

Cesar wrapped his hand around the back of Saxon's neck and crushed his lips against Saxon's. All heart and no finesse. "I never imagined you'd take me back."

"I missed you." The pain in Saxon's voice nearly ripped Cesar in two. He'd done that. He'd caused that pain.

But never again.

"Jesus, Sax." Cesar rubbed his nose along Saxon's as they breathed the same heated air. "I love you so fucking much."

Saxon sniffed and managed a watery, "Love you, too."

Straightening in his seat, Saxon clicked his seatbelt into place. "Now hurry up and take me home."

CESAR DRAGGED SAXON INTO HIS HOUSE, KICKED THE DOOR CLOSED with his foot, and slammed Saxon against the wall, not hard enough to hurt, hard enough to get his attention.

Bring it on.

Cesar's hands linked with Saxon's and hit the wall above Saxon's head, and a soft grunt escaped him. Cesar's eyes darkened, and his nostrils flared.

Fuck. He couldn't wait to have Cesar buried so deep in his ass that he couldn't tell one body from the next.

While Saxon loved Cesar's sweet nature, to say he didn't find this aggressive, possessive side of him intoxicating would be the lie to end all lies. Cesar slipped his thigh between Saxon's legs, and Saxon rutted against it as Cesar's hard cock pressed into his hip.

Cesar's mouth crashed down over Saxon's, their tongues dueling—a match Saxon had no intention of winning. He wanted Cesar to take him, claim him, make him his.

Cesar's groan came from deep within his chest, and he broke apart as if it were the last thing he wanted to do.

"Don't stop." Saxon's breaths came in short, rasping gasps like Cesar's. When Cesar curled Saxon's hands into his chest and touched his forehead to Saxon's, his nerves pinged with a familiar panic.

Had Cesar changed his mind?

Was something wrong?

Saxon's erratic heartbeat took a tumble and stalled out in his chest, and his diaphragm refused to function.

"What? What's wrong?" Stars floated in Saxon's peripheral

vision, but with the tightness banding his chest, he couldn't take a much-needed breath.

"Nothing's wrong." Cesar kissed Saxon's lips, so tender, so full of love that Saxon's heart had to grow three sizes to accommodate it. His breath drew in, and the stars vanished.

Shit. What else could they do? *Think.*

"D-do you not want to do this? I mean, if you don't, that's okay. I mean, I get it. We just made up. I don't expect… you know… We could sit on the couch and cuddle or—or—or—"

Thank fuck, Cesar shut him up with another one of his tender-ass kisses that sucked the thoughts out of his head. The type of kiss that fed his soul and chased out all the darkness until there was nothing but light. It was a great place to be, and Saxon never wanted to leave.

Cesar traced a finger along Saxon's cheek and continued down the slope of his neck, over his collarbone, until his finger snagged on the top button of Saxon's dress shirt. He kissed the tender spot under Saxon's jaw that had Saxon reaching for Cesar's belt.

"I *want*," Cesar said, doing nothing to stop Saxon from undoing his belt, unfastening his pants, and sliding down the zipper. "But I don't want this over quickly. I want it to last. I want you to know, to *feel*, and never doubt how much I love you."

Saxon swallowed hard, his hands going to Cesar's hips and pulling him in tight. "I never doubted for a minute you didn't love me."

Taking a step back, Cesar held onto Saxon's hands and walked backward, guiding him toward the bedroom. On the way, Saxon saw the pile of empty beer bottles and fast-food containers on the coffee table, the stack of dishes in the sink, the explosion of dirty laundry on the floor and the back of the couch, the refrigerator door standing open for some inexplicable reason.

In the bedroom, Cesar's sheets and comforter lay in a tangle at the foot of his bed as if he'd tossed and turned and tumbled in fitful sleep.

"Oh, sorry. Hang on," Cesar said as soon as he saw the bed. He went to straighten all the bedding, and Saxon stopped him with a hand on Cesar's wrist.

Seeing the visible toll their separation had cost Cesar made it challenging to talk. "It-it's fine. I don't care if the bed is messy as long as you're in it with me."

Cesar grinned. *Jesus.* Saxon had missed the way that smile filled him with the simplest joy. Saxon flopped on the bed, taking Cesar with him. They landed in a tangle of arms and legs and other body parts. Saxon would have a bruise where Cesar's elbow landed in his ribs. A problem for future Saxon to deal with.

Cesar struggled to balance on one forearm and unbutton Saxon's shirt one-handed. "Maybe we should have ditched the clothes first."

Saxon kissed him on the end of his nose. "Brilliant plan."

They scrambled out of bed and stripped faster than Saxon could say *Fuck me already*. They laid down together, Saxon on his back and Cesar straddling his hips. Their cocks aligned, and warm precum dribbled onto Saxon's abdomen.

He reached down, ran a finger through their mixed mess, and sucked his finger clean. "We taste good together."

Cesar groaned and bent down for a kiss, swiping his tongue through Saxon's mouth to get a taste. Before Saxon could take the kiss deeper, Cesar broke it and started working his way down Saxon's body.

The light but masterful kisses were unlike anything Saxon had experienced before. Don't get him wrong, the sex between them had always been explosive, but it had never moved Saxon the way Cesar's kisses did now. There was an adoration there.

A reverence.

The backs of his eyes stung, but he blinked the tears away, not wanting to miss a second of watching Cesar worship his body.

There were no other words to describe it.

Saxon raked his fingers through Cesar's hair and cupped the back of his head, encouraging him as he sucked and licked his way down Saxon's body. He'd missed Cesar's mouth on him. More than that, he'd missed the way Cesar made him feel like he was Cesar's number one.

Cesar sank to the level of Saxon's belly button, his tongue swirling in the sprawling hair surrounding it before continuing his exploration.

"I need your mouth on me," Saxon managed.

Cesar chuckled and nipped at the crease of Saxon's thigh. "My mouth *is* on you."

"You damn well know what I mean."

"*Mmmm...*" Cesar hummed. "I suppose I do. You have to be patient. You get grumpy when you're desperate."

"I'm out of pa—" Saxon nearly swallowed his tongue when Cesar went down on him, taking his aching cock to the back of his warm, wet mouth. "*Mmpf.*"

Cesar chuckled as best he could with his mouth and throat stuffed full. Working him over the way Cesar knew he liked it best, Saxon lost all ability to think, and words became a jumble of indiscriminate letters in his head. He couldn't even be sure they were the English alphabet. Could have been Sanskrit for all he knew.

Cesar cupped Saxon's heavy balls and must have felt them draw up with Saxon's impending orgasm because Cesar pulled off and wiped the corners of his mouth. "You're not getting off that easy."

Motherfucker. He'd been so close. So—

Cesar leaned across him, and he heard Cesar's bedside drawer opening, and the *snick* of the lube lid opening mollified him for a second. He'd give up coming with Cesar's mouth around his dick for having Cesar fuck him into the mattress.

Sitting back on his heels, Cesar dribbled the lube into his

palm and spread it over his fingers. Saxon folded his hands behind his head to watch the show. "You're so fucking sexy."

As if to prove the point, Saxon's dick hardened even more and nearly stood straight out from his body. Cesar grinned as he covered his cock with the lube and moved to slick up Saxon's hole. "You should see yourself from this angle. I'll never get tired of seeing you splayed out for me."

Saxon groaned. "Hurry up already."

Cesar readjusted and settled between Saxon's legs. Saxon brought his knees to his chest, and Cesar couldn't help diving in for a quick taste. Saxon's head fell back, pushing against Cesar's probing tongue.

"As much as I love your mouth *on* me. I want your cock *in* me."

Cesar nipped at one of Saxon's ass cheeks and straightened, riding his slick finger along Saxon's crease and easing one finger inside to open him up. Saxon didn't have time for that. Cesar may have wanted to slow things down, but Saxon couldn't wait.

He batted at Cesar's hand. "I don't need that. Just go slow."

"You don't know what you're asking." Saxon raised a brow, and Cesar added, "About the going slow part."

Even as Cesar said that, Saxon reached down and lined Cesar up. Cesar dropped down on his hands, nipping and sucking Saxon's bottom lip. "Let me know if I hurt—"

Saxon flexed his hips, forcing Cesar past the tight ring of muscle. Cesar's head dropped between his shoulders and muttered a string of sexy, strangled curses that brought a smile to Saxon's lips. He loved how he could make Cesar lose all sense of himself the same way Cesar could do it to him.

Saxon encouraged Cesar on with the grip he had on Cesar's ass, taking Cesar in an inch and backing off again to take him even deeper the next time.

When Cesar fully seated himself, he groaned, dropping down on his elbows and kissing Saxon as if he never wanted to stop.

Saxon wrapped his legs around the back of Cesar's thighs, holding him close, reveling in the fullness, in the unshakable knowledge that, no matter what, Cesar had his back.

"I love you," Saxon said.

Cesar rose higher on his arms with a playful, expectant grin. "Why do I hear a *but?*"

Saxon nipped at his nose. "*But…* if you don't start fucking me into the mattress, I may have to find someone who can."

Cesar laughed at Saxon's blatant lie. He pretended to pull out. "Should I leave now?"

With the lock Saxon had around Cesar's thighs with his ankles, Cesar wasn't going anywhere without dragging Saxon along. "Not on your life."

Snickering, Cesar trailed open-mouth kisses along Saxon's neck, but being the intelligent man he was, he started to move. Slow at first, then Cesar went to his knees, hooking his arms around Saxon's thighs and driving into him. The mattress squeaked, the headboard thumped against the wall, and the musky scent of sweat and sex filled the room.

Saxon dropped his legs. "Harder."

So. Damn. Close. Saxon's hand dropped to his dick, and Cesar batted his hand away and pulled out. He felt the emptiness all over. "What the fuck?"

Cesar smiled down at him, swiping a finger through the precum puddling on Saxon's abdomen and feeding it to him. Saxon licked the digit clean, his dick straining for friction.

"Not yet," Cesar said.

"Yes, *yet.*"

Cesar shook his head, and Saxon almost called him a bastard, but that would have only made Cesar's smile turn smug. "You only come when I say you can."

"*Mmpf…*" Saxon's head fell back as Cesar's words rolled through him. Goosebumps stacked up on his skin, and he shuddered.

They'd never played with those types of power dynamics, but considering how his body reacted and how his dick turned into a faucet, spilling precum until that puddle turned into a lake, he was into it.

Again and again, Cesar drove him to the brink, then hauled him back over and over and over. His heart had nearly maxed out, his lungs couldn't keep up, and sweat poured off them.

Just when Saxon thought he'd never be allowed to come again, Cesar shifted, changing the angle and the length of his strokes to aim at his prostate. Saxon shuddered. When he reached for his dick, Cesar beat him to it.

Cesar worked the deep purple crown, slicking the precum down his shaft as his climax built until he couldn't hold back. He gripped Cesar's hips, held on for dear life, and tumbled over the other side.

One or two thrusts later, Cesar stiffened above him, the cords taut in his neck as he spilled deep inside Saxon. He collapsed on top of him, neither one able to move or talk, only breathe.

When their heart rates dipped below stroke levels, Cesar slid off Saxon, lying face down on the mattress. He reached over and patted Saxon's chest. Then his hand fell to the sheets, apparently having used up what remained of his strength.

"Love… you," Cesar managed.

Saxon grunted in return because he couldn't muster the words. At least that way, Cesar knew he'd heard it and hadn't fallen asleep.

Sometime later—Saxon didn't know how much later, but the cum on his belly had mostly dried—he rolled to his side. "We should shower."

It was Cesar's turn to grunt. Then he turned his head toward Saxon. "Give me a minute."

Saxon pulled a pillow under his head and relaxed into it. The next thing he knew, Cesar kissed him on the forehead. "I just want to sleep."

"Wake up, sleepyhead. It's almost twelve."

"AM?"

"PM. As in noon. As in, we slept half the day away, and I'm afraid if we you don't get up, you may be permanently stuck to the sheets."

Saxon's stomach grumbled a complaint. He rolled to his side and allowed Cesar to help him to his feet. They showered off, still too exhausted to do more than some heavy petting and kissing before toweling off, slipping on underwear, and padding into the kitchen. Cesar poured them bowls of cereal.

He sniffed the milk before shrugging and pouring it into the bowls. "Smells okay. Sorry, I don't have anything else. I haven't been to the store in a while."

"It's fine." Saxon shoved dirty dishes to the other side of the table to make room for them. Once they'd rested, he'd help Cesar clean up since he felt partially responsible for the mess after leaving Cesar in relationship limbo.

They ate in silence, Cesar flipping through the email on his phone while Saxon read the back of the cereal box and worked through the kid's puzzles. His mind drifted to the night before, remembering how Cesar had said he wanted to be the one handing Saxon the swords.

Had he meant that?

He looked at Cesar, watching the muscles in his stubbled jaw worked as the cereal crunched with each bite. Cesar must have felt him staring because he glanced over and winked at him.

If it were possible to melt on the spot, Saxon would have. How did he get so lucky to have this man love him the way he did?

He cleared his throat. "Can I ask you something?"

Cesar swallowed and sat back, the seriousness of Saxon's tone drawing his attention out of his phone. "Anything."

Clearing his throat, Saxon asked, "Can you come with me to confront my father?"

29

Cesar dropped his spoon in his bowl with a clatter. He wiped his mouth on a napkin to give him extra time to compose his thoughts.

Never in a million years after he'd nearly ruined their relationship did he expect Saxon to ask for help where his father was concerned.

And to be honest, it scared the hell out of him. Would he be able to bite his tongue and not berate Melvin about everything he wanted to? The first of which was *How could you betray your son's trust like that?*

Cesar laughed at himself. *You're a fine one to talk. You betrayed him as well.*

At least he'd been attempting to protect him, not prey on him.

Saxon's face flushed, and he cut his gaze away. "Never mind. It was a bad id—"

"No. I want to go."

Saxon perked up. "You do?"

You can do this. You can support him without taking over the situation.

"Of course, I do. When do you want to go?"

"Now?"

Cesar glanced down at his bare chest and underwear. "Can I at least get dressed first?"

Saxon looked him up and down. "I don't know. I like you nearly naked almost as much as I like you fully naked."

"Goof." Cesar wrapped a hand around the back of Saxon's neck and pulled him in for a chaste kiss. Then Cesar sobered. Needing to clarify a second time, he asked, "You really want me to go with you?"

"Yeah," Saxon said. "I do."

"Okay." Cesar stood and helped Saxon to his feet. "Let's do this."

They dressed and climbed into his car in less time than Cesar thought possible. At mid-day on a Saturday—the busiest day of the week for the lot—they weren't concerned Melvin wouldn't be there when they arrived.

Saxon fidgeted in the seat beside him, and Cesar reached across the center console to take his hand. He rested their joined hands on his thigh. "Do you know what you're going to say yet?"

"Not a clue." Saxon's thumb traced quick circles on Cesar's hand. "I think I'm going to wing it. I don't think I have anything to lose."

"I'm sorry." Cesar squeezed his hand. He didn't know what else to say.

"Yeah. Me too."

On Saxon's insistence, they pulled into a drive-through to get coffee on the way. Cesar didn't know if he needed the caffeine or was stalling. Saxon took one sip, his hand went to his stomach, and he set the cup in the cup holder.

"Does it taste that bad?"

"It's not the coffee. The way my stomach is churning, I'm afraid I'll throw it up in your car."

Cesar moved the cup to the holder in the back out of Saxon's immediate reach. "Let's not risk it."

They pulled into the lot, a few more cars in front of the building than Cesar was used to seeing. Several people were looking at cars in the lot, and at least one was talking to a salesman in the showroom.

Cesar shifted into park, and Saxon immediately popped the door latch. "Hang on a second."

Saxon's knee bounced while Cesar dug through his center console. He knew what he was looking for had to be in there somewhere. One by one, he took out the contents and handed the items to Saxon. Napkins, fast food condiment packages, pens, a notepad, and a tangle of electronics cords. You know, the usual.

"What are you doing?"

Cesar glanced up at Saxon's exasperation. "I know it's here."

"What's here?"

Cesar continued rummaging, then spotted the hot pink piece of plastic that had been floating around in his center console for so long that he couldn't even remember how it got there.

"Found it. Here." Cesar handed the prize over to Saxon.

It took Saxon a second to realize what it was. He laughed, and his knee stopped bouncing. "God, I love you."

He pulled Cesar in for a kiss and slipped the plastic sword you got in one of those fancy drinks into the back pocket of his pants and patted it. "My good luck charm."

They climbed out of the car, and the nervous man that had ridden with Cesar the whole way seemed to have melted away, replaced with a confident man who wouldn't take shit from anybody. Not even his father.

Cesar held the door open, and they approached the man behind the reception desk.

"Can I help you?"

Saxon didn't answer. Had the nerves come back? Saxon reached out and linked his pinky finger with Cesar's, his other hand drifting to his back pocket with the pink sword. "I'm Saxon Gray. I'm here to see Melvin."

The man looked from Saxon to Cesar and back again. "I think he's with—"

"Buzz him."

Cesar almost growled at the authority in Saxon's tone. Fuck, that was sexy as hell. He settled on squeezing Saxon's finger.

The man reached for the phone, his eyes on Saxon the entire time as he hit one of the autodial buttons. When it connected, he said, "There's someone here to see you."

"Tell them they'll have to come back." Even with the phone to his ear, Melvin's voice carried enough for them to hear. "Cancel my appointments. I'm heading over to my son's—"

They heard Melvin's voice in stereo and turned to see Melvin coming down the hall. The receptionist hung up the phone and started shuffling papers as if he had something important to do besides listening in on the conversation.

A customer came in, and the one talking with the salesman walked out.

"Saxon…" his father approached. "What are you doing here?"

"I think you know."

Saxon brushed past him and headed for his office. And since Saxon had a tight hold on Cesar's pinky, Cesar also brushed past Melvin.

They stood in front of Melvin's desk, not bothering to take a seat. This conversation wouldn't be a long one. Melvin walked in behind them, picked up the receiver for his desk phone, and hit the intercom. "Hold my calls."

"Have a seat." Melvin gestured toward the chairs and went to sit.

"We'd rather stand."

Melvin caught himself and stood back up. Saxon opened his mouth. Before he could get a word out, Melvin held up a staying hand. "I deserve everything you're about to say and probably more, but can you give me one second?"

After a beat or two, Saxon nodded. Melvin visibly relaxed,

reached into the inside pocket of his suit coat, found a thick envelope and held it out to Saxon.

"What's that?"

"What you came for, I imagine."

Saxon dropped Cesar's finger and took the envelope. He ran his finger across the seal, revealing the stack of bills inside.

He took out the cash. Before he could count it, Melvin said, "It's not all there."

Cesar shifted, about to say *Why the hell not*, but Saxon put a staying hand on his arm. "I'm listening."

Melvin's hand went to the back of his neck. "Can we sit? Please?"

Cesar patted Saxon's back. "Let's give him a minute."

Look at Cesar, being the unexpected voice of reason when what he wanted to do was wring a certain someone's neck.

Saxon sat, and Cesar followed suit, doing his best to be Saxon's moral support.

Silent moral support.

"It wasn't supposed to be like this," Melvin started.

Cesar snorted. And Saxon and Melvin both stared at him. He cleared his throat. "Sorry. Continue."

Wait… was that a hint of a smile tugging at Saxon's lips as he turned back toward his father? He was so damn proud of Saxon. The words bubbled up, and he had to swallow them down. There would be plenty of time for that later.

"I borrowed that money in good faith." Melvin stopped and looked at Cesar as if he expected another outburst. When none came, he continued. "Shortly before I was to send the money, I got a message from the shipper saying they were having a problem with their account and to not send the money until they had it sorted. I figured their problem might have bought me a few days. I thought that if I could get a little more money, maybe I could buy one of his smaller shipments as well."

Saxon's brows drew together. "More money. How?"

Saxon's voice dipped to a dangerous level that Cesar had never heard before. He shifted in his seat because, *fuck*, who wouldn't be turned on by a growly, sexy Saxon?

Melvin squirmed. "I played the horses."

Saxon sucked in his breath and shifted in his seat. Cesar put a staying hand on his shoulder. He didn't want to have to call Kellon to help him bail Saxon out of jail for assault—as justified as it might be.

"The horses," Saxon repeated. It wasn't a question or a statement. More of a stunned clarification. Not that either of them had needed one because Melvin had spoken clearly.

"I lost a lot of it. And I've been trying to get it back ever since."

"And the cars?"

Melvin scrubbed a hand over his face. "I managed to buy a different lot of cars. Not as expensive. Not as good." Melvin pointed at the envelope in Saxon's hands. "That's the profit from selling those cars. I'll get you the rest of the money. That's a promise. I just don't know when."

Saxon waved the envelope. "How much is here?"

"Forty-two hundred."

Saxon sputtered and turned a shade of white reserved for people who needed blood transfusions. His gaze searched Cesar's as if asking what to do.

"What do you want?" Cesar asked. He'd do just about anything.

"I don't suppose you know how to break kneecaps, do you?"

Melvin laughed, his nerves making it short and humorless.

"They didn't teach that in PI school, but it wouldn't take much research to figure it out." They both turned their attention to Melvin.

"I-I...Um..."

"Relax," Cesar said, "Violence isn't Saxon's style."

Saxon might have muttered *pity*, but Cesar couldn't be certain.

"I'm going to pay you back the rest," Melvin said.

Saxon appraised him. "You know, for the first time since I've lent you the money, I believe what you're saying."

Cesar schooled his face. Melvin might have sounded sincere, but he didn't see what had made Saxon so certain. But that wasn't up to him to decide.

Melvin relaxed enough to lean back in his seat. "You won't regret this, son. I've made a lot of boneheaded mistakes in my life, and this one tops all the others. I finally have you in my life, and I ruined it."

"*Almost* ruined it," Saxon said.

"Wait…" Melvin's eyes shifted to Cesar's, then back to Saxon's. "A-almost?"

"I'm not gonna lie," Saxon said, "you obliterated my trust." He waved the envelope. "But this is a small step in rebuilding our relationship if that's what you want."

"I do. Maybe I could take you to lunch and—"

Saxon put up his hand. "I'm going to need a little more time. I want contact, but right now, it needs to be at my pace and comfort level. A probation period, if you will. If that's not okay with you, then—"

"No. It's fine. Whatever you want."

Saxon nodded, and Cesar stood when Saxon did. "We're—" Saxon's voice broke, and he just hitched his thumb over his shoulder, indicating they were leaving.

"Wait." Melvin stood. "Thanks for giving me another chance. I would have understood if you didn't want anything to do with me."

Melvin seemed to have shrunk two sizes, and Saxon's eyes swam with unshed tears. He had the biggest heart of anyone Cesar had ever known. He'd made it clear he wouldn't let Melvin take advantage of him again, but he'd left the door open to build their relationship in the future. And Melvin seemed to understand that their future rested in his hands.

Saxon swallowed hard. No words came. Instead, Saxon opened his arms, and his father stepped into the embrace. By the time they broke apart, no one in the room had a dry eye.

Cesar and Saxon walked out of the showroom, hand in hand. Cesar drove them back toward Stonewall House in comfortable silence, both lost in their thoughts.

"You alright?" Cesar asked as he parked behind Saxon's car.

Saxon reached across the center console and took Cesar's hand. "Better than I thought I'd be. I know he owes me a lot of money, but at least now I can order the furniture for the third floor."

Cesar must not have schooled his expression as well as he'd hoped because Saxon narrowed his eyes. "What is it?"

"Nothing." Cesar leaned across the console and kissed him. "I love you. That's all. Now let's get inside before everyone thinks I've kidnapped you."

Cesar stopped in the driveway beside Saxon's car and looked in the windows. Saxon still had partially unpacked boxes, one of his pillows, and a spare cat bed in the backseat. He'd been back at Stonewall House for a couple of weeks but never finished unpacking.

Saxon slid in front of him, blocking Cesar's view of the interior. Cesar grinned. "You haven't unpacked." Saxon scrunched up his nose, and Cesar kissed it. "Makes it easier for you to move back in."

Wait. What? "You want me to move back in?"

Cesar wrapped his arms around Saxon's waist. "I never wanted you to move out."

Saxon thumped his forehead on Cesar's shoulder. "I'm sorry."

Cesar lifted his face with a finger under his chin. "You don't have anything to be sorry for. *I* crossed a line. That's on *me*."

Saxon relaxed against him, then remembered the sword Cesar had given him. He took it out of his pocket and held it out to him.

"You don't want it?"

"I want you to hold onto it. You know… for next time."

Cesar smiled and tucked it into his pocket. "For next time, then."

Saxon opened Stonewall's front door to an explosion of cardboard boxes all over the floor in the den and the entryway. Kai and Phoenix came out of Saxon's room with an armload of clothes each.

"You're back," Phoenix said. "Just in time to see the finished product."

Addi came out of the room with books in their arms and Kai's backpack slung over their shoulder. "You're not supposed to be here."

Saxon didn't know which question to ask first, about what they saw or why they weren't supposed to be there. He decided to work his way backward. "Why aren't we supposed to be here?"

"Because I bet you two wouldn't drag yourselves out of bed until tomorrow. It's not even five. Now James wins the pot."

Cesar chuckled. "Should I be horrified that everyone was thinking about us having sex?"

"Ew," Sophia said as she came out of the bedroom with a box of Kai's belongings. She shuddered. "Trust me. No one wants to think about their program director having sex. But *betting* on it is a different thing."

Saxon and Cesar laughed, and Saxon stuck his arm out to keep Phoenix from heading up the stairs. "Can someone explain what's going on here? What am I just in time to see? And what are all these boxes doing here?"

"The furniture came," Addi said. "*Duh.*"

"Furniture?" Saxon turned to look at Cesar. "What furniture?"

Cesar shrugged and rolled his lips inward as if trying to stifle a smile. "I don't know what they're talking about."

Everyone started up the stairs as Saxon turned on Cesar. "You know, for a guy who has to lie for a living with his job sometimes, you're really bad at it."

"You wound me." Cesar couldn't stop the smile. He didn't look the least bit wounded. "And I'm an amazing liar. I'm just not as good at it when it comes to you."

Cesar bumped his chin toward the stairs. "Why don't we go see what all the fuss is about?"

Saxon followed Cesar up the stairs. On the last flight to the third floor, he heard everyone joking and laughing, and he'd never heard a sound that he loved more. Not only were the people in his program surviving, they were *thriving*.

"Wow," Saxon spun in a circle to take everything in. All the new beds were in place. Two for each of the two larger rooms and one in the smaller one Kai had taken over.

A love seat and two overstuffed beanbag chairs were in the small sitting area. Each half of the bedrooms had a dresser and area rugs on the floor. James was busy in one of the rooms, hanging bookshelves above each dresser.

Saxon turned to Cesar. "You did this."

"I can neither confirm nor—*ouch*." He slapped his hand over his side where Saxon had pinched him. Cesar gripped Saxon's wrists to protect himself. "Okay, okay. I might know something about this. But it wasn't all me. Derek kicked in money as well."

"Wait…When did you order all this?"

"Does it matter?"

"Humor me?"

Mango came out of Kai's room, his meows deafening as if affronted no one had told him Saxon had arrived. Saxon picked him up and kissed the top of his head before pinning Cesar with a hard gaze.

"A week… ten days maybe? I would have to look at the receipt to know for sure."

"We weren't together then. Why would you—"

"Because we wanted to. Because what you're doing here is worthy whether we're together or not."

Saxon backed Cesar against the nearest wall, nearly crushing poor Mango between them, who escaped before certain injury. "Every day, I find another reason to love you more."

Cesar took Saxon's face in his hands. His kiss started sweet and tender and quickly morphed into something much hotter until Addi's voice broke their tiny bubble.

"You two need a room. But not one of these because we haven't even put the sheets on the beds yet."

They broke apart, but that heat in Cesar's eyes definitely said *later*.

They stood in the doorway of Kai's room, over-crowded with Addi, Sophia, Kai, and Phoenix. James had already installed the shelves, and Phoenix was busy organizing the book spines by color. Sophia was folding Kai's clothes and putting them in the dresser, and Kai and Addi were hanging a picture that looked like James had drawn.

"This looks amazing," Saxon said. "All of it. You didn't have to do this alone. I could have helped."

"You did all the hard work," Sophia said. "We wanted to do this."

"And I like the idea of my own space. Your room was great and all, but..." Kai shrugged. Saxon understood.

"Thank you all," Saxon said.

There came a round of *sures* and *your welcomes*.

Then the front door slammed, shaking the house. Oliver's feet pounded on the steps as he ran up. "You guys have to see this."

Everyone piled out of Kai's room, and James put the hammer and level down.

"What is it?" Phoenix asked as soon as Oliver stepped on the landing.

Oliver held out his phone to a news report, but with so many people gathering around it, it was nearly impossible for anyone to see the screen.

"Braden was arrested for assaulting his new girlfriend, and his father's being investigated for trying to bribe the arresting officer into dropping the charges." The smile on Oliver's face only widened.

"I can't believe someone called them on their shit." Phoenix took the phone and scrolled through the article. "And it says at the bottom that people are already calling for the mayor to resign."

"We can only hope," Saxon said. Then maybe the city could elect a mayor who protected its citizens the way the mayor protected his son.

When the excitement died down, James stepped forward, wringing his hands. "Um... since everyone is here, I have an announcement."

"You're pregnant?" Addi threw in, breaking the ice and making James laugh.

"No. But..." James took everyone in, the uncertainty returning. "I'm moving in with Hamish. We're pretty serious, and I figure that way it'll open up another bed here."

A round of congratulations and hugs went around, and even though Saxon was happy for him, he had a lump in his throat. "You don't have to do that. You know that, right? You can stay here as long as you need."

"But that's just it," James said. "The program did what it was supposed to. It got me off the street. I have a good job, and my boss said I qualified for the manager training classes. I can work and train and get paid. I couldn't have done it without all of you and Stonewall House, but it's time for me to move on."

Saxon took a moment and then another. He knew this day would come. James would be the first person to leave the program, and as proud of James as he was, it hurt in a weird way.

"We're going to miss you." Saxon pulled him in for a hug. "And if you ever need anything, we're always here."

When they broke apart, Cesar hugged him as well. Everyone had so many questions for James. Saxon turned to Cesar and tipped his head toward the stairs.

Cesar followed him down. Mango must have seen them leave because he zipped past them on the stairs. At the bottom, Cesar took Saxon's hand and led him into his old room, where it was quiet. Saxon plopped down on the bed's bare mattress.

"You okay," Cesar asked as he sat on the bed beside him.

"Yeah. I mean, I knew this day would come. I wasn't expecting it so soon, though."

"I'm so fucking proud of you." Cesar pulled him to his side and kissed his temple. "You're making a difference here."

"I guess this means I can move back into my room."

Cesar stiffened and held Saxon at arm's length. "Is that what you want?"

Saxon couldn't quite read Cesar. Did Cesar want him to move back into his room or not? "I-I don't know?"

Cesar chuckled. "You don't know? Is that a question?"

Before he could answer, Cesar added, "Don't answer that."

What was he up to?

"I have a better idea." Cesar took the envelope of money out of Saxon's back pocket and set it in his lap.

Saxon picked up the envelope. "I don't understand."

"I think you should use that money to buy two beds and another dresser for this room. That would be two more people you could help."

"Where would I be?" Saxon asked, the smile coming to his face because he suspected he knew the answer.

Cesar stood, drew Saxon to his feet, and brushed a kiss across Saxon's lips. "With me."

"I can't stay with you forever."

Cesar's brow furrowed. "Why the hell not?"

"I-I..."

"Wait," Cesar said. "That didn't come out the way I wanted it to." Cesar tipped Saxon's chin up, and Saxon held his breath. "I love you. For now. And forever. I'm unsure of a lot things in this life, but that isn't one of them. Move in with me. For good. What do you say?"

"I..." Saxon wanted to be the voice of reason. To say they should wait. But... he didn't want that. "I want that, too."

Cesar scooped Saxon up and swung him around until Saxon's foot got hung on the mattress, and they both crumpled to the floor laughing. Saxon finally caught his breath and palmed Cesar's cheek. "I love you so fucking much."

"I love you, too." Cesar smacked a kiss on his lips and joined their hands. Cesar held them in the air, and Saxon noticed the second something popped into Cesar's head. "I've got an idea. Do you trust me?"

A valid question, and despite what had happened between them, Saxon honestly answered. "A hundred percent."

Cesar jumped to his feet and hauled Saxon to his. "Run upstairs and tell everyone we're heading out for a few hours. I'll meet you at the front door."

Saxon didn't know what Cesar had up his sleeve, but he was there for it. In record time, he ran up and then down the stairs. No one seemed to care that they were headed out.

They drove for about fifteen minutes, Cesar refusing to tell him where they were going. Finally, he pulled into the parking lot of the strip center that held Truman's tattoo shop, *Pigment of the Imagination.*

"What are we doing here?"

"Truman's giving us tattoos."

"Truman has a waiting list two months long. We can't just go in there and—"

Cesar shut him up with a kiss, and Saxon wouldn't lie, it was his favorite way to be shut up. "You said you trusted me."

Saxon rolled his eyes. "Fine."

They walked into the waiting room. Several people were in the seats waiting for their appointment, but as soon as Tavi saw them walk in, he escorted them to Truman's station. Though nerves made Saxon's stomach light—neither one had a tattoo—he was there for whatever Cesar had planned.

Truman met them with one-armed hugs and invited Saxon to sit. "You ready for this?"

If it had to do with Cesar, the answer was, and would always be, *yes*. Cesar might have made a mistake by looking into his father without Saxon's permission, but Saxon knew that this man would always love and protect him with everything he was.

Cesar had learned and grown from that, and Saxon couldn't ask for a better man to have at his side. "Ready."

Truman reached behind him and handed Saxon a blindfold. He took it with a glance at Cesar. "A blindfold. Really?"

"You don't have to do this if you don't want to."

Saxon covered his eyes in answer. Truman took Saxon's left hand and went to work. It didn't take long, though it seemed like it took forever for Truman to do Cesar's since Cesar made him keep the blindfold on.

Finally, Truman finished and sent them on their way. Cesar guided him to the car and helped Saxon get seated. "Both of our tattoos are done. Why can't I take my blindfold off? Are they that bad? Am I going to have to wear a blindfold forever?"

Chuckling, Cesar leaned in and kissed him. "Be patient, only a couple more minutes."

Cesar closed the car door, walked around, and climbed into the driver's seat. He started the car, took Saxon's newly tattooed hand over the center console the way he always did, and threaded their fingers together. It hurt a little, but he didn't care.

"Okay. You can look."

"You sure?"

Cesar took the blindfold off. "I'm sure."

Saxon glanced down at their joined hands, at the two perfect halves of a rainbow heart on the pad of their thumbs. It formed a full heart when they held hands like that.

"*Fuck*," Saxon managed, closing his eyes and letting his head fall against the headrest.

Cesar squeezed his hand. "You hate it."

"No. You're going to make me cry again."

Saxon opened his eyes and blinked Cesar clear, and Cesar did the same. "I love it."

"You know this means you're mine now, right?"

"No." Saxon leaned over to kiss Cesar. "This means you're mine."

A LETTER TO MY READERS

Dear Reader,

Thanks for coming along for Saxon and Cesar's story. But don't fret, you haven't seen the last of the Valley Boys. Kellon and Gideon's story is in the works. You can keep up to date on all my upcoming books and releases by signing up for my newsletter at http://bit.ly/V-W-T.

If you haven't already, you can read **One Shot**, the first book in the **Black Stallion Studio** series. It's were this world started.

Your next adventure starts here: One Shot (Book 1)

Romantic Suspense

Lazy S Ranch Series
Cowgirl, Unexpectedly (Book 1)
Cowboy, Untamed (Book 2)
(Previously published as Must Love Horses)
Cowboy, Undone (Book 3)

(Previously published as Hot on the Trail)
Cowboy, Undercover (Book 4)
Cowboy, Unbridled (Book 5)
Cowgirl, Unbroken (Book 6)
Lazy S Ranch Box Set (Books 1-3)
Lazy S Ranch Box Set (Books 4-6)

Steele-Wolfe Securities
Wyoming Confidential (Book 1)
Dealing With the Devil (Book 2)
Sweet Justice (Book 3)
Steele-Wolfe Securities Box Set (Books 1-3)

Wright's Island
Don't Look Back

CONTEMPORARY ROMANCE

Rockin' Rodeo Series
Luck of the Draw (Book 1)
Photo Chute (Book 2)
Reined In (Book 3)
Rockin' Rodeo Series Collection (Books 1-3)

MM ROMANCE

Black Stallion Studios Series
One Shot (Book 1)
Key Grip (Book 2)
Best Boy (Book 3)
Black Stallion Studios Box Set (Books 1-3)

Valley Boys

Art of Love (Book 1)
Flight of Fancy (Book 2)
Den of Thieves (Book 3)
Breach of Trust (Book 4)
The Valley Boys (Books 1-3)

ABOUT THE AUTHOR

Vicki Tharp makes her home on small acreage in south Texas with her husband and an embarrassing number of pets. When she isn't writing, you can usually find her on the back of her horse—avoiding anything that remotely resembles housework—smelling like fly spray and horse sweat.

Join my newsletter at: http://bit.ly/V-W-T
Join my street team and receive free Advance Reader Copies of my upcoming books at: http://bit.ly/S-W-S-T
You can find my website at: www.VickiTharp.com
I love to hear from readers. You can email me at vwtharp@VickiTharp.com

Or you can stalk me at:

facebook.com/VickiTharpAuthor
instagram.com/author_Vicki_Tharp
bookbub.com/authors/vicki-tharp
amazon.com/author/vicki_tharp
twitter.com/vwtharp